BEAUTY
FROM
ASHES

Is. 61:3

Lynnette

THE WYLDHAVEN SERIES
by Lynnette Bonner

Not a Sparrow Falls – BOOK ONE
On Eagles' Wings – BOOK TWO
Beauty from Ashes – BOOK THREE
Consider the Lilies – BOOK FOUR
A Wyldhaven Christmas – BOOK FIVE
Songs in the Night – BOOK SIX
Honey from the Rock – BOOK SEVEN
Beside Still Waters – BOOK EIGHT

OTHER HISTORICAL BOOKS
by Lynnette Bonner

THE SHEPHERD'S HEART SERIES

Rocky Mountain Oasis – BOOK ONE
High Desert Haven – BOOK TWO
Fair Valley Refuge – BOOK THREE
Spring Meadow Sanctuary – BOOK FOUR

SONNETS OF THE SPICE ISLE SERIES

On the Wings of a Whisper – BOOK ONE

Find all other books by Lynnette Bonner at:
www.lynnettebonner.com

BEAUTY
FROM
ASHES

Book Three
WYLDHAVEN

Lynnette BONNER
USA Today Bestselling Author

Pacific Lights

Beauty from Ashes
WYLDHAVEN, Book 3

Published by Pacific Lights Publishing
Copyright © 2019 by Lynnette Bonner. All rights reserved.

Cover design by Lynnette Bonner of Indie Cover Design, images ©
  Depositphotos_232384046 - Flare
  Depositphotos_21219423_DS – Texture
  AdobeStock_606424995 – Décor and Dividers

Other images generated by Lynnette Bonner using Midjourney and Adobe
Photoshop.
Book interior design by Jon Stewart of Stewart Design
Editing by Lesley Ann McDaniel of Lesley Ann McDaniel Editing
Proofreading by Sheri Mast of Faithful Editing

Scripture taken from the New King James Version®. Copyright © 1982 by
Thomas Nelson, Inc. Used by permission. All rights reserved.

ISBN: 978-1-942982-12-8

To the Weary and Broken:

Do you feel like your life is nothing but ashes?
There is One who longs for you to know the truth.
Ashes are temporary.
In fact, they are often used to fertilize ground that
needs refreshing.
From the ashes of hardship comes wisdom, prudence,
and maturity.
Out of burnt soil comes new life.
God longs to take your ashes and give you beauty in
their place.
Do you know Him?

If not, but you would like to know more
please visit:
www.peacewithgod.net

Isaiah 61:1-3

"The Spirit of the Lord God is upon Me,
Because the Lord has anointed Me
To preach good tidings to the poor;
He has sent Me to heal the brokenhearted,
To proclaim liberty to the captives,
And the opening of the prison to those who are bound;
To proclaim the acceptable year of the Lord,
And the day of vengeance of our God;
To comfort all who mourn,
To console those who mourn in Zion,
To give them beauty for ashes,
The oil of joy for mourning,
The garment of praise for the spirit of heaviness;
That they may be called trees of righteousness,
The planting of the Lord, that He may be glorified."

iora Fontaine stood in the yard of her newly constructed log cabin, hands propped on her hips, and satisfaction coursing through her. She admired the way the de-barked red cedar walls gleamed creamy-gold against the sun-kissed reds and ambers of the Cascade mountain valley. Soon the logs would gray and weather, but for today they still shone bright, just like her hopes and dreams for this place. God was going to do good things here. He was going to use *her* to do good things here.

A pile of cedar chips, notched from the logs to form good tight corners, lay at her feet. She bent to pick one up and inhaled deep of the tangy, woodsy scent that embodied all her dreams. The crew who had been helping to add the finishing touches were just packing up their wagons, about ready to head to their homes. Tonight, she would spend her first night in her very own home, thanks to the generous-hearted men of Wyldhaven.

A reminder flitted through her of the way Mrs. King's eyes had narrowed when her husband had proclaimed his plan to help build Liora's cabin. But she pushed away the discouragement the memory brought. She refused to let herself become disheartened at a time like this. Even if the men had in all probability only banded together to help her because of the urging of Deputy Joseph Rodante, she was going to choose to be thankful that they had.

Her mind went back to the day this dream had all started. The winter of 1891 had been cold and blustery. Determined not to go back to working for Ewan McGinty as a bar-girl-and-more, there had been days at the beginning of that winter where she'd wondered if she would make it to the spring alive. She'd been surviving on odd jobs and scraps of food, and if she were honest, she'd been wondering if God really did care about her plight. But then, thanks to the urging of Miss Charlotte Brindle, Deputy Joseph Rodante had told her that Dixie Pottinger was looking to hire help. To this day, no one in town probably realized that job had been a literal life saver.

That same winter, Parson Preston Clay had come to town. Back then, the town's services had mostly been held in Dixie's dining room. Occasionally on a sunny day, Parson Clay had held services across the street in the field where the church building now stood.

Whether services had been outdoors or in, Liora had most often crept into the back of the gathering just as the services started, and then scooted out right as they ended, wanting so badly to be there and yet knowing most of the townspeople would frown on her presence.

One such day, Parson Clay had spoken about the Lord being able to turn past sins into a beautiful testimony that could be used to reach others. In that moment, it had felt like a heavenly presence had wrapped her in a warm hug, and she'd suddenly known what she wanted to do with the property she'd inherited from her deceased outlaw of a father.

It had taken her eighteen months of hard work at Dixie's boardinghouse, and saving every penny she could during those months, but it had all paid off. And now she couldn't wait to get started with her mission.

She spun in a circle, taking in not only the log cabin, but

the garden plot she had staked out. The area where she would soon have a chicken coop built, and the small lean-to barn— nothing more than a pole hung between two trees with a thick layer of pine boughs leaning against it—that would at first only house a few goats and maybe a sow if she could afford one.

Yes. This was all such a dream come true. She felt her lips tilt into a smile.

"You're looking happy." Deputy Joseph Rodante stopped next to her, slapping a pair of gloves against one palm. He didn't glance her way, but focused instead on the shake roof he'd spent the day nailing down.

"I'm *so very* happy. I couldn't have done this without your help, Joe." She would have liked to have thrown her arms around the man's neck in a platonic show of her gratitude, but knew she didn't dare. Once the men got home and told their wives what she'd done, there would be no end to the wagging of tongues. And she valued Joe's friendship too much to tarnish his reputation in such a manner. She settled instead for clasping her hands behind her back.

Joe pulled a face and looked back to where the wagons were starting toward town.

Liora waved an arm over her head to the departing men. "Thanks again!" she called.

Several men acknowledged her thanks with return waves.

"Lots of townsfolk pitched in. I think you'd have done just fine without my help." One lock of his dark hair, which was trimmed short and close at the sides but a bit longer on the top, poked out at an angle, making her want to reach over and smooth it.

Liora returned her hands to the firm clasp against her spine. "It was your work that cut most of those logs out of the back half of my property. Your urging that got the crew together.

Your management that made the construction go so smoothly. Even your idea to give it an indoor pump and working powder room." She felt her face flame at the slip.

With his usual thoughtfulness, Joe let the impropriety pass without so much as a hitch. "Anyone in town would have done the same. I just stepped up first, is all."

She looked at him then, wondering if he knew how much she valued his friendship. She'd thought about telling him many times, but had never been able to come up with the right words. She didn't want him to think she wanted more than simple friendship. "Yes. You did."

His gaze darted to hers for the briefest of seconds before he turned his focus back to the cabin. "Turned out real nice."

"It's the most beautiful home ever built!"

He chuckled at that and started tugging on his gloves. "I'm glad you like it. You sure you're going to be all right out here all on your own?"

"It's only a few miles from town. Besides, how many times did you test the lock on that door?" Liora quirked a brow.

He rubbed the back of his gloved hand over his chin. "Yeah, I guess I did check it out pretty thoroughly. It's a good strong deadbolt."

"Indeed. And I have the pistol you gave me." She wouldn't admit that she had no idea how to work the thing. But if it came down to it, maybe just pointing it at someone would have the desired effect.

He still looked uncertain.

"And I'll be at Dixie's for work first thing in the morning, just like always."

"I can come out and give you a ride into town, mornings."

She took in the way his feet shuffled, knowing how much that offer had cost him. "It won't take me more than three quarters of an hour to walk in, and the weather's been beautiful. Now that I have the cabin built, I plan to start saving up for a horse and buggy so I won't have to walk that far for long."

He tipped a nod of acquiescence, without argument.

Was it a relief to him that she'd declined? Probably. The man had been politeness itself since the first time she'd met him, but he'd never crossed the line into anything that could be mistaken for interest, which was why their friendship had flourished.

Though he was obviously ready to ride out, he still stood quietly by her side. "Dixie says that you've asked for evenings off?"

Liora swallowed. *Tread carefully.* "Yes. I have another... project I'll be taking on in the evenings."

His gaze snapped to her, and even though she kept her focus on the cabin, she could see from the corner of her eye that his lashes lowered searchingly. "Another project?"

Yes, Deputy Rodante, and I won't be telling you a thing about it until I absolutely have to. Out loud all she said was, "Something to keep me busy. 'Idle hands are the devil's workshop,' as Mrs. King would say."

Joe slacked one hip, his scrutiny still calculated. "Mrs. King would do better to quote proverbs about wagging tongues."

He said it so dryly she knew he hadn't meant it humorously, but she couldn't help but chuckle. "Perhaps. At any rate, I'll see you at Dixie's in the morning for breakfast?" She needed to urge him on his way before he pried any further into her business, for he would surely try to talk her out of her mission.

He hesitated for a long moment, gaze still fixed on her as though he knew she was keeping something from him. Then finally he tipped her a nod. "See you in the morning."

Liora watched him unhook his Stetson from the saddle horn, mount up, settle the hat on his head in that unhurried way of his and, finally, give it a tug in her direction before riding away toward town.

Her heart constricted. She usually shared everything with Joe and it somehow felt underhanded to keep this mission from him. Yet she knew without a doubt that he would try to talk her out of it. And dangerous though it might be, she also knew that God had called her to it.

And follow her calling, she must.

Mist rose around Joseph Rodante as though night were releasing its soul at the first touch of sunlight. Dewdrops, hanging fat and full like berries just waiting to be picked, glinted bright, shattering sunrays into shards. A chorus of birds chirped their morning adulation.

He hung back just far enough inside the edge of the trees for Liora not to see him, but close enough for him to keep an eye on her. His well-trained horse didn't make a sound. It wasn't safe for a beautiful woman like her to be walking this road alone, especially this early in the morning. But it wasn't his place to make her see reason. And he couldn't escort her into town without setting tongues aflame with insinuations about where he'd spent his night.

His jaw clenched at that. No matter how many years had passed since Liora had worked for Ewan—and for two short weeks at that—the townsfolk had long memories and small penchant for accepting her as an upstanding Christian woman. He needed to protect both her current reputation, and his own.

Liora was singing "I Hear My Savior Saying," the hymn they'd sung in services on Sunday.

He maneuvered his horse around a fallen tree and searched his memory. He hadn't remembered seeing her there, but she must have been, because according to Parson Clay, the hymn had been written by his personal friend James Kirk only recently, and wasn't in any psalters yet.

Joe considered on that. He was fairly observant. His job had taught him that. So he would have noticed even if she'd eased onto a back pew just after services started.

He checked the road behind her—still all clear.

Back before the church was built, he used to see her slip up to the back of the crowd and then leave again right before the service ended. But he hadn't seen her at church since the building had gone up. Why had he thought that meant she had quit coming?

O Lord, I'm so glad Thou dost love me so,
To deign to walk with me here below;
Thy sweet, tender love has won my heart,
And now we shall never, never, never part.

His horse brushed up against a bush and he jerked the animal to a stop, holding his breath. That was what he got for letting his mind wander. Had she heard?

Out on the road, Liora stopped walking and turned to face the forest. Her eyes were wide and searching.

He thought through his options. Could she see him? He might not want to give the townsfolk something to gossip about, but even more, he didn't want to frighten her.

He urged his mount forward and rode it out into the light.

Liora pressed one hand to her chest. "Land's sakes, Joe! You nearly scared a year off my life!"

He felt a little sheepish and swept a hand over his face. "Sorry about that. I just wanted to make sure you got to town safe, is all."

She narrowed her eyes. "You can't ride out here every day to ensure my safety! I know you have late rounds. You'll never get any sleep!"

He fiddled with the reins. She was right about that. This early morning jaunt had cost him two hours of a night that had been short on shuteye already. But instead of replying, he merely dismounted and motioned for her to mount.

At his silence, she crossed her arms. "You can't be seen escorting me into town."

Didn't he know it. And yet the truth of her words irritated him. He jutted his jaw to one side. "Doesn't mean I can't escort you most of the way."

"And if someone comes riding along the road?"

"My horse is a good mountain-bred mustang. He'll let me know if someone is coming." He motioned her closer.

Liora searched the road up and down before finally giving in and stepping close to the saddle.

He curved his hands around her waist, swallowing away the tightness in his chest at the feel of her so small and close. He hoisted her onto the saddle. She didn't weigh much more than half a sack of grain. He let her go as soon as he felt certain she had gained her balance.

His horse wasn't used to skirts flapping at his flanks, or to a rider sitting sideways, but after a couple of balking steps and a bob or two of his head, he settled down and Joe set off, leading the mustang down the road.

After they'd gone several paces in silence, Joe tossed a look at Liora over his shoulder. "That hymn you were singing—we sang it in church last Sunday."

She shifted uneasily as he searched her face.

After a moment, she lifted her chin. "So, not only were you spying on me, but eaves-dropping too?"

He scrubbed a hand at the smile that wanted to break free at her indignation. "Wasn't spying. Just keeping you safe. And I wasn't trying to eavesdrop either. I was simply surprised to learn that you'd been to the service, since I didn't see you there."

She squirmed in the saddle and refused to meet his questioning look.

"You've been coming, but staying out in the entry, haven't you?"

She took a moment to tug at the cuffs of her coat. "Maybe I learned the hymn somewhere other than church, did you think about that?"

His eyes narrowed. "You can't have, because Preston— Parson Clay—said that the hymn was written by his friend and wasn't even in any books yet."

Her gaze flicked to his, surprise reflected there.

This time he did let his grin slip free. She'd obviously snuck into the back of the building after the parson had told that story. But as he thought over the ramifications of *why* she felt the need to hide her church attendance from everyone else, a hard knot of anger settled into his stomach and the smile slid from his face. "You have just as much right to be in church as anyone else, you know."

Her shoulders seemed to slump, even though she hardly moved. "I just don't want to cause trouble, is all."

"If it causes trouble for a repentant soul to enter God's sanctuary, then Parson Clay has more problems on his hands than you can solve by hiding in the entry."

"That may be true, but I just don't want to be the one to light the match to the tinder. I'm sure you understand."

iora couldn't help but feel gratified when Joe made a disgruntled sound and said, "It's not right."

She adjusted herself to a more comfortable position in the saddle. "That may be, but I don't mind. I'm used to it. I've talked to the parson, and he put a chair in the entry near the coat rack just for me. People think it's for sitting on while they remove their overboots, but it serves me well. I can sit out of sight and listen to the sermons and then leave again without anyone ever knowing I was there."

"You shouldn't have to do that."

Instead of countering again, Liora pulled the horse to a stop. They were almost to town. "We'd best part ways here."

Joe lifted his hands to help her from the saddle. His grip about her waist was firm yet gentle as he swung her down, but as ever it sent apprehension worming through her. She held her breath, hoping he couldn't feel her trembling. The fear wasn't of him. He'd never given her cause for such. Just the opposite, in fact. It was simply that any time a man made a point to touch her, unappeasable fears of what might come next stampeded through her. She'd done her best to quell it many times, knowing most men would never hurt her, but with the haunting memories from her past she hadn't been able to conquer it.

Did his hands linger a little longer than propriety allowed? Or was that just her anxious imagination?

Before the thought hardly had time to take root, he loosed her and stepped back. He took up the reins and slapped them against one palm, tipping a nod toward town. "Go on. I'll watch from here to make sure you get to the crest of the ridge all right. And then I'll cut through the woods and come into town from the south."

It felt sneaky and deceptive, especially when they were doing nothing wrong, and yet for his sake, she mustn't ponder on it. His reputation would be trampled if they arrived in town together at this hour of the morning.

She started up the road, but then paused and looked back at him. "Thank you for coming out to escort me in."

He nodded. "Of course."

There was no "of course" about it. It had probably not even crossed the mind of any other man in town that she would be walking in from her new property this morning. No one except Joe.

Gratefulness spread through her. And that was her cue to turn and keep walking, because lately he'd been looking at her with a bit of a different light in his eyes. She couldn't quite peg it. Certainly it wasn't the same lustful assessment men used to give her when she worked for Ewan. But it set her on her guard, nonetheless. If she let him see all the appreciation she felt, he might mistakenly think she harbored a whole wagonload of other emotions. That would undoubtedly complicate matters. And the last thing she wanted was to hurt her best friend's feelings.

Dixie was already in the boardinghouse kitchen when Liora arrived and let herself in through the back door. She hung her wraps on the peg by the door and strode to the sink to wash her hands.

"Morning," she offered.

"Morning," Dixie returned with a smile. "How was your first night in your new place?"

Liora couldn't have withheld the smile that bloomed on her face if she'd tried. "It was lovely. Simply lovely." She marveled at how the Lord had not only planted a dream in her heart, but had also given her the resources to bring it about. And much of that was due to the wonderful woman who had employed her for the past eighteen months. "And it's all due to you."

Dixie blew out a sound of disagreement and waved away the comment. "You've done more to help me than I ever could repay. I've been so blessed to have your help. You were a godsend, just when I needed you."

Liora stepped near and threw one arm around Dixie's shoulders. "The feeling is mutual. Now"—she pulled away and grabbed an apron from the hook by the counter—"what's on the menu this morning?"

"This morning's options are flapjacks with bacon, oatmeal with fresh apples, or The Platter."

The Platter, a meal offered each day, was Dixie's most requested breakfast, though Liora had never been able to fathom how the men put away such an enormous spread. Two large biscuits, three eggs, four thick slices of bacon, a side of hash browns, four flapjacks—with the option to add more at just a penny apiece—and as much coffee and milk as they could drink. And men routinely ate every last scrap and put in orders for two or three more flapjacks. It boggled Liora's mind. However, she and Ma used to live in the camps, and well she remembered the long hard days that many of the lumberjacks put in. And for many of the men who breakfasted at Dixie's, it might be the only meal they ate until they arrived back in camp each evening.

Dixie's prices were more than fair and her meals delicious,

which kept the men coming back in droves. Sometimes the tables filled and emptied so fast it was almost more than the two of them could do to keep up. Dixie always took the orders and interacted with the customers while Liora cooked in the kitchen—an arrangement Liora was more than happy with since she much preferred the silence of the kitchen to the snide comments many of the men sent her way. None of them dared speak to Dixie, the doctor's wife, in such a manner however, so the arrangement worked out for the best, all around. The only time she had to go out into the dining room was when Dixie needed help clearing tables, or sweeping up.

"Right. I'll get the first batch of flapjack batter made up."

Dixie touched her arm. "Before you do that, there's something I want to tell you. I've hired Kin Davis to do some work for us. Charlotte says he's completed every lesson she could think to teach him a year early. And he wants to save up some money so he can attend university. He's going to do the running and fetching and gathering of the eggs, sweeping and mopping, and maybe even clearing some of the tables three days a week—if I can train him to do it and still keep my dishes intact."

Liora chuckled. "I think he'll do just fine. And that will be a relief."

"Oh good." Dixie seemed to relax a little. "I worried you would fear that I was trying to replace you, which is not the case at all. We've just been running ourselves so ragged lately that I thought it might be nice for us to have the help."

Liora pulled out the bin of flour. "I'm all for that. When does he start?"

"This morning. He should be here any minute."

"Wonderful. I'll at least get a break from fighting with that mean old rooster of yours." Liora pulled a face as she swept a gesture toward the chicken coop.

Dixie smiled. "I'm sure Roscoe will miss sparring with you on a regular basis." She pushed through the batwing doors into the dining room then, and Liora heard her open the exterior dining room doors and greet the first customers of the day.

She set to whisking together the flapjack batter, and smiled at Kin when he stepped into the room a few minutes later.

In his typical serious way, he gave her the barest of nods in greeting.

"Dixie's busy taking some orders right now, but if you don't mind, could you gather the eggs?"

"Yes, ma'am."

Liora watched him go. When had she last seen the boy smile? Probably not since he'd lost his father a couple years back. Her heart went out to the young man. At seventeen he seemed a lot more world weary than someone his age ought to be. Liora knew the parson had tried to do his best by the boy. And she had to admit that Kin was always polite and courteous. She just wished he would smile once in a while. Maybe now that she worked with him, she'd have a chance to encourage him a little.

She flicked some drops of water against the griddle, pleased to see them dance and sizzle across the surface. Hot enough to start frying the flapjacks.

Dixie swept through the doors with several orders, and the day was off to a start.

Much as Liora enjoyed her job at Dixie's, today she felt a mite restless.

She could hardly wait for her shift to be over. Because as soon as she purchased the supplies she needed, she would head out to Camp Sixty-Five and see who the Lord would lead her to.

For, just like Joe had at one time rescued her, she knew without a doubt that God had called her to rescue other women. She just hadn't told anyone yet. Would the men of the town have been so helpful if they'd known she wanted a cabin so she could have a place to care for rescued camp girls? She hadn't been sure, and thus had kept that information to herself.

But today... Today was the day. Hopefully, after today there would be no more hiding her intentions because she would have one or more women living under her roof. Women she could teach about the love of the Lord. Women she could nurture and restore. Women who were in so much need of a Savior.

Perhaps because of her excitement, the day seemed to drag on. And yet, once the lunch dishes were washed and the kitchen cleaned, she glanced at the small watch she kept in one pocket to find it was thirty minutes earlier than normal. No doubt due to Kin Davis's hard work and quick recognition of what she and Dixie needed, almost before they did themselves.

Not long ago, just before she'd asked for evenings off, Dixie had offered her the job of overseeing the boardinghouse dinners, but Liora felt more thankful now than ever that she'd turned down the extra hours. She'd felt bad, knowing Dixie wanted more time at home in the evenings with her new husband. But it had worked out because Dixie had hired Susan Kastain, whose husband had never quite recovered from the gunshot wound he'd sustained from Liora's now-deceased father. The Kastains needed the income much more than she did, and she was thankful the job had gone to the hardworking mother of five, in addition to giving herself time to follow her calling.

She greeted Susan, who was just coming in as she left, and then stepped out into the glorious sunlight. She'd always loved a sunny day. She glanced longingly at the bridge leading across Wyldhaven Creek. If only she had time to go up to the rose field. She'd passed many a wonderful day up there, sitting on the roots of an old oak tree, reveling in the scent of wild roses in full bloom while she read the little Bible Joe had gifted her. But there was no time for that today.

Liora started across the street toward the mercantile. She grinned as she remembered the battle Miss Brindle had gone through just the month before, trying to get Mr. Hines to correct his sign which read 'Merkantile.' But the man had wanted nothing to do with Miss Brindle's updates. So his sign still hung crooked and misspelled. When she pushed through the door into the store, Mr. Hines looked up from behind the counter with a smile on his face, but his greeting faded when he noted her.

She smiled at him, nonetheless. The man was always congenial to her when he wasn't under the watchful eyes of his new pinch-lipped wife. His first wife had passed away several years ago—long before Liora had ever come to town. And everyone in Wyldhaven had been quite surprised when he'd greeted the stagecoach one day last fall and announced that the fancy woman descending the coach steps was to be his wife.

"Good afternoon, Mr. Hines. Mrs. Hines." She nodded at the woman she could see peering at her from the supply room before turning her attention back to the proprietor. "With my newly completed home, I'm here with quite an order today." She pushed her list across the counter toward him.

The man's mouth thinned a little as he picked it up. His gaze flickered toward the supply closet, not quite making it all the way there before coming to rest on her list, once more. "I'm afraid I can't offer you credit, Miss Fontaine."

Liora kept a smile pasted on her face, ignoring the sting of his distrust. "That's not a problem. I have cash."

He swept a scrutinizing look the length of her as though

trying to assess if she spoke true. She could hope it was an act for his still-spying wife. "Cash?"

The question might as well have accused her of thievery.

Liora reached into her reticule and pulled out several bills—more than enough to cover the cost of the items she needed. She raised her voice so the woman in the storeroom could hear her. "Yes, sir. I work for Dixie in the boardinghouse kitchen, as I'm sure you know."

"Very well." The words were wan. "Give me a moment." He disappeared into the back, her list in hand.

She could hear furious whispers and shuffling. And then silence fell. Mr. Hines had obviously won this round.

Liora eased out a lungful of relief. She'd hate to have to make the longer journey to Cle Elum for supplies.

It wasn't until he started piling her things onto the counter that Liora realized she was going to have quite a time getting all of it home. The items hadn't seemed that numerable when she'd written them down the night before, but the fifty-pound bag of flour alone would be almost more than she could carry.

What was she going to do? She glanced around the store, searching for a solution. A wheelbarrow! Of course! And she would need one anyhow for the garden. She would just have to remember to bring it with her in the future on days when she needed to buy supplies from the mercantile. She wandered toward the shiny red barrow to check the price, then winced as she saw the amount on the tag. Three dollars and seventy-five cents seemed like robbery, but she didn't have a choice and it was a good sturdy one that should last her for years to come. She rolled it toward the front of the store and pulled the extra money from her reticule.

Mr. Hines tallied her purchases and accepted her money, but then he headed into the back room of his store, leaving her to load everything into the wheelbarrow herself. And when she got to the top step just outside the door, she realized she'd made a mistake. She couldn't take the full wheelbarrow down the steep steps to the road without dumping the whole load of dry goods into the street. With a sigh, she started unloading all of the sacks and cans onto the treads.

"Here, let me help you with that."

Liora looked up at the familiar voice. "Joe, you don't have to help. I'll be fine."

Joe ignored her. "You take the handles, and I'll grab the front here near the wheel. Then we can carry it down the stairs together without worry of everything spilling."

She felt anxious to get on her way, and he'd already been seen speaking to her by anyone who was paying attention—which anyone with windows along the Main Street of town probably was—so she didn't suppose accepting his help could do much more damage. "Fine. Thank you."

They lifted it down the stairs and it only took them a moment after that to get the rest of her supplies loaded back into the wheelbarrow. Liora stepped behind it and hefted it by the sturdy wooden handles. "Thanks for your help." She started off down the street.

And Joe waved farewell without comment, but she'd only just made it past the crest of the hill outside of town when he appeared from the woods and swung down from his horse. He handed her the reins. "Here, you take this and let me push that."

Liora gave in to his demand with a little more thankfulness than she probably should feel. She hadn't realized just how heavy the wheelbarrow was until she'd been forced to push it up the long hill. She'd been dreading the five-mile walk out to her place. Her arms already ached. She pulled a handkerchief from the pocket of her dress and dabbed at the moisture on her brow. "Thank you."

He nodded and leaned into the weight of the wheelbarrow to maneuver it over a rut. "How was your day?"

"Fine. And yours?" She clucked to his horse and led it down the road, walking beside Joe.

"Fine," he answered with his typical briefness.

They walked for a few more minutes until the silence felt too companionable and made Liora squirm. "Dixie has hired Kin Davis to help out at the diner. He started today."

He dipped his chin. "Heard that."

"He did a real fine job. He's a hard worker."

"Good to hear."

Liora turned her face away from him before she rolled her eyes. Fine, if he wanted to walk in silence, they could walk in silence, companionable, or no.

But after they'd gone a mile in complete quiet, she couldn't take it any longer. She glanced over at him, paused, and plunked her hands on her hips.

His lips quirked as he set the wheelbarrow down and adjusted his gloves. "You're kind of quiet today."

"Oh, so you did notice?" She raised her brows at him. "It takes two to converse, in case you'd forgotten."

He attempted an injured expression. "What? I'm too short on words for your liking?"

She laughed. "Well, that might be one way to put it."

Joe angled her a sly look. "Okay, how about you tell me what it is you plan to do with the free evenings you seem so reluctant to discuss?"

Liora bit her lip and started walking down the road once more. Why had she twitted him about his silence? Behind her, she heard Joe resume pushing the wheelbarrow. He pulled up beside her and pinned her with his scrutiny. "What is it you don't want me to know?"

She tried for nonchalance with a wave of her hand. "It's nothing. Just with a place of my own I'll have more to attend to. You understand. Gardening. Washing. Canning." She flicked the roll of chicken wire in the wheelbarrow. "I'm hoping to get a chicken coop built soon. And I also hope to buy a sow from the Kastains and maybe a mid-sized hog so I can set some pork to smoking later this autumn." She couldn't bring herself to meet his gaze during her entire explanation.

"I see." A note of suspicion still lingered in his tone. "Nothing else?"

She bit her lip. At one time in her life she wouldn't have hesitated to lie to him. But ever since she'd given her life to the Lord, she'd realized that truth was the commodity of respect and trust. And she didn't want Joe to think he couldn't trust her. "There's more, but for now I'm asking you to let me have my secret. I'm sure it will come out soon enough."

Joe plunked the wheelbarrow down again and turned to face her, hands propped on his hips. "Are you courting someone?"

"What?! No! Whyever would you ask that?" Simply the thought of it resurrected the tremor in her middle.

He swept the back of one gloved hand across his chin, and then took up the wheelbarrow again and headed down the road at a faster clip than before. "No reason. Just can't figure out why you want to keep whatever this is from me, is all."

Liora sighed. It was obvious by the tenor of his tone that she'd hurt him. But, despite that, she couldn't bring herself to tell him her plans. She knew he wouldn't approve of her heading out to the logging camps on her own. And certainly not to take on the likes of John Hunt. For John would see what she planned to do as nothing less than a challenge to his power should she get caught. Which was why she would need to be very careful.

John Hunt ran the area's largest string of brothels. Liora's mother had been one of his girls, right up until the day death had freed her from his clutches. Liora still regretted that she hadn't been by her mother's side during her last hours. But there wasn't much she could do about past failures. All she could do was live her life in such a way that hopefully ten years from now she'd be able to look back and have no regrets about the years between here and there. And that was what she aimed to do.

John liked to recruit his girls young. She'd been fifteen the first time he'd tried to ensnare her into working for him. Her mother had spared her from it by offering to work more hours in her place. Not that her mother's sacrifice had prevented Liora from ending up in the life anyhow, but at least she'd been a little older. And at least Joe had rescued her from the life only a couple weeks after she started. Most girls didn't have anyone to come to their rescue nor any other options, John tended to ensure that. He picked girls with no family and no other way to support themselves. And once they got a little older and realized there were other possibilities in life, if he ever sensed that they might want to get out, he set into motion an endless cycle of owing him for this or that favor and having to put in one more month of work to pay it off. Right up until the grave opened up and accepted the girls into the darkness of its bosom.

But Liora intended to give the girls who would trust her another destiny.

It just wasn't time to share that intention with anyone yet. Not even Joe.

Could she change the subject? "I hear Charlotte has decided

that the town will have boardwalks by the end of this summer. She came into the diner today while school was on lunchbreak with a collection can."

Joe pegged her with a knowing look. But then he must have decided to let the matter drop. "Yes. I've heard the same. Even donated to the cause when she shook that can in my face yesterday." He smiled ruefully.

"If anyone can make it happen, it's her. And I must say that I'll be more than thankful to have them, especially come winter. Those muddy streets are murder on dress hems."

The conversation stalled again, and Liora felt a rush of relief when her cabin came into view only a few minutes later. She motioned to the kitchen steps. "You can just park that by the back door and I'll unload it in a few minutes."

Joe's lips twisted. "I promise to help you unload without doing any more prying if that's what you're worried about."

It had been what worried her. "Very well. Thank you." She tied his horse to the front rail, pulled her key from her reticule, and unlocked the door. "I don't know yet where I'm going to put everything, so you can just stack it all on the sideboard there." She motioned toward the secondhand sideboard that Mrs. Callahan had given her. It was broad and made of solid maple, and separated her kitchen from the dining area just beyond. Joe and the men had made her a table and benches from hand-sawn pine. The remainder of the great room had been designated as a parlor of sorts. It contained the secondhand settee she'd purchased from the Kings when they'd decided on a new one, a trunk which sat beneath the far window, and a rocking chair. Sparse, but functional. Both the kitchen door and a door in the living area led out onto the porch that wrapped around two sides of the house.

It only took Joe and her a few minutes to get the wheelbarrow unloaded. And then he tipped his hat in her direction. "Have a good evening now. I'll put this in the lean-to for you, and then be on my way." He motioned to the chicken wire that still remained in the wheelbarrow, and lifted the handles once more.

She couldn't just let him leave with this tension hanging between them. "Joe?"

He paused and looked at her.

"Thank you for not pressing. It will all be clear soon, I assure you."

He worked his lower lip as he studied her. "Just promise me you aren't planning to do something dangerous."

Liora hesitated. With John Hunt in the picture, she could promise him no such thing.

Joe dropped the wheelbarrow and hooked his thumbs into his beltloops, narrowing his eyes. "You see, that hesitation right there tells me a whole lot more than you think it does. What are you up to?"

She scrambled for an explanation that would satisfy him. "Have you ever felt the Lord calling you to do something, Joe?"

His gaze softened and lifted to the scar she knew remained visible on her forehead for the briefest of seconds, before he glanced at the ground and scuffed his toe into the dirt. "You know I have."

Yes, she did indeed. It was only his intervention at the urging of the Holy Spirit that had saved her from certain suicide. "Then you understand that we don't always have a choice—I mean, if we follow what we feel called to do. God doesn't often ask us to do easy safe things."

Joe stepped closer to her and his voice emerged soft and low when he asked, "And what are the hard, unsafe things you feel God calling you to do?"

A wave of something indefinable curled through her. She

studied his face. His gaze drilled into hers, focused and intense. There was no give in the subtle jut of his jaw. And yet a softness lingered about his eyes and tugged at her. She longed to step closer. To confide in him. But to do so might give him the wrong impression which would only hurt him in the long run. There could be no possible future for them—her past with all its baggage ensured that. And she cared too much for him to impress him otherwise.

And yet, *not* confiding in him, though it may be for his own good, would hurt him also. So what ought she to say? There was naught for it but to think of his future.

"Joe." She kept her voice soft and steady, suddenly feeling the burden of her past mistakes with such clarity her legs threatened to crumple beneath her. She looked away, unwilling to witness the impact of the blow she was about to impart. "You have no more business here. I'll ask you to leave now."

From her peripheral vision, she saw him scrub one knuckle over the dark stubble on his chin. And she could almost feel the hurt radiating off him. But after a moment, he lifted his hands in an 'I surrender' gesture, then stalked toward the lean-to, pushing the wheelbarrow ahead of him.

Battling the tears that threatened to blind her, she turned for the house. Her foot missed the first step, and she fumbled to find it, then rushed into the kitchen and pushed the door shut behind her. She leaned there, head tilted toward the ceiling, and simply let the tears fall. *Father, am I ever to live life on my own? When will this plaguing fear dissipate?*

She was so weak. So selfish. She would love to have the strength to yank open the door, dash across the yard, and beg him to support and protect her in this mission she felt the Lord calling her to. Yet she knew that might lead to more, which terrified her.

Besides, to entangle her life with his... That would be unthinkably self-seeking. Even should God miraculously take away her fears, she would be asking Joe to give up his good standing and reputation in Wyldhaven. And she prayed that her fondness for him would remain strong enough that she'd never be willing to cause him such harm.

oe battled with himself as he mounted his horse. Did he linger and follow her to ensure her safety? Or did he leave her to herself as she'd requested? He sat, staring off toward the horizon. It was his duty to protect all citizens of Wyldhaven, and yet she'd very specifically told him she didn't want his help. *You have no more business here.*

He refused to analyze the pain that burgeoned in his chest at the reminder.

Realizing he still loitered in her yard by the lean-to, he angled a glance toward the cabin. Despite his responsibility, he knew his desire to protect her probably went beyond his obligation to mere duty. He'd never even been tempted to follow any other citizen of Wyldhaven just to make sure they didn't come to injury. He might be able to fool others, but he'd never gone in for trying to fool himself. So what was it about her that made him feel so protective? Why did he feel obligated to go out of his way to help her, when he didn't do that for most others? Was it merely the fact that he'd at one point saved her life? Did he have an underlying fear that if he wasn't around the next time, he might not be able to do the same? Ridiculous. He had no concerns that Liora still wanted to take her own life. She was an entirely different woman now that she knew the Lord.

He resettled his Stetson. How far was too far when pushing

protection on someone who didn't want it? She'd made it more than clear she didn't want him tagging along.

And normally he would never force his help on anyone. Heading back to town was probably best because, in addition to Liora not wanting his help, the town wouldn't stand for him spending too much time with her. Mrs. Hines had already brought up that issue at the last town council. And she was right that he'd spent a good number of his off-duty hours out at Liora's property. He'd also urged the townsmen to help build Liora's cabin. There'd been no denying it. Thankfully, the vote had fallen in his favor. But would it the next time? Pushing to help Liora could cost him his job, he had no doubt of that. Unfair as that might seem, it was the reality.

He jutted his jaw to one side, and then clicked to urge his horse out of the yard.

Halfway back to town, he yanked on the reins with an oath of frustration. He sat for a long moment considering the consequences of what he was about to do. Liora would be upset with him, but she would get over it. And even if it cost him his job, he'd never be able to live with himself if he rode away and something happened to her.

He nodded.

Whether she wanted his protection or not, she was going to get it.

Pulling the horse around, he slapped his reins against its rump. "Get up, now." He dug his heels in too, until his horse settled into a distance-eating gallop.

But when he arrived back at her house, Liora was nowhere to be found. A sinking sensation settled into the region of his heart. She must have departed the moment he'd ridden out of the yard. And she hadn't been on the road toward town, or he would have encountered her while coming back. Where could she have gone?

To a neighbor's house? Out to the logging camps? If so, which one? She could have gone in any number of directions.

Joe leaned on the pommel and pondered. He could take the time to track her and go after her. But with all the activity that had taken place here recently, it likely would take him a good hour to pick up her trail and by that time she'd be so far ahead of him she might be returning home.

There was also the consideration that she might be en route to meet a beau. She'd denied as much earlier, yet...a beautiful woman like her had to have plenty of interested suitors. And it would be some awkward to track her down only to find her passing time with another man.

With a grunt of frustration, he reined his horse toward the road and headed back to town.

He would come out in the morning to escort her in to the diner.

Until then, he would have to content himself with praying for her safety.

From her position on the front bench of the carriage next to Reagan Callahan, who was driving, Charlotte Brindle withheld a sigh.

Seated on the back bench just behind Reagan, the new Mrs. Hines hadn't ceased prattling for the past hour.

Charlotte couldn't help but wonder what Jerry Hines had seen in the woman he'd married last year. Certainly, he'd probably been lonely after the death of his first wife, but how could anyone be *that* lonely? She almost laughed at the irreverent thought. Of course, perhaps Jerry hadn't quite known what he was getting into since the woman had been a mail-order bride.

Even Reagan, who was normally much more patient with people than she, had his jaw clamped so tight she could practically hear his teeth grinding together.

Charlotte covered her mouth and looked away, lest the laugh break free despite her efforts. She shouldn't be so ungrateful. When Pricilla Hines had heard that Charlotte planned a trip to the mining camps to try to raise more funds for the town boardwalks, she'd simply wanted to help. And Charlotte might even dare say they had raised more money with the woman's help than they would have without it. Several people had plunked coins in Charlotte's can simply to be shut of Mrs. Hines's incessant babbling, she felt certain. Never mind that Charlotte had been looking forward to spending an afternoon alone with Reagan. Instead they'd been chaperoned. And neither of them had been able to get a word in edgewise for hours.

The woman was currently in the midst of expounding on the differences between butterflies and moths. A conversation that had been spurred by the innocent curiosity of a monarch that had flown near the carriage.

Reagan glanced over and caught her attention. Humor crinkled the corners of his eyes and he reached over to clasp her hand.

"Ah, ah, ah!" Mrs. Hines leaned over the back of the bench and smacked the knuckles of Reagan's hand with her folded-up fan. "You see, it is a good thing I came along with you two. You may have been courting Miss Brindle for nigh on two years, Sheriff, but you are not married yet." When Reagan didn't immediately let go of Charlotte's hand, the woman barked. "Release her hand, if you please!"

Charlotte squeezed his fingers in a quick gesture of camaraderie, before tugging her hand back into her lap. There was no sense in them giving the woman further ammunition for the gossip she willingly spread to anyone who entered Jerry's mercantile.

Pricilla gave a satisfied hum to have them both once again firmly on their own sides of the carriage seat, and then launched into a tale about a couple she'd known back in New York who had "most scandalously" ridden through the park without chaperones. "It was really most shocking. Most!"

Charlotte so wanted to insert, "This from a woman who traveled west to marry a man sight-unseen." But she managed to restrain herself.

A movement ahead caught her eye at the same moment that Reagan spoke low to the horses. "Whoa there." He pulled the carriage over to one side of the road.

Liora Fontaine walked along the road with a basket over her arm, heading toward the logging camp they'd just left.

From the back bench Mrs. Hines gasped softly.

Reagan nodded to Liora. "Afternoon to you."

"Hello." Charlotte smiled her own greeting.

Liora returned the greeting cordially and then offered, "I'm heading out to Camp Sixty-Five for a bit."

Reagan nodded. "We're just coming from there. How was your first night in your new place?"

A snort emanated from the back seat.

Liora's feet shuffled as her gaze darted to the woman.

Charlotte's irritation with Pricilla Hines mounted.

"It was lovely. Thanks for asking. So wonderful to see the fruits of my labor finally coming to bear." Liora's smile seemed a bit thin around the edges, but there was no denying the sparkle in her eyes.

"We're so happy for you." Charlotte infused as much enthusiasm into her words as she could. "You've worked so hard for this. We're all so proud of you!"

A louder snort from Mrs. Hines this time.

Liora looked down and adjusted the basket on her arm. "Yes. Well. I'd best get going if I'm going to make it back home before dark."

Reagan touched the brim of his Stetson. "Evening to you, Miss Fontaine." He clucked to the horses, and with that they parted company.

The wheels on the carriage had barely started rolling when Mrs. Hines emitted a shocked exclamation. "Well, I never! You surely aren't going to allow her to continue on without challenging the blatant immorality of what she's doing, are you?!"

Charlotte clenched her hands together and clamped her teeth over her tongue. The woman was insufferable.

"Blatant immorality?" By the underlying tone of Reagan's words, Charlotte could tell that he planned to have a little fun with Mrs. Hines. "Last I checked there were no Biblical laws about walking along a road minding one's own business, Mrs. Hines."

"Oh! Go on with you. You know exactly what I'm talking about. She used to be a woman of...well...a woman of... Oh! You both know very well what she used to be. And there can be only one reason she'd be heading out to the camps at this time of night! Why Camp Sixty-Five is so heathen I'd lay money on the fact that not even the Lord can bring Himself to search it out!"

Reagan's jaw bunched. "If you and I can find Camp Sixty-Five, Mrs. Hines, I'm sure the good Lord certainly can."

Charlotte busied herself with brushing invisible dust from her skirts to keep from laughing at that.

Mrs. Hines gasped her outrage and craned around to watch Liora disappearing into the distance behind them.

But Reagan wasn't done. "And in case you hadn't heard,

Miss Fontaine has repented of her past sins and found a new life in Christ. In my book that makes her a sister in Christ and someone to be respected and admired. Certainly no more of a sinner than someone who, say, makes a habit of gossip, for example."

"Well-well, yes," Mrs. Hines sputtered. "But actions do speak louder than words. If she were *truly* repentant, she wouldn't place herself in such a questionable situation!"

"The only thing questionable I see, Mrs. Hines, is your rush to judgement in a situation you know nothing about."

Charlotte pulled in a breath and held it, lest she be tempted to cheer Reagan on.

"Well! I never!" Pricilla flounced against the back of her seat with enough force that the carriage shifted. Then she set to mumbling. Most of what she said was incomprehensible, though Charlotte did think she caught "backwater" and "heathen" and "God forsaken" in the diatribe.

The road took Liora through acres of clear-cut land, with nothing but stumps and small saplings no higher than her knees. A squirrel, cheeks stuffed so full that he must have just come from robbing an entire grain field, dashed across the road in front of her and leapt up to study her from the flat of a stump, nose and tail twitching. After a moment, he turned and continued his mad dash up the hill.

Here and there a few lone tall trees had been left uncut to reseed the area. She knew that many logging companies didn't give a care for such things. Each tree left on the land was considered a loss of money. Yet she couldn't help but be thankful that Mr. Heath apparently gave thought to the future as well as to the present.

The road wound up a steep hill and topped out above Camp Sixty-Five. She paused and settled a hand over the trepidation worming through her stomach.

Just the sight of the camp nestled in the valley below, which she hadn't visited since she'd left almost three years ago, nearly took the strength from her knees. In all that time, naught seemed to have changed. Though most logging camps were built only as temporary housing, and this one had certainly started out as such, it had far outlived the quality of the first shelters that had been erected. Those, amazingly enough, still stood on the far end of the camp—row upon row of windowless structures, the farthest of which appeared to nestle up against the green wall of timber that towered just beyond them. These thin, gray, canted buildings looked as though a good stiff breeze could topple the whole section of them like so many dominoes. Timber walls, so thin that they frosted up on the inside in the deepest part of winter, were weather-stripped with other, narrower, boards nailed over the gaps. The buildings stood so close together that conversations were often carried on right through the walls from one shanty to the next. Smoke streaked from many of the round, black stovepipes which protruded from each cedar-shingled roof. Mean and lean as these shanties were, they housed crew foremen and loggers who had worked for the company long enough to be awarded one of the coveted abodes.

Closer to the middle of the camp stood three log cabins that, though small, Liora knew to be much warmer and more comfortable than the shanties. These housed the top three crew chiefs and their families, if they had any.

The rest of the camp consisted of scattered tents, covered wagons, and tent houses—timber walls about three to four feet high, topped with canvas ceilings.

Her eyes were drawn to the largest of the tent houses, even as the sick feeling in the pit of her stomach doubled. There, nearly at the very heart of the camp, John Hunt ran his brothel, each room separated by nothing more than a bit of thin canvas.

The women who worked for him were each "awarded" a small lean-to in the thinned copse of trees just at the edge of the camp. These were nothing more than a few boards nailed together and leaning against the trunks or branches of the trees.

On rainy nights, bedding became damp clear through. And Liora remembered sitting up many a night, arms wrapped around her knees, rocking and trying to keep warm by their small fire, while her mother worked. During the winter, never warm. During the summer, never cool. Constant thirst. Constant dirt. And always the fear.

Several times, Mother had tried to leave John. One time they'd even made it a good way into the forest that grew up thick and wild beyond the thinned area, but always John's guard, who patrolled the lean-tos, had caught them and forced them back to their hut. Prisoners in their own home.

It was this last thought that currently made Liora's stomach turn. Because her one reason for coming here was to help women escape. But the *how* of it, she had been grappling with.

And what would she do if John caught wind she was in the camp? He'd never liked the fact that she'd refused to work for him. Could he force her into his brothel? And who would stop him if he tried?

Joe.

She pushed the thought away before it could take root.

Still, she hesitated. How would she even decide which women to help? Her limited resources meant that choices would have to be made. Maybe this hadn't been the best idea. Maybe she should come back another day, after she'd worked out a better plan.

The canvas flaps of the main brothel entrance burst apart and a man lurched into the square in front of the building, hauling a dark-haired woman by one arm. She clutched at her bodice, which had been torn from collar to midriff, trying to keep it clasped shut with her one free hand. The man tossed her to the ground and leaned over her.

"I want my money!"

The woman shook her head and attempted to scramble back from him. Her reply emerged too soft for Liora to hear from this distance.

Like ants converging on sweet fruit, people started pouring into the square from every direction. They surrounded the couple, but no one moved to help the woman.

And then Liora saw him.

John Hunt stepped out of the crowd, his tall ten-gallon hat an unseemly white slash against the sepia and gray tones that painted every other surface of the valley below, from dirt roads to dusty canvas. He hooked his thumbs into his belt and spat a stream of tobacco to one side. "I'll know what's going on here." His words dropped into the sudden silence that had settled.

The bruiser flashed a gesture at the woman still lying at his feet. "She stole my whole poke when I were washing up."

Again, the woman shook her head, her eyes darting up to John. Even from the hill above, Liora could see the woman's terror.

John strode to her, squatted to the balls of his feet, and said a few words.

Another shake of her head, and again words too quiet to hear.

One moment John was simply looking down at her, the next his hand cracked across the flesh of her cheek so fiercely the sound seemed to echo off the surrounding hills.

Liora's hand flew to cover her own cheek.

John stood and spat another stream of tobacco directly onto the woman's skirt. He motioned to one of his guards. "Toss her room. I'll not have a thief working for me. If you find his wallet, bring it." To the patron he offered a handshake, while reaching into his vest pocket with his left hand. "We can make this right. How much did you lose?"

The man hesitated. Only for the briefest of moments. But in this situation, it changed the whole atmosphere.

John froze and looked up at the man, his money clip half way out of his vest pocket.

"Ten dollars. And a couple bits," the man rushed to say.

It was almost the end of the month. And the loggers were paid only once each month on the fifth. The likelihood of a man such as this still having ten dollars to his name was slim, Liora knew. And obviously, from the look on John's face, he knew it too. His eyes narrowed in a telltale way. He returned his money to his vest and propped his hands against his hips.

His guard returned at that moment. "Didn't find anything, boss."

John regarded the client for a long moment before nodding the guard toward the woman, who hadn't dared to stand in all this time. "Search her."

The guard yanked the woman to her feet. After a very thorough and invasive search of her clothing and body, he turned once more to face John with a shake of his head. "Nothing."

Without another word, John drew the pistol from the holster at his hip and leveled it at the accuser's chest.

A gasp rose up from the crowd. Everyone standing behind the man scattered.

"Now wait just a min—" He didn't have time to say more.

John shot him where he stood and he crumpled to the ground.

Chapter Four

Liora jolted. John couldn't just do that, could he? She scanned the crowd. Most were studying the ground. Feet shuffled, but no one challenged him.

Into the thick silence, John said, "I'll not tolerate anyone who lies about my girls." He holstered his pistol and swept a gesture from his guard to the body in an indication that the man knew what he needed to do. John started to walk away, but paused by the prostitute's side and gave her shoulder a gentle squeeze. "You go on and get cleaned up now."

The woman tugged her shoulder from his grasp, still clutching her blouse closed, but John didn't seem to notice either her contempt or the state of her dress. He adjusted his hat, strolled up the street, and disappeared into a tent that housed one of the camp's saloons.

Slowly, the crowd disbursed and the woman limped her way past the brothel toward the lean-tos beyond.

Liora's feet, which up to that moment had seemed iced to the ground, came free, and she moved to keep track of the woman. Sticking to the trail that skirted the ridge above the camp, she hurried toward the northeast, eyeing the woman's progress as she made her way through the lean-tos. Liora reached the head of the path that led down into the copse of trees, thankful that winter frosts had stripped most of the deciduous trees of their leaves. She watched until she caught a glimpse of the woman ducking inside one of the structures, and then scrambled down the hill.

She passed the lean-to she and Mother used to live in, willing down the urge to rush away to safety. If John caught her here... But she had no time to dwell on that now. Besides, she'd seen him go into the saloon. If he still stuck to his patterns, he likely wouldn't emerge till nearly midnight or beyond.

And why had she come, if not to help? The medicines in her basket would help the cut on the woman's cheek, if nothing else. And maybe, just maybe, the Lord had sent her here with rescue on His mind. The least she could do was try. There would be no better time to make an escape than now with John's goon busy getting rid of a body.

Liora tapped on the thin door of the home and when the woman opened it, she still clutched her blouse together with one hand.

Her eyes widened a bit and she took Liora in from head to toe.

The new green day-dress she'd purchased only last month from Mrs. Callahan gave her away as a stranger to camp life.

"You ain't from these parts. What you want?" The woman's voice was surprisingly soft and mellow. Or maybe it just seemed more so, juxtaposed with the harsh surroundings and the violence Liora had just witnessed.

Liora clutched her shawl more tightly at her throat and tossed a glance over her shoulder. "I'm not from around here anymore, but I used to be. I have some medicines, and I'd like to help you with that cut if you'll let me."

The woman's gaze drifted to where Liora's own scar marred one side of her forehead. She let her look, knowing that a lack of defensiveness would be the quickest way to gain this woman's trust.

Now that she stood closer and could see her more clearly, "woman" probably wasn't quite accurate. The brunette before her was likely closer to seventeen than twenty-five, though the hard life of the camps tended to age a person so she might even be younger. Liora could see why she'd been drafted into John's brothel. She was beautiful in a breathtaking way that would stop most men in their tracks. Obviously of mixed race, her porcelain skin, golden-brown touched with cream, accentuated dark-lashed blue eyes that seemed to carry the weight of the world. Liora wondered where her parents might be.

After a long moment, the girl stepped back. "Don't see's how you can make things worse."

That was the only invite Liora got, but she was fine with that. She ducked under the lintel and shut the door behind her. She moved to set her basket on the room's small table. A strange looking pistol with a fat handle lay atop it.

Liora froze. Her gaze sought out the girl who had sunk onto the only other piece of furniture in the room, a small cot.

The girl looked down. "Don't worry none, I ain't got the courage to use it. I done tried so many times, the devil just laughs when I pick it up now."

Heart full with the knowledge that the Lord had indeed brought her here, Liora nudged the pistol to one side and set her basket down. Was this what Joe had felt like all those years ago when God had woken him from sleep and sent him to rescue her from herself?

Lord, give me words. She turned to face the girl. "May I know your name?"

"Teresa. Teresa Trenton But mos' just call me Tess."

"Both are beautiful names." Liora smiled as she tugged off her shawl and held it out to the girl. "Do you have another blouse?"

Tess swallowed, and accepted the shawl with a small shake of her head.

Liora glanced at the cut that still seeped along Tess's cheek. It was too dark in here to clean it properly. "Do you have a lantern? Or a candle?"

A barely perceptible shake of her head was the only response.

That was probably fine because Liora felt a keen urge to be gone from this place. She dug for one of the clean cotton bandages in her basket. "Water?"

Tess lifted a half-filled canning jar from the floor near her feet.

Liora wetted her cloth and stepped closer to the girl. She dabbed away the blood and dirt. "You don't have to stay with him, you know. He doesn't own you."

Tess's lips pressed into a hard thin line. "Easy fo' a white woman to say. He won't let me leave. I done tried."

Liora stepped back and made sure she had Tess's full attention. "Come with me. Right now. I have a place about five miles from here. John is in the saloon and"—she waved a hand—"whoever he has working for him right now is off burying that body."

Suspicion narrowed Tess's blue eyes. "You tryin' to start competition fo' John? Cause he ain't gonna like it none."

"No! Heaven's no. I just want to help you."

"Why?"

Liora paused. There wasn't time to offer her whole story. She settled for, "Because someone once did the same for me."

Tess's eyes widened and she took Liora in from head to toe. "You was once a whore?"

Liora felt the stab of regret that always accompanied the reminder. She nodded. "I was."

"And you just offerin' to he'p me?"

"I am. In fact, it's exactly why I came here."

"What I gots to do?"

"I'll have rules. But only about helping keep the place clean, the garden weeded, that sort of thing. You won't be expected to...entertain anyone."

For one brief moment, hope lit the girl's eyes, but then her shoulders slumped. "He never gonna let me go. No matter that I ain't nobody's slave. Jus' the way things be."

Liora had to admit she felt much the same way. "I understand. More than you know, because my mother used to be one of John's girls. But we can try."

Tess gave her little shanty a long scrutiny, and Liora knew the moment she'd made her decision. She wrapped the shawl about herself, forming a covering like a corset, picked up the pistol from the table and thrust it into her skirt, and then propped her hands on her hips. "Fine. We go."

Liora scrambled to thrust everything back into her basket. "You don't have anything else you want to bring?"

Tess gave one last look around. "Only other thing here is the blankets, and I'll leave 'em for the next gal, if you don't think we need 'em."

Liora's heart softened to the girl. "That's very thoughtful of you. Okay, wait here a moment and I'll make sure all is clear." She cracked open the door and assessed the area just in front of the shanty. Seeing nothing out of the ordinary, she stepped outside to give the area a once-over. No one seemed to be paying Tess's little lean-to any mind, so Liora tapped on the door. "Let's go."

With Tess on her heels, she hurried through the copse toward the dirt path that led to the top of the ridge. If they could just make it onto the road that led to Wyldhaven, they should be able to make good time. If they hurried, they should be back at her cabin before anyone even realized Tess had gone missing.

Liora lamented all the other women in all the other shanties. But she couldn't save everyone at once. She would have to come back for more another day.

Hoisting her skirts, she devoured the hill with large strides, Tess scrambling to keep up just behind her. Once on the path at the top of the ridge, she wanted nothing more than to run to the connecting trail that would take them back home, but she forced herself to walk calmly, knowing that anyone who looked up to see two women running out of the camp would immediately raise an alarm. Thankfully, there were some patches of brush that kept them from being seen from below by turns. But each time they came to a clearing, Liora held her breath, listening intently for any outcry.

She could hardly believe it when they reached the road leading back to Wyldhaven. Just a short section down the hill through a few trees and then they would be in the cleared acres where they would be able to be seen for a good ways in either direction.

Her heart pounded. She hadn't thought of that. If they noticed that Tess didn't arrive back at work and went looking for her...

Now that they were out of sight of the camp, there was nothing for it but to run. Liora took hold of Tess's arm and urged her forward. "Run!" They had to put distance between themselves and the camp.

For a little way, Tess kept up, but they hadn't gone nearly far enough before she stumbled to a stop and propped her hands against her knees. "Can't. Keep. Runnin'."

Liora's heart panged her. The girl had been surviving on a subsistence diet, even though John did make sure to feed his girls well enough to keep them just above skin and bones. She wasn't in any condition to be running five miles back to the cabin.

She glanced behind them. Still no sign of pursuit. She took a breath and slipped her arm through Tess's. "All right. We'll walk, but we need to walk as quickly as possible."

Tess nodded, still fighting for air. But as they set out, Liora was thankful to see that the girl really did understand the need to hurry.

An hour later, with the sun hanging in the sky above the mountains to the west of Wyldhaven, a shout echoed down the ridge from behind them.

Tess's eyes grew wide, and Liora could feel a tremble in her arm. She spun to look back.

Barreling toward them on a steel-dust-gray Appaloosa, John's guard had a hard glint in his eyes.

Nothing but open fields surrounded them, and the house was still fifteen minutes away. They had nowhere to go. Nowhere to hide.

Liora tucked Tess behind her, lifted her chin, and sent up a fleeting prayer.

Joe hadn't been able to relax for a moment since he'd gotten back to Wyldhaven. Agitation had him pacing through his rounds of the town. All remained quiet, which was probably good for the criminal element of the area because in his current state of mind he itched for a fight. He headed back to the jailhouse, but only sat for two minutes before he lurched to his feet and took to the street again.

Walking was infinitely better than sitting and wondering. Not that it stopped the wondering. But at least it gave the pent-up energy thrashing around in his chest a form of release.

He had just started on his fifth round of Wyldhaven when he saw Reagan drive back into town and help Mrs. Hines down from the carriage in front of the mercantile. Charlotte was also in the carriage so Reagan would probably head to his mother's place next, since Charlotte rented a room there.

Joe tipped his hat to Charlotte when she glanced his way, prepared to stroll on by and continue his pacing. However, Reagan lifted a hand and motioned for him to approach.

"If you'll give me but a moment, Mrs. Hines," Reagan said as Joe stepped over, "I'll escort you to your door."

Mrs. Hines offered a curtsy of acceptance. She tugged on the lace at the wrists of her gloves and gave Joe a once-over.

He tipped his hat to her, wondering what Reagan needed.

Mrs. Hines busied herself with swiping invisible dust from her skirts and tried to look like she wasn't paying attention, yet obviously paying attention was the only thing she *was* doing. She might as well hold an ear trumpet in their direction.

And Reagan didn't seem to want to let the town's biggest gossip in on their conversation, whatever it might be.

Reagan clapped him on one shoulder. "Join Charlotte and I in the carriage, would you? There's something I'd like to discuss with you. I'll be back in just a moment."

Joe ignored the huff that emanated from Mrs. Hines, and swung up to the back seat of the carriage.

"Good evening, Joe." Charlotte turned to him and offered a nod.

He snatched off his hat and pressed it to his chest, returning her greeting. The polite thing to do would be to fill the silence with conversation while they waited for Reagan to return from escorting Mrs. Hines right to her door, but worry still churned through him and made small talk illusive.

He watched Reagan escort Mrs. Hines up the mercantile steps.

Should he have taken time to find Liora's trail and gone after her? Despite the fact that it would have been overstepping, he couldn't help but feel it had been a big mistake to leave her on her own. There were all manner of dangers that could befall a woman. Especially one as beautiful as... He gritted his teeth and crimped the crown of his Stetson.

Reagan stood to one side of the door to the mercantile now, hat pressed to his chest, obviously waiting for Mrs. Hines to enter, but the woman groused about something in a low voice, leaning in to make sure Reagan understood her concerns. From this distance, Joe could only hear a strident note every once in a while, not make out her exact words.

Reagan said a few low words of his own, then leaned past the woman to unlatch the door and nudge it open. He actually put his hand to her back and, despite the heaviness of his own heart, Joe had to bite down on a grin as Reagan practically pushed Mrs. Hines into her husband's store and shut the door behind her.

Reagan had barely reached the carriage and swung aboard before Joe noticed Mrs. Hines' face in the window above the mercantile. She peered down at them, cheek practically pressed through the glass in her attempts to see them best. He looked down, scrubbing at the grin that wanted to break free. The woman had made singularly excellent time up to the home she and her husband and stepson shared above the store.

Reagan clucked to the horses and snapped the reins. "Get up now." He waited only until the carriage was rolling before giving Joe a glance over his shoulder. "Liora say anything to you about going out to Camp Sixty-Five today?"

Something like a boulder fell into Joe's stomach. He shook his head. "She told me she had plans, but didn't want to say what they were."

Reagan scratched at the stubble on his chin, jaw jutted to one side. "Might be best for you to ride out to her place to check on her. We ran into her on our way home. She was walking out to the camp. I didn't think much of it at first, but the more I think on it, the more something doesn't feel right. I'd just feel better if we made sure she was all right tonight."

Joe didn't need a second urging. "I'll go right now." And as Reagan slowed to take the turn onto his mother's street, Joe leapt from the carriage and sprinted for his horse at the livery.

As he galloped out of town, he saw the curtains above the mercantile flutter.

He shook his head as he snapped the reins against his horse's haunch. Mrs. Hines wouldn't rest until she learned what had taken him down the road at a gallop. She'd probably made it halfway across town to Jacinda Callahan's already.

He only hoped he wouldn't have to bring back word of a tragedy.

iora stood her ground, Tess trembling at her back, as John's thug rode up and dismounted. He slapped his reins against one palm and gave her a once-over. "The girl there works for John Hunt."

Tess's feet shuffled.

"She quit." Liora thanked the Almighty that her voice emerged steadier than she felt.

"She can't quit."

"Last I heard, slavery has been outlawed in this country."

The man huffed a sound halfway between a laugh and a grunt of disgust. "She ain't no slave. Just under a contract, of sorts—and she gets paid."

The response riled her. Liora knew just exactly how much John's girls got paid and it could hardly be called pay at all. "Is that right? Did she sign a paper?" She glanced at Tess over her shoulder. "Did you sign anything?" She swallowed, knowing that sometimes John did make girls sign a paper. Yet other times he overlooked it. Was Tess legally bound to him?

Eyes wide with fear, Tess shook her head.

Liora took a breath, relief coursing through her. "There, you see? She never signed anything. So, she can quit whenever she wants." She spun on her heel, took firm hold of Tess's arm, and set out at a good clip. "We bid you good day, sir." She leaned close to the girl and whispered fiercely, "Give me your pistol!"

She tossed a glance over her shoulder. The man still watched them, one hand fisted against his chin.

Tess fought with the material of her pocket, but was finally able to remove the gun and hand it over. Liora assessed it. She'd never seen anything quite like it. The gun was so old that the wooden grip had cracked in several places and separated a bit from the metal housing. There was a little ramrod-looking piece that she didn't remember seeing on the gun Joe had given her, and the barrel of the thing looked about as rusty as a crosscut saw blade left too long in the rain. Why hadn't she thought to bring along the pistol Joe had given her? Because she had no idea how to use one, that was why.

"Is it loaded?" she whispered to Tess.

Tess gave a dip of her chin.

Liora used both thumbs to lever back the hammer and glanced at Tess with brows upraised.

Tess nodded affirmation.

"I said she can't quit!" The angry words were accompanied by the unmistakable sound of a rifle cocking.

Liora and Tess froze.

Tess's blue eyes flickered in fear from the gun to Liora's face. She pressed close to Liora's shoulder. Her barely audible words quavered. "I should just go back with him. I'll be in powerful trouble as it is. If I cause more problems, things will only get worse."

"They can't *force* you to work for them!" Liora whispered. "Just stand your ground. He'll have to leave us alone." She patted the pistol. "Especially when he sees this." *Or shoot me and take her back by force.* The thought did nothing to comfort. Especially when *or take us both* followed fast on its heels.

Summoning every ounce of courage she possessed, Liora spun to face the man once more. She kept the pistol carefully hidden in the gathers of her skirt. "Mr.—I'm sorry, I didn't catch your name?"

"Pike." The man spat a stream of tobacco against the embankment, eyeing her over his rifle. "Burt Pike. But civilities ain't gonna help you none."

"Well, Mr. Pike, please return to Mr. Hunt and let him know that Teresa Trenton no longer wishes to remain in his employ."

"Can't do that. You've got exactly ten seconds to hand her over or I'm going to drop you where you stand and take her anyhow."

Liora raised the pistol to arm's length and pointed it right at the man. "Not if I drop you first." If only her arm would stop trembling!

Pike blinked, took in the weapon, and then burst out laughing. "You'd be lucky if that old musket worked to club a mongrel over the head." His voice and expression lost all traces of humor. "Now drop it, or I will shoot."

Liora lowered her aim, and pulled the trigger, hoping merely to maim the man in the leg. But the gun only emitted a soft click as the hammer fell into place. Liora's heart stopped.

Pike, who had momentarily flinched away from them, set to swearing so loudly that a hawk perching on one of the seed trees took to flight. He raised his own rifle to his shoulder and Liora had no doubt she was about to enter into eternity.

Tess gasped and leapt forward to spread her arms wide in front of Liora. "I'll come. Don't go shootin' her now. I'll come!"

But at that moment another voice spoke from behind them. "Drop the gun. Now."

Liora's eyes fell closed in relief at the sound of that oh-so-wonderful voice, even as she tugged Tess behind her once more.

Pike jolted and searched the hills beyond them. "Who's there?"

Liora chanced a glance. Not a soul in sight. Just the clear-cut fields of rolling hills. But there were any number of stumps or low-lying bushes he could be behind, she supposed.

"Deputy Joseph Rodante from Wyldhaven. Don't make me tell you again."

The reply allowed her to pinpoint the place where Joe must be, but a search still didn't reveal him.

"Show yourself!" Pike's tone rose almost as high as a schoolboy's.

Joe's reply came in the form of a shot that knocked Pike's hat from his head.

The man cursed, and lunged behind his horse.

"Get on your horse and ride back to camp. Let Hunt know that both these ladies are now under my protection." Joe may as well have been discussing the price of wheat.

Despite his calm, his statement made her heart lurch and her mouth go dry. What had she just done? No way could he protect them and keep his distance. This could very well mean the end of his reputation—something she'd been fighting hard to protect for quite some time. But she could consider on that quandary another day. For now, she'd like to get Tess to the cabin in one piece.

Joe's boots now crunched through the brush on the hillside and Liora glanced back once more to see him descending toward them, rifle held ready, his eyes never leaving Pike. A three-foot-tall stump must have been his hiding place.

"Coward!" Pike challenged.

Joe didn't miss a step. "If you'd like to put your weapons down and step over here, we can see just which one of us is the coward."

Pike swung astride his horse. "You want me to deliver a message to Hunt, or do you want to fight?"

"Any man who forces a woman to do something against her will is the coward in my book. And you can tell Hunt I said so." Joe's voice remained low and steady, but there was a tightness about it that told Liora he remained on high alert. He stepped between them and Pike now, putting himself in the line of fire should the man decide not to comply with his orders.

But Pike only reined his mount around and kicked his heels into its side.

Joe didn't move until the man had ridden out of sight, and then he turned and gave her a hard look. He thrust his chin in the direction of her cabin. "Let's go." A muscle bulged in his jaw. "And give me that." He snatched the pistol from her hand. "Don't you know that you should never point a gun at someone unless you plan to actually use it?"

"I *did* use it. It just didn't shoot."

Joe pulled back the hammer with his thumb and then looked over at her. "You didn't put on a percussion cap."

"A what?"

Joe only narrowed his eyes on her, jaw bunching. "Where did you even get this thing?"

"It's Tess's."

Joe's hard gaze flicked to Tess, who still cowered behind her, peering out at him with wide eyes. Something in his expression softened subtly. He motioned in the direction of Liora's cabin. "We need to go."

Liora took a breath, the sting of his reproach settling in the region of her heart. She'd never seen Joe this angry before. But there was something she needed to say. "Joe, John Hunt shot a man."

"What?"

She nodded. "Just a bit ago. In Camp Sixty-Five. In front of a whole crowd of people."

Beside her, Tess nodded.

Joe scrubbed at his jaw and studied the road in the direction of camp. "He dead?"

"I think so. Though I can't be certain. I followed Tess to her cabin and didn't see much of what happened after."

"All right. I'll look into it. First, let's get you home."

She put one arm around the girl's shoulders. "Come on. Everything is going to be all right now. Joe won't harm us. Let's get home."

The problem was, she felt very certain everything was *not* going to be all right.

At least not for Deputy Rodante.

And the fault for it lay squarely at her feet.

Joe whistled for his horse, and waited as the mustang descended the hill. Gathering up the reins, he counselled himself to take deep breaths, then trudged down the road behind the scurrying women.

He could still feel his heart beating so hard that his pulse throbbed in his throat. He could honestly say he'd never been so scared about anything in his entire life, and it had nothing to do with facing down a man with a gun.

No. Not at all.

He'd faced down gunmen plenty of times and he'd never had that wash of terror wing through him.

Earlier when he'd swung by her cabin and found it empty, he'd cut across the back of her property and taken the shortcut to the road. When he'd come out on top of the ridge and seen Liora below with a gun pointed at her, the fear had been instant and strong enough to make his legs weak when he'd quickly dismounted from his horse.

And that had been the moment he'd known...

Despite all his efforts over the past few years, he'd gone and fallen in love with a woman he could never have. At least not if he wanted to keep his place in polite society.

And yet what had he done only a moment later? Declared that both Liora and this other woman were under his protection. It wouldn't take long for word of that to spread back to town.

Still, he'd do it all again. And maybe he could pass it off as just a deputy doing his job of protecting the citizens of his town. Maybe. But after only a moment more of consideration, he gave a soft huff. He'd be a fool to think he could pass this off as just a deputy's duty. Like it or not, Liora's actions today had sealed his fate as well as hers for the days to come. Because she would need protection. And he wasn't about to leave her without it again.

By this time tomorrow, the people of the town would be demanding his resignation, or worse, voting on his termination.

Teeth clenched, he paused to study the road and hillsides behind them. The last thing he needed was for Pike to double back and take a shot at them from a hidden position. The tight ball of tension in his gut eased only partially when all seemed quiet.

A few minutes later, he followed the women across the yard and up onto Liora's porch.

Liora used the key he had given her, and unlocked the door.

Thankfully, she'd at least taken that much of his advice, earlier. But he couldn't fathom what had made her think going out to the camps without a man to protect her had been a good idea.

Blast. He was still shaking like a dry leaf in a full-blown

autumn windstorm because a picture just wouldn't release him. A picture of Liora lying in the roadbed, eyes staring lifelessly, and blood seeping across her chest. If he'd been too late...

Stepping through the kitchen, Liora nudged the girl toward one of the spare rooms she'd specifically requested be built into the cabin.

He scrubbed his hand across the back of his neck. She had been planning this all along, hadn't she? Anger burgeoned. He yanked off his hat and tossed it onto the kitchen sideboard. Pressing his palms against the cool surface, he let his head hang and pulled in a calming breath. This anger coursing through him was not a normal emotion for him. And he knew the emotion had been born out of fear.

Grabbing up his hat, he banged back out the door, and tugged his horse toward the three-sided lean-to. It wasn't even tall enough for the Paint to have some cover. Hard as he'd ridden the animal from town, it needed some rest before he rode out to Camp Sixty-Five. He would ride out after dinner. The horse might need rest, but *he* needed anything *but* rest. He knew Liora planned to build a barn. Maybe he could work off some of his pent-up emotions before having a conversation with her. But they *would* be having a conversation.

He tied the Paint off to a bush and looped a feedsack over his head. After rolling up his sleeves, he took up her shovel, and set about clearing the area that would make a good floor for the barn.

He wasn't sure how long he had been working, but it had been at least an hour, when Liora poked her head out of the cabin door to announce dinner was ready.

He rested his arm on the shovel's handle and used his bandana to wipe the sweat from his face.

She still watched him, hands tucked behind her and leaning

against the wall next to the door, when he started toward the house.

He paused, then resumed his course.

She didn't move, simply watched him with those soft blue eyes of hers.

He propped the shovel against the porch railing and folded his arms, unsure how to begin the conversation they needed to have, or even if this was the right time for it.

She made the decision for him. "I've made you angry."

He lifted his gaze to hers, surprised to see a glimmer of moisture in her eyes before her rapid blink whisked it away.

And just the sight of her near to tears made him feel like the lowest of any low-down scoundrel he'd ever run across. He was a cad. He adjusted his hat, took the steps up to her level, and looked down at the porch boards beneath his feet. "Only because I felt so terrified when I came up over that hill and saw Pike with his gun trained on you."

He heard her sniff. And then a dry chuckle escaped her. "I confess to being a mite terrified myself."

"What were you thinking?" The words were out before he could consider better of them. And the hardness of his tone compounded the mistake.

She spun to yank open the screen door, tossing her retort over her shoulder as she disappeared inside. "Best come in before dinner goes stone cold."

Instead of following her immediately, he turned to face the yard, leaning into the rail. *Lord, I don't know why you stuffed me full of these feelings that I can't do anything about. But I can see that if I'm going to reach her, I need to take a step back and approach this with a lot less fire. Just help her to see that my main concern is for her safety. And help me to know how to best protect her and keep my reputation intact.*

With that, he turned and opened the screen door, paused to wash up at the kitchen sink, and then stepped over to the table. He set his hat on the end of the bench Liora indicated, and sank onto his seat.

From the pinched-lip looks on both women's faces, this would be just about the longest meal he'd ever endured.

iora forced herself to think of anything but how discomfited she felt over Joe's anger. She'd expected him to be hurt that she hadn't taken him to the camp with her, but she hadn't expected him to be so angry about it. In fact, if the truth were told, she'd halfway expected him to admire her desire to help girls like Tess.

It pleased her that the blouse she'd given to Tess fit her well. The girl would eventually need more clothes, but for now, she was taken care of.

Tess squirmed in her seat, making Liora realize she hadn't yet made introductions. "Teresa Trenton, this is Deputy Joseph Rodante from Wyldhaven. Joe, Teresa prefers to be called Tess."

Seemingly all politeness now, Joe tipped Tess a nod as he tucked his napkin into his lap. "Miss, nice to meet you."

"Yessuh," Tess murmured, her eyes never leaving the tabletop, and awkward silence settled as Joe looked back to Liora. With Joe's focus no longer on her, Tess seemed to take in every detail of the room, the table, the silverware set at each place, even the material of the tablecloth which she fingered with a bit of an awed expression.

Liora realized it had probably been a good long time since the girl had sat down to a properly set table. Why, she herself wouldn't even have known what a properly set table looked like, had she not worked at Dixie's boardinghouse.

Tess's stomach rumbled loudly through the stillness and her face pulled into a grimace of embarrassment.

Chagrinned that she'd delayed dinner due to a dread of facing Joe, Liora fidgeted. "Joe, say the blessing, would you?"

His blessing was short and to the point, and Liora was left to once more fill the quiet. Fine, she didn't have to talk to Joe. She didn't quite know what to say to him anyhow. What had spurred his anger? He'd said he'd been terrified. But there had to be more to it than that, didn't there? Surely, his anger didn't stem from her desire to help women who were fallen, like she had been? The thought was too painful to consider. She pushed it away and focused her attention on Tess as she passed the bowl of potatoes to her. "I hope your room is satisfactory?"

Tess nodded, and quickly swallowed the bite of biscuit already in her mouth. "Yes'm. Thank you, kindly."

"Of course. I'm happy to help. At some point there will probably be one or two more girls who will need to share the room with you—"

Joe's fork clattered against his plate, and she felt the hardness of his dark gaze settle on her.

She pressed ahead, pretending she didn't notice. "But we'll arrange for more beds when that time comes. After dinner, I'll show you around the place, but there's really not much here yet, except for this cabin. Joe and the other men from Wyldhaven helped build it for me. For us." Liora picked up her fork and lifted a bite of mashed potatoes and gravy.

Tess's gaze darted to Joe, but rebounded to study Liora's movements. Instead of adding to the conversation, she carefully lifted her fork in mimicry of Liora and tasted the mashed potatoes and gravy. Her eyes closed and Liora couldn't help but smile at the look of heavenly bliss on Tess's face as she savored the flavor of the food.

She would be utterly enjoying this, if only the silence didn't ring with Joe's disapproval! He was usually easygoing and a pleasure to converse with, but today he was all prickles and spines. Not even when he paused for a moment to take in Tess's enrapture, did a smile reach his face.

Liora searched for something else to talk about. She'd seen the girl eyeing the small bookshelf near the cabin's front door earlier. "Can you read, Tess?"

Tess came out of her reverie and looked down at her plate. She pushed her fork into the potatoes but didn't lift another bite. "If I can't, do I have ta go back?"

Liora's gaze collided with Joe's across the table, and then she rushed to reassure the girl. "No! Of course not. But I can teach you to read, if you'd like." That was one thing she'd been blessed with. Ma at least had taught her how to read before their lives had gone all to pieces.

Such a look of wonder filled Tess's features, that Liora couldn't suppress a smile. "I'd like that, ever so much, Miss Liora."

Liora took a moment to compose her voice, because her throat had suddenly tightened and gone a bit scratchy. She took a sip of water, then she nodded. "You can dispense with the 'Miss' and just call me Liora, and I'll be more than happy to teach you to read. We can start first thing after morning chores tomorrow."

Liora gave up on keeping a conversation going after that, and simply allowed the rest of the meal to play out in silence.

When she and Tess had cleared the last of the dishes, Joe stood. "Tess, you mind washing up those dishes while I talk with Liora outside?"

Tess nodded, blue eyes bright. "I'm right good at dishes, yessuh."

Liora glanced from Tess to Joe, wondering if he understood how amazing it was that the girl seemed so comfortable around him despite how irritable he'd been since meeting her.

Tess continued. "Stella from Stella's Spirits used ta hire me ta wash the dishes at her saloon on the nights she served food. Was better 'n..." Her face flamed, and her gaze suddenly fastened to the floor. "Well, better 'n workin' for Missah John."

Liora couldn't withhold the question that had been plaguing her for most of the afternoon. "Where are your parents, Tess?"

Pain pinched the girl's features. She pressed her lips together before finally lifting her gaze to Liora's. "My pa, he owed Missah Hunt money. He done borrowed it so's we could plant our fields. But some men came, middle o' the night, and rousted up all the seed soon after it sprouted. Pa 'spected Hunt's men, though he could never prove it. Then Missah Hunt had him killed when he didn't pay on time." Tears brimmed on the girl's lower lids. "Missah Hunt, he was gon' make my ma work for him. But she done took her own life 'fore he even got one night outta her. Then he done come for me."

Liora reached out and pulled the girl into an embrace. "How long ago?"

Tess pushed back and swiped at her cheeks, obviously uncomfortable with the offer of comfort. "That be last month."

"Thank you for telling me. I know that must have been hard." Liora gave the girl's shoulder a gentle squeeze. She hesitated to leave her alone after such a revelation. Her stomach churned at the injustice of her story. But more than that, she knew that Hunt wouldn't want such a one left alive to spread her story to the world. What were they going to do?

Joe's feet shuffled.

Tess pulled back and Liora let her go.

"You can see to the dishes now. We'll only be a moment."

Joe met Liora's gaze and tipped his head toward the porch.

She willed down her irritation over his high-handedness and the fear that mingled with it at the thought of his departure. What would she do if John Hunt and his men returned in the middle of the night to finish the job Joe had prevented them from finishing earlier? Her gaze darted to the mantel where she'd put the pistol he'd given her earlier this year. If only she knew how to use the thing. Maybe then the thought of the long dark hours between now and morning wouldn't hold so much terror.

Joe cleared his throat, drawing her attention back to him.

She sighed. Fine. He didn't seem to be offering a choice in the matter. He lifted her shawl from the peg by the front door and held the door open. A swing of his hat indicated he would follow her out.

She settled her shawl around her shoulders, but didn't remain on the porch. Still half hoping to hurry him on his way and half dreading his departure, she started toward the place where she'd last seen his horse. She reminded herself to be strong. She'd gotten herself into this mess—and at the urging of the Holy Spirit. Surely, God wouldn't abandon her now, just when she needed protection!

And it would certainly be better if Joe got going right away. Come morning Mrs. Hines would already be full of juicy tales. Liora had taken note of that certain gleam in the woman's eyes when she'd seen her walking to the camp earlier today. She didn't want Joe embroiled in any of the kerfuffle sure to follow. And if anyone found out he'd even had dinner here, things wouldn't go well for him.

Maybe walking over to his horse would do the trick. But his

horse was not waiting for him. He'd stripped it of its saddle and staked the mustang in the middle of the field to the east. Her brow furrowed. But before she had time to register why that gave her a bit of unease, Joe spoke.

"He needed some rest. I'll ride out to the camp and poke around a bit tonight, but then I'm going to need a blanket..."

The words, paired with the sight of the picketed horse, sent realization coursing through her and a jolt of shock to her core. She spun to face him.

He blinked at her abrupt movement, but kept going. "At least for tonight, if you have an extra? Tomorrow after I escort you into town and drop you off at work, I can get my own things from McGinty's."

A tremor threatened the solidity of Liora's knees and she tightened her grip where it clasped the shawl closed at her throat. "You can't stay here."

He would lose everything! Besides, where would he sleep? She didn't even have a barn to offer him, and the lean-to barely offered enough room for the wheelbarrow it contained.

A muscle bunched in his jaw. "You may not want me around, but John Hunt is not a man who will take a seat while being crossed. And like it or not, cross him you did. Not to mention that apparently you witnessed a murder. I'm assuming Tess saw it too?"

Liora nodded.

"Well if you think I'm going to simply ride back to town and leave you defenseless, you don't know me very well."

Liora whirled away from him, pressing one hand to her forehead. "Joe, I know we've danced around this issue in the past. But associating with me can bring you nothing but heartache. It's not that I don't want you around. It's that I care about you too much—as a friend, you understand." She hoped he would believe the truth of that statement. "The town won't stand for it."

"And I care about you too much to let a few town gossips put your life in danger. But if it bothers you that much, there's one thing that would make them move on to gossiping about some other poor souls. Marry me."

She heard him swallow, even as her astonishment spun her to face him once more.

He couldn't seem to meet her gaze. In fact, he looked a bit taken aback and his face pulled into the briefest of grimaces— he tried to hide it with the swipe of one hand, but she saw it nonetheless—like he couldn't quite believe what he'd just said. His feet fidgeted as he lifted his Stetson and ruffled his fingers through his just-this-side-of-too-long brown curls. Then he spent a few seconds resetting the hat on his head and kicking at a clump of bunch-grass near his boot. After a long moment of taut silence, he lifted his gaze to hers. "Well?"

Liora's jaw gaped. She couldn't help it.

She looked up at the hills surrounding her cabin, needing to break eye contact and give herself a moment to think. *Marry him? A man who'd obviously only made the offer out of duty?* She would rather die from one of John Hunt's bullets piercing her heart. And yet what other sort of offer was a girl like her ever going to get? Especially from a man as good as Joseph Rodante? And yet marriage would mean...*intimacies.* A thought that made everything inside her crawl with dread.

On the other hand, she didn't want to remain single for the rest of her life, did she? And yet, to saddle a good man like him with her past? Did he realize what it would mean for his future? Being known as "the man who has the former whore for a wife."

Behind her, his boots scuffed over gravel. "I can see your

mind turning every which way. Despite my bumbling words, I mean to care for you like you deserve. Neither of us is getting any younger. And I feel we've grown into good terms over the past few years. I'd even consider you a friend. Many a marriage is built on less. You'd have my protection and our reputations will be salvaged. And well, I guess I'd get some land out of the deal."

A hot little lump started to roil in the pit of her stomach. He made it sound so practical. Dutiful. Businesslike. And for some reason she couldn't quite fathom, that made her more than a little angry. She marched toward the house. "No, Joseph Robert Rodante, I won't marry you! And you can't have a blanket! Go home!"

Something pinged off the ground at her feet, kicking up a puff of dirt. She heard the report of the rifle as Joe dove on her. The hard and unyielding ground took the breath from her. She coughed for air and scrambled on all fours toward the house with Joe yanking her forward and yelling indecipherable commands in her ear.

She barked a shin against the steps, and then he was shoving her through the front door. He locked and barred it. "Tess, lock the kitchen door. Now!"

Liora was thankful to see Tess scramble to do as instructed because all she could seem to do at the moment was stand and stare and feel numb.

Joe took her arm and gently pushed her onto the settee in the sitting room. "Tess, bring Liora a cup of coffee, would you?"

His words snapped her out of it. She didn't want to be the one needing to be coddled during a time of crisis. She shook her head. "No. I'm fine. Truly. What do we do now?"

Joe's mouth firmed into a grim line. He stalked to the mantel and took down her pistol and the box of shells. Striding back to her, he thrust them into her hands. "You're going to need these. Which reminds me, why didn't you take the gun with you to the camps?"

Liora swallowed. "I don't know how to use it."

With a huff, he took the pistol back. "Come over here and I'll teach you how to load for me. We're going to be in for a long night."

Aurora McClure worked her fingers over her long braid, one shoulder planted into the support post of the shanty, as she watched Dr. Griffin working over Ma. Her insides were all aquiver. And her knees felt a bit like the pudding Ma had made for her once when she was just a tyke. She could still remember the creamy sweetness as the delicious warm treat had spread across her tongue. Even now it made her mouth water, but that might have something to do with the fact that she hadn't eaten since Ma had taken this turn for the worse two days ago.

Mr. Hunt's man, Pike, had come by yesterday morning and let her know that Ma had fallen a week behind on her rent and that if Ma passed, Mr. Hunt had said Aurora could work off their debt herself.

At the recollection of the way the man's eyes had lit up and skimmed her, ever so slow, from head to foot, her stomach churned.

She'd gone for Doc Griffin herself, after that. But now she almost wished she hadn't. It was the look on his face that told the truth. The weary droop of his shoulders. The way he wouldn't look at her as he packed his things back into his black bag.

She chewed the side of her finger. A nasty habit that Ma would reprimand her for, but the anxiety was about to be her undoing. "Well, Doc?"

The puff of air that escaped him hammered home the final nail in the coffin of her hope. "Aurora, I'm sorry to be the giver of such news, but I'm afraid your mother won't likely make it through to morning." The gentleness in his eyes let her know he truly did feel sorrow at the news he'd just imparted.

In that moment, all the dismay and trembling just sort of melted away. A numbness moved in to take their place. Her focus returned to Ma, barely budging the coverlet with each shallow breath. Gone by morning?

John Hunt would come. He would make her work in Ma's place.

Her attention flitted back to the doctor, who still watched her with that soft sorrow in his gaze. She forced strength into her voice. "What's she got?"

He rubbed a hand over his face slowly. "It's..." He gave a little motion in the general direction of the whore house. "From her...time working for Hunt."

Aurora's jaw clenched. So not only had Mr. Hunt made Ma's life a living hell these last few years, but he'd killed her too. And she would be next.

The time had come for the doctor to leave and she suddenly realized that she didn't have a cent to pay him with. Chagrin weighed down her head. "I don't have any money to pay you. I'm sorry."

The latches on his bag made a soft clicking sound. "Please don't worry yourself. I certainly didn't become a doctor for the money. Or the hours." Those last words were accompanied by an expansive yawn and a wink of gentle humor.

Aurora couldn't help but give him a little smile in return.

She liked the man, despite the bad news he'd just shared. "I'll try to make it up to you, sometime."

He gave her shoulder a gentle squeeze as he passed. Just before ducking out the door he paused. "Send word once she expires and I'll fill out the appropriate papers."

Expires. Such a final word. Aurora nodded.

He gave her a tip of his head, and then disappeared into the evening gloom.

Flynn sent up a prayer for Aurora McClure as he mounted his horse and turned its head toward Wyldhaven.

A weight hung heavy in his chest. The girl was in for a rough time of it. John Hunt and his kind did nothing but steal, kill, and destroy—much like the Good Book said of the devil. In fact, "devil" would be an apt description for the man and his cronies. Without money, and carrying her mother's debt to the man—something Hunt always seemed to have on his side in situations like this—what would the girl's chances be? The law would be in Hunt's favor, hard as that seemed to imagine.

If only Flynn weren't already run off his feet, he would start a home to help Aurora and girls like her. But only last month he'd put himself flat in bed for a full week because he'd overworked himself and gone for too long without any sleep. He'd collapsed from exhaustion—thankfully just as he'd arrived at the diner where he now lived with his wife Dixie and her first husband's mother, Rose. But he had scared ten years off of Dixie's life, to hear her tell it, and she'd been harping on him ever since not to work so hard.

He wished he could listen to her demands, but there was little he could do about the number of hours he was putting in. The region could use two, if not three more doctors. He'd sent letters to as many people as he could think of—former colleagues, medical schools, and hospitals—asking for doctors to come, but until the Lord laid the region on someone's heart and they decided to take his appeals seriously, he remained on his own. One doctor with fifty square miles of patients. And many of those miles housed people living in the dangerous and illness-inducing conditions of the logging camps.

But no matter his level of exhaustion, it wasn't conscionable to stand by and do nothing when he knew that predator John Hunt would pounce on a girl like Aurora the moment her mother passed. He sighed. For tonight, she would be fine. But he should go to Parson Clay and see what could be done. He wouldn't be able to rest until he'd at least asked the parson to check in on her.

With a click of his tongue, he urged his mount into a trot. Dixie would have fresh biscuits and stew waiting when he got home. Then he'd have a hot bath, and hopefully get a few hours of sleep tonight—instead of the two he'd gotten last night—before someone came banging on his door.

The road wound through the rolling hills which as recently as last year had been thickly forested, but now had been stripped of timber. With the growing populations all the way down the coast to California needing lumber, Zebulon Heath had bought into the timber industry at just the right time. The bare hills appeared desolate right now, but in fifteen years they would be covered with new growth fifteen to thirty feet tall.

A herd of deer grazed about halfway up one of the hills and Flynn enjoyed the sight of the graceful creatures. Munching from a patch of green grass, they watched him attentively with wide curious gazes, but didn't seem inclined to flee—until the first shot rang out.

Flynn froze. His horse whickered and danced in agitation.

Scanning the hills around him as the deer bounded over the crest of the rise, he tried to assess where the shot had come from. It wasn't close. Nor directed at him. Another shot—and this time he could tell it came from down the road a bit.

Near Liora's new place! The realization shook him.

"Get up." He kicked his heels into his mount and set out at a gallop down the road. When he got closer to the house, he led his bay off to one side of the road, ground-hitched him, and then, taking his rifle, soft-footed it to the top of the ridge that would give him a good look down on Liora's place.

Smoke spiraled from her chimney, and nothing seemed to be out of place in the yard... except that Joe Rodante's Paint was staked in a field several paces from the cabin. What was he doing here at this time of evening? Maybe Liora had invited him for a meal as thanks for all he'd done to help her build this place? At any rate, everything appeared normal.

Flynn frowned. Had the shots really been coming from here?

A curtain at one of the cabin windows moved and another shot rang out. Dust puffed from the log wall just to the right of the window. The curtain went still.

Flynn flinched and scrutinized the area where a flare of light gave away the shooter's location. Someone had Liora pinned down in her cabin. And likely Joe Rodante, too. Who could it be and what did they want? Liora wouldn't hurt a fly, and Joe was a fair and upstanding lawman.

Flynn pondered what to do. He could stay here and try to scare off whoever was taking the pot shots. Or he could ride for town, where Sheriff Callahan and Marshal Zane Holloway would know better what to do. They had more experience with this sort of thing and could be back inside an hour. But what if they arrived too late? He scrubbed at his eyes, wishing he'd managed to get more than a couple hours of sleep last night.

Giving himself a shake, he scrambled back down the hill to his horse and retrieved his binoculars from his saddlebag. Back at the crest, he scanned the hill across the way where he'd seen the flash of light. Sure enough, a man lay on his belly, sighting down his rifle toward the cabin.

On a hunch, Flynn methodically scanned the rest of the surroundings. He found two more men, and with the terrain being what it was, there were probably more.

Flynn dropped the binoculars and considered the angle of the sun. Whoever these men were, they likely wouldn't attack until full-on dark. And he could be to town and back with Reagan, Zane, and a posse of men before that time. But only just.

Decision made, he hurried to his mount and set it at a gallop toward town.

And as he rode, he reminded himself not to forget to mention Aurora's situation to Parson Clay.

harlotte Brindle sat correcting papers at Jacinda Callahan's dining table. She sighed in irritation as she realized that she'd just read the opening line to Zoe Kastain's paper about the current state of politics in Washington DC for probably the sixth time without really reading it.

She couldn't concentrate for her curiosity over Reagan's strange behavior this evening.

This morning on their ride out to the camps to solicit funds for the boardwalk project, he'd seemed fine. Acted like his usual self.

But then, after they'd talked to Joe about Liora going to Camp Sixty-Five and Joe had leapt from the carriage and taken off as though someone had lit a fire under him, Reagan had turned suddenly pensive. And when he'd dropped her off at his mother's house, instead of coming in for a piece of pie, as was his usual habit, he'd barely even offered a parting word before leaving her standing on the top step of the porch to see herself inside.

And then he hadn't arrived for dinner. That wasn't uncommon, because his work often took him away from town at odd hours, but combined with everything else, it made Charlotte uneasy.

Had she done or said something wrong? She'd racked her thoughts and come up empty.

Ever since Mr. Heath had given them permission to court, nigh on a year and a half ago now, Charlotte felt like her relationship with Reagan had grown comfortable and easy. She loved that he accepted her without trying to change her. He'd even said he understood that she wasn't ready to give up teaching yet to become a wife and mother.

But had she held him off for too long? Had he decided to pursue someone else? If so, she really had no idea who it might be because he'd given her no reason to doubt his loyalty at all over the last years. Which brought her full circle to her puzzlement over what had suddenly changed about his attitude today.

She sighed and set the papers aside. Perhaps a cup of tea would help.

In the kitchen, she filled the kettle and nudged it closer to the center of the stove, then added a few small sticks of wood to the firebox and blew on the coals below them until she had a good fire going. Just as she reached for the tea cannister, Jacinda breezed into the kitchen.

"There you are. Someone is here to see you." She made a shooing motion with her hands. "In the parlor. I'll finish up the tea."

Charlotte frowned. "Who—"

But Jacinda cut her off with an uplifted palm. "I'll join you in just a few minutes." She turned her back before Charlotte could get a good read on her expression.

Curious over her behavior, Charlotte made her way to the parlor and cautiously peered around the door casing.

Reagan paced before the fire in the fireplace, one hand working at the muscles along the back of his neck.

Charlotte's dread mounted. There really *was* something wrong. What had she done? Hands smoothing the pleats on the skirt of her dress, she stepped into the room. "Good evening." Her voice cracked and she cleared her throat.

Reagan spun to face her. One hand remained at the back of his neck, the other dropped against his hip. "Evening." He nodded.

Silence settled between them. His gaze bored into hers. He obviously had something to say but couldn't quite decide where to start.

Charlotte worried her lower lip. This tension between them was a strange new thing. "Reagan, I feel I may have done something to upset—"

With two swift strides, he stood before her and took her hand, shaking his head. "I'm sorry. I'm bumbling this rather badly." His fingers curled around hers, broad and blunt. Warm and oh-so-familiar.

Charlotte felt her brow lower. "Bumbling what?"

Reagan glanced up toward the ceiling, then down toward his boots—everywhere but right at her.

"Reag—"

He dropped to one knee and reached for something in the pocket of his shirt, finally focusing directly on her.

Charlotte's eyes barely had time to widen before a loud banging practically shook the house. "Sheriff?! You in there? It's me, Doc!"

Reagan glanced from Charlotte to the parlor door and then back again, lips twisted in frustration.

In the entryway, the outer door creaked open and then Jacinda gasped. "Land sakes, Doc, that horse looks done in."

"Rode pretty hard to get here. Is Reagan inside? McGinty said he saw him heading this way a bit ago." Doc's words grew progressively louder, likely because Jacinda had admitted him entrance.

Reagan sighed and held up one finger to Charlotte. "Don't go anywhere. I'll be right back." He clambered to his feet and strode toward the entrance.

Charlotte realized that she had one hand pressed to her chest and dropped it to her side. She felt all aflutter inside. Had he really been about to ask... Yes. He had. Was she ready for that?

She paced to the fireplace and took up the poker, then prodded at the wood. A shower of orange sparks shot up and rose through the chimney. Her hand trembled, but she kept prodding.

It would mean giving up teaching. But somehow, she suddenly knew she would be just fine with that. She truly did love her students, but the truth was that lately she'd been dreaming about what it might be like to have little boys at her skirts with soft blue eyes just like Reagan's. Or maybe a little girl in pigtails with her own slightly upturned nose and green eyes.

Charlotte felt a burn in her cheeks that had nothing to do with her proximity to the fire. She thrust the poker back into its holder and settled one hand over the flutter in her belly. She reminded herself to breathe. She didn't want to faint from excitement, or bring on a breathing attack, before the poor man had even had the chance to ask her.

She forced herself to tune in to the conversation taking place in the entry.

"I don't know," Doc said. "But it looked like real trouble. I think we better hightail it back there with as many men as we can raise right away."

"All right. Get Zane from the boardinghouse, and as many trustworthy men from McGinty's as are willing to help. Then, meet me at the livery. I need five more minutes here."

Doc must have agreed silently, because the next thing Charlotte heard was the house door clicking shut.

She smoothed her skirt and tugged at her sleeves.

Reagan stepped back through the door, a "V" of concern furrowing his brow.

"Trouble?" She moistened her dry lips.

He nodded. "Some trouble is brewing out at Liora's new place. I need to ride out there right away. But first"—a hint of humor relaxed his face and softened his eyes—"I want to finish what I started."

Charlotte couldn't help the smile that tugged at her lips. "I really wish you would."

His face turned immediately serious. "Do you?"

"I do." She willed him to believe her with a look that must have done the job, because he strode toward her and dropped to one knee before her once again.

"Charlotte," he pulled a gold band from the pocket of his shirt, "I've been thinking on this for some time, but then today when Joe went off halfcocked the moment he heard Liora might need his help...well... I'm not exactly sure what it was about it that made me realize I didn't want to spend another day without you by my side, but it did. I know I'm not the richest man in these parts, nor am I likely the one most worthy of your devotion, but I promise you that for all our days I will do my best to love you and to put your needs before my own. And it would be my great honor if you would agree to be my wife."

And Charlotte couldn't help a chuckle, because despite the fact that she'd only a moment ago reassured him that she wanted his proposal, a tight uncertainty still lingered around his eyes.

She bent forward and took his face in both her hands. "Yes, Reagan Callahan. The honor would be all mine."

His face broke into the hugest of grins. He gave her a quick peck of a kiss and then reached for her hand and slid the ring into place.

She examined it as he stood to his feet. "Isn't this supposed to wait until the ceremony?"

He waved away her concern. "I want all the men in these parts to know that you are spoken for and that they'd better keep their distance." He grinned and tugged her close for a lingering kiss, settling his hands at the small of her back.

Charlotte savored the feel of his lips working over hers, the strength of his arms around her, the feel of his heart pulsing beneath her palms. If only they could stay this way forever, but she knew he needed to get going, so she pushed back from him, but only far enough to admire the ring sparkling on her hand where it rested against his chest. After a moment, she looked up. "I love you, Reagan."

He stroked her cheek with the pad of one thumb. "As do I you, Charlotte. You blew into my world like a tornado, but I find that I've rather come to enjoy the sensation of mountain-uprooting winds."

Charlotte rolled her eyes and smacked him gently but firmly. "Oh, do go on with you."

One lid lowered in a conspiratorial wink. "I wish I didn't have to, but I do need to get. Be all right if I come by for breakfast in the morning?"

Charlotte raised up on her tiptoes and gave him a quick goodbye kiss. "I'll look forward to it. And please be careful?"

He reached for his Stetson where it lay on the side chair. "I always am, darlin'. Don't you worry any about me."

And with that he exited, leaving her staring dreamily at her left hand in the parlor.

Joe paced from one window in the cabin to another, trying to see from which direction Hunt would likely mount his main attack. Thankfully, enough light still shone outside that Hunt and his men wouldn't be able to see into the cabin past the glass, but that only gave the slimmest of benefits in this situation. He remained careful to keep to the side of the windows in case one of them decided to just start blasting away—and he was wary not to bump the curtains because clearly they were aiming at anything that moved. He'd instructed the women to do the same.

He currently had Tess stationed in the last bedroom down the hall, watching the back of the house.

No more shots had come since a few minutes after he and Liora had made it into the house, but that seemed only prudent. Hunt's men knew they had them pinned down and were conserving ammunition. Nothing would pierce the log walls of the cabin.

After assessing the terrain surrounding them, Joe figured Hunt's men would just wait till dark, when one of them would sneak up to the southwest corner of the cabin where there were no windows, and no line of site from inside the house. They would light a fire and smoke them out.

And blast if he could figure out a way to prevent it.

The only solution he'd come to was that they were going to have to make a run for it the moment it grew dark enough. If they were lucky, the moon would be hidden by some cloud cover and the men wouldn't see them. Once he had the women to safety, maybe he'd even be able to soft-foot through the dark and catch the thugs off guard, one by one. And if further luck was on their side, he might even be able to save Liora's cabin.

But if they were unlucky and the moon shone unhindered, they would be doing good to escape with their lives.

He prayed for clouds, but if the Good Lord didn't choose to send clouds, he prayed that the only loss would be Liora's cabin.

Pacing to the kitchen, he poured himself a cup of the coffee Liora had set to perking on the stove, then studied the yard outside.

He lamented the fact that his horse stood picketed in the open. If Hunt's thugs decided to kill the mustang, there would be nothing he could do to save him. Though he hoped they wouldn't try since horse thieving was still a hanging offense in these parts, if they did, the mountain-bred Paint, a good sure-footed horse, wouldn't be easy to replace—emotionally or physically.

Behind him, he heard a soft intake of breath, and turned to find Liora looking past him to the Paint.

He still couldn't believe he'd asked her to marry him. The farthest thing from his mind this morning when he'd woken up had been that he might be a committed man come evening, and yet, he couldn't deny the hurt that had curled up and lodged in his gut when she'd turned him down flat. His head told him it was likely better this way. But his heart seemed to have other ideas, and that perplexed him.

Ever since he'd been a kid and Father had hammered into him the importance of a man's reputation, he'd determined that the woman he one day chose to love would also be an upstanding and respectable person. The sound reasoning persisted. When he thought of Liora, his rational side reminded that other men had gone before him. It screamed that it would be better for his future if he turned his attentions to a woman society wouldn't shun. Not only for his own protection, but for his future children's, as well.

And yet...here he stood, considering marriage to her. Repentant though she may be, she was barely tolerated by most in town because of her sinful past. He'd always prided himself on his friendship with her, and been irritated—angered even—by the fact that many women of the town shunned her. They treated her as though she wasn't a new creation in Christ; as though God's grace wasn't sufficient to cover her sins.

Something crimped in his stomach. Wasn't his refusal to even consider her as an eligible marriage partner, the same form of prejudice? She had proven herself to be a changed woman, so no danger existed of becoming unequally yoked in this situation. The thought that his actions and thoughts were no better than those of the disapproving gossips in town, dropped a rock of self-disgust into his heart. All this time he'd been harboring a judgmental attitude, yet he himself had mistreated her just as badly!

His jaw jutted to one side and he massaged it, considering.

Something had broken open inside him this morning when he'd blurted those two words. *Marry me.* And the fissure revealed a side of himself that he didn't much care for.

His actions toward Liora had been just as bigoted, just as misrepresentative of the true gospel, as the actions of those women who crossed the street when they saw her coming to avoid having their skirts brush hers. That thought alone nearly took him to his knees.

Only compounding the matter was the fact that he knew Liora had tried to guard his reputation on more than one occasion by distancing herself from him. *She'd* been trying to protect him, when *he* should have been the one protecting her.

What must it be like to be in her situation? Unable to undo the sins of her past, and yet knowing that because of them she would never be accepted by many?

He was a cad! The lowest of the low.

No wonder she had turned him down with such vehemence.

And yet, it wouldn't help her any to add fuel to the town gossips' fires. The very fact that they were likely going to have to pass the night together—no matter that Tess was also here—would set off a veritable tornado of prattle in town.

Yes sir, any way one considered it, Liora had opened up a whole can of worms the moment she'd decided she wanted to help women escape the likes of John Hunt.

"I'm sorry I got you into this, Joe. Do you think they'll hurt him?" Her voice emerged soft and full of concern. Her gaze remained on the Paint outside.

Even in this situation her thoughts were first and foremost about him and his horse. *You're a fool, Joseph Rodante.* Where in the world would he ever find a better woman than this one? She was waiting for him to reply so he said, "Not sure. I hope not. But there's nowhere for me to put him, even if I could get to him under cover."

Tears brimmed in her eyes and she started to spin away. Before he could think better of it, his hand shot out to stop her from fleeing. Her wrist felt warm and smooth beneath his fingers. He loosened his grip just enough to let her know she was free to go if she really wanted to make her escape, but still tight enough that she would know he wanted her to stay. Because he desired more than anything for her to stay. He needed to prove to her that he could be, *would* be, a better man for her than he had been these past months.

When she didn't try to pull away, he dared to let his thumb stroke the inside of her wrist. He'd never touched her before—at least not in the way that a man touches a woman, though he'd been plenty aware of her and that was certain. Her skin slid softly beneath the pad of his thumb as he traced a blue vein down the inside of her wrist to her sleeve.

If he could just keep the women alive through the night and bring the law into this come morning, John's options would be severely limited. He would have to be a lot more cautious after that, knowing that he would be the first one scrutinized.

But even if Joe managed to keep Liora and Tess safe through the night, his pulse hammered with the realization of what John Hunt could do. He could take Liora to court—accuse her of theft, not of Tess herself, because slavery was no longer legal, but of the income Tess owed him, and maybe even of the income she would have provided for him in the years ahead. And with their current circuit judge—a man who had proven his friendly view toward many of the outlaws in the area— there was no telling how the ruling would be handed down. John would bring in character witnesses of her past conduct to prove how low she'd been willing to stoop. And he would say she had coerced Tess into fleeing with her—maybe even accuse her of trying to start her own whorehouse.

Yet if she married, she would fall under her husband's protection. And Hunt was just enough of a coward that he wouldn't want to harass her if he knew it could come back to bite him. And Joe would make certain he knew it would come back to bite him.

The truth was, Liora agreeing to marry him would solve a lot of her problems. Simply because of the situation they found themselves in, she was already in danger of the town gossips running her out of town on a rail. Mrs. Hines wouldn't tolerate her shopping at Jerry's Mercantile after tonight, or him for that matter, and that would leave them needing to ride all the way to Cle Elum for supplies. But if they married, the town chatter would soon turn to something else and everyone would forgive—

if not forget—the fact that they'd spent a night together before marriage. So...how did he go about convincing her?

He brought himself back to the present and realized Liora's breathing had grown louder. Still caressing her wrist, he lifted his eyes to hers.

She trembled from head to toe.

Alarm darted through him and he released her. Had she thought— "I'm sorry. I didn't mean to alarm you."

"Joe..." Her tongue darted over her lips. "There are many reasons why you and I could never marry." She wrapped her arms around herself, and so much pain radiated from her gaze that he felt it in his core. "It wouldn't be fair to you. Do you understand?"

He didn't understand. But words seemed elusive. Joe's heart thudded several times. He took in her pale face. The dots of moisture on her forehead. The taut skin around her wide eyes... He straightened, his heart kicking about in his chest like a green-broke bronc with a bur under its saddle. "You know I would never hurt you, right?"

"Yes."

"But I scared you just now, didn't I?"

A moment of pause was followed by a softer, "Yes."

He searched through his actions trying to figure out what he'd done to cause her fear. The only thing he'd done was reach out and touch her to keep her from fleeing. And yet with her history... He was every kind of a fool. "Liora, I'm sorry. But we can get past—"

"We can't, Joe." She shook her head.

He felt confusion tighten his brow. He'd been about to say they could work past her fears. "We can't what?"

She shook her head again, more forcefully this time and took a step back.

But when she started from the room he said, "Don't go. Please?"

She stopped at the threshold, her back still to him. A fawn poised to flee.

He looked down and clasped his hands, which suddenly felt so barren. "Talk to me, Liora. We have some time. They won't attack again until dark. What can't we do?"

"Marry, Joe. It will never work. I have too much...brokenness."

That made despair surge, but he pushed past it. Maybe he could still convince her. "My mother used to say that time was a gift God gave for our healing."

She made a little sound and raised one hand to her forehead. "There are some things one simply doesn't heal from."

"I remember the beating you took, Liora. I'm sorry I wasn't there to prevent it."

She flinched. Brushed a strand of hair off her neck. "You were off helping my ma."

True as the words were, they didn't change his regret. He considered her reaction and thought back over their years of friendship. He'd hardly ever touched her. Only in the last couple days had she needed the escort into town. And prior to that, on any occasion where they'd had contact, she'd been stiff and guarded. His heart ached with the realization. And yet if there was one thing he believed in, it was the healing power of God, for mind, soul, or body.

And if she had only ever known the touch of a man as harsh, oppressive, and hateful, maybe he ought to show her what the touch of love felt like.

His mouth went dry and he rubbed his palms down his thighs.

She still hadn't moved.

He needed to see her face. More than he needed air. He strode over and eased around her.

He waited patiently for her to lift her gaze to his. "Do you trust me?"

She licked her lips, eyes wide. After a long moment, she nodded.

Slowly he raised one hand, giving her plenty of time to withdraw.

She trembled, but held her ground, only flinching slightly when his fingers grazed along her cheek. He settled his hand there and simply took in her beauty, willing her to experience love. Patient. Kind. Unselfish. Unflappable. Pleasurable.

"Joe, you can't look at me like that." Her words were barely audible.

"And how am I looking at you, exactly? Like a man who has suddenly recognized what a dunce he is and that he owes you an apology?"

She frowned. "An apology for what?"

He swallowed, forcing himself to admit the humiliating truth. "I've mistreated you. For years." He hurried on when she started to shake her head. "Yes. I have. Just like the town gossips."

Her denial was forceful. "No, Joe. You haven't. You have been the kindest, most—" She broke off and tore her gaze down to his chest. "And I care for you too much to let you—"

He dropped his thumb over her lips. "Don't say it." Softly, he stroked the dip below her mouth. Awe and wonder mixed together inside of him like the convergence of two rivers. "I want to marry you." It was a breathy statement, more revelation than declaration. And even more assertion filtered through the next words. "And you need me."

He felt her tremble before she took a step back. "This is exactly what I'm talking about, Joe. You can't do this."

He eased after her, making sure to keep his movements slow

and allow her time to escape, if she felt the need. "Why not? Don't you want me to?" He curved a caress around the side of her neck and rested his thumb against the skittering pulse in the hollow of her throat.

Those amazing dark-lashed blue eyes of hers widened a little, and her tongue darted out to moisten her lips again.

He pressed on before she thought to make another escape. "If you marry me, you'll have protection. Not only from John and his men, but from the town gossips."

Liora's jaw jutted to one side, and her arms dropped into a firm, protective clasp before her. "So that's the reason I should marry you? For protection?"

He felt her pulse thrum beneath his caress. "It's a start."

She rolled her eyes and spun away. She yanked several potatoes from the barrel by the sideboard and set to scrubbing them with a fierceness he hadn't known she possessed. "I need to get breakfast preparations going. Tess!" she called, even as she thunked several potatoes onto the cutting board. "Come and help me, please? I'll teach you how to prepare the potatoes, like I promised I would."

A clear dismissal.

He sighed and strode over to peer out the dining room window.

By all the cedar in the mountains! He couldn't believe he hadn't seen his growing feelings before today. And yet here he was, a man in love with a woman. She needed him now more than ever, yet still she refused him. He turned back to study her once more. She continued to scrub furiously at the potato in her hand.

He grinned and took a large slurp from his cup. At least she hadn't turned him down flat this time.

iora had scoured the potato in her hands until the skin was nearly off. She passed it to Tess and forced herself to concentrate.

Tess chopped nice even slices out of the potatoes.

Liora gave her a nod. "Good job. Just like that. You are doing fine." She turned to the stove and thrust two more sticks of wood into the firebox. At least they had enough wood inside that they would be able to stay warm through the night—if they held out that long. But by the way Joe was acting, he didn't think they had till morning.

Joe... She gritted her teeth, holding back a growl. It irritated her, his logic that made so much sense. If they married, it would solve a lot of her problems. But she had always thought that if she could ever get past her fear of being intimate with a man again, she would have a marriage with a foundation of love. And if not love, at least something stronger than duty and obligation. Yet her own poor decisions had brought her to this place. If she had never been a prostitute herself, the people of the town would likely champion her decision to help girls like Tess. Even John Hunt would probably think carefully before attacking a woman if he knew she was highly respected and revered.

But ashes begat ashes, it seemed.

And now, she found herself trying to determine which

decision was the more foolish—to turn Joe down, or to let him
step in as the protector he offered to be. The answer might be
easy if she didn't want to shrivel up inside and die each time
she thought about a man touching her like the men of her past.

And yet, Joe's touch just now...when he had curled his hand
around her neck and asked 'don't you want me to?' she'd felt
a warm sensation deep inside that she'd never expected to feel
around a man ever—especially with his hand at her throat—and
that had confused her. Maybe she could make a marriage to Joe
work, after all? An unfamiliar shiver swept down her spine.

On one hand, she knew that even were she to wait and search
for a thousand years, she would never find a man more kind,
considerate, or God-fearing than Deputy Joseph Rodante. On
the other hand, she knew it wasn't fair to saddle Joe with the
burden of her reputation—or her fears which would certainly
cost him, as well as her. For the stench of her past would never
quite evaporate. Even if she and Joe could work past her fear
of intimacy, in the eyes of most townsfolk she would never
measure up, and she didn't want to burden Joe with that. Yet
that was something he already knew. He was a grown man, and
it wasn't like she had coerced the offer from him.

He'd even said he wanted to marry her. But he didn't know
what he was asking. What if she could never release her fears?
And besides, in all the years she'd been friends with Joe, he'd
never once expressed an interest in her. That was why she'd
been so comfortable with their friendship. So, wasn't it more
likely that he simply wanted to be close enough to her to
protect her at all times? Joe was nothing if not conscientious
over the safety of those under his purview. And that was
most probably what he'd actually been feeling. She nodded to
herself. The fact of the matter was that Joseph Rodante was
simply a good-hearted man who couldn't stand to see anyone

in danger. His proposal had been based on that and nothing more. And later he would come to regret his rash decision. She must protect him from that.

So therein lay her dilemma. She could do worse. A lot worse. But he could do better. A lot better.

She rolled her eyes at herself and blew a hank of hair out of her face.

"He done hurt you, ma'am?" A genuine note of concern rang in Tess's question.

Liora startled back to the present and gave a wave of one hand. "No, I'm fine. Sorry. I simply got lost in thought for a moment." She reached for her large bowl and the bottle of vinegar. "See the pump here? We need to pump out the tepid water until it turns really cold." She demonstrated by working the lever and indicated Tess should feel the water temperature. "Feel how cold it is now?"

Tess nodded.

"You put one tablespoon of vinegar into the bowl, like so. Then fill it halfway with water." She demonstrated. "The vinegar helps keep the potatoes from turning brown in the water. And keeping the water really cold helps too. After that, we scoop the potatoes into the bowl and then we put it in the ice box."

Tess's eyes rounded in fascination when Liora opened the lid on the insulated bin that Joe had built right into the kitchen for her. "The ice comes at a bit of a dear price, so I do try to keep the icebox lid closed as much as possible..." Liora put the bowl inside and shut the lid. "Of course, we could slice them up come morning, but I find that doing them this way the night before saves time in the rush of morning chore—"

The kitchen window shattered. Shards of glass shot inward. And then the crack of a rifle shot echoed off the walls.

On instinct, both of them dove to the floor. Tess sobbed, and Liora absentmindedly plucked at the shards of glass in the girl's curly dark hair as she fleetingly thought how much this moment represented the mess she'd made of her life.

A shot rang out just as Reagan, Doc, Ewan McGinty, Washington Nolan, and Zane Holloway—the hastily assembled posse—started to climb the last hill before Liora's cabin. The men dove from their mounts and hunkered down in the brush, and Reagan felt thankful to be working in a town with sensible men who could be called on in an emergency without worry that they would jump into ill-considered action.

Washington Nolan looked ready to take on the world, and Reagan felt the weight of the burden of keeping both his posse and Liora and Joe safe.

Motioning for the men to stay back, Reagan belly-crawled to the lip of the hill and used the new binoculars Ma had given him last Christmas to study Liora's house and the hills surrounding it. In a gully below him, four horses had been tethered to a rope strung between two bushes. One man stood guard by them. Reagan trained his glasses on the man, but didn't recognize him. He turned next to studying the animals. Each had a different brand, but the sight of one of them raised the hair along the back of his neck. The large Appaloosa mare belonged to a man named Burt Pike. Pike was known to do John Hunt's dirty work. A hard man with a mean streak a mile wide, there wasn't a fight he hadn't started, or finished, and he had the scars to prove it.

Reagan lowered the glasses and pondered for a moment. If Pike was here, this likely had something to do with John Hunt. Did Liora owe the man money? Was he trying to force her to come work for him? Or was there something else going on here?

Reagan shook his head. Answers would have to wait. Four horses meant four men. One lay just below. Where would the others be? He lifted the glasses once more and it didn't take him long to find Pike and the other two.

Obviously, Hunt's men were not expecting any sort of resistance, because none of them had even bothered to keep their positions hidden. Though the only damage to the cabin seemed to be a broken window, Reagan could also see that Joe would have a time of it defensively, from down there. Of course, Liora hadn't built the cabin with a mind toward holding off attackers.

A hot sensation curled through Reagan's stomach. John Hunt had always been a man who irked him, but in this situation, "irked" didn't even come close to describing how he felt. A man who would go after women was nothing but a coward. But Reagan knew that he would find no traces of Hunt here. And likely he would deny any association with these goons once they'd been rounded up. It would be their word against his. And sadly, Reagan knew whose word would be believed in a court of law.

With a sigh, Reagan pushed himself back to where his posse waited for his instructions. They would have to content themselves with getting Liora out of this current situation and trying to catch John Hunt off guard another day.

Very quietly, he instructed his men. He motioned for Zane and Ewan to take the knoll on the far side of the cabin. He held up two fingers. "There are two of them over there. Wait for my signal." He touched his pistol, indicating what kind of signal it would be. "We have to take them all at once."

Zane nodded and clapped one hand onto Ewan's shoulder.

"Ewan." Reagan spoke before the men could leave.

Ewan met his gaze with bland curiosity.

"I expect that you will handle yourself in an upright manner and bring your man back in one piece."

Ewan's only response came as a slight smirk and a two-fingered salute. The two men melded into the brush and slipped away.

That left two of Hunt's men on this side of the cabin who still needed to be taken care of, so long as he hadn't miscalculated. Reagan turned his gaze to Doc. "There's a man just below us on the other side of this hill. You take him. I'll get Burt Pike. He's over to our right."

Doc nodded.

"What about me?" Wash whispered, feet shifting with anticipation.

"You stay here and guard our horses."

Washington's shoulders fell but, to the kid's credit, he didn't backtalk or moan.

Reagan started away then paused, realizing the parson was missing from the men who had volunteered and that wasn't like him. "Where's Parson Clay?"

Doc pulled a face. "Kin was in McGinty's again when I got there. I took him home before rejoining you all."

The implication in his words was clear. Not only had Kin been in the alehouse, but he'd imbibed plenty of Ewan's rotgut liquor to boot. Reagan's eyes shifted to Wash.

The boy lifted his hand and shook his head. "I was right glad to have Doc come along. I'd been trying to get Kin out of there for quite some time." He scrubbed one hand along the side of his neck. "McGinty just keeps pouring so long as Kin plunks down the money, no matter how much I ask him not to."

Reagan sighed, but nodded and motioned that they should get on with capturing their quarry. Doc moved off, and he did the same, yet he couldn't help but ponder on Kin's wayward ways. Of all the people in town, shouldn't the son of a man who'd died in a drunken fit be one who wanted to stay as far from McGinty's booze as possible? And yet, time and again, Preston had been forced to fetch the boy from the alehouse to sober him up.

Releasing a breath, Reagan pushed the thoughts away to be dealt with another time. Right now, he needed to concentrate on capturing his quarry.

Pike lay hunkered down by a boulder, sighting down the barrel of his rifle toward the house.

Reagan shucked his pistol and scrutinized the terrain he would need to cross to get to the man. Pike had chosen as good a spot as any to make his stand. There was no way for Reagan to sneak up on him from behind without knocking bits of shale down the hill with his steps. He wouldn't be able to even get close without alerting him to his presence.

But a good thing came from having others helping him. He didn't have to sneak up on the man. In fact, the more noise he made the better it would be for Zane, Doc and Ewan.

He reached down and hefted a good-sized rock into one hand. He waited another thirty seconds to make sure the others had plenty of time to find their own quarries and then he chucked the rock good and hard so that it landed to Pike's right. At the same moment, he leapt down the hill on his opposite side, firing two shots into the air.

Pike heard him coming, but he was off balance because he'd spun toward the sound the rock had made, and before he could even half way spin around to bring his rifle to bear, Reagan had slid to a stop by his side and pressed his pistol behind the man's ear.

"I'd think very carefully about my next move if I were you."

Pike grunted as he climbed to his feet and gingerly held the rifle out to one side. "Got others with me. They'll hunt you down, you so much as ruffle my whiskers."

"I suppose that's a chance I'm going to have to take, Burt Pike."

Reagan's use of his name seemed to give the man a start. Hands still carefully lifted by his shoulders, he peered at Reagan, clearly wondering how he knew his name.

Reagan chuckled at that. Let him wonder. Despite his humor, Reagan felt his caution rise as he took in Pike's size. The man was huge. Reagan hadn't quite realized how huge until standing this close to him. Pike had a good eight inches and at least seventy-five pounds on him—and he'd heard the man could move fast. He would have to watch himself. "I'm Sheriff Reagan Callahan from Wyldhaven." Reagan slung Pike's rifle over his chest and patted him down for other weapons. He removed a derringer from one boot and a hunting knife from the other, then motioned for the man to precede him up the hill. "Nice and slow. Any sudden moves and I might end up doing something you'll regret. You here working for John Hunt?"

Pike took three careful steps before responding. "No sir."

Reagan practically rolled his eyes. "That so? Well we'll just see what all your other friends have to say."

"You got them too?"

Reagan carefully placed his feet so as not to slip while they climbed toward the crest of the hill. "If my posse has done its job."

Pike's shoulder flinched. It was the only warning Reagan had before the man spun, swinging a sledge-hammer fist.

On instinct, Reagan dropped to one knee.

Pike's fist knocked Reagan's hat off, missing the top of his head by no more than a hand's breadth. The force of Pike's punch carried him too far around and the shale rolled beneath his boots. One of his legs slid wide and Reagan heard his intake of breath as he comprehended his mistake.

Pistol gripped tightly, Reagan threw his punch from the shoulder. The barrel of the Colt connected with the inside of Pike's extended and vulnerable knee. Bone crunched. The joint buckled.

Pike went down screaming, clutching at his leg. He slid some ways on the rocky ground, and for one moment Reagan thought he would slide all the way to the valley floor, but then he got hung up on a juniper bush. "You busted my leg!" He cursed Reagan soundly and continuously for the several minutes that it took for Reagan to navigate the terrain to his side.

Leaning carefully into the angle of the hill to keep his balance, Reagan paused, looking down on him. "One of my posse is Dr. Griffin. Way I see it, you've got two choices. You can stop your belly aching and let me help you to the top of the hill where he can patch you up. Or I can walk away and leave you here to find your own way.

Pike glowered at him, but he did reach up one hand for Reagan's help.

Reagan didn't move. "You try anything and I won't go easy on you just because you are hurt."

Pike grunted, hand still outstretched. "You didn't shoot me last time."

"I never said I'd shoot you. I said I'd do something you'd regret."

Pike gave an impatient swipe of his hand. "I ain't gonna try anything. Just help me up."

By the time Reagan got him to the top of the hill, the others had each returned with their own captives. Ewan's man looked a little worse for the wear with a large gash over one eye and a good-sized lump on his head. Reagan gave Ewan an assessing look.

Ewan simpered. "What? I'm acting on behalf of the law, ain't I? And at least I didn't bust this cuss's leg!" With a rough kick to the back of the man's knees, he shoved his captive, whose hands were already tied behind his back, down onto the ground.

Reagan let the matter slide. He helped Pike to a seat on a low boulder, motioning to Doc that he needed attention.

It wasn't long until they had all the men bound. Reagan had a lot of questions he wanted to ask them, but it would be better to do that once they were in the security of a barred cell. And he first needed to check on Joe and Liora to make sure no one had been hurt. He looked to Zane. "Can you get this lot back to town? I'd like to ride down and check on the house."

Zane nodded, resettling his hat on his head. "I've got me a haircut and a slice of pie waiting back in town, anyhow." He grinned at Reagan.

With a roll of his eyes, Reagan clapped Washington on one shoulder to indicate that he could come with him, then mounted and headed down the hill to Liora's. He knew Zane had been goading him a little about the fact that he and Ma had been spending quite a bit of time together lately, but what the man didn't know was that Reagan was more than happy for his ma to have found another man to love. Especially one as respectable and upstanding as Zane Holloway.

Now to see if any of those shots they'd heard had done any damage.

Liora and Tess were still cowering in the kitchen when Joe half-scrambled half-dove past the heavy oak sideboard. He landed on his belly, rifle clattering against the boards, and skidded almost all the way to the rock fire-break beneath the stove. He caught one glimpse of them, alive and well but trembling below the kitchen window, and slumped forward until his forehead rested on one fist against the floor. He only remained there for a heartbeat before he lifted his focus to Liora once more. He skimmed her from head to toe as though to reassure himself she truly was uninjured.

A warm sensation begged to find root in her heart, but she pushed it away. She tore her gaze from his. She had Tess to think about. Now was not the time to ponder the crazy turmoil this man had foisted upon her today with his proposal. She'd never before longed for the freedom to allow a man to enfold her in the safety of his embrace.

Tess still sobbed almost uncontrollably. "I'm sorry. I'm right sorry," she kept repeating. "I done brought so much trouble."

Liora smoothed the girl's hair back from her face and pulled her head onto her shoulder. "Hush now. This is not on you."

She met Joe's gaze across the room. His jaw worked back and forth and she knew his soft heart was being ripped asunder by Tess's predicament.

Outside, two more shots rent the air. Tess flinched and they all three froze for a moment. But no more windows shattered. And no more shots came.

Joe eased across the room and peered over the lip of the windowsill by the table. Only a moment later, he jumped to his feet.

Liora's heart stuttered. "Joe! Be careful!"

He brushed aside her concern. "It's Reagan."

Hope drew her to her own feet. She eased Tess onto one of the benches at the table and stepped to Joe's side. Sure enough. Up on the hill, she could see Reagan helping a man. They disappeared from sight for a few minutes, and then two men rode over the crest of the hill, headed their way.

Joe blew out a breath of relief. "That's Reagan and Wash. Likely coming down to see if we are all okay. Someone must have heard the shooting. Thank God."

Liora nodded. "Yes. Thank God."

Joe turned to look at her. His focus honed in on something near her hairline. He raised his palms in an I-mean-no-harm gesture, then reached toward her slowly, a question in his eyes.

She worried her lip. But it was silly to fear Joe. She gave him a nod.

He dabbed at a spot on her forehead. When his thumb came away with blood on it, her brow lifted. Only then did she feel the pinch of the cut. She reached toward it but Joe stilled her hand.

"I'll get it." He spoke softly as he laid his rifle across the table and stepped closer. "You've got some glass..."

The gentle brush of his fingers plucking at her hair sent ripples of awareness over her scalp.

Heart thudding, she started to look away but the angular contour of his jaw, bristling with a day's worth of stubble, seemed to have a powerful grip that refused to release her. It drew her attention to the cleft in his chin, and then upward to full lips that would have been Garden-of-Eden-perfect were it not for the small scar that puckered a white line from his lip to where it disappeared just below one eye. It was so faint that she'd never noticed it before. But then again, she'd never been this close to him—

He stilled.

Her gaze darted to his.

A muscle ticked beneath his eye at the point where the scar

disappeared. "Had a nasty run-in with a blackberry bramble when I was seven." His words, soft and laced with a bit of gravel, jolted a breath from her and knocked her focus down to where his Adam's apple bobbed on a heavy swallow.

His fingers were still laced in her hair, but they remained motionless. Unmoving for so long that her gaze involuntarily rose again to see what he might be doing.

He also studied a scar. *Her* scar. The one she had inflicted on herself the night she had intended to end it all and Joe had burst into her room and saved her life. The night that had changed her life for the better.

Ever so gently, his thumb traced over the mark on her forehead, but though his gaze remained on her forehead, he didn't seem to be seeing the mar any longer. She knew memories of that night had also gripped him.

She could still feel the cold press of the gun barrel beneath her chin. Remember the way her hand had trembled as her finger curled around the trigger. Then Joe had kicked in her door just before she'd pulled the trigger. Her startled flinch had saved her life. The bullet she'd hoped would end all her problems, ironically had done just that. More accurately, the incident had brought Joe into her life and he had introduced her to the Word, where she'd discovered a God who loved her more than she would ever be able to fathom in this lifetime.

And now he was offering to love her himself in a way she never could deserve. Could she accept that? Allow him to make that sacrifice?

With a blink, he returned to her again, and this time his eyes drilled directly into hers. They held an intensity that told her he was a man on a mission.

She tried to swallow but her mouth offered no moisture. She shook her head. Took a step back. "Joe—" Her voice failed her.

"Hello the house!" Reagan called from outside. "Everyone okay in there?"

Joe reached out and gently squeezed her hand. "We're not done here," he said softly. Lifting his rifle once more, he released her, giving a nod toward Tess. And then he headed for the door.

Liora hurried into motion, fetching a cup of coffee from the kitchen for the girl. Maybe the bitter black brew would comfort and return Tess to reality in a way that Liora hadn't seemed to be able to do since the first shots had broken.

It only took her a moment to decide that she needed a cup herself. Her hands were trembling as though she hadn't eaten in days and she doubted that even half of her agitation could be credited to the fact that John Hunt had practically declared war on her today.

War she could handle.

It was Joe Rodante she didn't know what to do about.

oe met Reagan and Washington in Liora's yard. He held out a hand to his boss. "Sure was glad to see you riding over that ridge. Thanks for coming."

Reagan nodded. "Anytime."

"Wash." Joe shook his hand.

"Sir." Wash returned his greeting with a nod.

"Anyone hurt?"

Joe shook his head. "We're all fine. You catch them all?"

Reagan nodded. "I think so. Rounded up four men. Know for a fact one works for Hunt. Know why they were shooting at you?"

Joe swept a hand of weariness over his face. He filled Reagan in on as much as he knew of the story.

"Liora and this girl, Tess, witnessed a murder?"

Joe nodded. "Apparently a...patron accused Tess of stealing from him, but when it was proven untrue, Hunt shot the man. They said there was a whole crowd of witnesses."

Reagan studied the last rays of sunlight disappearing through the trees. "Well, it's too late to ride out there tonight. And chances are that one of the four men we've just captured was there."

"Was one of the men you arrested named Pike?"

The men turned to find Liora huddled into her shawl on the front porch. A ferocious determination glittered in her eyes.

Joe offered the question to Reagan with a look.

Reagan nodded. "Pike was one of them, yes."

Liora trembled visibly. "He's the one John told to deal with the body."

Reagan met Joe's gaze. "All right. We'll start with him, then. Maybe we can get him to give us some information beyond the reason why he was here shooting up the place. Meet me in town mid-morning? That will give me some time to question them. Then we can ride out to Sixty-Five?"

Joe gave him a nod.

Reagan tipped his hat to Liora and then reined his horse around toward town. "Till then." He kicked his big black into a canter, Wash following in his wake.

When the doctor had left the evening before, Aurora had turned back to find Ma's eyes open and fixed right on her. For one moment. hope pushed aside everything she knew to be real. She hurried forward and took Ma's hand, kneeling by the cot. "Ma! You feeling better?"

Ma gave a weak nod. But Aurora knew it was only for show. With a trembling hand, Ma reached up to smooth her hair back from her face. "My...beautiful...girl..." The words were so weak they barely carried sound and Aurora leaned closer so she wouldn't miss a word. "So kind and generous." Ma's lips thinned into a smile. "I'm sorry to be leaving you so soon."

Aurora blinked hard to hold back the tears. "Hush, Ma. I'm going to be fine."

"I've done everything I could to keep you from the life."

Aurora knew exactly what life Ma meant. "I know, Ma. Don't worry about me, please. You just rest."

But Ma was already shaking her head and lifting a weak

finger to shush her. "Lis...ten. Whoring will...kill you, baby girl. Run. Hide. Don't let him find you."

Aurora had no doubt who her mother meant she should hide from. But where would she go? John Hunt had people everywhere. And Ma owed him a lot of money. He would chase her down and drag her back.

Ma's strength flagged but she gestured insistently toward the small trunk that contained the only possessions they'd retained of her father's. Everything else, they'd had to sell after he'd died in a logging accident. One of the mules in his team had balked at a snake on the roadway and sent the entire wagonload of logs into the ditch, taking Papa with it. He'd been crushed instantly. That had been three years ago midwinter. Aurora had been a gangly girl of fourteen. Ma had tried to find work, but John Hunt had liked her looks and he'd forbidden anyone in the camp from giving her a job or selling them a wagon or a horse. In the middle of winter, they hadn't dared try to leave without a wagon for cover. In the end, Ma had no choice but to go to work for John.

And Aurora wouldn't either.

But she did as Ma wanted and pulled the trunk closer to the bed, opening the lid. Her heart lurched at the sight of Papa's violin case lying on the tray inside. Her hand traced over the smoothness of the hard case. How many times had she wanted to pluck the strings, to hear the bow sing a sweet note along a tight string? But Ma had forbidden her to play it after the accident. It reminded her too much of Papa, she'd said.

Ma's hand trembled when she motioned that Aurora should lift the inset tray of the trunk.

Aurora set the tray to one side, watching Ma carefully to see what might be in the trunk that she wanted Aurora to pay attention to.

Ma motioned to a stack of clothes in one corner. "Been sa... ving...these." Her breaths were coming in short shallow puffs now.

"Ma, you need to rest. We can do this later."

Ma gave a firm shake of her head. "No. Just..." She motioned emphatically that Aurora should lift the stack.

Torn between forcing her to rest and upsetting her by refusing to do as she asked, Aurora gave in and reached for the clothes. "These?" She lifted the top item. A man's shirt, but likely too small for any man she knew.

Ma nodded and seemed to relax back into her pillow a bit. "For you."

Aurora frowned. She held the shirt up to herself. It was exactly the right size, but why would Ma think she would need a man's shirt? The next item in the stack was a pair of denim pants, complete with brass studs, just like Papa used to wear for work. Again, cut down to Aurora's size. Two more shirts, and a pair of Sunday-go-to-meeting pants were also in the stack. These she recognized and a realization suddenly hit Aurora. None of Papa's clothes remained in the trunk. Ma had taken all of Papa's things and cut them down so that they would fit her. A frown pinched at her brow. The question remained. Why?

Her gaze settled on Ma.

Ma struggled to inhale, then wheezed. "You run!"

Aurora understood then what Ma's intentions for her were, and a thought struck her. "Did you know you was dying?"

"Were...dying."

Aurora couldn't help a teary-eyed smile. Even with her last breaths, Ma expended energy to correct her grammar. "Yes, ma'am. Did you know you were dying?"

Air rattled at the back of Ma's throat. She nodded.

Aurora's tears blurred her vision. "You should have told me, Ma."

Ma shook her head and squeezed Aurora's hand. "Not...your burden...to bear, love."

Aurora clutched Ma's dry, wrinkled hand between her own. "Life's not fair, Ma." A sob escaped her.

"Shhhh," Ma soothed. "Can't go back. Only...forward." Her hand tightened around Aurora's and she gave it a little shake, drawing Aurora's attention to her once more.

Aurora dashed at her tears so she could see better.

Ma lifted one hand to touch Aurora's braid. "Razor's in... the trunk."

Aurora's eyes widened. Surely she didn't mean...

Ma's next word cut through the space between them, sharper, more agitated. "Run!"

Aurora nodded. "Yes, Ma. I'll run, I promise."

"Before...the weather...turns."

"Yes, ma'am." In fact, Aurora knew that if she were to escape John Hunt she would need to run even before news of Ma's death spread through the camp.

Relief seemed to sap the last of Ma's strength because her hand fell back to the coverlet and her whole body seemed to sink into the thin tick on the cot. Her eyes fell closed.

Aurora wept long into the night, alternating between listening to Ma's rattling breaths and rising to wipe the death foam from her lips. Ma coughed and sputtered, and Aurora patiently helped her turn on her side so some of the liquid slowly drowning her could drain away. In the wee hours, Ma grew too weak to even do that, and despair over her inability to relieve Ma's suffering collapsed Aurora to her knees. She shoved the knuckle of her first finger into her mouth and bit down hard to keep from screaming her anguish to the entire camp. Aurora curled into a ball on the floor beside the cot and buried her weeping into her fist and the crook of one arm. And just as dawn washed the sky with pink, the torturous wheezing stopped. Ma breathed no more.

Aurora lay quietly for a few more minutes. Waiting. Half hoping Ma would breathe again, half hoping she finally lay at rest. The silence was soon penetrated by the sound of the camp coming to life. Ma was indeed gone.

Aurora's stomach rumbled loudly, bringing with it a pang of hunger that reminded her she needed food. Yet there was none in the shanty.

Pushing herself up to a sitting position, she studied Ma's still form, a numb sensation wedging indecision between the twin needs of escaping to freedom and seeing Ma safely to her final resting place. If Pike or even Mr. Hunt, himself, found out about Ma's passing, her chance to run would be snuffed out before it had even begun. After several moments of weighing her options, she decided on a compromise. She would run, but not before she had washed and prepared Ma for her grave.

With the wooden hairbrush, she combed out Ma's long brown locks and braided them into careful plaits that she then wrapped around her head like a crown. She washed and dressed her in her Sunday best dress, which Aurora hadn't actually seen her wear since she'd been forced to go to work for Hunt. She tried to put on Ma's pert black boots, but had to give up because she couldn't get them over her heels. She settled for covering her feet with a pair of the warm woolen socks they had knitted for each other last Christmas.

Aurora had just stepped back to take one final look, when a knock sounded on the door. She spun to face it, feeling her eyes go wide.

"Aurora? 'S me, darlin'. Joanie Pence."

Aurora gritted her teeth. Joanie was almost as bad as either of the men. Everyone in the camp knew that she was John Hunt's eyes and ears. She couldn't know that Ma had passed, or she would go straight to Mr. Hunt with the news. But neither could Aurora not answer the door, for the woman would take that as a sign that something was amiss.

Aurora scrambled to her feet and cracked open the door, doing nothing to disguise the fact that she'd spent a good portion of the night crying, but also not allowing Joanie a good look into the shanty's interior.

Joanie's face pulled into a forced expression of sympathy. "Aw, look at ya, poor dear. A corpse warmed over'd have more color. Bad news from the doc yesterday, then?" She craned to see into the interior behind Aurora.

Aurora pulled the door tighter against her shoulder and nodded. "Doc says it's a contagion. Ma must have caught it from a john. Doc says she only has about a week, and that I likely have it too and should stay away from the rest of the camp."

Joanie's eyes widened and she took a large step back, then another. She lifted her arm to cover her nose and mouth. "That so? Well, I'm right sorry to hear it!" With that, she scrambled off as though the angel of death himself were chasing her.

Aurora clicked the door shut and glanced around. She'd bought herself some time, maybe a day, before someone came back around to check on her, or they conferred with Doc and found out she'd made the story up. But she needed that time to get her head start. There was not a moment to waste.

Picking up the scissors, she paused before the small hand-mirror that Ma had hung from the shanty's central post. The small mother-of-pearl backed mirror had been a gift to Ma from Papa on their wedding day. That thought drew her eyes past her dark braid to the corner of the room. She fingered her plait for a moment while she studied the still form on the bed.

The lump in her chest threatened to take her to her knees, a hot burning mass that bade her to scream her pain to the world. Instead, she stuffed it further down inside and purposefully turned her attention to cutting her hair. It took several hacks with the scissors to sever the braid at the base of her neck. But she didn't stop there. If she was going to don a disguise, she would go all out. She snipped away bits until her hair was as close cropped as she could make it on all sides with just a bit more length on top. The way Papa had worn his hair before he passed. And, with surprise, Aurora noted that a good deal of him now stared back at her from the mirror. She had Ma's pale green eyes and upturned nose. But it was Papa's broad forehead and blunt chin that showed up so well now that her hair had been cut. One finger drifted up to touch her reflection and the cold press of the glass brought her back to the present. She needed to hurry.

The pile of hair would give away her plan to anyone who entered the shanty, so she carefully swept it up and dropped it in the fire, ribbon and all.

Her next task was to don the men's clothing and boots. The britches felt foreign and stiff. Confining and much too revealing. But she tried to see herself as others would. Skinny as she was from the lack of food they'd had in recent months, her curves were minimal. Still, she needed to do something about them. She tugged off the shirt and used one of Ma's head scarves to bind her breasts as flat as she could. This time, when she tugged the shirt back into place, she felt more satisfied with her presentation. There wasn't much she could do about her small waist or hips.

At the fireplace, she took up a piece of charcoal that had

fallen to the edge. A few smudges around her eyes, made them look a bit more sunken. Some streaks near her mouth would hopefully draw people's attention to them instead of to her full lips that looked anything but masculine.

She tilted the mirror this way and that, studying herself, and finally put it back on its hook. Anyone who had known her well, would likely still recognize her, but hopefully the disguise would trick those who had only seen her in passing. She wished she could take the mirror with her as a memento, but a boy wouldn't pack around such a thing, so it would have to stay. As would Papa's violin. John Hunt could sell them to cover Ma's debt. The violin on its own was worth far more than Ma owed.

Gathering up the rest of the clothes Ma had cut down for her, she tied them into a bandana.

And then it was time to leave.

A sob clogged her throat as she looked once more to where Ma lay so still and pale. Her skin had turned rather gray and Aurora spun away, wishing she hadn't taken that last look.

In her hurry to get out of the shanty, she almost used the front door, but right before she yanked it open, she froze, heart pounding. If she went out the front, anyone who saw her leaving would immediately recognize her. The back of the shanty had a loose board that she could push through. The gap was small but she could fit through it. And it would release her into the cascading branches of the tall lilac that grew at the back of their shanty.

She shoved the bandana of clothes out first and then, giving a careful look, wriggled out after it. All around her the sounds of the camp continued as though the world had not come to an end just now. Up on the road, she could hear the men talking loudly as they climbed aboard the wagons that would take them out to their logging sites for the day.

Dawn had seeped away to a barely perceptible pink against a vibrant blue sky.

Snatching up the bandana, Aurora sprinted toward the back edge of the camp. If she could just make it to the forest beyond, she would figure out what to do next. But she hadn't gone more than twenty paces when a craggy voice called for her attention. "You there! Boy! What you doin' runnin' around back 'ere?"

Aurora froze. She recognized the voice as that of the elderly Mr. Whitehall. She'd forgotten about him. And about Mr. Heath's program that kept the boys of the camp employed from dawn to dusk.

"Shirkin' your duties, no doubt." The man grumbled as he ambled closer.

Mr. Whitehall had always been nothing but kind to her, but was known to be a bit hard on the camp's boys. On more than one occasion, he'd confided in her that all boys really needed was a man with a good firm hand to shape them into men.

Heart in her throat, she turned to face him. This would be a good test of her disguise. "No sir. I don't actually live here."

"Nonsense! Don't give me that. What you doin' in camp at this time of mornin' for if'n you don't live here?" The white-whiskered man didn't even blink at her appearance. Of course, he was known to be more than half blind. Before Aurora could take another step, Mr. Whitehall had her firmly by her upper arm. "Hmmm. Scrawny one, ain't ye? Well, no mind. A few days of hard work and good food will put some meat on your bones and maybe even teach ye not to prevaricate." Without ceremony, he hauled her toward the center of camp.

Aurora lost her grip on her bandana and her bundle of clothes tumbled to the ground and rolled a few turns, but the man didn't seem to notice and wouldn't release her arm so she could go back for it. "My things," she protested.

"They'll still be there when you get done with work. Your folks must be new to these parts, eh?"

Aurora opened her mouth, but he barreled ahead before she could even utter a sound.

"Your pap working for old Heath? Or is your mam one of that snake Hunt's women? Never mind." He waved a hand that indicated he didn't really care about the answers to any of the questions he hadn't let her answer. "I'm old man Whitehall—leastwise that's what all the lads call me—and I'm in charge of the boys about camp by day. We've got wood to stock and I dare say you wouldn't turn down some breakfast, hmmm lad? Skin and bones is all that's on ye. Skin and bones."

Aurora would have fled when he released her at the meal tent that sat at the center of camp, but the mention of food presented too much temptation. Her stomach was so empty it didn't even rumble. It just ached and pleaded.

Mr. Whitehall pushed her none too gently through the slit in the canvas. She'd seen the tent every day, but had only ever entered on the days she and Ma served the thin porridge that was part of the boys' pay. To keep the boys in his camps from raising too much mischief during the day while their parents were off to work, Mr. Heath put them to work for themselves from very young ages. Even boys eight to ten years old were strong enough to gather wood for fires and older boys laid walkways or hacked back brush that threatened to encroach on the camp. Two cents a day was given to each boy who worked. And it was Mr. Whitehall's job to make sure they all worked.

He shoved her onto a bench at the closest table. "Sit. You'll eat. Then I'll show you what your job will be for this week."

Aurora despaired of escape. And other boys in the room were eyeing her like fresh meat ready to be tenderized. She squirmed in her seat and tried not to lick her lips when one of the matrons—Mrs. Rojas—clunked a bowl before her. She kept her eyes averted from the woman, the wife of Camp Sixty-Five's foreman. But the woman hardly gave her a glance. The porridge was plain—no sugar or butter—but it easily took the prize as the best thing Aurora had tasted in a long time, and a cup of sweet milk, fresh from the cow, accompanied it. She savored her bites slowly, washing each one down with a sip of the milk.

None of the boys at her table spoke to her, but when Mr. Whitehall stalked further into the tent to deal with some infraction at one of the other tables, the boy across from her—the son of one of the recently-arrived sawyers, she thought—reached over and snagged her still-half-full bowl, leaving his empty one in its place.

Aurora offered no challenge. She merely studied a knot in the table-board before her. The last thing she wanted to do was get in a fight with the boy. And besides, it mattered not. Her stomach was already fuller than it had been all week. And for that she would choose to be thankful.

The meal soon finished and Mr. Whitehall waved them all outside. "Right lads. Get to work now. You there, new boy, wait for me," he instructed.

Aurora paused outside the tent, trying to decide what to do while other boys streamed past her and headed for their various chores. The longer she remained in camp, the more chance there was of someone recognizing her and reporting her to John Hunt, so she should make her escape at the earliest opportunity. On the other hand, John wouldn't likely think to search for her here in camp right under his nose and maybe she could make enough money to hire someone to take her to a nearby city.

Each of the boys grabbed an apple from the small barrel

that sat outside the tent door as they went by. That would be their lunch, then. Mr. Whitehall came out, but his attention was immediately taken by two boys who had set to scuffling over one of the larger apples.

Still undecided over whether to stay or flee, Aurora figured that an apple would be a benefit no matter what she did. She took one up and turned, but ran smack into the chest of the boy who'd stolen her porridge. He was a large boy for twelve. And since his arrival a few days ago he hadn't let any of the other boys forget it. She'd seen him picking on younger or smaller boys several times.

He knocked the apple from her fingers and gave her a challenging look. One eyebrow cocked. And his gaze slipped over her from head to foot, brow furrowing.

Her pulse tripped. Did he recognize her?

After a long moment, he must have given up on whatever thought he'd been pondering because he gave her a shove and stepped closer. "You only get an apple after you've proven that you are a good worker, greenhorn."

Aurora looked around for Mr. Whitehall, but he would be no help. He was at this very moment hauling the two delinquents in his charge back into the tent, holding each one by an ear. She raised her hands to indicate that she wanted no confrontation. "I don't want to fight you. How about we both simply withdraw?" She started to ease away, but the bully hooked one of his legs behind hers and shoved her hard.

She sprawled onto her back in the dirt. Right at the feet of a horse.

"Whoa!" The rider pulled his mount to a stop. It danced sideways a few steps and then the man leaned over and peered down at her.

With dark hair that curled out from under his Stetson, a

close-cropped beard that accentuated an angular jaw, and eyes as green as morning dew on spring grass, he was probably the best-looking man she had ever seen. But his lips tilted up into a slant of a smirk that set her teeth on edge and her blood to boiling. What kind of a man found humor in a predicament like this?

Teeth gritted, she leapt to her feet and folded her arms over her chest.

Her decision was suddenly made. She wasn't going to stay in a camp where boys were treated like this!

reston Clay had ridden through the morning mist toward Camp Sixty-Five with Kin Davis riding beside him—well, more like grudgingly, barely keeping up. Kin was in what Preston's gran would have termed a 'foul as a rooster destined for the pot' mood. And Preston had to admit that, with his patience running thin, he might have been a bit short with the kid this morning. But Kin's backtalk and rebellion were getting a little old.

Preston rubbed a hand over the nape of his neck and blew out his frustration. At twenty-five, he wasn't old enough to know how to handle the bad attitude of a contrary teen. Kin may have lived with Preston since the death of his father when he was fifteen had left him an orphan, but that didn't mean it had been easy. And the truth was, two years hadn't done much to improve the kid's wayward ways.

No matter how much Preston forced him to read the Word, or lectured, or prayed, Kin seemed determined to persist in his penchant for choosing trouble. At first his antics had been over more innocent things like skipping school to go fishing. But recently his rebellion had taken a more sinister turn, as evidenced by the fact that Doc had found him in McGinty's last night—again. Kin had earned seventeen cents from tips at Dixie's Boardinghouse the day before and of course McGinty, a man who saw the world in dollars and cents, had been happy to take it from him. Dixie had promptly fired Kin when Preston had taken him to her back door this morning, and Preston was honestly thankful for Dixie's quick decision. Kin had always admired Dixie. She had always been kind to him and offered him jobs whenever he had need. Preston figure that maybe getting fired by her would shake up the kid's world a bit.

No wonder the kid was in a foul mood. He'd lost the respect of one of his favorite people in town and he likely had a headache that felt like a crosscut saw at work.

Preston smirked and set to whistling—loudly.

Behind him, Kin grunted.

Preston led the way over the last rise and down into the shanties on the near end of camp. Doc had said the girl would be in one at the center of the encampment beneath a wild lilac tree. What had he said her name was? Preston thought he had said, but he'd been so frustrated with Kin, who had been grinning drunkenly at him, that he couldn't now remember it. No matter, she could give it to him when he spoke to her.

A commotion off to his left drew his attention.

Two boys of about fourteen had faced off. One of them appeared to have ganged up on the other. He gave the smaller boy a shove and he sprawled on his back in the dirt right in front of Preston's horse. "Whoa!" he called, hauling on the reins.

For one terrible moment, he thought his mount had stepped on the kid, but then his horse sidled sideways and the boy was still there, breathing and all in one piece. Dirt smudged the kid's face and he presented such a forlorn picture that before Preston thought better of it, a smile tugged at the corner of his lips. It never ceased to amaze him how God brought him 'the least of these' to help.

The kid on the ground scrambled to his feet and folded his

arms over his chest, digging at the ground with the toe of one scuffed boot.

"What's going on here?" He dismounted.

The other boy continued to glower at the kid.

Kin pulled his mount to a stop, but only leaned on his pommel looking bored. He likely wouldn't be any help if this came to blows.

The bully, fists still balled, tipped a nod to the kid who'd been on the ground. "He's new 'round these parts. I caught him skulking 'round. Just was letting him know we don't put up with no troublemakers."

"I ain't no troublemaker!" The new kid kept digging at the ground. He looked younger than the other. Smaller. Lighter. With a voice that hadn't changed yet. Pale, gaunt cheeks. Hungry looking.

Preston's stomach crimped. Well he remembered what it was like to go days on end without food. "What's your name kid? You hungry?"

Wide pale green eyes flashed to his for a fleeting moment before returning to the ground. After another moment of hesitation, the boy said, "Rory. And yes, sir. A little bit, sir."

The kid's hesitation made Preston wonder if that really was his name, but what mattered at this moment was saving him from the bully and then maybe getting him some food.

"You got a ma and pa around?"

The boy shook his head. And was that a sheen of tears casting that highlight in his eyes?

Preston motioned from the boy to Kin. "Why don't you join us? You can ride behind Kin there. I just have one stop to make and then I can get you some food."

The kid glanced toward the tent behind him and seemed to think on it for a moment. His gaze bounced between the bully,

Kin, Preston, and the hole his boot continued to dig in the dirt. Finally, he nodded. "All right."

Preston felt unaccountably relieved. He nodded the boy toward Kin's horse. "Go ahead. That's Kin. He looks meaner than a wild dog with a broke leg, but he doesn't bite. Much."

Kin rolled his eyes, but he did motion the kid over and reach down a hand to help him swing up behind his saddle.

Preston tipped his hat to the bully. "You have a nice day now. I'll make sure the kid stays out of trouble."

The chubby red head puffed out his chest. "See that you do!"

Preston hid a smirk. He had half a mind to give the boy a fistful of his own medicine, but could also remember what it was like to feel protective over the few possessions he had called his own as a kid.

Only a moment later, they were on their way again and it wasn't hard to find the shanty under the area's only lilac tree.

Preston swung down. "I'll only be a moment—" he started to explain, but, behind Kin, the kid's eyes were so wide and his face so pale that Preston paused. "You okay, kid?"

The boy nodded. He gave a little squirm on the horse and his voice was barely audible when he said. "What are you doing here?"

Preston's heart went out to the kid. Maybe he feared their intentions.

Kin released an audible sigh. "Heck, kid, relax! The parson there ain't never hurt a fly!"

At his purposeful use of such slang, Preston's teeth set together. Kin was just trying to bait him. And now was not the time for an argument. Instead, he would choose to be thankful that Kin had actually stood up for him. As for 'never hurt a fly...' well, that was a talk he hadn't worked up the courage to have with Kin. One day God would make him tell that story, but not today...

He offered the boy a nod and a reassuring smile, gave Kin a look that he hoped said 'don't try to ride away while I'm not looking, and be kind' all in one, and then approached the shanty. He knocked. No one answered, and he was just about to knock again when a woman stepped out of the next shanty over.

"What you lookin' fer, mister?"

Preston pressed his hat to his chest as he faced her and gave a sketch of a bow to show respect. "Morning ma'am. I am Parson Preston Clay. I heard that a woman in this shanty was feeling poorly and that her daughter might need some... assistance."

The woman appeared only somewhat appeased by his introduction, but she did give an attempt at a curtsy. "Joanie Pence at yer service, Parson. And 'tis true enough what ye say. I done spoke to Aurora jus' this mornin'. The doc done said her ma had only a week to live and that she herself was likely contagious, poor lass. She ain't answering? She has to be in 'cause I ain't seen her leave yet today."

The kid behind Kin suddenly seemed very interested in something on the other side of the encampment away from the woman. Preston tried to see what might have caught his attention. Nothing seemed out of the ordinary. Was the kid running from home? Did he have parents out looking for him? Preston looked again, but he didn't see anyone frantically searching the encampment for a lost kid, just people going about the hum-drum everyday tasks of camp life.

Preston brought his mind back to his present task. He would have to grill the kid about the details of his life later. Right now, he needed to try and find the girl Doc had said needed some help. He knocked on the door again. When he still received no answer, he motioned for Kin to wait, and made his way around to the back of the shanty. But there was no back door, and there wasn't even a slit of a window to peer through like some of the other shanties had. Completing a full circle, he pondered what he ought to do.

But Joanie Pence took the decision out of his hands. Eyes widening, she started to back away from the shanty as fast as her legs would take her, one arm swinging up to cover her mouth and nose. "They done both died then? Aurora done said the doc told her whatever her mama had was deadly. But she—only an hour ago she—" Joanie seemed to have run out of words.

Preston frowned. Doc had said nothing to him about it being contagious. Kin looked a little wide-eyed when the woman turned and ran away, but Preston held up one palm and patted the air a few times.

Turning the handle on the door, he gave it a push. It squeaked inward. He proceeded cautiously lest he might be barging in on someone who was sound asleep, but it was soon apparent there was only one person in the room—and she had passed on. A quick check showed that the girl—Aurora, he mentally thanked Joanie for the reminder—wasn't in sight. Had she gone to get someone to carry out her mother? A touch to the woman's throat found her cold. So she passed sometime in the night, then. If that were the case, the girl should have returned by now...

He stepped back out into the morning light, hat pressed to his chest and a furrow on his brow. Somewhere in this camp there was a young girl whose life would be torn apart if John Hunt got hold of her. And hang it all if he knew how to go about finding her without making things worse for her.

Aurora stood next to the newly opened hole on Camp Sixty-Five's boot hill, teeth clench with the reminder to withhold her tears.

Much as she'd wanted to run in terror when the minister had insisted on searching out John Hunt to let him know one in his employ had passed away, and to see to the burying, her fear of being caught had held far less weight than her desire to see Ma safely into her final resting place.

Hidden as she'd been for most of the day behind the rather broad back of Kin Davis, it hadn't been hard to keep out of John and Joanie's sight, and she wasn't too worried about any of the others—none of them would expose her, even if they recognized her, though none had even given her a second look. Not even when Parson Clay had asked the women to go in and prepare Ma for burial, and none of them had wanted to go inside since Joanie had already spread her story through the camp, so Aurora had volunteered to help the parson. Kin had rolled his eyes at her, clearly thinking the boy, Rory, was only sidling up to the minister to get on his good side, but she'd ignored him and followed the man inside the shanty. The parson had seemed much relieved when he'd noticed that Ma was already washed and prepared for the grave. And Aurora had been touched by how gently and carefully he had handled Ma. He'd wrapped her in the quilt from her bed, tucking it about her as though he might be tucking in a small child for a night of sleep. It had been all Aurora could do to keep herself from collapsing into a fit of sobs at the small table she and Ma had shared for so many years.

Throughout the day, it had been quite clear the minister was looking for her. He had asked several of the camp wives if they had seen where she might have gone, and she'd overheard him tell one that Doc had told him she might need his help. Which was true enough. But he *was* helping her. And revealing her identity to him while Hunt and his men were still about would only ensure a fight that a kind man like the minister was sure to lose. So, she kept her silence and watched.

The minister said some nice sounding words over Ma, though Aurora had to admit she didn't quite understand the meaning of them all, and then before she realized so much time had passed, the camp folk were heading back to the camp.

What would he do with her now? Her stomach rumbled a, reminder that the only thing she'd had to eat all day were the few bites of gruel this morning. And yet somehow, she didn't feel like she could swallow anything without the danger of it coming right back up. The forced withholding of her emotions was making her literally queasy.

But the parson must have heard her stomach, because he stopped by her side and ruffled her hair. "Never did get you any food, did we lad?"

Aurora felt weary to the bone. She only wanted to sleep. Sleep for years and never wake up.

"Come on, kid. Back on the horse. You look all done in." He grabbed one of her arms with one hand, and her backside with the other, and boosted her up behind Kin's saddle.

She gave a little squeak of surprise and turned away before he could see the flush that she could feel warming her cheeks. Having spent the day with the man, she had no doubt that he would never manhandle a woman in such a manner. She reminded herself that he didn't know she was anything other than a grubby kid who needed his help. But none of that erased the memory of the feel of his hand on her backside.

Nor did it eliminate the question of what she would do after the man fed her and sent her on her way. Where was she going to go? How was she going to survive? She had no skills. Sure, Ma had tried to do her best by her. She'd taught her the basics of sewing and cleaning and instilled in her the importance of working hard for anything she got. But she had no real-world skills. Nothing that would convince someone to give her a job. Nor even any knowledge of how to go about attaining a job.

All of the questions had her pulse thrumming and her lungs tighter than the scarf about her chest. And over top it all, a heavy weariness draped, making the answer to each question harder to come by and the sight of the deforested hills around them naught but a blur that urged her to close her eyes and cease the battle, even if only for a few moments.

For now, she was safe. She would relish in that, and take the next days and hours as they came. She slumped forward and rested her cheek against Kin's back, and let the world fade away.

Joe propped his hands on his hips and gawked at Liora, who was busy kneading a loaf of bread at the table. Tess sat at one end, nursing a cup of coffee and glancing between them.

Reagan and Wash had just ridden away and Liora had denied Joe's request for a spare blanket so he could bed down outside.

"I mean it, Joe." There was a flash of irritation in her blue eyes. "Since you and Reagan don't plan to ride out to the camp until tomorrow, go back to town. Tess and I will be fine now." The tremor in her hands belied her words.

Joe felt like a steam engine about to explode. He reminded himself to gentle his voice. "You either have a death wish, or you have no idea what Hunt is capable of."

She swept a strand of hair off her forehead with one wrist. "I assure you that I'm neither pining for my grave, nor naïve enough to take my eyes off of a snake like John Hunt. But he won't even hear about his men's arrests till morning. We'll be fine."

"Well that's not a risk I'm willing to take. You don't have to give me a blanket, but know that I'm not leaving."

She blew out a breath, hands stilling in the dough. "Joseph Rodante, be reasonable! I'm only trying to protec—" All her attention plunked back to the dough, and her hands set to pummeling it again.

Everything in him stilled. "Wait a minute. You're not worried about *me* are you? I can take care of myself."

"I'm not worried about you being able to handle John Hunt. It's just... Never mind. Just please, go back to town." Defeat washed her tone.

He watched her butter the loaves and shape them into the loaf pans. And realization struck. It was his reputation she was concerned about. Hadn't he just been pondering on the fact that she'd gone out of her way to guard his reputation on multiple occasions? This was all his fault. If he hadn't been so stand-offish with her. If he had treated her like she deserved to be treated, she would know what a treasure she was in the eyes of God and maybe the townsfolk would have seen it too, by now. Sometimes people simply needed someone to lead the way.

He strode to where she rinsed her hands at the sink. She stiffened at his approach so instead of turning her to face him, as he'd intended, he only said, "Look at me, please?"

She searched his face quizzically, water dripping from her hands into the sink.

Taking up the towel, he thrust it toward her. "Tess? Can we have a moment?"

The girl complied without hesitation. "I'll just get on to my room."

Joe had been prepared to launch into a lecture, but now that he stood alone with her, words failed him. Mostly because he suddenly realized how much he wanted to declare his love for her.

Love? Hang it all. He was *in love* with the woman. When was that going to sink in and feel real?

Liora plunked her hands on her hips, one of them still gripping a towel. She tilted him a look. "Joe, you are acting all-fired strange today. What has gotten into you?"

"I told you I wanted to marry you. But what I didn't say is that I'm in love with you." The words blurted out before he could lasso them into submission.

Her eyes shot wide and she spun to face the sink. "No, Joe. No, you can't—You *don't* love me!" She set to working the pump handle for no apparent reason.

Joe's hands trembled and he thrust them deep into his pockets. "Liora, you tell me you don't have..." He ground to a stop. It would be too easy for her to lie undetected if she wasn't facing him. "Look at me. Please?"

She angled a glance over one shoulder.

He would have preferred to take her face in his hands to ensure she couldn't look away, but he wanted her to have her freedom. Holding her gaze with his own, he swallowed and started again. "You tell me you don't have any feelings for me and I'll not press the issue. But I'm begging you to be honest."

White teeth clamped down on her lower lip. "Joe, of course I have feelings for you."

His heart started an elated pounding, but caution held him in place.

"You've been a good friend since the moment we met. And it's because of you that I came to know the Lord."

She paused and he held his breath. Some of his elation seeped away. He sensed a "but" coming.

"But this thing between us can never work. I could never... I'm simply not...wife material. And for your own sake, I hope you will abandon this foolishness."

Again, he was filled with a sense of discouragement over how he had failed her. She truly saw herself as unworthy. Unworthy of others' respect. Unworthy of love.

There was nothing he could do about the past, but he intended to change the future. The problem was he knew it was going to be difficult to convince her that he spoke the truth when he said he loved her. He would just have to show her. Starting now.

"I know you don't want me to stay here. And I know that's because you worry about what the townsfolk will think, both of you and of me. But the truth is, not one of those folk would begrudge another woman protection if something like this happened to her. So I can't see why things should be different with you. And I couldn't live with myself if something happened to you. So you'll pardon me for refusing your request that I go back to town tonight."

Her eyes were as wide as a newborn calf's, and he knew he needed to depart before he gave in to the urge to pull her into his arms and show her just how ardent his feelings for her were. He tipped her a nod and pushed out into the night.

Liora felt her jaw drop as Joe closed the door behind himself. That stubborn man! He was going to shatter his reputation and there obviously wasn't a thing she could do about it.

As he clicked the door shut, the icy draft of his departure swept in around her ankles and it struck her how cold he would be on this autumn night, sleeping outdoors without cover.

She rushed across the room and flung open the door. "Joe, wait."

Before he even turned, she sped toward the trunk beneath the parlor window and withdrew the two thick quilts she had set aside for future girls. She reached the kitchen door as Joe was stepping back onto the porch.

Holding the bulky quilts with one hand beneath and one atop, she thrust them toward him. If he was going to be stubborn enough to stay, at least he could be warm while he did it.

"Thank you." He reached to take the bedding and his hands covered hers, top and bottom. He paused right there. His gaze drilled into hers and one corner of his mouth tipped up.

She snatched her hands back to her sides, doing her best to ignore the tremor that swept up her arms and seemed to squeeze the very air from her lungs. Oh how she wished she could appreciate it when a man looked at her thus. Yet naught but terrible memories accompanied such a look.

He cleared his throat softly and took a step back, but he didn't release her gaze. "Wanted to ask if you'll be busy tomorrow after work?"

Caution made her hesitate. Why would he want to know that? "No. Not really. I'd planned to stop by Mrs. Callahan's before work and ask if she might have some darning to employ Tess with, so I might need to swing over and pick her up when I get done at Dixie's, but other than that, I'd only planned to return here."

He gave the barest hint of a nod. "Good. See you in the morning." And with that, he slipped off the porch and disappeared into the darkness.

Liora shook her head and returned inside.

She had planned to spend the evening talking to Tess to see what sort of skills she might need to teach her, but the girl hadn't come out of her room since Joe had asked for some time alone with her, and she supposed they'd had a trying enough day that the girl was probably already sound asleep. She would leave her be for now. Lord knew she was tired enough to fall straight into bed herself.

In fact, as soon as she banked the fire and swept up the kitchen, she might do just that. And hopefully she would be able to sleep and not worry about one stubborn man sleeping in the elements just so he could ensure her safety.

Chapter Eleven

"Reagan Callahan!"

At breakfast the next morning, Reagan sipped from his coffee and grinned at Charlotte over the rim of his cup. Hang it, but she was beautiful when she was riled. He wasn't going to let a murder investigation or the nefarious deeds of any outlaw taint this moment.

Still standing next to his ma's table with her hands on her hips, she tilted him a look that, if he were smart, would have sobered him right up. But he was feeling courageous, perhaps even as brave as the prophet Daniel must have felt just before descending into the lions' den, so he stood his ground. "I don't see why we have to wait a whole long while. Your family could be out here from Boston by the end of the month, and..." He reached for her hand and tugged her closer, giving her a pump of his brows. "Now that we've made the decision, I find I'm rather looking forward to being an old married man." He stood and settled his hands at her waist. "So? What say you?"

Her cheeks had turned a rosy pink. Her lower lip pooched out slightly and she tapped his chest with one finger. "You don't play fair."

He grinned. Had he actually won her over that easily? "So you agree to my suggested date, then?"

Still she hesitated and he could see her considering and checking things off on one of her perpetual mental lists.

He didn't mind the wait. He could hardly believe his fortune to have a woman such as this agree to spend the rest of her days with him. How had he gotten so lucky?

Finally, she lifted her gaze to his. "All right. I'll telegram Mother and Father to see if they can make it that soon."

"They'll make it." Reagan settled more comfortably into his heels, pushing away the small niggle of concern over whether her parents would like him or not.

Charlotte looked pensive. "I can hardly believe that it's been nearly two years since I saw them last."

"I'm sure they've missed you just as much as you've missed them."

"I'm certain you're right. It's only that I hate to have them come all this way and then have us head off on our wedding tour only a few days after they arrive."

Reagan pondered. "We could delay our tour for a couple weeks? That would give us time to get settled into our place, and time to visit with them before we all go our separate ways again."

Charlotte wrapped her arms around Reagan's neck and leaned back to look up at him. "I think that's why I fell in love with you, Sheriff. You are such a thoughtful man."

He grinned down at her and then lingered over a kiss, wishing he didn't need to get to the office first thing this morning. By the time he'd gotten back to town last night, it had been so late that he'd decided to leave his interrogations until today. And then he'd have to ride out to confront John Hunt about the attack and the possible murder Liora and Tess had witnessed.

Reluctantly, he pulled away. "I'd best get. It's going to be a long day." He lifted the Seattle newspaper that had come in with yesterday's mail, and tucked it under one arm.

Charlotte turned and picked up her satchel from where it waited by the door. "Yes. Me too. Poor Belle Kastain is going to be devastated when I walk into the classroom today with this ring on my finger." She tossed him a wink.

He rolled his eyes. Charlotte was forever giving him a hard time about the girl, but the truth was, Belle had acted like a perfect lady toward him ever since her father had been shot that fateful day nearly two years ago now. The man still lived, but he'd never been the same since. Reagan playfully kicked Charlotte out the door and she scampered ahead of him giggling like a little girl.

He escorted her to the church, which now functioned as a schoolhouse during the week, and then made his way back across the street and pushed into the jailhouse.

Four sets of eyes glowered at him from the two cells at the back of the building.

He didn't envy them the night they had all spent on the small uncomfortable cots. "Morning, gentlemen." He plunked the newspaper onto his desk and set about making a pot of coffee, letting the spoon do plenty of clanking against the pot to ensure he had all their attention. "First one of you who's willing to tell me what you all were doing out at Miss Fontaine's place yesterday gets a nice hot cup of coffee. I also have cream and sugar, if you like." Judging by the hungry looks on all their faces, he added, "I'll even throw in a plate of bacon and flapjacks from Dixie's Boardinghouse." A moment of pause emphasized, "It will be Ewan's porridge for the rest of you." He allowed a few beats before he tacked on, "I also heard there was a murder in Camp Sixty-Five, yesterday. Would any of you know anything about that?" He pinned his gaze on Pike.

The man didn't flinch under his scrutiny.

However, a man in the adjacent cell, the one who'd been left in charge of guarding the attackers' horses at Liora's the day before, shuffled his feet.

Burt Pike growled audibly and looked at the smaller man in the cell next to his. "Don't you say a blamed thing, Tom. Not a blamed thing!"

Tom swallowed and eyed the pot of coffee, his belly yowling loud enough that Reagan could hear it from across the room.

Though his normal practice was to fetch McGinty's porridge for any prisoner in his jail at this point of the day, today he thought he'd let his point settle a little. He deliberately sank into his desk chair and propped his boots atop the far corner. He pulled over the newspaper he'd brought with him from Ma's and snapped it open.

It wasn't long before the scent of fresh coffee wafted through the air. Without a word, he rose, poured himself a cup and returned to his desk. He slurped noisily and smacked his lips, pretending great interest in the paper that didn't really have anything interesting in it at all.

Reagan was only on his second sip when Tom blurted, "I'll tell ya whatever ya want to know."

Burt Pike surged to his feet and grabbed the bars between the cells. "I said you don't say a word, Tom." He motioned the man who shared the cell with Tom, toward the smaller man. "Shut him up, Harry."

Reagan let the cocking of his pistol do his talking.

Everyone froze and looked his way.

He gestured Harry away from Tom with the point of the Colt.

Harry took three reluctant steps, each at the prodding of the gun barrel.

"That's better. Now, Tom you go on over and sit on that cot next to the wall over there."

Tom hustled over and did as he was told, wrapping his skinny arms around knees that were so knobby they looked pointed beneath his denims.

Reagan kept his voice low. "Harry, over here by the cell door, please."

Harry glowered at Tom, but did as he was told.

Reagan slowly opened the cell door and motioned Harry out with the point of his gun. Then, keeping the gun trained on him, he locked the first cell and unlocked the second. This time sweeping his aim to keep all three men in their places, he eased open the door of the second cell. "In." He motioned Harry into the cell.

With a glum twist of his lips, Harry complied. And thankfully, the other two men were smart enough to hold their places.

It only took Reagan ten minutes to return with the food. He shoved three bowls of McGinty's porridge beneath the bars of the cell where Pike, Harry, and the third man paced.

Pike had been speaking vehemently to Tom when he'd returned, and for a moment Reagan feared that they might have changed Tom's mind about spilling what he knew, but when he withheld the man's plate and asked "You still going to talk to me?" Tom nodded his head vigorously.

Reagan opened his cell door and stepped inside.

Tom's hands trembled as he reached for the plate, leaving Reagan to wonder when the man had last eaten anything.

Reagan let him eat for a few minutes, and then dove into his questions. "Know anything about the man that was shot in camp yesterday?"

Tom shook his head. "I don't know nothing about that."

Reagan considered. Maybe he'd work his way back around to that question. He pressed ahead. "All right... Want to tell me what you boys were doing out at Miss Fontaine's place yesterday?" Reagan had a good idea, but what he really wanted was some evidence that pointed to John Hunt.

Tom sopped up the last of his syrup with the last bite of flapjack. "We was hired to retrieve...some personal belongings."

Reagan's jaw bunched. "You saying that Miss Fontaine took something that belonged to your boss?"

Tom smacked his lips and slurped down the last of his coffee. "In a manner of speakin'."

"What did she take?"

"'Twer'n't a what, but a who."

"Tess? The girl who was at Miss Fontaine's house?"

"That's the one."

Reagan clasped one wrist behind his back, willing down the anger that wanted to boil over in a pummeling for all four men before him. The girl Tess, whom he'd met the evening before, couldn't be more than seventeen, if she was a day. "So who does this Tess belong to?"

Reagan held his breath. The word of this no-account wouldn't hold much weight in court, but it would give him enough evidence to do a little poking around in Hunt's business. Reagan would like nothing more than to arrest the man and send him away for a good long stretch, but he'd never been able to catch him doing anything illegal.

Tom folded his arms, a smug look overtaking his features. "Well now, I said I'd talk, but that don't mean I planned to tell you everything."

Reagan moved so fast, even he was a bit surprised by his actions. One moment he was standing in the cell with Tom and the next he grabbed the man by his shirt and shoved him up against the bars that faced his desk.

Tom's feet scrabbled for purchase. "Hunt! She belongs to John Hunt!" he hollered.

Curses erupted from the other three men.

"Tom, you're a fool!"

"Hunt will bury you."

"Idiot!"

Reagan kept Tom pinned to the bars. "What about the man who was shot?"

Tom trembled. Shook his head. "Don't know nothing, like I said. I was out in the woods sawing with my crew all day. And when I got back to camp, they said they needed someone to guard their horses and that it paid a dollar. I said I'd do it. That's the Lord's honest truth."

Satisfied that the man really was telling the truth, Reagan plunked Tom back onto one of the room's cots, and then shut and locked the door behind him.

"It's not what you think," Pike spat. "Hunt doesn't own her. The girl simply owes him some money."

Reagan spun to face him. "How much?"

He shook his head. "Not my business. I don't know."

"You know anything about the man that was shot in camp?"

Pike shook his head and the other two followed suit. "Didn't see anything like that, Sheriff."

Reagan collected the bowls and utensils from everyone, and then banged out into the autumn morning.

He had a man to visit about a girl. And questions still lingering about a murder.

oe tried not to think about how little sleep he had gotten the night before as he escorted Liora and Tess toward town the next morning, leading his horse behind him. Instead he chose to concentrate on the good.

It was one of those fall mornings that could almost make a man forget that summer was behind him. The sun already warmed them, even though it was just past seven, and all around them dew drops fractured shards of light into rainbow prisms. Mist rose up from the ground cloaking them in a veil that reminded a man of a bride on her wedding day.

He clenched his jaw and angled a glance toward Liora. Okay, maybe only a man like him, who had been turned down flat by his prospective wife the day before.

She marched primly by his side, tugging on the cuffs of her gloves as though they hadn't quite gone on right the first time. He recognized the gesture for the nervous one it was. The crest of the hill just this side of town had come into view a few minutes ago—the one where he always left her to walk the rest of the way into Wyldhaven by herself. And he knew by the way she kept opening her mouth like she wanted to say something and then snapping it shut again, that she was worried he wasn't going to do the same today.

And she'd be right.

Come what may, yesterday had marked a turning point in their relationship that he didn't intend to shy away from.

He'd lain awake long into the night pondering on their relationship—from the earliest days when he'd only seen her as a hurting woman who needed someone's help and friendship, to the more recent days in which he'd thought of her each time he had something he wanted to share with another. He'd come to her first when Reagan had agreed to let Marshall Holloway headquarter in these parts and he'd been concerned over losing his job. She'd reassured him that Reagan was a fair man who would never go behind his back on something like that. He smirked at that memory now, because what did he plan to do first thing when he got into town but resign his job as deputy.

It was going to take all his time and effort to guard Liora from here on out, at least until John Hunt was dealt with. Things would be tight for a while since he didn't want to dip too deeply into his savings, but he could make it.

And she was worth it.

All his pondering the night before had made him realize just how much he'd come to care for Liora over the years. His love had grown slow and steady. Each time he'd watched her marvel over something new the Lord had revealed to her through His Word. Each time she'd acted unselfishly and given of her time or money to help another. Each time she'd listened quietly as he'd unburdened himself. Each time he'd listened to her own cares and concerns. Their friendship was like a deep river, running still and slow. And now it was time for him to stir things up. Get the waters moving a little. Show her that she truly was worthy of love and respect.

But they had a few obstacles to get past. And he knew exactly the place to take her to start the conversation.

He couldn't help but grin a little in anticipation.

Liora glanced his way and narrowed her eyes.

He scrubbed one hand over his mouth and glanced behind them, feeling the bite of her irritation. This transition wasn't going to be easy, and that was certain.

Tess trailed in their wake. She seemed to be taking everything in as though she'd just been released from years of living in a dark cave and was seeing the light for the first time.

And maybe she was. How long had Hunt been forcing the girl to whore for him? His gut cramped. Lord forgive him, but there were some men who didn't deserve to take one more breath this side of eternity.

They'd reached the crest of the hill now and Liora stopped. "We'll be fine, from here on in, Joe. Thank you."

He kept his expression bland and ignored her clear dismissal. "I know."

When he didn't move to head off into the woods like she'd expected him to, she spun to face him. "Joe?"

He adjusted his hat to block the rays of sunlight that had just broken over the tops of the trees. "I've never condoned hiding truth, Liora. It was one thing for me to let you walk into town on your own when all I'd done was ride out to escort you, but I'll not hide the fact that I stayed out at your place last night. It's the truth, though we did nothing wrong."

Moisture gathered on her lower lids, and that was almost his undoing. "This is exactly what I've been trying to keep you from for all these years. Don't throw away all that effort."

Uncaring that Tess was right there watching him, he dropped his mount's reins, and stepped toward her.

She gave a little gasp and stepped back.

The flash of fear in her eyes stopped his intention to cup her cheeks and swipe away her tears with his thumbs. He propped his hands on his hips. Studied her.

Face flushed now, she looked away.

He decided to let the matter drop. If he wanted to gain her trust, he was going to have to take this slow. Be smart and thoughtful. "I never should have let you worry about my reputation. Spending time with you has been my privilege. And it's not something I'm ashamed of."

"I know that. It's just—"

"Liora." He looked deep into the blue of her eyes. "Everything's going to be fine."

Her lips pinched together. She stepped farther back, shook her head, and opened her mouth, but her gaze flicked to where Tess had stopped several paces behind. The girl was bent in study of something in the grass beside the road. By the look on Liora's face, she didn't want to have this discussion in front of the girl.

Nevertheless, it was probably best not to give her more time to debate. He retrieved the Paint's reins, and started walking again. For a long moment he thought she wouldn't follow, but then he heard her release a sound that was half sigh and half growl. An instant later, her slapping footsteps resounded in his wake.

He bit back a smile of victory.

When they walked into town, Mrs. Hines was out sweeping the mercantile steps. Of course she was. Because the woman seemed to always turn up where she wasn't wanted. Joe had hoped they might be able to ease into this transition, maybe explain their side to a few of the more reasonable people in town before the news spread from someone else, but it didn't look like they were going to get that chance.

Mrs. Hines' broom froze, and her beady gaze followed them all the way to the alley that led to Jacinda's place.

He waited while Liora ushered Tess into Jacinda's. She wasn't gone long, but when she returned, a world of discouragement weighed down her shoulders.

"What's the matter? She not have any work for Tess to do?"

"No, Joe, it's not that. Jacinda said she'd be happy to teach the girl to sew and pay her too."

He fell into step beside her as she started toward Dixie's. "So why the long face?"

She marched into the alleyway and for several steps he thought she wasn't going to answer, but then she stopped and spun to face him. It was all he could do not to crash into her.

"She saw us, Joe. And word's going to be all over town before noon."

He nodded. "Without a doubt."

Liora's shoulders slumped. "You're likely going to lose your job. And I might lose mine. Why are you doing this? Things have been just fine. We've been—"

"Because you're worth it." The words emerged straight from his heart. "And I haven't been treating you like you deserve."

Her blue eyes narrowed a bit as though she were trying to determine what language he was speaking. She shook her head. "I don't understand. You've always treated me with the utmost of care."

"Have I? Enjoying your company when we are on our own, but then parting ways before we get back to town?"

The furrow on her brow deepened. "But I've never been hurt by that, Joe. In fact, I think it is wise."

"Why?"

She gave him a blank look.

"Why is it wise that I not be seen with you in public?"

Her shoulders slumped. "You know why."

"Maybe you would have been right at one point in time. But you are no longer that same woman, are you?" When she only scuffed at the ground with the toe of one boot, he pressed on. "No. You aren't. You've been made new. Changed from the inside out. And you are worthy of both respect and love—have *always* been worthy of love, even if it wouldn't have been right for me to spend time with you back then—no matter what those around us might say."

She sighed. "Maybe, yes. I'm certainly glad the Lord used you to open my eyes to His love. But what ought to be, doesn't change what is. I just hate to see you throwing away everything you've worked so hard for."

"Listen, Liora." He took a step closer to her. "You might be right about the town council voting me out. But I plan to quit my job this morning anyhow." At her gasp of protest, he held up a hand to stop her interruption. "Dixie is not the type who is going to fire you over something like this. Any reasonable person in town is going to see that you need protection and I'm giving it. Please don't worry further."

If her shoulders drooped any more, she was going to be bent half way to the ground. "Maybe I made a mistake helping her escape him. Maybe I should have thought things through a little better."

Blast if he didn't want to pull her into his arms and show her that everything was going to be all right. He contented himself with words instead. "It's never wrong to help out a person in need. And don't you worry any more about it. I plan to give Hunt a visit today. And I think he and I will come to a clear understanding." *A very clear understanding.*

Alarm tightened her features and she searched his face.

This time he couldn't resist. He reached for her hand, but the moment his fingers grazed hers, she folded her arms and stepped back. He pushed the wave of discouragement away and adjusted his hat to a more comfortable position. "Don't worry about me. I'll be fine. We're both going to be fine. You did the right thing. Don't give up on that now." It was time to lighten the mood. He gave her a quick wink. "And don't forget you promised me you wouldn't be busy after work today."

He was happy to see a glimmer of curiosity replace some of the discouragement in her eyes. "I haven't forgotten."

"Good." He started walking before she could ask any questions—and before he could give in to too long a contemplation about what it might feel like if he had the freedom to drop a kiss against those soft-looking lips.

He escorted her to Dixie's kitchen door, bade her farewell, and then shored up his gumption with a deep breath. It was time to go quit his job. Reagan wasn't going to be too happy about that. They were already shorthanded, but there wasn't much he could do about it. Liora's safety would come first every time, in his book.

Reagan was just exiting the sheriff's office as Joe started up the steps. He retreated to the roadbed. Maybe he should find out some details before he quit outright. "Did they tell you anything?" He nodded to where he knew the men arrested the evening before were locked up in the cells inside.

Reagan shrugged. "Nothing that I didn't already suspect. I was just heading out to have a chat with John Hunt. See if I could learn anything about the man Liora and Tess saw him shoot."

Joe considered. Speaking to Hunt as part of the law would certainly hold more weight than if he were simply to approach the man on his own. "I'd like to come with you if you don't mind." He pushed away the niggle of guilt that said he might be taking a bit more advantage of his current position than he ought to, considering he'd been ready to turn in his badge not five minutes ago.

Reagan pegged him with a look. "Are you too close to this one?"

Joe raised his hands and allowed a quirk of his lips. "I promise to be on my best behavior."

Reagan didn't look like he much believed him but he gave him a nod anyhow. "All right. You can come along. I just need to let Zane know that he's going to be in charge in town while we're gone."

They found Zane at Jacinda's place, eating pie at her kitchen table—a fortuitous turn of events for Joe since he needed to ask if Tess could stay a little later than Liora had planned. He also gave Jacinda the order he'd penciled out and asked if she'd be willing to surreptitiously get it to Dixie a bit later. He couldn't deny that he felt a bit of relief when she agreed to both requests. But he could concentrate on that surprise later. For now, he needed to focus.

It didn't take them long to get to Camp-Sixty-Five. Nor to find John Hunt. He was at his usual place, leaned up against the bar in his favorite saloon.

Just the sight of the man had Joe's anger at a near boil. Reagan must have sensed his mood because he cleared his throat softly. Joe gave him a nod and willed himself to keep it under control.

Reagan stepped to the man's side and leaned his arms on the bar. "Morning, Hunt."

Hunt tossed back his whiskey and lifted his finger gesturing for the bartender to pour him another. "Callahan," he greeted as the bartender complied.

"You know anything about a scuffle that took place at Liora Fontaine's place last night?"

Hunt's glass paused halfway to his lips.

Joe had to admire the way Reagan had thrown the man

off his guard. He'd probably expected questions about the shooting.

Hunt gave a snort that was more air than sound. "And if I do?"

"If you do"—Reagan turned to face the man—"then you should know that I have four of your men down to my jail for shooting up the Fontaine place. And one of them tells me that a girl named Tess owes you some money. What can you tell me about that?"

"What I can tell you is that a man's business is his own." Hunt started to rise.

Reagan's hand shot out and clamped onto his arm. "Not when it comes to the peace in my jurisdiction, it's not."

Hunt stared at Reagan's hand for the span of several heartbeats, his eyes slitted up like a rattler's.

Joe reached down and slid the strap off his pistol.

Hunt must have seen the gesture from the corner of his eye because he settled back into his seat. "Can't say as I rightly have any men, leastwise not the way you meant it. But I may have mentioned to some friends of mine that a girl named Tess did run off while she owed me some money."

Joe's fists clenched. He folded his arms and settled in to his heels, reminding himself to proceed calmly. "How much does she owe you?"

Hunt swiveled a quarter turn on his stool and assessed Joe from head to toe and back again.

Joe held his ground and John's gaze.

Finally, Hunt gave a flip of one wrist. "I would have to check my books. There are a lot of people that owe me money." His mouth tilted up at one side.

"We'll wait."

Hunt didn't move, but leveled him with an assessing squint.

Joe pulled in a calming breath. "I'm here to pay what she owes you. But I'll want to see it in writing."

Hunt gave a soft chuckle, yet there was a hard glint in his eyes that told Joe he didn't like his interference. Not one little bit. His look was likely meant to cow Joe into backing off. But Joe met him gaze for gaze without flinching. After a long moment, Hunt lifted one finger to a man at a table just to their left. The man scurried over with a leather accounting book in his hands and laid it on the bar.

With a long-suffering release of air, Hunt dropped the cover of the book open and ran his fingers over the alphabetized tabs along the right edge. He flipped open the "T" section and turned pages until he came to *Trenton, Teresa.* "It says right here that she owes me thirty-three dollars and two bits."

Thirty-three dollars and change? Joe gritted his teeth. For an average month's worth of pay, this brigand had been willing to go after two women, endangering not only their lives but the lives of everyone around them!

Joe reached into his back pocket and pulled out the bills he'd tucked away there. He'd been prepared to pay more. He counted off the proper amount and then dug into his front pocket for the two bits, then slapped all of it onto the bar before Hunt. He leveled the man with a look to make sure he had his attention. "Consider her debt paid in full."

Hunt didn't look too happy about it, but he did start to gather the money.

Joe leaned close and spoke low. "I also want you to know that both Tess and Liora are now under my personal protection. If there is even a rumor of danger where they are concerned, I'm coming for you, do you understand me?"

There was a flicker of something in Hunt's eyes, and Joe knew in an instant that the man was going to swing. And sure enough. Hunt swung. He swung fast. And he swung hard. But Joe's half second of advantage stood him in good stead. He ducked under the blow and landed two solid punches of his own to John's exposed solar plexis.

Air whooshed from the man's lungs and he bent double in pain.

Joe grabbed Hunt's arm and twisted it up high along his back, shoving him down on to the bar until his cheek pressed against the wood. "I'm going to overlook the fact that you just tried to assault a man of the law, Hunt. We came here peaceful-like. And I don't intend for it to go down any other way. So you just let me know when you are ready to act peaceable."

"Fine!" John growled. "Now get your hands off me."

Joe let him go, keeping his guard up, but he was thankful to see that the man seemed to have settled down some. He eased back.

Reagan stepped forward and clapped Joe on one shoulder. "Right. We'll just be on our way then, Hunt. Seeing as how we are all feeling so peaceable now. Teresa Trenton is no longer any of your concern. Understand?" Without waiting for a reply, he gave Joe a firm nudge toward the door of the tent.

Anger still spiking his pulse, Joe shook him off the moment they were outside.

Reagan plunked his hands on his hips and quirked a brow at him.

Joe pulled in a slow breath. "You didn't ask him about the man he shot."

"He's not going to tell me anything. And I didn't want to give him advance notice that we're looking into it. It would only give him time to threaten everyone into silence. We're going to be fighting enough of that as it is. You sure you're not going to do something for which I'll have to arrest you?" Reagan's look was pointed.

Joe chuckled. Threw up his hands. "I know. I shouldn't have lost my temper. But I don't like being punched—even if it was only an attempt."

Reagan sighed and swung into the saddle. "Better to take a punch than to injure a man like that one's pride."

Joe wished he didn't agree. But he did. And an injured predator was always more dangerous and unpredictable.

iora had just finished the last of her shift at Dixie's and stepped outside the kitchen via the side door, when she heard a loud commotion coming from down the street. A mix of dread over what she was about to see and curiosity that wouldn't let her turn the other way drew her around the corner.

She had been in a morose mood all morning. One moment telling herself that Joe was right that she was forgiven and should therefore be accepted by the other women in the church, and the next, rebutting with the realization that every action carries consequences, and she therefore ought never to expect to be treated in the same way as a woman who had kept herself pure.

She'd gone so many rounds with herself, that exhaustion seemed to have settled into her very bones, and yet she was no closer to an answer than before.

The commotion grew louder as she made her way down the street. In front of the sheriff's office, a group of women had gathered. Mrs. Hines and Mrs. King were at the front of the pack.

Of course.

Guilt jabbed her for the uncharitable thought.

She paused on Dixie's porch, before she approached too near.

Reagan and Joe were just arriving from the direction of the livery in Joe's wagon, which gave her a moment of hesitation. Normally, they rode their mounts when going out on rounds. And hadn't Joe told her he aimed to quit his job first thing this morning? Yet his deputy's star still glinted sunlight from the pocket of his shirt.

The group of women took note of the men's approach and quieted, but they may as well have been hawks, ready to swoop in and devour carrion.

Joe, his gaze fixed on Mrs. Hines, had a pinched-lip look that let Liora know his anger was riding close beneath the surface. He pulled the wagon to a stop and both men dismounted. Joe set to tying the reins to the hitching post, while Reagan approached the group.

"How can I help you, ladies?" Caution heavily weighted his voice.

Dread mounting, Liora scuttled a few steps closer. She knew what this was going to be about!

Feeling like a coward, she huddled behind one of the large log pillars on Dixie's recently-constructed porch. Any woman who looked her way would likely be able to see her skirts protruding from behind the column, but at least this way she wouldn't have to meet anyone's gaze, or read their dour, disapproving expressions, and with the pillars in front of McGinty's Alehouse also running interference, she might just escape without notice.

Mrs. Hines was the first one to respond to Reagan's question. "Sheriff, a concern of grave proportions has come to our attention regarding...well, regarding Mr. Rodante here, and we thought it only right that we should bring it immediately to your attention."

Liora could hear Reagan's keys jangling as he unlocked the jailhouse door.

"Very well. Give it to me straight."

"Well, you see, it's just that..."

The sound of boots scuffing against the jailhouse steps revealed Reagan's irritation. "If you don't mind Mrs. Hines, I have a busy day ahead of me. So do you have an accusation to bring against Deputy Rodante, or not?"

"Well yes we do, Sheriff."

"Then I would appreciate it if you would come out with it."

"We think your deputy is engaged in unsavory activities with Liora Fontaine." The words rushed out of Mrs. Hines' mouth so fast that they might have been all one word.

Liora cringed and settled one hand over her heart. It was exactly as she had feared. And it hadn't even taken half a day for the town gossips to bring her worst fears to life. Whether he quit or not, Joe was going to lose his job. Had already lost his good reputation. And it was all her fault.

"And I suppose that you have spoken to both Deputy Rodante and Miss Fontaine to confirm these suspicions of yours?" There was a hard edge to Reagan's voice. "We do live in a country where people are innocent until proven guilty."

"First I've heard of it," Joe said. His voice sounded like it was a lot closer than he'd been the last time she'd looked. Maybe he had joined Reagan on the steps. She was tempted to peek out to see where he was, but feared being caught eavesdropping.

Mrs. Hines sputtered. "Well no. We did not speak to them, because of course what are they going to do but deny it?"

"I do deny your accusation of unsavory activities, Mrs. Hines. However, I do not deny that I spent the night out at Miss Fontaine's place." His next words were spoken over top of the gasps of the gaggle of women. "Outside. By myself."

The jailhouse door squeaked and Reagan spoke. "There you

see, ladies? Seems like we don't have anything to worry about. Now if you'll excuse me..." The door clicked shut with decided finality.

"Well! I never!"

This time, Liora did peek out from behind the pillar, she couldn't help herself. Neither Joe nor Reagan were in sight. The group of women stood for several long moments gaping at the empty space before them.

Then Mrs. Hines hoisted her skirts and marched out at the head of her pack. "Come on, ladies. It is clear that we are going to have to take this up with the town council."

Mrs. King glanced toward Dixie's, and Liora withdrew behind the safety of her pillar. Soon the sound of the women's footsteps and outraged babble disappeared beneath the clanging of the mercantile's bell.

"You going to cower behind this pillar all day? Or were you coming to let me know that you were finished with work?"

Liora gasped and spun around. She felt her face flame with heat at having been caught eavesdropping. "I thought you went inside the jailhouse with Reagan."

Joe only grinned. "Saw you hiding out over here and didn't figure I ought to leave you to fight the wolves alone. Went down the alley and cut through Dixie's from the back." He motioned that he'd only just come out of the door behind her.

Liora despaired of a solution to their situation. "What are we going to do?"

"Well first I need to go in and tell Reagan that I need to quit my job. And then..." He hefted a basket that she only now noticed by his side. "I picked this up on my way through the diner. You and I are going to go on a picnic."

Liora's heart stuttered. "A what?" If gossip were flames of fire, it looked like Joe planned to ignite the whole town. The appreciative look in his eyes would have sent her running had it come from any other man, yet coming from Joe it was... intriguing. She fiddled with the collar of her blouse. "I have to go pick up Tess."

He held out a hand that urged her toward the jailhouse. "I already spoke to Jacinda. She said Tess is more than welcome to stay until we get back."

She should decline. Every rational thought in her said that going on a picnic with Joe Rodante, especially when confusion muddled her every thought where he was concerned and her only aim was to protect his reputation, was a very bad idea indeed. But her traitorous heart was racing with anticipation. Besides... He'd already set the match to his reputation. And she knew there would be no talking him out of quitting his job at this point. Under those circumstances, what could one little picnic hurt?

Joe was studying her. "So...you'll come?"

"All right." Her mouth felt as dry as the dust of the street.

"Such enthusiasm," he teased. "But I'll take it." He directed her toward the wagon and hefted the basket into the back. "It's probably best for you to wait here. Reagan still has Hunt's men in the cells in the back. I'll only be a moment."

He assisted her up to the wagon seat, and then, true to his word, was only a couple of minutes inside the jailhouse before he stepped back out and strode her way.

She studied the empty space on his pocket, and then lifted her gaze to his as he climbed up onto the seat next to her. "How did he take it?"

Joe shrugged. "Said he understood. Said there would always be a job waiting for me if I wanted it back. Said if I ever needed any help just to give him a holler."

Liora smoothed her hands over her skirt. That was a relief

at least. If they could get past all this hullabaloo, perhaps Joe could go back to work. She voiced something that had been concerning her ever since he mentioned quitting his job. "Joe? I appreciate you wanting to help, but... I don't... I can't afford—"

He held up a hand. "I've got considerable savings laid by, and I wouldn't take a penny from you even if you could afford it. I've had a hankering to buy a few broodmares and maybe start up a stable. This will be the perfect opportunity to see if I can make a go of that."

She felt relieved to know she wouldn't be responsible for making him destitute. "Did you find out anything about the man that was shot?"

Joe sighed. "Unfortunately, no. Not one person was willing to speak of the matter. I did however pay off the amount Tess owes him. So, she'll no longer have that hanging over her. Not that it will stop Hunt from trying to get her working for him again."

It was in that moment that she recognized how relieved she was that Joe had not taken her words at face value. Much as she hated for him to have lost his job, she would have been terrified to face down John Hunt alone. And face him again she would because she knew beyond a shadow of a doubt that rescuing Tess, and any future girls like her, was exactly what she ought to be doing.

"Joe?"

"Yeah?"

"Thank you."

He remained silent for several moments before he finally nodded. "Like I said earlier, you're worth it." There was a bit of gravel in his voice, and the intensity in the gaze he turned on her sent her pulse skittering in a most unfamiliar way. She swallowed, unsure if it was a good feeling or a bad one.

She scrambled for a change in topic. "So where are we going?"

"You'll see." He tossed her a quick wink.

She pulled in a breath. This flirting was not like the Joe she knew at all, and yet she couldn't deny that she was fascinated by this new side of him. And that in itself terrified her. When she'd left off working for Ewan, she'd sworn never to let a man touch her again. Yet Joe had always beguiled her. Even back when McGinty was paying her to lure men in, she'd tried to seduce Joe on more than one occasion.

Just the reminder of it sent flames to her cheeks.

And yet after Joe had purchased her contract and freed her from that life, she'd only ever thought of him as a friend—until he'd asked her to marry him. Somehow with that one question he had resurrected feelings she'd thought long buried.

And that realization made her heart race. So much for trying to change the subject to spare her pulse.

Chapter Fourteen

They settled into a comfortable silence as they rode further up into the mountains, the horses' hooves clip-clopping a rhythmic beat that settled Joe's nerves. Or maybe it had nothing to do with the sound of the horse hooves and much more to do with the company of the woman who sat on the bench beside him.

He glanced over at her. She sat with her hands folded primly in her lap, taking in the scenery. He followed her gaze. All around them the mountain foliage had turned from the beautiful green shades of summer to the glorious vibrant colors of autumn. Maple trees fluttered bright red in a gentle breeze. Aspens now wore cloaks of gold. And even the pine trees had taken on a golden green hue with the old needles dying off.

Joe was content to let the silence ride. All day long he'd been praying about the conversation he wanted to have with Liora, and he was thankful for a few more minutes of prayer. He didn't want to mess this up.

He turned the horses off of the main road where it widened out, and set the brake. Wrapping the reins around the brake handle, he tipped his chin toward the faint path visible through the underbrush. "There's something I'd like to show you just this way if you don't mind walking a bit?"

"I don't mind."

Joe came around to her side of the wagon and helped her

down from the seat. Much as he would have liked to, he didn't let himself linger over the task but instead turned immediately to take up the basket from the wagon bed.

Anticipating Liora's reaction to what he was about to show her, he led the way through the thick underbrush. And he wasn't disappointed.

When they came out into the small clearing, Liora caught her breath in awe.

Joe allowed a smile of satisfaction. He loved this place! The sound of the bubbling brook could be heard just across the way. But he'd brought her here because of the shoulder-high sunflowers that grew so thick in this field that he'd had to chop a path through them earlier.

"Joe, these are beautiful!" She reached up and fingered the vibrant gold petals of the nearest bloom.

He smiled at her. "I remembered that you said one time how much you like sunflowers."

Nostalgia washed her features. "They were my ma's favorites."

Pain washed through him. Some would say that was a coincidence. He knew better and it was just further confirmation that he had done right to bring her here. He cleared his throat. "My mother's too."

He took her hand and led the way through the sunflowers until they gave way near the bank of the creek, then removed the blanket he'd begged Dixie to loan him from the basket and spread it on the ground. He motioned for her to sit as he pulled the large tin vase—again, borrowed from Dixie—from inside the basket. He dipped it into the creek and filled it halfway with water and then used his pocket knife to cut the stems of several of the sunflowers. He deposited the flowers into the vase before he sank down across from her with a shrug. He was no hand at flower arranging, and that was certain. But he wanted to get to the heart of why he'd brought her here before he lost his nerve.

"I'm not much good at this," he said. "I guess... I just wanted to share this place with you because..." He cleared his throat. "My ma was the one who planted this field of sunflowers."

He realized that in all the years he had known Liora, he had never once spoken to her of his family. Painful memories were mostly best left in the past, but if he wanted a future with her, she deserved to know where he came from.

"Your family was here? Near Wyldhaven?"

He nodded, swallowing down the lump of aching reminder. "We settled here when I was just a boy. My pa was a trapper. After they birthed me, my ma and pa tried for many years to have more children, but they never could. Then, finally, when I was about fourteen, my ma got in the family way, but things were hard for her from the beginning. She had to rest a lot." He took a breath and forced himself to continue. "One day while Pa and I were out checking traps, a grease fire started in the kitchen."

"Oh no."

He pressed ahead. "Ma was able to escape, but there was no saving our cabin. It sat right here on this very knoll." He tapped the blanket they sat on. "It was spring, and unseasonably warm that year, so we lived in a tent while Pa and I kept the traps going and sawed logs every day for a new cabin. Ma, she planted the sunflowers that spring. She said God had reminded her He could bring beauty from any ashes. She even went so far as to say she felt God had told her to plant the sunflowers." His voice broke and he looked out across the creek, willing away the emotions before they turned him into a crying fool. "I scoffed that God would do such a banal thing. Especially when the baby tried to come early just a few weeks later, and Ma, well, she didn't make it. The baby, either."

"I'm so sorry, Joe."

He nodded. Scrubbed at the back of his neck. Best he get on with the telling. "Pa...he just...never seemed to recover from Ma's death. We never did get that cabin built and he died only a couple years later." He plucked a blade of grass and began shredding it methodically. "I thought often about Ma's proclamation. God told her to plant sunflowers? Beauty from ashes? I didn't understand. Nothing beautiful seemed to have come from our ashes. And I figured Ma had just been spouting romantic nonsense, as she did from time to time. She wasn't here to see the sunflowers when they bloomed, but bloom they did. And they were beautiful. Are beautiful still. I've come to see them every year. And every year, I've prayed for God to help me understand. And then it hit me last night, maybe you're the one they were meant for."

"Me? Whatever do you mean?" Liora tucked her feet up beside her and leaned against one arm, a furrow trenching her brow as she studied the field of flowers.

He waited until she returned her focus to his. He looked right into her eyes, because he really wanted her to hear what he was about to say. "Not long ago I was reading in the book of Isaiah."

She nodded. "That's one of my favorite books."

Joe leaned closer to ensure he kept her attention. "It's in chapter sixty-one, verse three. And the writer speaks of what salvation does for us. The main part of verse three says 'to give them beauty for ashes, the oil of joy for mourning, the garment of praise for the spirit of heaviness; That they may be called trees of righteousness, the planting of the LORD, that He may be glorified.'"

He waited for her eyes to light with understanding, or a smile to break out on her face, but she only frowned at him.

An urgency to make her understand swept over him. "Don't you see, Liora? At salvation, we all come to Christ broken. We have ashes. We have mourning. We have spirits of heaviness to offer. And God accepts those and returns to us beauty, joy, and an attitude of praise. All to be used for His glory."

A light of dawning lifted her brows.

He pressed forward. "Your life may have been ashes in the past because of your choices, but that's no longer what you are. Christ's righteousness has transformed all that." He reached down and plucked a handful of grass from beside their blanket. Tossing it aside, he dug a little deeper and came up with a handful of ash-black dirt. Reaching over, he cupped her palm and funneled the dirt into her hand. "You are no longer this, Liora. Now you are beauty! You are a sunflower standing tall and strong." He swept a gesture around them. "And *that* is why you—and everyone in creation—are worthy of respect and love. Not because of anything you have done, but because of what Christ has done."

Tears burgeoned in her eyes and spilled over.

He frowned. Tears, he hadn't been expecting. Smiles. Laughter. Shouts of joy, yes. But not tears. "I'm sorry. I didn't mean—"

And then through her tears she laughed. "These are happy tears, Joe."

Liora laughed some more when Joe's frown deepened. He was obviously having a hard time reconciling her tears with happiness. But she truly was overjoyed. In fact, she didn't remember feeling this light and joyful ever.

Beauty for ashes. What a worthwhile barter. *Thank you, Jesus.* For a long moment, she studied the dirt Joe had poured into her hand. Sooty-black and gritty, it reflected no light. What a picture of what her life had been like before she'd given everything to God. She sprinkled the dirt back into the grass beside the blanket, rose, and washed her hands in the creek.

Joe joined her. He was still studying her like he was worried he had broken something inside her.

Patting her hands dry on her skirt, she tucked them behind herself and looked up at him. "I'm fine. Thank you for sharing what you did. You have no idea what a burden it's been to feel like I was somehow *less* due to mistakes of my past. It will probably take some time, but I will try to see myself the way Jesus does from here on."

Relief shining from his eyes, he started to reach for her and she felt the familiar jitter of fear she always did when a man looked at her in such a way. He paused when she pulled back.

She met his gaze, hoping to ease the sting of her withdrawal. "You never finished your story. What happened to you after your father passed?" She returned to her seat on the blanket.

He shrugged. "Not much more to tell... I was so green behind the ears, I had no idea what to do with myself. I was living here, basically in survival mode, when Zeb arrived and claimed he was going to set up the town. I told him I'd work at doing anything he needed done if he would give me a job. And that eventually worked into me becoming deputy." He glanced up and met her gaze. "I realized the other day that I'd never given you much of my history. And I figured that you should know if we are ever to..."

Marry. Her mouth went dry merely at the thought. And she willed down the skittering of her pulse.

Joe captured and held her attention. "You think any more on that?"

Liora tore her gaze away and brushed a few bits of grass off her skirts. The truth was, she hadn't thought on much else since the moment Joe had voiced the idea. "I have." The words were barely a whisper.

Joe cleared his throat. "And…?"

Liora scrambled for words to explain herself. "And… It seems as though the damage is already done. You've already quit your job. Though, thankfully, Reagan has said it will be available to you again in the future if you want it. And the women of the town are already convinced that we have done wrong. So, it doesn't seem as though marrying will solve any of our problems." She wouldn't tell him that she didn't want to saddle him to her for the rest of his life. She wouldn't mention that she didn't want him to wake up a couple years from now with regret over the fact that he'd married her during a crisis. And she certainly couldn't mention that just the thought of any man ever touching her again—the way a man surely would expect of a wife—sent waves of dread through her.

"And what of marrying for a good old-fashioned reason? Like love?" His words were soft and settled like a warm fire on a cold winter's day deep inside her.

She blinked at him. This was the second time he'd mentioned love. Yet he deserved so much more than she could bring to a marriage.

One of the sunflowers in the vase rolled slightly and tilted toward her.

She studied the bloom, her heartbeat growing stronger and stronger until it resembled a tympani in her ears. Surely God wasn't trying to tell her…

"Never mind. It wasn't my intention to badger you. Forgive

me." Joe flipped open one side of the basket and started pulling food out.

"No. It is I who should beg forgiveness, Joe. It's just that for so long I've lived with the notion—and been content with it, if I'm honest—that my future would be lived on my own. Well, with the exception of the women I plan to help. And my mind cannot seem to fathom that after years of mere friendship you've suddenly had a deepening of feeling for me."

He stilled and lifted his gaze to hers. "Believe it, Liora. Because never has there been a truer fact."

She worked her teeth over her lip, wishing beyond reason that she didn't need to disappoint him. Yet the truth could not be hidden. "Joe, I might be too broken to be mended. Do you understand?"

Such pain transposed his features that she had no doubt but that he truly did comprehend her meaning. But he was already shaking his head. "There is nothing so far gone that God cannot fix, Liora. And I hope you know that I don't expect anything from you—wouldn't expect anything from you—until you're ready."

Warmth shot through her and she looked down to brush at invisible specks on her skirt. Yes, he indeed understood. Would there—*could* there—ever come a time when she would welcome a man's touch?

Beauty from ashes.

Something gave way inside her—like the first spade of soil for a new garden had just been turned over. And in that moment, she felt the first stirrings of hope. She lifted her focus to Joe, once more. Her breaths came short and shallow. "Don't give up on me, Joe."

He gave her the gentlest of smiles. "Don't worry. There's no fear of that. Now"—he gave the basket a tap—"I hope you don't mind eating food that you likely helped prepare this morning?"

She laughed. "I do not mind."

His abrupt change of topic was both a liberation and a consternation, yet she couldn't deny that she was relieved to leave the strained conversation behind, at least for the moment.

unday morning, Liora knocked on Tess's door. "Tess, we leave for Sunday services in thirty minutes. Will you be ready to go?"

Liora willed down the apprehension cramping her stomach. One day she hoped to be able to attend services without getting this sick feeling inside, but she could never seem to get past the slight edge of panic induced by the thought of potentially bumping into Mrs. Hines and Mrs. King.

The girl cracked open the door, her long curly hair still cascading nearly to her hips. Brush in hand, her expression appeared hesitant, yet her eyes shone with more light than they had since her arrival. Rest and good food were doing her some good, it seemed.

"I be ready come time, yes ma'am."

"Remember, it's just Liora. No need for formalities."

Tess nodded. "Yes ma'am—Miss—Liora."

Liora gave her a smile and a nod, then started for the kitchen where she had eggs boiling, but Tess's next question stopped her.

"Do you think someone like me be...allowed to attend services?"

Liora's heart fell. Oh, how she understood the desire to be accepted. Oh, how she wished that she could promise the girl that the love of Christ would be the only thing she would encounter at services today. But she wouldn't allow herself to lie. Yet how to explain it to Tess?

She pondered for a long moment before she said, "We must remember that people don't always represent the love of our Lord perfectly. But Christ's love for us is always perfect."

Tess's expression softened with a touch of disappointment. "I see."

"Parson Clay allows us to sit in the entry..." She knew there was no need to elaborate the reasoning.

Tess pondered for several beats but wasn't long in nodding her understanding.

"Eggs will be ready in a moment," Liora said.

Tess nodded again.

Liora settled one hand over her midsection as she headed back to the kitchen. Now she was not only concerned about keeping herself out of sight, but keeping Tess from getting hurt too.

Joe knocked on the back door just as she stepped into the kitchen. "Come," she called, removing a loaf from the breadbox on the sideboard.

He stepped inside and headed straight for the coffeepot on the back of the stove. "Morning," he murmured. "Wagon is hitched and ready to go."

His hair was still damp from where he'd slicked it back at the pump outside. His sleeves were rolled up nearly to his elbows, and the morning light caught and played in the ridges created by the muscles along his arms.

Liora swallowed and forced her eyes back to the task of slicing bread. It only took her a moment to have several slices buttered and layered onto the hot griddle. They would soon be toasty and warm. That task done, she checked the clock. Thankfully, the eggs were done. She carried the pan to the table and scooped two eggs onto each plate next to the slices of ham she'd already placed there.

Joe ambled to the table with his cup and sat, angling his chair slightly toward the window. Tess bustled in with her mass of curls now piled atop her head, and he rose out of his seat until the girl sat and then retook his chair.

Liora's heart expanded tenfold to the man for such a gesture. She noted Tess studying him quizzically. She doubted the girl had ever been in the presence of a true gentleman before, much less been treated like a real lady.

After Liora had fetched the toast, and they'd cracked and peeled their eggs, breakfast was consumed in silence and the ride into town was more of the same. If she hadn't been dreading a potential run-in with the discouraging-duo, Liora would have found the silence comfortable and warm.

Joe paused the wagon to drop them off at the door of the church, and Liora realized she'd been too distracted to take note of how early they'd actually left the cabin. Normally, she waited till she was certain everyone would already be inside before arriving.

Liora looked over at Joe.

He gave her a nod. "Beauty from ashes."

She rubbed a hand at the queasy spot in her middle. "Just because the good Lord sees me as a new creation doesn't mean the townsfolk do."

"True. But I think if you give them a chance, most of them will come around to the right way of thinking."

When she still didn't move, Joe gave her a look. "Why don't you two wait for me inside? I'll park the wagon and be right back."

Liora glanced at the line of people headed this way from town. The Hineses were at the front of the group. "How about we ride with you to park the buggy and walk over together?"

Joe glanced toward Mrs. Hines, who was in the process of chastising her stepson and yet had her full attention fixed on their wagon. He gave Liora a nod. "All right. We can do that."

Thank you, Lord. Maybe everyone would already be inside by the time they returned. Then she could simply tell Joe that she and Tess would remain in the entry.

Unfortunately, when they got back to the church her chair was not in its normal place in the cloakroom. She spun to face Joe, her hands plunking on her hips.

He gave her an unrepentant grin. "Yeah I might've had something to do with that." He swept a gesture with his hat towards the entry at the back of the sanctuary. "There's always plenty of room."

Though he didn't prod her further, there was a light in Joe's expression that urged her to strength. To trust. Not only in him, but in God's promises.

Tess didn't seem to know what to think about this clash of their wills. She glanced back and forth between them, clearly unsure which side to take.

Liora would have argued with him further but she had a feeling he was going to win this battle, and she didn't relish walking into the service late. "Fine." She made a little impatient gesture to indicate he should lead the way.

With a smile of triumph, he gave her a bold wink. "Right this way."

Liora could literally feel her pulse beating in her throat as they stepped through the double doors and started down the aisle.

From their left, there came a gasp, and Liora didn't have to look to know it was Mrs. Hines seated with her family near the back. Her steps faltered. Joe paused and moved to the side of the aisle, allowing Tess to pass. A muscle bunched in his jaw as Liora looked at him. There was compassion in the expression he directed toward her, but when his eyes flicked in Mrs. Hines' direction, a distinct hard glitter settled into their depths. Despite that, Liora wasn't sure she should go further. The last thing she wanted was to cause a scene here.

Joe stepped to her side and settled one hand at her back. Holding out his hat to urge her down the aisle, he spoke low. "Don't let her tell you who you are. Only God has the right to tell you that."

And somehow Liora found comfort in the gesture. Reassurance and the strength in his words. At least enough to keep walking.

With each step she took she could feel the woman's glower drilling into her, and Mrs. King's pinched-lip expression wasn't any more welcoming when she caught Liora's attention from the other side of the sanctuary. Liora might have wavered again, but just then both Charlotte and Dixie, who were seated together toward the front right, looked back and gave her beaming smiles. Reagan also looked back and smiled from where he sat by Charlotte's side. Since Dr. Griffin wasn't here, he must be out on a call. Liora offered the three a nod and hurried to catch up to Tess.

Joe directed them to an empty bench halfway down the aisle on the left. He stopped and motioned for them to seat themselves. Tess scooted in first and Liora followed, with Joe bringing up the rear.

He leaned close. "You're doing just fine."

Liora wasn't so sure.

Several people throughout the room whispered to each other. Were they talking about her? Liora cast a sideways glance at Joe, but he had opened his Bible and was reading a passage, seemingly unconcerned.

She oughtn't to have had time to wonder more, for just then Parson Clay stepped to the pulpit and asked them all to rise for the first song, but when the sermon ended, Liora felt chagrinned to note that she hadn't heard one word for all her worrying.

"I have an announcement I'd like to make." Parson Clay beamed a large smile toward Reagan and Charlotte who sat across the aisle.

Liora was already smiling before the parson could even say another word. Beside her Joe grinned too. "Well, I'll be," he murmured.

Charlotte squirmed in her seat and blushed to the roots of her hair, and Reagan raised a gesture of triumph above his head that caused a ripple of laughter.

Parson Clay chuckled. "I can see that several of you have already caught on to what this announcement is going to be. And it is my great pleasure to inform you that you are correct! It seems that our beloved sheriff has gone and popped the question to the lovely Miss Brindle."

Huzzahs and cheers erupted throughout the room.

"And Miss Brindle has had the good sense to accept the man's proposal."

More cheers.

Liora realized she had one hand pressed to her chest in excitement and tucked it back into her lap where she clasped it with her other to keep it in place.

"Moreover, it is my further pleasure to announce that the wedding will be held just before Thanksgiving, only five weeks from yesterday!"

This time the congregation gasped and then a thick silence fell.

The parson hurried on. "Miss Brindle has asked me to

reassure you that your students will be in good hands. She is still in the process of working out all the details with our founder, Mr. Heath, but will send word to you all next week about the future of the school. So for now, let us wish them both well!" He started clapping and it was only a moment before the congregation regained their enthusiasm. The crowd surged to their feet as everyone scrabbled to congratulate Reagan and Charlotte.

The parson fought his way down the aisle so he could greet people at the back.

Ben King and Doc Griffin—who must have come in at some point while Liora was lost in thought—smiled at Joe and approached to shake his hand. And Dixie came over to give her and Tess a hug and say how happy she was to see them here today. Liora didn't correct her assumption that she hadn't been attending church previously.

With the surge of people still clamoring to speak to Reagan and Charlotte, she and Tess had become separated from Joe. She stood on tiptoe and saw him halfway down the aisle. He gestured that he was headed to pick up the wagon and he would be right back. She gave him a nod, her stomach immediately crimping into a painful fist. Somehow this had all seemed easier with him by her side. No matter. She and Tess could just leave right now and wait for him outside.

But with Parson Clay at the back greeting each person as they left, the going was slow. And amazingly, several families greeted her warmly and told her how happy they were to see her. Each time she introduced Tess, the girl seemed to relax a little bit more. And Liora was surprised to note that the cramping in her stomach had mellowed to mere queasiness. Maybe Joe had been right. Other than Mrs. King and Mrs. Hines, everyone had been most pleasant.

Liora had searched the room for any of the other women who had been in Pricilla's little mob the day Joe had quit his job, but she didn't see any of them. Though she didn't know the women by name, she felt sure she would have recognized them. Perhaps of those women, only Ethel King and Pricilla Hines attended services.

She and Tess had almost reached the parson now. By his side was a teen boy that caught Liora's eye. Something tugged for her attention. She frowned. Something about the boy seemed... what? She couldn't quite place it. She smiled at him, and he gave her a shy nod before turning his focus to the ground near his feet. Who was he and where had he come from?

Parson Clay cleared his throat and Liora gave herself a little shake. It was her turn to speak to him. She quickly stepped forward.

He smiled at her and his handshake was warm and firm. "It does my heart good to see you this side of the doors today, Liora. I've been praying for quite some time that you'd find the courage for just such a step."

Liora swallowed. "You have?"

He nodded.

She fiddled with her cuffs. "Well, I'm relieved to hear it, if I'm honest. I was concerned what you might think."

He leaned forward and took her shoulders. Sincerity shone from his expression when he said, "What I think is that God's Word says we are all sinners, and that His blood can cover us no matter how far gone we were. It also tells us that God can take our shortcomings and turn them around for His glory."

Liora tilted him a look. "Have you been talking to Joe?"

Parson Clay chuckled. "I have not. But rest assured that the good Lord can speak to us in any number of ways and through any number of people. He is not required to use a parson who has fallen just as short of His glory as any of the rest of humanity. So if Joe has been telling you something along the lines of what I just said, I would say he's probably hit the truth right on the head." He cocked a brow at her to hammer home his point before his gaze flicked to Tess. "And who do we have here?"

"Oh, forgive me. Parson, this is Teresa Trenton. Tess to her friends, as I'm sure you'll be. Tess, this is Parson Preston Clay."

Tess gave a little dip of her knees, but didn't lift her gaze any higher than the parson's shirt sleeve.

Preston leaned forward, took her hand, and pumped warmly.

Liora couldn't help but smile when Tess lifted wide eyes to scrutinize the man's face.

He gave her a nod. "It is a great pleasure to have you here with us today, Miss Trenton. I hope you'll join us again next week."

"Yes, suh."

"And may I introduce my new charge Rory to you both? Rory will be staying with me and Kin for a time."

Liora smiled and stretched out one hand to the boy. He had the most beautiful jade-colored eyes she'd ever seen.

He shook her hand but did not speak or look her in the eye.

"Good day to you." Liora bade him farewell, then led the way through the coat room and down the church steps. She moved to one side of the stairs to wait for Joe.

Pricilla Hines and Ethel King stood talking just ahead. Pricilla's voice was sharp and loud enough to carry to anyone on the church lawn. "As if one soiled dove isn't bad enough, now she's dragging her like into—"

Ethel noticed Liora and Tess descending the step. Her eyes widened and she shot out a hand to stop Pricilla mid-sentence.

Ethel exhibited enough compassion to look embarrassed at her friend's blatant rudeness.

Pricilla glanced their way and scanned them up and down. Her lips curled like they might have been muddy cats who had wandered onto the lawn.

After giving them only the briefest moment of her time, she returned her focus to Ethel. "Wasn't that *such* a divine message today?"

Ethel nodded, her feet shuffling uneasily. "Indeed, it was."

Liora met Tess's gaze. It was obvious from the girl's expression that she was well aware of just what the two women had been discussing before they'd come out. Liora rested one hand on her shoulder, hoping to offer encouragement and solace.

Pricilla gave Ethel a very unsubtle nod that said "follow me" and both women hustled away without even so much as a greeting. They scurried around to the side of the church. Pricilla's voice sliced sharply. "The last thing poor little David and the boys like him need is to face the temptation of fallen women. In church! On a Sunday!"

Ethel King's voice was a little quieter when she said, "You really should guard your tongue a bit, Pricilla."

"What?" Pricilla was obviously taken aback by the rebuff. "You think my boy should have to look at those, those, those *women* every Sunday?"

Ethel sighed. "I meant your words about Liora and her friend."

"Well... They're only whores. It's not like they have feelings." Pricilla tittered a laugh.

There was a moment of pause and then Ethel spoke again. "Isn't that a fine kettle of fish about Miss Brindle marrying the sheriff? She is going to leave us without a teacher right in the middle of the school year!"

Tess and Liora had walked all the way to the edge of the road, but the women's voices still carried as clearly as if they'd been standing close by. It was nigh impossible not to overhear the conversation.

The distinctive sound of Pricilla's fan snapping open preceded her reply. "Is Charlotte in the family way, do you think?"

Liora felt her fists clench as Ethel gasped. "Well I wouldn't know, but they've never been suspected of impropriety."

"It's just strange. Mighty strange. And did Dixie speak to you a moment ago? She's wanting all of us to have a congratulatory gathering ahead of the wedding! Should we even be congratulating them if there is a child on the way?"

Liora swallowed and glanced around for Dixie. She felt badly for wanting to dodge an invitation to bring refreshments, but the last time she'd brought a dish to a church gathering, Mrs. Hines had pushed it to the very back of the table and tossed a towel over it. Liora had tried to tell herself she didn't care and that it had meant more leftovers for her, but in truth she'd been hurt by the action. Since then she had chosen not to participate in community gatherings. But this one was for Charlotte and Reagan, both of whom had been nothing but kind to her through the years. She should seek Dixie out and offer to bring something. Instead, she nudged Tess toward the large oak at the far end of the church lawn. They could wait for Joe there and hopefully remain out of Dixie's line of sight.

Beside Liora, Tess's feet shuffled.

Liora looked at her.

"Why those women talkin' such?"

Liora shook her head, looped her arm around Tess's shoulders and gave her a squeeze. "Don't worry about them. They are a couple of old gossips. Reagan and Charlotte are both upstanding God-fearing folk."

Tess gave her a pointed look that indicated she knew she'd avoided the fact that the women had been disparaging them as well.

Liora sighed. "We can't change the past, Tess. Time only marches one way. You can't walk forward with your focus on the past or eventually you will bring about your own demise. Yet that's all some people seem capable of doing."

She swallowed her discomfort as her conscience pointed several fingers in her direction. Beauty from ashes... Could she bring herself to a place of accepting the beauty God offered?

After a beat of silence, Tess asked, "What that means? God-fearing?"

"To fear God means that you take Him at His Word and know that if you don't live according to His principles there will be consequences. We can talk more about that later. Here's Joe to pick us up."

There was a certain gleam in Joe's eyes even though he smiled cordially as he helped first Tess and then Liora up to the wagon's seat. "Wasn't that a happy turn of events? I couldn't be more pleased for Reagan and Charlotte." He held onto her hand a little longer than necessary, locking his gaze with hers.

Liora's breath caught. And then her heart set to hammering. Because a realization had just coursed through her. For the first time ever, it was not fear that had made her breath catch at a man's touch, but anticipation.

She snatched her hand back and settled her skirts. "Indeed."

She needed anywhere to look but at the alluring and somehow knowing smile of Joseph Rodante. Her gaze fastened on her clasped hands. She heard him give a little chuckle and then the man whistled his way around the end of the wagon toward his seat. Joe whistling? She'd never heard the man whistle a day in her life.

Beside her, Tess squirmed again. And it was in that moment that Liora noticed how thin and threadbare the girl's dress was. The autumn wind had picked up and it was icy and cutting. She swept up the bench blanket and swung it around the girl's shoulders.

She would need to order her a couple of new ensembles, but it would have to wait until her next pay day. Her stomach knotted. Providing clothing for the girls she rescued hadn't been an expense she'd considered. Perhaps she shouldn't have turned down the extra work at Dixie's after all.

That thought sent her mind back to the two women they'd just left. Why was it that she couldn't seem to win them over? No matter how she tried to be friendly and pay back right for wrong, she couldn't seem to make a friend of either Mrs. Hines or Mrs. King.

Joe glanced over at her. "Something weighing on your mind?"

"It's noth—"

"Those two ladies was downright awful to Miss Fontaine and me, and that be stated kind." Tess's chin lifted a fraction with each word of her sentence.

A muscle bulged in Joe's jaw. He flicked the reins with a sharp snap against the horse's rump. "I see," was all he said, but Liora got the feeling there was a whole lot more going through the man's mind.

urora stood outside the chicken coop with the bucket of cracked corn clutched against her pounding heart and the bucket of leftover vegetable scraps by her side. The parson had told her in no uncertain terms at breakfast that it was time she started pulling her weight with helping out around the place. And he was likely right. It had been a full week, and the ache inside from missing Ma had been so strong, she'd hardly been able to get out of bed some days. She scratched at an itch beneath the waist of her britches.

After Ma's service, she had been able to go back to retrieve her bundle of clothes. But she'd been too scared to change out of the set she'd had on ever since because the parson and Kin both shared the parsonage's only bedroom. They each had a bed against opposite walls and they'd put down a pallet for her between them. At first, she'd been terrified by that prospect, but that first night she'd been so tired that she'd fallen onto her pallet the moment they'd laid it down and been sound asleep before either of them came in to bed. Since then, she'd made sure she was tucked safely under her covers before either of them retired for the night. That way she could pretend to be asleep and keep her eyes closed so she hadn't seen anything she oughtn't have. While the bedroom did have a door, she'd never felt comfortable enough to change. Since there were only men in the house—or so they thought—they were in the habit of simply barging through doors without knocking. She'd thought about trying to change a few times midday, but the parson had rarely left the house with her in it. She hoped she might get the chance today because he'd said he had some visiting to do, but he hadn't left yet. Just the thought of a bath and clean clothes had her anticipating his departure like a kid anticipating Christmas.

But first she was expected to enter this coop—and chickens, quite frankly, terrified her. Scaly heads. Beady eyes that always seemed to be watching. And leathery feet with long claws. What was there not to be terrified of?

But the parson had been very specific. She had to go into the pen and sprinkle the corn and scraps in the trough on the other side.

Kin tromped out of the barn, pushing a wheelbarrow. He paused, frowned from her to the chickens and back again. "You may as well get it done, kid. I've never known him to be happy if his instructions aren't followed to a T."

Aurora swallowed. Easy for him to say. He didn't have to wade in amidst filthy fowl.

Kin started around the barn with his load, but then stopped and grinned. "You afraid of them, kid?"

Aurora thinned her lips. She'd been a bit worried how he might treat her when she'd first arrived, but he mostly ignored her. And that had been just fine with her. At least he wasn't being unkind. She hoped he wasn't about to start now. She chose not to answer his question, working instead on gathering her courage for the task at hand. All she had to do was open the gate, hurry across, dump the corn, and then—

"Here. Give me that." Kin was beside her reaching for the bucket.

She gasped and sprung away from him. Corn arced in a golden rainbow and scattered at their feet.

Kin raised his hands by his shoulders. "Whoa, kid. I'm not gonna hurt you. Was just aiming to help is all."

Feeling sheepish for startling so easily, Aurora bent and set to gathering as much of the corn as she could back into the bucket. She wasn't sure what to say. She couldn't very well admit to being terrified of chickens because the likelihood of a boy having that malady were slim to none.

Kin stalked away, probably figuring she was a lost cause. But only a moment later, he returned with a broom and dustpan. "Watch out." He brushed her aside and started sweeping up the spill. "The chickens are just going to scratch this out of the trough and through the dirt anyhow. A little extra dust won't hurt them none." He dumped the corn back into her bucket and leaned on the broom handle for a moment, studying the chickens along with her. He bumped her with his shoulder. "Tell you a secret?"

Aurora pressed her lips together and nodded. Despite the fact that he was a bit rough around the edges, she liked Kin Davis. At least as one "boy" to another.

And that reminder brought a wave of guilt. The parson's whole message the day before had been about the importance of truth and honesty. She'd been trying *not* to think on it, ever since. But the nagging impression that she should confess who she really was hadn't left her since she'd walked out of the service. She didn't think the parson would send her back to Hunt. Yet, what *would* he do with her? *That* was the question that had kept her silent. She realized Kin was talking and she hadn't heard a word he'd said.

"Anyhow, all that to say... I'm not much of a chicken lover either. But they make a mighty tasty meal, all fried up and slathered in gravy. So kid, what you've got to tell yourself is that all you're doing is fattening up those fluffy varmints for the pan." He gave her a wink. "Leastwise that's what I tell myself. Now go on, get." And with that, he gave her a brotherly slap on the backside.

Aurora couldn't stop a squeak of surprise. His slap was so strong that it knocked her forward toward the pen. Eyes wide, Aurora continued to the gate.

Behind her, Kin guffawed. "Did you just *squeak*, kid? We're gonna have to toughen you up some, I see."

Aurora half-cringed, hoping he didn't plan to begin right this moment.

But Kin only laughed and trundled the wheelbarrow around the side of the barn.

Aurora sighed. She'd hoped he would do the chore for her. But it looked like there was no escape. "All right you little tasty meals. I'm coming in. And you all better stay back or you won't be getting any of this fine corn today. Or these ever so tasty leftovers." She curled her lip as she bent to retrieve the bucket of slops.

The chickens only clucked and pecked at the dirt. One cocked his head and seemed ready to pounce on her the moment she opened the gate.

Aurora rolled her eyes at herself and took deliberate hold of the latch. "Right. On three."

She counted down, then dashed across the pen. Chickens squawked and scattered right and left. She dumped out the corn, almost dropping the bucket in her hurry. After pitching the vegetable scraps out on the ground, she nearly trampled a hen trotting toward the corn in her haste to make her exit.

But she'd done it. She grinned and slammed the gate home. The chickens were making quite the racket now as they gobbled and cackled. But she was safely on the outside of the fence. And she didn't have to face them again for another twenty-four hours!

When she turned for the barn, she gasped. Deputy Rodante was grinning at her as he tied his mount to the hitching rail. She'd met him yesterday when the parson insisted on introducing her to everyone at the church. He opened his mouth, glanced at the chickens, then seemed to give himself a little shake and change his mind about what he'd been about to say. "The parson around?"

Aurora was struck by what a good-looking man he was. Dark hair. Dark eyes. Stubble-shadowed jawline. Of course, the parson with his green eyes and dark skin was some hard to beat in the looks department, but the deputy could give him a run for his money, at any rate. He was handsome in a clean-cut sort of way, and if Ma were still alive and Aurora were able to live as a girl right now, she might even have been tempted to give him more space in her thoughts. But, of course, none of that was an option. At least not while she was pretending to be someone she was not.

Deputy Rodante's feet shuffled and she suddenly noticed that he was squinting at her in a way that made it clear he was trying to decide if her mind was all there.

Flames licked at her cheeks. Hoping the deputy wouldn't notice, she spun toward the barn and reminded herself to lower her voice when she said, "He's in the house."

Studying for next Sunday's sermon. Which would likely once more point out the severity of her shortcomings. Behind her, she heard the deputy's footsteps crunching toward the house. With a sigh she hung the feed bucket back on its hook and retrieved the pitchfork she had been instructed to use to add clean straw to the stalls Kin had finished mucking earlier.

Kin had to get out to one of the logging camps to hunt for a
new job, so the parson had told her she would need to finish
the task.

As though her thoughts had conjured him, Kin returned
with the now empty wheelbarrow. "All right, kid. I have to get.
She's all yours."

Aurora couldn't deny her relief as she watched him walk
away. She liked him, but she was used to being alone, and
whenever she was around Kin—or anyone for that matter—
over the past few days, she always had this lingering fear that
she was going to be found out. What would they do to a girl
who was posing as a boy? No matter that she'd done it to
escape being forced to work for Hunt, she had a feeling the
parson wouldn't like it one little bit.

She glanced toward the house. What had the deputy come
to talk to the parson about? Had they somehow discovered
her true identity? Was that what the deputy's squint had been
about a moment ago?

She recalled that the parson had pushed open the window
by his desk when she'd left the house to do her chores. He liked
to have the bracing air to keep his head clear, he'd said.

Before the thought had hardly registered, Aurora leaned the
pitchfork back against the wall and started across the yard.
She instinctively reached to lift her skirts, only to be reminded
that she wore the slim-fitting breeches. She rolled her eyes at
herself.

Once she reached the side of the house where the parson's
window was, she slowed. The last thing she wanted was to step
on something that would alert the men inside to her presence.

Pressing herself to the side of the cabin, she slid toward
the window. The low murmur of voices slowly clarified into
understandable words.

"You're sure I can't offer you some coffee?"

"No. No. Thank you. I won't take but a moment of your time. Truth is, I've been putting this off since Sunday, I'd just like to get to it, if you don't mind."

The parson's chair creaked as he sank into it, and Aurora could envision the way he was likely even now stretching his legs out before him and setting fingertips to fingertips in a gesture that offered those who visited his full attention. "Very well. What can I do for you today, Joe?"

The deputy cleared his throat. "I'm actually here about Liora."

"I was very glad to see her work up the courage to come into the service on Sunday."

"Yes. About that... I wondered if you might be able to speak to... There seems to be... It's just that..."

"What is it, Joe?" The parson's words carried compassion and concern.

"It's just that some of the women in town have not made it very easy for Liora. And I feel like the church especially should be a place where any repentant soul finds welcome and acceptance."

"I see. And you don't feel like Liora has received that from the congregation?"

"Not when she feels the need to sneak into the back of the service and sit on a chair in the coatroom, no, if you'll pardon me for saying so."

There was a long pause. And finally the parson spoke with a bit of dejection in his tone. "I think you are right. I've failed in my duty to make everyone welcome to the house of the Lord. I will—"

"I'm not blaming you, you understand, Parson."

"No. No. I understand. But nonetheless, it is my duty to

make sure I'm teaching the principles of God's Word. And I believe you are right, this is one area where I have fallen short. I was trying not to force Miss Fontaine to do something she found uncomfortable and yet still give her the opportunity to hear the Word, which is why I offered to put the chair in the entry for her. I never paused to consider that it might be the actions of some of my congregants who were causing her hesitation in the first place. Therein lies my failure."

"I believe it is only a couple of the women and they are very careful to...appear genuine on the surface."

"Please say no more. I think I likely know just who you may be referring to. I will try to find the time to make some visits around town this week."

"Thank you."

Aurora realized that the deputy would be leaving at any moment and that she oughtn't let herself be caught dashing back to the barn. She turned and hustled back to the corner of the house. Giving a quick look toward the door, she was satisfied that the men hadn't opened it yet, and made her run across the yard for the barn.

She'd barely taken up the pitchfork and started in on the first stall when she heard the deputy retrieving his horse. Relieved to have him gone, she turned to fetch another forkful of hay and dropped the pitchfork with a gasp.

For there, standing with arms folded in the barn doorway, was the parson. His head was tilted in that way he had when he disapproved of something. Usually it was Kin on the receiving end of that look. Today was the first time she'd seen it directed at her.

She bent to retrieve the pitchfork. "You gave me a fright."

The parson's lips thinned. "Was it me standing here? Or your guilty conscience that gave you the fright?"

Her heart thumped. "What?" She tried to pull off innocence, but her mind raced. Had the deputy said something to him before she'd reached the place where she could hear? Did he know about her deception?

His green eyes hardened. "Listen, lad."

The word "lad" filled her with relief.

"If there's one thing I won't tolerate it is lying, do you understand?"

She couldn't seem to tear her eyes from his. The air all around her suddenly seemed thin and inadequate. Even if he didn't know about her now, when he did find out he was going to be some put out.

"I saw you just now darting across the yard as the deputy was leaving. Were you eavesdropping on our conversation?"

The ache that had slowly been building in her chest since yesterday's sermon squeezed tight. She'd never liked to disappoint her elders. Maybe she could deny it. "N-no sir."

His eyes narrowed further and he took a step toward her.

She threw up her hands. "Yes! Yes sir. I was under the window." She'd seen that look on John Hunt's face many a time just before he or one of his men thrashed Mama for some infraction or another.

The parson hesitated. Stilled. Seemed to relax a little, though the way he settled into his heels and folded his arms didn't give her much reprieve. His jaw bunched. "Why?"

She only looked at him. She couldn't very well admit that she'd been worried the deputy was here to talk about her, now could she? Especially not when he'd just made his feelings on deception so very clear. But he seemed determined to wait her out, so she offered. "I don't know." She prodded at a clump of hay with her boot.

A look crossed his face that was almost her undoing. It was

a look of such disheartenment that it nearly stole her breath. She'd hurt him. He'd taken her in. Given her a place to stay. Three square meals a day. And she'd repaid him with this. She could see all that cross his features.

She swallowed. "I'm sorry."

He nodded and glanced around the barn. His hands settled against his hips, fingers splayed in a very masculine way that she should *not* be noticing right now. But notice it, she was, much to her chagrin. In his eyes, she was just a lad. He could have easily given her a sound thrashing, yet he'd restrained himself despite his obvious anger. That fact only made him all the more a man to be admired.

His green gaze settled back on her. Hard. Unmoving. "Well, if you were my kid, I would give you a thrashing you wouldn't soon forget."

Then again, maybe not. Her heart pounded from the region of her throat, cutting off her ability to inhale.

"But you're not. And I wouldn't presume to do that to someone else's child. Especially since I don't know that you've been taught about the evils of deception." He pinned her with a look that said she had now been apprised of his feelings on the matter and future situations would take such into account.

She nodded her understanding. Her tension eased only slightly.

"But punish you, I must. So..." He swallowed and seemed to search his mind for an appropriate punishment. "You will get no dinner this evening."

She almost sputtered a laugh. Would there be anything else?

"And don't do it again. You understand?"

She nodded, lips pressed together.

With that, he turned and stomped back to the house.

She released a breath she hadn't realized she'd been holding.

No dinner? That was it? She'd had more food in the past few days than she'd had all last month. She could handle missing out on dinner and hardly even notice.

And the deputy hadn't been here to discuss her. So she was free and clear there as well.

If only the parson wasn't so against deception, she might go to him right now and tell him who she really was. But based on his sermon yesterday and his reaction today, she thought it might be better if she just up and disappeared out of his life one day. It wasn't like he could help her with her situation anyhow. He'd helped her, unwittingly or not, escape John Hunt, and that was all she could ask for. If the weather wasn't so cold at night now, she might leave right away. But it would be smarter to hold out and wait till spring. Then she could travel in warmth until she figured out a good place to settle and a good job to make her living.

She wouldn't find a better place to winter than here. Kin treated her a bit gruff, but like a little brother. That she could handle. And the parson had just proved that he wouldn't manhandle her.

She would be safe here till spring.

And that was enough to bring tears to her eyes as she turned back to forking the hay into the stalls.

ohn Hunt had let his anger simmer for several days. But he was still sore aware that Deputy Rodante had punched him in the gut right in his own saloon, and every time he thought of the incident his pride hurt him even worse. He must be getting old. There had been a day when no man would've been able to take him off guard like that. There had been a day when he never lost a fight that he started.

He stood in the street outside the Timber Saloon with his hands propped on his hips surveying the camp around him. Why was he letting this eat at him so? The truth was he didn't need the girl. There were any number of other beautiful women to take her place, and those right willingly. But this was about more than just the money. This was about saving face. A man didn't dare let anyone perceive him as weak, because then the vultures would all start swooping in. No indeed, this was about so much more than money. He had a reputation to uphold. And that was of a ruthless man who didn't let anyone undermine him.

And Rodante had definitely tried to undermine him.

Then, what had happened right about the same time as the attack but that the McClure girl had found her courage and up and disappeared? He couldn't figure where she might have got to. He'd had his men scouring the area for days but they'd all come up empty. It vexed him. People ought to know their place.

For the past few days John had pondered. How did he go about patching up his reputation? Ruling by fear was easy so long as you came up with new and better ways to make people fear you. He had let the problem simmer. He'd stirred it and turned it and flipped it around. How did he go about saving face in a way that left him an out in the eyes of the law, but also in a way that everyone round these parts would know he was a man to be feared?

And then yesterday he'd been in his usual place at the bar in the saloon when he'd overheard two loggers talking.

"Heard the wedding's gonna be right fancy. She was originally a rich girl from back east you know."

John had strained to hear the other man's reply.

"That's what I heard too. I bet the church will be packed to the gills."

A third man had joined them. "Who you speaking of?"

"The sheriff. He's set to hitch himself to the pretty schoolmarm from over in Wyldhaven. There's supposed to be some big shindig this Saturday. A pre-wedding celebration of sorts."

And just like that, John Hunt had known how he was going to get his revenge. Even now he grinned to himself as he pushed through the tent flap and into the Timber. Yes indeed, maybe a few other folk would be collateral damage, but as a bonus it was likely that all the local law enforcement would be in attendance. And it certainly wouldn't hurt his feelings to be done with the likes of them.

What better way to leave himself innocent in the eyes of the law than to take them all out in one fell swoop? And if done right, it would certainly leave everyone in the community knowing just who had pulled it off. Yes sir. This was exactly the opportunity he'd been searching for.

Now he simply had to decide who to enlist to help.

Kin Davis rode into Camp Sixty-Five with the weight of all his mistakes riding on his shoulders and the thirst for a drink nagging at his mind. He ground his teeth. Why was it that he kept going back to that? He knew what that life had done to Pa. Yet no matter how hard he seemed to try, the need for just one more drink always built up until it was near to busting up his insides.

He was supposed to be here looking for work. Best he stay away from drinking tonight.

He reined to a stop in front of a large tent with a hitching rail out front and swung down. Above him chains squeaked, drawing his attention. An etched board sign swung between the posts that rose on either side of the tent's entrance. *Timber Saloon.*

His mouth watered. He could look for work in a saloon, couldn't he? Maybe one drink. What could it hurt?

Before he could change his mind, he strode forward and ducked inside the tent.

A few lamps hung from the central beam of the tent and the liberal scattering of ashtrays at every table filled the room with haze. Over in the corner, a man plunked out a honky-tonk song on an out-of-tune piano. And a woman wearing a bright red dress with ruby-painted lips smiled at him from just ahead. She swayed toward him, black feathers wafting from the boa that graced the expanse of skin below her neck.

He swallowed. The parson would tell him to shutter his eyes, but she was right in his space now, touching his chin with a slim cool finger, and she smelled divine.

"Hi, sugar." She batted her long dark lashes and worked her fingers down his chest in invitation. "You look like you could use a little relaxation. Hmmm?"

He should leave. He propped his hands on his hips. Closed his eyes. Willed himself to have the strength the parson said he could have if he only trusted God enough. But he made the mistake of breathing in. Her perfume called to him. Like someone doused her in a little bit of heaven. He looked at her again. Her impish smile certainly promised a taste of heaven.

"I-I'm really here about a j-job."

She giggled and took his hand, sidling backwards towards the bar as she drew him after her. "A job, is it? What kind of work would a handsome man like you be looking for in a place like this?" She didn't give him time to answer before leaning forward and whispering playfully in his ear, "I could give you a job, sweetie." Her giggle and her implication were clear.

Kin felt a wave of heat wash over him. Back at McGinty's, all he got was rotgut liquor. This place was already a decided improvement. "What's your name?"

She tittered and led him closer to the bar. "The name's Adelle, sweetie. What's yours?"

"Kin."

She pulled out a barstool and eased him onto it, then set about massaging the muscles of his shoulders and neck. "My but you are a muscled one, aren't you, Kin?" she giggled. "Now what'll you have?"

Kin felt his ears burn. Truth was, he had no idea what to get. McGinty offered one drink that he made in his own still out back of the alehouse. "What do you recommend?"

She draped an arm around his shoulders and blinked up at him with a coy simper. "Well now, that depends on if you are looking for just a plain good time, or a really good time, Kin."

He grinned at her. "Let's start with a really good time and go from there."

She touched his nose and offered a knowing wink. "I knew you were a smart one. I truly did." She lifted a hand to the barkeep and the man plunked two small glasses in front of her and Kin and splashed a golden-brown liquid into them.

Adelle lifted her glass toward him in a salute. "Bottoms up, handsome."

Kin returned her salute and then slung the liquor to the back of his throat. He choked. Then coughed. Everything burned like he'd just set his insides on fire. His eyes watered.

Adelle's laugh tinkled in his ear. "Welcome to the big house, honey. Now tell me what kind of a job you want?"

Kin shook his head, hoping to ward off the buzzing in his ears. "Anything really. I just need to make enough money to get out of town."

"Aw, darlin'. Your pappy a bruiser, is he?" She lifted her hand to the bartender again.

Kin frowned. "My pa died."

"I'm right sorry to hear that."

The bartender refilled both glasses.

"So... You on your own now?"

Kin shook his head, then gave her a wry grin. "I live with the parson over in Wyldhaven."

Adelle shook her finger at him like he was a naughty child. "What would the man say to find you here enjoying my company?" She slung her arm around his shoulders and lifted her glass toward his. "To getting out of town."

Kin smiled. "I'll drink to that."

John knew fate had smiled on him the moment he entered the

Timber and heard the kid at the bar next to Adelle bellyaching about Wyldhaven.

He'd been pondering how to pull off his plan and now, here, right on his own home turf, the answer had presented itself.

He sank onto the stool next to Adelle and peered around her at the kid who was barely remaining upright on his stool. "Who is he?"

She caressed her finger around the rim of her glass. "Just some poor kid who needed to blow off some steam. Said he lives with the parson in Wyldhaven." She chuckled gleefully. "Ain't that something?"

"How much does he owe?"

Adelle sighed and rolled her eyes. "Don't worry. I've been making him keep caught up on paying. But he's out of money now."

John considered. He tapped the bar and watched the kid for a few more minutes. He was mumbling unintelligible phrases into the top of his shot glass.

Satisfaction worked through John. This was exactly what he needed. He bumped Adelle with his shoulder. "Let him have three more without paying."

Adelle gave him a pointed, searching look. "He'll be passed out by then."

John grinned. "Yes." *And by this time tomorrow, he'd have the kid firmly by the scruff of the neck.*

Chapter Eighteen

iora leaned over the table and peered past Tess's shoulder.

The girl's fingers moved painstakingly slow as she traced out a perfect letter "A," her tongue caught between her teeth.

Liora couldn't hold back a huge smile. She patted Tess on the back. "Perfect! That's the best one you've done yet. And see here it is, right in the fifteenth chapter of the book of First Corinthians that we read in our morning devotions. 'Adam.'"

"A-d-a-m." Tess drew her finger carefully over each letter as she pronounced the sounds.

"Yes! You'll be reading like a teacher in no time."

"What that all mean about the first Adam and the second Adam?"

"Well the first Adam was the one created by God at the beginning of all time in the Garden of Eden. We are all like him because we are human, made in the image of God. The second Adam, is Jesus. We can all choose to be like Him and be reborn spiritually. We simply need to believe He died for our sins, that He was the sacrifice who saves us all. Just as God gave that first Adam physical life in the garden, so He can give all of us a new life, spiritually."

Tess pondered for a moment. "I like that. My daddy, he used to say that verse. Her finger touched down on the page.

"'We are sewn perishable, but raised imperishable.' I never understood. But I think I do now. He meant these first bodies is like Adam. They gonna die and be no more, but when we trust Jesus, He gives us new bodies, like them seeds this chapter talk about that get new bodies when they go into the ground and die."

Liora smiled. "That's exactly right."

Tess took a breath. "I'm glad Jesus chose to do that for us. Them other whores back there workin' for Mr. Hunt? If I could sacrifice somethin' to give them a chance to have a better life, I would want to do that too. Like you done for me." Her gaze lifted to Liora's. "Thanks ever so much."

Liora squeezed Tess's shoulder. "You're welcome. And maybe you'll get the chance sooner than you think. After this hubbub with John Hunt dies down, I plan to go back. You can come with me. We'll save women from that life, together."

Tess lifted pain-filled eyes to Liora. "You think Jesus can forgive me for the way I've lived? I didn't want to live that way, mind you," she hurried to say. "I jus' didn't feel like I had no choice. But maybe I coulda fought harder, resisted more."

Liora bent down until she was on eye level with Tess. "Jesus can forgive anything. All you have to do is ask Him."

A large smile touched Tess's lips. "I'll do that."

Liora gave her a nod, and stood just as a knock sounded on the front door of the cabin.

Liora reached for the ties of her apron and glanced at the clock with a frown. Who could that be at this hour of the afternoon? Joe was out working near the lean-to so whoever it was, he must have directed them to the house to speak to her.

When she swung the door open, she was surprised to see Parson Clay standing on the porch, hat in hand.

"Parson." She stepped back and motioned him in. "What a

pleasant surprise." She gestured toward the secondhand settee in the corner. "If you'll have a seat, I'll fetch you some coffee?"

He motioned for her to wait and then spun his hat through his fingers. "Please. There's no need. I'm making rounds and if the truth be told, I've had more coffee in the past few hours than a man should have in a month of Sundays."

Liora chuckled. "Very well. How may I help you?"

She was surprised when he suddenly looked uneasy. He studied and fiddled with the brim of his hat for a moment before lifting his eyes to hers once more. "If I'm honest, I feel that I owe you an apology before getting to the other reason that I'm here."

Liora frowned. "An apology? Whatever for? Please, shall we sit?"

"Yes. Thank you." The man lifted a gesture of greeting toward Tess as they stepped farther into the room.

Tess nodded, but quickly ducked her head back to her studies.

When they were seated next to each other on the settee, the parson settled his hat on the side table and then looked over at her. "My apology is for not seeing that it was some of the women in the church who've been making you so uncomfortable that you didn't want to come into the service."

Liora felt her face blanch. How had he heard that? She hadn't wanted to get anyone in trouble.

He held up a reassuring hand. "Joe came by to see me. He was very discrete, but open enough to let me know what you've been going through."

Joe. Yes, of course Joe. Liora smoothed her skirts. "In many ways, I feel like the treatment is somewhat deserved. The consequences of a life of sin, you might say."

From her peripheral vision, she could see him shaking

his head. "No. Being mistreated by fellow believers is never deserved. You've repented and turned from your sin. Sometimes, yes, there are natural consequences. However, mistreatment by fellow believers should not be one of them. And I apologize for not having seen it sooner. I plan to speak to Mrs....well, to some of the ladies."

Liora felt even worse on hearing that. "That's really not necessary, Parson. I have no desire to befoul anyone's good name."

"It is my duty to shepherd the whole flock, Miss Fontaine. Therefore, it is my duty to gently bring correction where I notice it necessary. And in this case, I believe there is a call for it. Please don't distress yourself. If the Holy Spirit is indeed at work in our lives, we should all be happy to learn and grow and become more like Christ." He gave a dismissive wave of his hand as though to say he was done with this part of the conversation. "Now let me move on to the other reason I'm here. As you may have heard, Dixie would like to have a wedding party for Charlotte and Reagan. It will be held at the church on Saturday and Dixie noticed she hadn't heard from you. She asked me to see if you'd be willing to bring a dish and a dessert."

Liora swallowed. "I'd be happy to."

"Wonderful. Thank you. And with that, I'll bid you good day, Miss Fontaine. I still have several stops to make before getting home and I left the new boy at the house writing a test Charlotte wanted him to take to determine where best to place him in school."

Despite her quick assurance that she'd be happy to help, Liora's heart squeezed into a painful rhythm as she bade the parson farewell and watched him ride away.

So much for all her efforts to keep out of Dixie's line of sight on Sunday.

She straightened her shoulders. This would be good for her. She simply needed to disregard Mrs. Hines and her cronies. She would make a pork roast and a berry pie.

But it didn't have to be done right now. What she *did* need to do was have a talk with one Joseph Rodante. She could already feel her pulse climbing in aggravated anticipation.

"Tess, I'll be right back." She hoisted her skirts and set out at a smart clip toward the lean-to. The closer she got, the more pressure she could feel building up inside of her until she fairly exploded upon reaching him. "Joseph Rodante! What in the world do you think you are doing?"

Ax in hand, Joe spun from the log he'd been stripping of bark. His eyes were wide and she could see him searching his memory for what he might have done to upset her. "Ah…" He scrubbed his wrist over his chin, then gestured to the log laying atop the sawhorses. "Stripping some logs so we can use them for the barn walls."

Liora trembled. "Mine!"

Joe looked confused.

She flipped a gesture to the tiny three-sided shed. "My lean-to." Another gesture encompassed the area he'd been clearing for a barn. "*My* barn." A sweep of her hand took in the house. "My house." She slammed fingertips to her chest. "My life! And I don't need you meddling in it!" It suddenly hit her how petty she sounded when he'd only been trying to help. That feeling was driven home by the hurt look that crossed his features. She took a breath and ended lamely. "No matter how good your intentions might be in doing so."

"I see." Joe presented her with his back, sank the ax deep into the log, and then turned to face her once more. Thumbs hooked in his belt loops, he studied her, letting his gaze drill deep into her own. She saw anger flash for the briefest of moments. She knew it was anger because she so rarely saw it in Joe.

She swallowed and took a step back, waiting for him to lash out with as much venom as she'd just used.

But then his emotions shifted. His features softened. And he took a step toward her.

She swallowed. What was that look all about?

His expression seemed warm and easy. His mouth set, but not in anger. His head tilted ever so slightly. And those gentle dark eyes... They made her feel things deep inside that she'd never felt before.

He took another step toward her, little crinkles appearing at the corners of his mouth.

She backed up a step, heart thudding with some sort of crazy unfamiliar emotion. Certainly not fear. She was all too familiar with that. No. This was something almost entirely opposite.

He continued his advance. His voice was ever so soft when he spoke. "You are so used to people rejecting you that you can't even fathom someone standing up for you, can you?"

"I didn't need you getting Mrs. Hines in trouble on my behalf." Her voice was gravelly and she cleared her throat as she matched his steps, withdrawing once for every advance he took.

"We all need someone else to stand up for us once in a while, Liora. I didn't do it because I felt you were weak."

His approach was steady and his strides longer. She was now backed up against the porch rail with no more room to retreat.

"Nor was I trying to get Mrs. Hines in trouble. I was standing up for the woman I love."

Something closed off her throat. She opened her mouth to tell him once more that he simply couldn't love her, but no sound would emerge. He was close. So close she could see that tiny scar again, and her fingers itched to trace it. Everything in her screamed, *too close*, while at the same time waiting in anticipation for him to come nearer. Why had she gone off half-cocked and yelled at him?

He hesitated, studying her. And she couldn't deny her relief. He wasn't going to come closer. Wasn't going to touch her.

But then he said, "I'm not going to hurt you, Liora, but you'll remember that you asked me not to give up on you, yes?" A bit of a roguish curve touched his lips as he slowly stepped forward.

Liora's mouth went dry and she felt a tingle of fire race along the back of her neck.

He closed the distance between them until she could feel the warmth of him invading her space. He propped both hands on the rail on either side of her, settling his weight there.

She could no longer handle looking into such depth of emotion. She closed her eyes. The disconnection brought immediate relief. But she could still feel him near. Still sense him studying her in that steady methodical way of his. Still smell the appealing scent of leather and evergreen that always seemed to accompany him.

The scent lured her forward. Her cheek brushed against the rough stubble of his. Her heart pounded, but she couldn't quite bring herself to retreat.

He didn't move. Didn't speak. Simply let her linger near.

After a long moment, she relaxed. Leaned further forward until his shoulder cradled her forehead.

She heard him swallow. Felt the gentle brush of his hand against her back.

"Joe?"

"Yeah?" She felt the warmth of the word against her neck.

"I'm sorry. I shouldn't have lost my temper."

He loosed a soft laugh. "I'll think on forgiving you."

She straightened, giving his chest a mock slap.

He chuckled and trapped her hand against the beat of his heart, letting his thumb caress over her knuckles. He regarded her with gentle humor. "You can get mad at me anytime, so long as it ends up with you in my arms."

Heat burgeoned in her cheeks. She looked down. Studying the broad expanse of his sun-browned hand that still held hers captive.

He remained where he was for so long, she peered back up at him to see what he was doing.

His gaze was fixed directly on her and his mouth tilted up in a lazy smile. "You are some beautiful of a woman, Liora. Some beautiful. But that's not why I love you. It's your kind heart and gentle spirit. It's because even when you are mistreated you do not choose to respond in kind. It's because even though you understood the danger, you still chose to rescue Tess, and will probably do the same for other girls. You've been my friend and confidante. And my feelings for you grew so slowly that even I was surprised to discover them the other day." His gaze roved from her hair, to her cheeks, to her lips where it hesitated for the briefest of moments before rebounding to her eyes. "I hope that when you examine your heart, you'll find that those same feelings have grown in you. And one of these days you are going to accept God's trade of beauty for ashes. When that time comes, you'll figure out a way to let me know, and then we are going to have a wonderful life together." And with that, he gave her hand a gentle squeeze and then strode back to his work across the yard.

Weak-kneed, Liora fumbled her way up the porch steps and pushed into the house.

It would probably be best simply to let Joe stand up for her from now on.

Besides, he was right. She somewhat liked it.

Who was she kidding?

More than somewhat.

She felt like her heart had been frozen for a very long time and Joe had just kindled a fire at its center.

Chapter Nineteen

A vice pressed hard against Kin's skull. Pounding pain made any movement torture. Someone groaned, and then he realized the sound had come from him. His mouth felt like it had been stuffed full of cotton all night long, and where was the outhouse? He needed it now. Even if it was right outside it was too far away. He squinted around the room. Where was the door? Someone pushed through the tent-flap entrance, sending a shaft of agonizing light straight through his eyes.

He stumbled forward, one hand raised to block the blinding rays.

Someone loomed before him. "Whoa, kid. You never paid your bill last night."

Kin assessed the man through the slit of one eye. The bartender. "I'll be right back." He made to go around the man.

But the bartender sidestepped to block his path. "You'll pay me now."

Irritation surged, but sharp on its heels a faint warning bell clanged. There was something he should realize, but he couldn't think for the need to get outside. "Look, mister. If you don't let me get to the necessary, you're going to have more to worry about than the fact that I haven't paid yet."

The bartender huffed a breath and stepped to one side, but not before waving another man over to follow him.

Kin didn't care if he had the whole town following him at this point.

Thankfully, one of the camp outhouses was just next to the saloon and was at the moment unoccupied. When he emerged, feeling much relieved, he almost barreled into the man who'd tailed him. And that was when realization hit him.

He didn't have any more money. The agony in his head pulsed like a couple of ax-wielding lumberjacks in a competition.

A sick feeling dropped into the pit of his stomach. How many more drinks had he consumed the night before? He remembered paying for the first two. After that, everything was a bit of a blur.

"You'll need to come with me." The man gave him a hard look.

Nausea swept through him in a consuming wave. But he knew there was no escape. He nodded for the man to lead the way. What was he going to say? What *could* he say? He had nothing. What would they do to him?

He could tell by the look in the bartender's eyes that he knew he didn't have the money.

Kin kicked at the dirt floor inside the tent. "What do I owe?"

"Thirty dollars."

Shock washed through him. "What?" There was no way he'd drunk that much!

The bartender shrugged an uncaring gesture. "You bought two rounds for the entire house. Since you'd been paying all along right up to that point, I figured you were good for it."

Thirty dollars. Kin sank back against a barstool and scrubbed one hand over his face. He searched the interior of the room. At the back corner, a drunk still slept on one of the tables. A few of the chairs were overturned throughout the room. Other than that, no one would believe how full the place had been the evening before.

The bartender eyed him over the glass he was polishing. "You're free to go, soon as you've paid up."

Kin shifted. It was probably time to fess up. "The thing is... I don't have it. Not even a penny of it."

The bartender wagged his head. "That's a bad spot to be in, kid. Mr. Hunt don't take kindly to folks what can't pay." He glanced toward the tent entrance and Kin heard the sound of scrambling feet behind him. Light from the opening of the tent flap momentarily cast a triangle on the floor, and then disappeared again.

Kin swallowed. Someone had just left the tent. Likely going to fetch Mr. Hunt. This was not going to be pretty. How did he get himself into these situations?

It was only a moment before Mr. Hunt stepped in, followed by the man who'd gone to fetch him.

Hunt folded his arms and leaned into his heels. He was a big man. At one time his girth had probably been all muscle, but now it was liberally padded with flesh. He had a white shock of hair and a skiff of a white beard covered his jaw like he hadn't quite had time to shave yet this morning. "McGuff here tells me you can't pay."

Kin felt sick. "No, sir."

"Thirty dollars. That's a lot of money."

"Yes, sir."

They would beat him now. But that was okay. If there was anything living with his pa had taught him, it was that he could handle a beating.

"By rights, I ought to beat you and make you work at shoveling outhouses around camp until you can pay me back. At fifty cents a day, that would be two months of work."

Kin felt a weariness drape over him. Always he failed. Always he made the wrong decisions. He didn't reply to the man. He knew that wouldn't do him any good. He kept his eyes down in a respectful manner and waited for the man to pronounce his judgement.

"But I'm not going to do any of that, kid."

Kin lifted his eyes, not daring to give the hope that had just sprung to life too much root.

John Hunt smiled, but there was something feral and wild about it that kept the light of it from reaching his eyes and sent a chill down Kin's spine. Hunt leaned closer, his narrowed eyes drilling straight into Kin's. "No, sir. I'm not going to do that because I've got a better way for you to pay me back, kid. And it will only take a couple hours of your time."

Kin swallowed. He didn't like the sound of this at all. "How's that, sir?"

Hunt's lips spread into a wide smile. "Why, kid, you are going to burn down the Wyldhaven church come Saturday."

Kin's heart stuttered and then quit beating altogether for a few moments before resuming again at double speed. Saturday was the day of the sheriff and Miss Brindle's party. At the church. Near everyone in Wyldhaven would be there.

He shook his head. "I'll have to do the outhouse shoveling for you, sir. I know that will take longer but—"

Pain exploded in his kidney. With a grunt, he fell to his knees. Hunt's man, McGuff, loomed over him from behind. Another blow shot arrows of fire through his ribs and sent him writhing to the floor. And then a boot stomped down on his thigh.

Anger surged, and he flipped onto his back, ready to leap to his feet and fight back, but one glimpse of his attacker and he knew that he was beat. The man stood over him with a long wooden club in his hands. He had it raised and ready to smash into Kin's face if he moved another muscle.

Kin lifted his palms. "All right. All right." He winced as he straightened the spasming muscle in his stomped leg. His mind scrabbled to think. He swiped at his lips with the back of his hand, more to buy time than anything, and was surprised when it came away bloody. He must have smashed his lips into something on his way to the floor. Climbing slowly to his feet, he leaned to the side and spat the metallic taste of blood from his mouth. What was he going to do?

John Hunt clutched him by the hair. He jerked his head back and glowered directly into his face. "Don't think, kid. That's not your place. Your place is just to do as you're told, understand?"

Kin wanted to tell him where he should go, but even more than that he wanted to be able to walk out of here. So he kept his mouth shut and merely nodded.

"Good." Hunt released him and patted his cheek as though he were a young boy. "Good. I knew we'd come to an understanding." He gave the bartender a nod.

Kin watched warily as the man reached under the bar. Beads of sweat suddenly dotted the man's forehead.

Kin frowned. Was the barkeep afraid of Hunt? He spat more blood and kept silent, knowing there wasn't much more he could do at this point.

The bartender stood slowly, one careful inch at a time. His attention remained fixed on whatever he was lifting from behind the bar, cheeks puffed out in careful concentration. A bead of sweat dripped into his eye and he blinked hard.

"Steady!" Hunt admonished.

The bartender eased out the air that had rounded his cheeks and ever so gently set a wooden box onto the bar.

Kin studied it. The box was only about six inches high. And it had nine smaller compartments that divided it into three even cubicles in each direction. In each small cubicle there was a glass vial surrounded by straw.

Hunt leaned forward and gingerly lifted one of the vials from its bed of straw. He held it up for Kin to see. "You know what this is, kid? We've been keeping it on ice behind the bar."

The vial contained a clear liquid that could have been water, except it looked a little thicker. Oilier. He shook his head.

"This is called nitroglycerin."

Kin's pulse shot into a gallop. He stepped back, but immediately knew the gesture was foolish. He'd studied about nitroglycerin. It was the ingredient that gave dynamite its bang, but was even more deadly in its liquid form. If the temperature rose by even a few degrees, a simple jostle of the container could cause an explosion the likes of which would leave this entire saloon nothing but a crater in the dirt.

Hunt took in his shock. "Ah, so you've heard of it, have you? That's good. That knowledge might actually save your life." He handed the vial in his hand back to the barkeep. "Prepare this one for travel with the lad here."

Kin felt woozy and nauseated. What had he gotten himself into?

"There's a party in town this Saturday, yes?"

Kin nodded. Swallowed. He couldn't seem to take his eyes off the vial that the bartender was wrapping in a red bandana. "Yes, sir. For the sheriff and Miss Brindle." Sweat slicked his palms and he rubbed them against his denims.

John nodded. "Just as I had heard." From the trembling hand of the bartender, he accepted the vial, now carefully wrapped and packed in its own small crate stuffed with straw. Cautiously, he handed it to Kin. "It's cold enough these days that they'll definitely build a fire in the stove. All you have to do is set this behind the stove. And"—he chuckled—"you might want to make sure that you find an excuse to skip the lovely party for the sheriff and his bride."

Kin took the box and looked into the man's eyes. "That's it? And then I don't owe you anything?" What was he saying? There was no way that he could blow up the church with the entire town inside it.

John shrugged and nodded. "That's it, kid."

Kin thought for another beat. He eyed the club in the hand of the man still standing next to John. He eyed the box in his hands. And then the thought hit him. If he declined to do what John wanted, he would surely take another beating and maybe even get blown up in the process. But if he agreed and took the vial and left, that didn't mean that he had to follow through. He could walk out of here right now and no one would have to get hurt. He would even have a chance to warn Reagan and Joe about Hunt.

He gave a short nod. "All right."

John folded his arms, settled into his heels, and gave him a hard look. "Don't think you can walk out of here and run off without me knowing."

Kin swallowed. How was he going to get out of this if they were watching him the whole time?

Hunt narrowed his eyes.

Kin realized he would have to figure out answers later. Right now he just needed to get away from here and give this raging headache time to clear so he could think. He nodded. "Yes, sir."

"Right then. Be off with you. We'll be watching, kid."

Kin eased out a breath and started for the exit.

"Oh and... I wouldn't risk the jostling of a horse with that nitro. Probably best if you walk back to town."

All the men in the bar cackled.

Kin felt moisture dampening his collar before he'd even gotten his mount's reins untied from the hitching rail. It was going to be a long walk back to town.

Chapter Twenty

A urora sat at the small kitchen table in the parson's cabin with her forehead propped in one hand. The numbers and words on the test the parson had left with her blurred and danced and fragmented through her tears.

As soon as the parson had left to do his rounds, she had hurried through a much too chilly bath, changed into fresh clothes, and then dumped the water at the back side of the house so the men wouldn't be any wiser to the fact that she'd bathed while they were out. Then she'd made the cookies as the parson had instructed for tomorrow's gathering in town. And then she'd sat down to take the test the Wyldhaven schoolteacher wanted her to take so she would know where to place her.

At first Aurora had been thrilled with the idea of attending school. She hadn't been to school since the year she'd turned ten. And Ma hadn't had the time to teach her much over the past several years. But she'd always loved learning and oh the joy that had filled her at the prospect of being allowed to return to school—even if she had to do so under the pretense of being a twelve-year-old boy. She'd planned to dumb down her answers to the questions on the test, but once she'd sat down to take it, she'd found the questions much harder than she'd anticipated. As a woman of seventeen years, she should know a lot more of the questions on the test, yet hard as she'd tried, she was utterly unclear on what some of the questions were even asking.

Under the geography section, one question instructed her to name and give the boundaries of the five zones. That had been the first question on the test that made her tear up. But it wasn't the only one, nor by far the last.

In the mathematics portion, one question wanted to know how much a man had paid if he'd purchased a cord of wood for eighty-nine and a half cents per cord and the pile of wood he ended up with had been twenty-four feet long, four feet wide, and six feet three inches tall. How was she to do that figuring when she had no idea the size of a cord of wood in the first place?

Under the grammar section, the test asked her to "Decline I." She couldn't even fathom what that might mean, but she certainly wanted to decline and that was certain. Decline the whole dad-blamed test!

Kin gingerly carried the nitroglycerin until he was far enough outside of Camp Sixty-Five that the chance of anyone stumbling across it and blowing themselves up was extremely minimal.

Despite the fact that Hunt had said he'd have men watching him, Kin hadn't seen hide nor hair of anyone. He searched carefully up and down the road. No one was in sight.

He stepped off the road, and tucked the box away near the roots of one of the seed trees. With that task seen to, he released a huge breath of relief and bent to prop hands against his knees. His legs were shaking worse than a newborn foal's.

Now he just had to decide how he was going to proceed.

He stood for a long time staring at the box. Hang it all if he knew how he was going to get out of this predicament. He sank into a squat and plucked up a pinecone. He set to shredding it bit by bit as he glanced back in the direction of Camp Sixty-Five.

Of course, he wasn't going to take the nitroglycerin and blow up the church tomorrow. The people of Wyldhaven had rallied around him when his father had died, and he would no more hurt any of them then he would a newborn pup. His first inclination was that he should just ride out of town and keep on going. Hunt couldn't hurt him if he couldn't find him.

But there were two problems he could see with that.

The first was that despite his having given Parson Clay as rough a time as he dared, the man had taken him in after Pa's death when he didn't have to. He'd made a home for Kin, and Kin knew that had come with sacrifices. What kind of appreciation would it show if he just rode away without even saying a fare-thee-well to the man? Plus, the horse he was riding wasn't his. And horse thieving was a hanging offense, even if riding off without goodbyes wasn't.

The second problem was that John Hunt would have a backup plan. Even though he hadn't seen anyone following him, Kin knew Hunt was too savvy to simply trust that Kin was going to follow through with his instructions. The man had obviously set him up. And he likely had men watching even if Kin couldn't see them. They were probably staying at a distance to keep from getting blown to pieces if something went wrong.

Was his reputation so besmirched that Hunt had actually thought he could force him into such a sickening crime? Kin's shoulders slumped. Whatever Hunt thought of him, he would never stoop that low. But maybe he could use that? If they thought he was low enough to do it, why not let them keep thinking that for a while longer? Because even if he could escape Hunt's men, if he left without giving warning, he would still be responsible if anyone was injured or killed. The right thing to do would be to ride into town and report what had happened.

After weighing out all of his options, he came down to the realization that he only really had one. And his gut crimped into a tiny hard ball because he had no idea how to pull it off.

He had to somehow escape Hunt's men without letting them know he was trying. Even this pause in his journey had probably already given them more insight into his reluctance than he would like. Maybe if he pretended to pick the vial back up, they would be fooled and keep their distance? He would take the road slow, like he was still carrying the nitro. Then once he got back to the forested area closer to town he would be able to lose them. He knew every little trail and gully in that area.

A tingle raced along the back of his neck. He searched the surrounding hills again, but still he didn't see anyone watching.

He huffed. Hunt was probably all bark and no bite. But he couldn't take that risk.

He stood, brushed off the seat of his pants, bent and pretended to retrieve the vial from the box. He hoped his own red bandana, tugged from his pocket, would fool whoever might be watching through blurry field glasses. He went through the motions of pretending to put the vial into one of his saddle bags, and reached for his mount's reins.

Pain pierced his side at the same moment the *crack* of a rifle shot resounded.

His mount whinnied and reared, yanking the reins from Kin's hand. The horse landed stiff-legged, and then surged into a gallop down the road.

Kin reeled a step back and glanced down. Blood seeped

through his shirt and already soaked the top of his pants. He'd been shot!

He had to get out of here. He took a step.

But behind him footsteps crunched.

Kin spun around.

The man who had, earlier, followed him to the outhouse loomed, rifle raised like a club. "You should have done as you were told, kid. No one would risk riding a horse with nitro in the saddle bags." The butt of the rifle smashed into Kin's face.

Everything went black.

By the time Preston arrived back at the cabin, he was bone weary and discouragement was no small part of the reason. He didn't like to be a failure. But no matter which way he tried to look at it he couldn't get away from the fact that he had failed and failed big. Thankfully, Liora had been very forgiving and understanding. But now he faced the task of confronting Mrs. Hines and Mrs. King and maybe a couple other ladies in the church.

He would have to do that tomorrow before Reagan and Charlotte's congratulatory party, because it was too late to ride into town tonight, and he still had to put the finishing touches on the speech he had been asked to give. Not to mention the lad Rory had already been on his own for long enough today.

He led his mount into the barn, stripped it of its saddle, and set to currying while he pondered the best way to go about said confrontation.

If he were honest, he probably should have just ridden straight to town and gotten the ordeal over with, but confrontation had never been something he enjoyed. This delay wasn't all bad, however. It would give him time to think through what to say to the women. And do some praying on the matter.

He scooped two scoops of oats into the horse's trough, made sure it had enough water, and then headed for the house.

The sniffling coming from the dining room was his first clue that not all was well with Rory. "Hang this whole dad-blamed test!" The sound of crumpling paper accompanied the words.

"Rory, lad?" He stepped into the dining room. "You all right?"

Rory scrambled to swipe tears from his cheeks and straighten from where he had been slumped at the table. He'd crumpled the test into one hand, but now rushed to smooth it out. "Yes sir. I'm fine. Had a bug fly into my eye is all."

Preston frowned as realization hit him. Here was another area where he had failed recently. The kid had told him that his ma and pa had died and that he was on his own. Preston had just assumed he'd been on his own for quite some time. But maybe the loss was more recent? The kid certainly had been very quiet since he'd come to stay. Preston had been so concerned with his search for the missing daughter of the woman who had passed away that first day, and then after that he had just sort of absorbed the kid into his world without really thinking too much about him.

Now he approached the table and sank into the chair cattycorner from Rory. He glanced from the test to the boy's face and back again. If only he was better at ferreting out information. Maybe he would be able to help the kid more competently. But it was obvious with Kin as an example, that he wasn't very good at that.

"Test a little harder than you expected it to be?"

The kid shoved the test away. "I've done fine on my own without schooling up to this point anyhow. Don't suppose I need it." The lad was obviously trying to fight his emotions, but the tears kept coming and he kept swiping at them fiercely.

Preston leaned forward to take up the test and that was

when his nostrils caught the distinct whiff of fresh soap. He drew the test closer to himself, leaned against the slats of his chair, and scrutinized the kid.

Rory's hair had been washed because where it had been slightly greasy this morning it looked clean and wavy. And he was definitely wearing clean duds.

The kid had taken a bath while he was gone? Well glory be! Kin had come to live with him when he was fifteen and it had taken several months of strong talks to get him to take a voluntary bath.

Preston's gaze skimmed over the light blue shirt. The kid must've had it stuffed in a bag because it was wrinkled like nobody's business. And he must've made the cookies that he had instructed him to make, because he had flour on the front of his shirt, and now that Preston took time to notice, the scent of baked sugar did linger nicely in the air.

"I see you got the cookies made. Thank you." Preston reached out to brush flour off Rory's front shirt pocket. The kid recoiled so violently that his chair tipped over backwards and slid for several feet across the floor.

"I'll get it!" Rory's voice was an octave higher than normal. Preston blinked.

The kid gave him a look that was at once apologetic and exasperated. "Sorry." He brushed the flour from the front of his shirt and his face was pinker than a fresh-sliced summer watermelon.

Something niggled at the back of Preston's mind. Something that he should be able to put his finger on, but couldn't. He shook the thought away and turned to look at the test the boy had been crying over.

The boy had been crying over... Had he ever known a boy to cry over a test before?

Slowly his gaze lifted from the paper to study Rory once more. The kid had his back to him and had bent over to retrieve his chair, his shirt stretched tight across his back as he leaned down and through the material of his shirt Preston could see the ridges of a lighter band of color right below his shoulder blades, like...

Preston's heart set to beating faster than a woodpecker on an insect riddled tree.

Dear God please tell me it's not so.

But as his gaze skimmed her once more, he knew. *Her...*

The lighter band of color was from a binding cloth used to hide her...womanly...ness.

Aurora turned from picking up her chair and froze.

The parson was gaping at her like she'd just grown a second head.

Panic slivered through her. She didn't know what had given her away, but she had no doubt that she'd just been found out. Her legs went weak and she sank into the chair she'd just put upright. What was going to happen to her now?

He shoved away from the table and set to pacing the room with his hands clasped behind his neck. "No! No, no, no! This can't be happening." He stilled and pegged her with a glower. "Tell me it's not so!"

Rory frowned. Swallowed. Couldn't quite bring herself to meet his gaze. Maybe she was panicking for no reason? "Tell you what's not so?"

His gaze drifted over her and then he fell to pacing once more. He mumbled to himself, ticking a few things off on his fingers, and then he froze. "Oh, I am every kind of a fool!" He nailed her with a look. "You're her, aren't you? The very girl I came to the camp to help!"

Rory swallowed, mouth so dry no words would form.

He continued his accusation. "That boy, the one who was beating you up when Kin and I rode into camp, he said you were new to these parts. But later, you seemed almighty set on keeping the neighbor lady from seeing your face. And then you were more than happy to help me prepare the body for burial. What other preteen boy would've done that for a stranger?" He anchored one heel as a pivot point and continued his pacing and self-recrimination. "Stupid blind fool, Clay!"

Aurora trembled. At least none of his anger had been directed her way. Yet.

He pulled in a gulp of air. Then another. And another. Finally, he exploded with, "How could you do this?!"

She flinched, half way expecting a blow, but it never came.

Parson Clay towered over her. His eyes glittered like the sparks of flame given off by flint. "I'm still waiting for an explanation that I can accept."

She wrapped her arms around herself. "I wanted to tell you, especially after your sermon on Sunday, but then you said..." The words withered and dried up beneath his parching glare.

He resumed his trek across the floor. "I can't believe— My congregation is going to—" He emitted a sound that could only be interpreted as a growl, propped the heels of both hands against the wall and leaned into stiff arms, head hanging.

Aurora swallowed and waited.

His next words seemed to be spoken to himself. "I could lose my ministry here in Wyldhaven. Not only that, something like this could follow me for the rest of my life!" The parson straightened suddenly and spun to face her. Anger still sparked in his eyes. "What? You wanted to tell me, but I said...what?"

Rory's lower lip trembled. "That you wouldn't tolerate deception."

Another growl escaped, this one even more feral than the last. "So, the very thing I said I would not tolerate, you did?!"

She had no reply for that.

"Why? Why didn't you tell me"—his hand swept from her head to her feet and back again in a gesture that indicated he couldn't quite come up with an appropriate way to voice her gender—"right from the start?"

Aurora's tears started again, but this time they were born more from anger. "I'd already made the decision to flee. My mother made me promise to, if you must know. And you, quite frankly, seemed like a godsend in the face of that boy's bullying. You certainly seemed less dangerous than John Hunt."

The parson's gaze sharpened on her. "John Hunt? What do you know about him?" His face paled and he stepped back. "Please tell me you're not a..."

Aurora shook her head. "No. But my mother was—not of her own choice, mind you. And he ensured she owed him money, which he would have demanded from me in the form of...services after she died." She hesitated, but there was a burning question she needed the answer to. "How did you know?"

The parson's shoulders slumped, as though shedding away the last of his hope. "I've never known a boy your age in my life who voluntarily took a bath! And you didn't want me touching your—" he swept a hand in the general direction of her shirt, his face turning red as a baneberry, and his accusatory glower, just as poisonous.

Preston stepped to the window and stared across the moonlit yard. Every curse word that he had ever banished from his vocabulary wanted to spill from his lips. He clenched his teeth. This could be the end of his ministry. He'd had a girl living at his house. A girl that he was not married to. A girl that Kin was not married to. A girl! Living with two bachelors! He released a groan. "And Mrs. Hines thought she had something to gossip about before!"

Rory gave a soft sob.

He turned to study her.

She swiped tears from her cheeks. Very womanly cheeks that tapered down to soft full lips. Combined with large green eyes framed by long dark lashes. He called himself every kind of fool. How had he not seen that she was a woman?

"I'm sorry," she choked out. "I wanted to tell you. Especially after last Sunday's sermon. It's only... I don't have anywhere to go. And I thought maybe I could make it through till spring."

"How old are you?"

She studied her clasped fingers. "Seventeen."

Seventeen. Practically a woman! Did that make this better? Or worse?

He couldn't think for the shock still coursing through him. All he knew was that she couldn't stay here with them for another moment. "Get your things." He gestured to the bedroom.

Her eyes widened. "You're going to put me out?"

"Yes, I'm going to put you out!" He noticed his voice had grown in volume and with it the fear on her face. He took a calming breath. "But not like you're thinking. Just get your things please, and meet me outside."

He started for the barn, but paused partway across the room. "Did Kin ever come home today?"

She shook her head.

Preston grunted. Perfect. Like he needed one more thing to worry about!

He turned for the door, grabbing up his coat on the way out. "Hurry up and get your things."

Hunt was seated at his usual place at the bar when his man, Samuel McGuff, entered and sank onto the stool next to him. Hunt sipped his drink. "Well?"

Samuel raised a finger to the barkeep, then pointed at the whiskey. "He wasn't gonna do it. He left the nitro at the base of a tree just outside of camp. He sat there for a while and I almost thought he'd changed his mind, but then…" He shrugged. "He tried to make a run for it. I had to shoot him."

Hunt cursed. "Did you kill him? What did you do with him?"

The bar keeper slid a half full glass into the space in front of Samuel.

Samuel shook his head. He downed the contents of the glass in one gulp before he replied, "He's not dead. I locked him in the stone storage shed out back. Figured I'd come in and see what you wanted to do. We leave him there and he'll most likely be dead by morning."

Hunt grunted. "Leave him. I don't have time to deal with such complications. But now I need you to ride to town and take care of this for me."

Samuel's eyes widened a little, but Hunt knew the man wouldn't let him down.

"You know where he left that vial of nitro?"

Samuel nodded.

"Good. The parson always leaves the church unlocked. All you need to do is put that nitro by the stove. But I got to thinking, you better hide it with something. Wouldn't want to take the risk of it being found before it blows. Maybe strap it to the underside of a chair. It might take it a few extra minutes to get warm enough to blow." He paused as a thought registered and he chuckled. "Unless someone decides to move the chair. Then it won't take long at all."

Samuel swallowed. "Right. Strap it to the underside of a chair near the fire."

Hunt nodded, then reached out and squeezed Sam's shoulder. "There will be a hefty bonus waiting for you when you get back. And I'll even guarantee you a week with Adelle, free of charge."

Samuel gave Hunt an appreciative smile. "You can count on me, boss."

Hunt smiled and sipped his drink as he watched Samuel step out into the dark.

Now it was time to start planning how he was going to expand his empire once the law was extinguished from this part of the country.

Chapter Twenty-one

$\mathcal{I}$t didn't take Aurora more than a minute to gather her belongings into the bandana they had been wrapped in when she first left Ma's shanty. She tied the four corners into a knot and tucked the bundle under one arm.

She paused in the main room and gave the place a scan. It was quite tidy for the home of two bachelors. Not that Kin could really be considered a bachelor yet. He was the same age as her, if she'd figured right. She realized that she was actually going to miss saying goodbye to him. It had been nice having a "big" brother while it lasted. She'd always been an only child, and now she recognized she'd liked the feeling of camaraderie that had existed between Kin and her.

She wasn't certain where the parson was taking her, but it seemed likely that she might not get to see Kin again. She wished he was here to give her a hard time about this whole situation. He would have known how to lighten the mood, somehow.

She rolled her eyes at herself. Best she get out to the barn before the parson came looking for her.

Parson Clay was waiting for her by the barn. She had hoped that the few minutes of separation would soften his irritation, even if only by a margin, but if anything, the hardness of his jaw and the glitter in his eyes indicated that he was even more angry than before.

"Can you ride?" he gritted, hardly even looking at her.

She nodded. "Well enough to stay on."

He dipped his chin and held out a hand to help her mount. Had the situation been less tense she might have chuckled, for he had tossed her into the saddle without ceremony several times since her arrival.

He led the way out of the barnyard, the horses' hooves making barely a sound in the dirt of the roadbed. Sparse clouds scuttled across the sky, blocking the starlight here and there. The breeze that blew was gentle, but in her thin shirt it seemed to cut like icicles. Though it didn't take them long to reach Liora's, Aurora was shivering by the time they arrived.

Again, like the most gallant of gentlemen, the parson helped her dismount. He glanced down at her. "You're cold. Why didn't you wear a coat?"

She shrugged. "The one I've been wearing at your place belonged to Kin."

His shoulders drooped wearily. "Yet another failure on my part."

Aurora frowned. Her heart pinched. She hated that she'd made him feel like a failure. "I didn't mean to—"

He held up a hand to cut off her apology. "I mean to say, I apologize. I should have noticed and offered you a coat." He wrapped the reins of both horses around the porch railing. "Let's get you inside."

Footsteps sounded in the yard behind them, and they both turned to find Joe approaching from the lean-to. Curiosity furrowed his brow. "Good evening."

Parson Clay nodded. "Joe." He glanced up toward the house. "Something's come up. Could I speak to Liora for a few minutes?"

Joe nodded. "Yeah sure." He led the way up the steps. "We just finished dinner. She and Tess are likely in the kitchen."

Joe knocked on the front door, and it was only a few moments before Aurora heard the latch sliding from its place. Liora peered out at them. "Parson! And Rory. Please come in." She stepped out of the way, holding the door for them.

Joe tipped his hat. "Evening to you." It was obvious that he was headed back to the lean-to.

But Parson Clay reached out a hand. "If you don't mind, I'd like you to stay. I might need your advice."

Joe's gaze bounced between Aurora and the parson. He nodded and followed them into the room.

"Rory's a girl."

Aurora studied her feet. Parson Clay didn't beat around the bush.

Audible gasps from three people filled the room. Aurora couldn't lift her gaze to any of them. She kicked at a knot in the pinewood floor.

"You Molly McClure's girl!" Tess exclaimed. "How'd I not see it?"

It was only a moment before Aurora felt Liora's arm slip around her shoulders. "Oh honey. I knew there was something I should've realized about you last Sunday but I couldn't quite pin it down. How old are you?"

Aurora chewed her lip and clutched her bundle of clothes a little closer. "Seventeen."

All eyes in the room fell on the parson. He was twisting the brim of his hat through agitated fingers.

Joe broke the silence with a chuckle. "Well, I'll be." He grinned at Liora. "Looks like you and I will be off the gossip train for at least a couple days."

The parson darted a razor-sharp glare at Joe. A muscle in his jaw bulged. "Cut it out, Joe. What am I going to do?"

Joe turned serious. "Seems like tomorrow's gathering might

be providential. You're going to announce what happened. Say you brought her to Liora's the moment you found out the truth. Which I assume is true?"

The parson looked hurt. "Of course it's true!" His gaze narrowed on Aurora. "I only found out the truth five minutes before we rode out to head this way."

Liora's arm about her shoulders tightened. "You poor dear. What distress has you disguised as a boy?"

Aurora wasn't sure she could get the whole story out without bursting into tears. And drat if just the thought of tears hadn't summoned them. She covered her eyes with one hand, biting on her lower lip in an attempt to ground herself in the moment. There was nothing to cry about right here and now.

But it had been a terrible month. She'd been strong when Mama passed. Strong when she'd helped the parson prepare her for burial. Strong as she'd walked away from her grave.

She swiped tears and sniffed, gritting her teeth and willing herself to get under control, but her voice was useless to her in this state.

The parson's voice was soft when he spoke. "She said she was running from John Hunt."

Aurora darted him a glance and was surprised to see genuine compassion in the green of his eyes.

Liora hissed out a breath. "I might have known that snake, Hunt, would be part of this. Do you owe him money?"

Aurora shook her head and managed, "Pa's violin...should have...covered what...Ma owed."

Liora wrapped both arms around her now, and squeezed Aurora to her side. "You did right to run. And I'm so glad that God brought you here. Come with me and I'll show you to your room. We'll get you some proper clothes to wear. Then you can tell me your story."

Aurora couldn't deny that donning a dress once more would be some comfort. She tossed a glance over her shoulder just before Liora led her from the main room. Joe and the parson were in deep conversation, and the parson's gaze hadn't left her.

But at least it had softened a touch.

Kin awoke in a dark room on a cold floor. He started to sit up, but then fell back with a cry of pain. With his fingers he carefully assessed the throb in his side. His shirt and pants were stiff and hard with blood. He guessed that might be a good sign. At least the bleeding had stopped.

He'd been shot?

He scrunched his eyes and tried to remember what had happened. Yes. He'd been shot. Then knocked out. He'd come to off and on as Hunt's man had hauled him back to town. Draped across the front of the man's horse, as he had been, the pain both in his head and his side had been severe and unforgiving. Each time he'd tried to stay awake, but each time a jostle or lurch had sent him back to the ease of blackness.

But now there was something he must think on. It swirled at the back of his mind, a phantom that couldn't quite be grasped. He tried to fight through the blur of his thoughts. Something he needed to do before morning.

Morning... That thought pierced him with awareness. There was a task he needed to complete before morning. He pressed a finger and thumb to his eyes, willing away the weariness from his long night of carousing and the agony from his injuries.

He needed to concentrate. What was it he needed to concentrate on?

The vision of a woman in a red dress undulated, just out of focus.

The saloon at the camp. The drinking.

His eyes widened in the darkness as memory flooded him.

John Hunt was going to blow up the Wyldhaven church, and Kin had to stop it.

He forced himself to sit up, gritting his teeth to block the groan that begged for escape. Outside he could hear crickets. And a bullfrog. That meant it was night.

His heart hammered. Which night? How long had he been out? Was he too late? Had everyone already been killed?

He had to try to escape and find out.

His eyes had adjusted to the dark a little now, and he could see that he was in a shed of some kind. But it contained nothing except some old rotting pallets. The walls felt like stone, cold and hard. But the floor was dirt.

Kin tried to dig his fingers into it, but it was packed hard. And so cold it must be close to freezing tonight.

He realized then that his body was shaking. Maybe the ground wasn't so cold as his body was feverish. And thirsty. He swept a dry tongue over dry lips.

Merely a sip of water would taste like heaven right about now.

Heaven. He snorted. It was the scent of heaven that had gotten him into this predicament in the first place. It was probably best he quit thinking about heaven and get to digging.

He fumbled through the darkness until he found a loose board. He could see a strip of moonlight coming in beneath the door. He pulled himself toward it. All the walls would have a foundation that he'd likely never be able to dig past. But the door... If it wasn't guarded, he might be able to dig out from under the door.

Holding his breath, he knocked on the wood. The crickets and the bullfrog stilled, but there was no other response.

"Anyone out there?" His voice rasped from thirst and lack of use. There still was no response so he called out again, a little louder this time.

Still no reply.

Kin relaxed a little and willed his fevered hands to grip the board. "God, if you're out there, I could really use a little help to save a group of good people. Your people."

There was no response to that either, but then, he hadn't expected one.

Kin set to scraping away at the floor in front of the door.

But it was slow going. The ground really was as hardpacked as he'd first thought.

Preston was still shaking his head by the time he arrived back at his parsonage. He unsaddled the horses and rubbed them down, then took time to clean the tack before heading into the house.

There was still no sign of Kin. This made the second night in a row that he hadn't come home.

Preston grunted. "Living for the world will suck the living energy right out of you and leave you dryer than ancient bones, Kin. One of these days you're going to ask me how I know."

A shiver swept over Preston's shoulders as a thought occurred. Kin would only be able to ask that question if he was alive. Preston gave his head a shake. He'd never been a worrier until he'd taken Kin under his roof, but there was something about being responsible for the well-being of another that burdened a person clean to their very heart.

And right now, that burden was burning in his chest like a holy fire.

"God, wherever he's at, get a hold of him, please. And

between now and then, keep him safe, would You? Even if he doesn't deserve it?" The worry eased a bit, but somehow Preston knew that a good deal of his night would be spent tossing and turning in prayer for his errant ward.

He stepped into the bedroom and sank onto the edge of his bed. As he tugged off his boots, his focus landed on the small pallet Rory had been sleeping on each night. *Aurora.* She had rolled it up and tucked it against the base of the wall.

He flopped back on the bed with a groan. Here was more to pray about.

"Lord, who knew that being a good Samaritan came with so many risks? I hope You're paying attention to my little corner of the world? Might be that this servant of Yours is about to be run out of the church on a rail. Sure would be nice if You paved the way for a little merciful understanding from the townsfolk, tomorrow. And if You'd give me the right words to say, that'd be appreciated too."

Kin's side felt as though it was on fire. And his fingers ached and bled. The rotting boards kept breaking after only a few scrapes against the rocky soil. The hole he'd managed to dig wasn't big enough for a good-sized dog to squeeze through, much less someone his size. Too bad he'd inherited his Pa's broad shoulders and height. If he was a smaller man, this task might be easier.

He collapsed back against the stone wall, energy nearly spent, and vision blurred with fever.

He wasn't going to make it. Already he could see the ground outside growing lighter. It was almost dawn, and he still had to find a way to get back to town.

His thirst demanded attention. His mouth was so dry

he could feel that his lips had cracked. His gaze fell to the small pile of dirt he'd pushed to one side of the doorway. He remembered a trick Pa had once told him about. He lifted a pebble from the dirt, rubbed it against his trousers to clean it as best he could, and then put it in his mouth. Sucking on the rock, soon drew needed moisture to his mouth and lessened his body's cry for water.

With renewed energy he went back to work on his hole.

But the board he was using snapped in two.

Kin flung the pieces across the room with a grunt of anger. "Why does everything in life have to be so hard?" He hauled himself back across the space to the pile of pallets.

It was the sound of metal clanking against wood that froze him. He patted his hand carefully across the ground in front of him. His fingers were so cold, he couldn't recognize the feel of anything. He brought his hands up to his mouth, blowing warm air against the aching digits. Then he tucked his fingers into his armpits and waited for a count of ten. He fumbled his hands across the ground again. This time his heart started hammering. His fingers wrapped around the hand-sized piece of metal and he scrabbled back to the door to examine it in the pale light. It was an iron log spike. The kind hammered into logs so they could be hauled behind a mule or horse. Pointed on one end, it had a flat metal loop on the other to chain off to.

Kin gripped the spike firmly in one hand, elation threading through him. "Thank God."

He set to digging with renewed vigor.

Chapter Twenty-two

Saturday morning arrived with sparkling sun glistening on the morning frost. Liora felt a thrill of joy wash through her as she basted egg whites on the top of her pie and popped it back into the oven to brown. She couldn't be more ecstatic for Charlotte and Reagan.

The water on the stove had come to a boil and she added the oats and gave them a stir.

Joe had offered to take them all into town a little early so that she could deliver her food to the church. He had spent the week cutting and stripping logs and now had enough that he had said they could start building the barn first thing come spring. He'd also added on to the lean-to to make a stall for his Paint and to add a fourth wall so that he would have a warm place to sleep this winter. Liora was thankful to have that worry off her mind.

And another thing to be thankful for was that neither John Hunt nor his men had bothered them all week. But—a shiver touched the base of Liora's neck—there was a feel of danger looming on the horizon. She felt it every time she stepped out the door. Of course, Joe's hyper-vigilance probably didn't help alleviate that feeling much. He rode out multiple times a day to check the perimeter of the property and make sure no one was waiting in ambush. And each time she or one of the girls wanted to go outside, he made them wait until he'd stepped into the yard and done a thorough scrutiny of the hills all around.

Tess stepped into the kitchen wearing one of her new dresses—the cornflower blue one that she had declared to be her favorite. She smoothed her hands over the front self-consciously. "Does it look all right?" Tess couldn't have been prouder when she had come home last evening and announced that Jacinda had allowed her to sew on the dress's buttons.

Liora grinned broadly and pulled the girl into a quick embrace. "You look absolutely beautiful. It really brings out the blue of your eyes!"

"And that's the truth." Joe stepped into the kitchen and gave Tess a quick wink. The girl blushed to the roots of her hair and busied herself at the sink.

"Is Aurora awake?" Liora hadn't seen the girl come out of her room this morning. "Breakfast will be ready in a moment." She gave the oatmeal on the stovetop another stir.

Tess shrugged. "Not sure. Her room's been mighty quiet."

"Have some porridge." Liora lifted the pot of oats to draw their attention to it, then set it on a trivet on the sideboard. "I'd best go check on Aurora." Liora nodded Tess's attention toward the stove. "Mind the pie, would you? It only needs five minutes to brown."

"Yes'm."

Joe poured himself a cup of coffee. "The wagon is hitched up and ready to go as soon as you ladies are."

"Thank you," Liora called over her shoulder as she hurried toward Aurora's room. She knocked on the door. "Rory? Can I come in?"

Silence rang in response.

Liora's heart rate picked up. Had the girl run off?

She turned the handle slowly and peered around the edge of the door.

Aurora lay on the bed, staring out the window adjacent. The sheets were fisted in one hand that trembled near her chin, and her eyes were red and glistening.

"Oh, darling. I'm so sorry." Liora sank onto the bed and smoothed Rory's hair back from her face.

"I'm not coming to town. I can't face all those people." Rory's voice was dry. Brittle. Barely audible.

Liora poured a cup of water from the pitcher on the nightstand and urged her to sit up. She really didn't want to leave Rory here on her own. "Here. Have a drink of water."

She was gratified to see Rory down the whole cup before she curled into her pillow once more.

Liora tried again. "I'd really like for you to come to town with us. It might not be safe here."

Aurora gave a sniff. "No. I'm not going to be there when that man tells everyone what a liar I am."

Liora's lips thinned. "He's not going to say it like that."

Aurora shrugged. Swiped angrily at her cheek. "It's what he thinks."

"I'm certain he was simply in shock last night. If he said anything unkind, I'm sure he'll be the first to offer an apology. It really would be safer for you to join us."

Aurora shook her head, jaw jutted in stubborn refusal. "I survived living in the camp in a thin-walled shanty where John Hunt could barge in whenever he pleased. I think I'll be fine here in a log home with doors that lock." There was a touch of bitterness to the words, and Liora's heart tugged at the sight of the girl's fresh tears.

She gave a sigh. She couldn't force her to come. She smoothed a hand over Rory's hair. "All right, you don't have to come. Only...I'm expected. You're sure you'll be all right on your own?"

Aurora sniffed. "I'll be fine." She tacked on almost as an afterthought, "Thank you."

Liora stood reluctantly. "I'll leave you a bowl of porridge in the icebox. You can heat it in the warming oven when you get hungry. And I'll bring you back a plate of food from the gathering."

Aurora's face scrunched further and her voice was tighter when she said again, "Thank you."

Despite Aurora's reassurance that she would be fine, Liora couldn't banish her disinclination to leave her at the cabin on her own. She eased the girl's door shut and hurried back to her room. She would ask Joe what he thought, but first she must hurry and dress. Joe and Tess were waiting on her.

Joe... She tried not to think too much on how she enjoyed having him pop into her kitchen each morning. Or about the warmth in his eyes as he'd watched her over the rim of his coffee cup just a bit ago.

She quickly changed from her workday dress into the green ensemble that she'd had Jacinda make for special occasions and then assessed herself in the mirror. She loved this outfit. The green fitted jacket had a large bow at the back, and the full skirt had three tiers of tassel-fringe around it. Perhaps a bit extravagant for the town of Wyldhaven, but it had appealed to her when Jacinda had presented her with the idea and each time she wore it she was glad they had chosen this design.

And today she would need the confidence boost.

She'd decided that for Joe's sake she was going to try to enjoy herself today. And she'd figured out a way to get her pie and roast to the church without anyone knowing they were hers, so that should make the enjoyment easier to come by.

The reminder of the pie sent her scrambling back to the kitchen, but Tess had already retrieved it from the oven along with the roast. "Aurora be all right?" she asked.

Liora wagged her head indecisively. "I suspect she's just feeling the loss of her ma now that she's giving herself some time to mourn." She met Joe's gaze across the table. "She says she doesn't want to come to town with us. Do you think we should let her stay?"

Joe twirled his coffee cup, staring out the window at the surrounding land. "I don't like it."

"I don't either. But I tried to encourage her to join us and she flatly refused."

Joe sighed. "I don't suppose there's much we can do about it then. As long as she keeps the doors locked, she'll probably be okay." He stood, draining the last of his coffee. "I'll get the wagon."

With one last worried glance toward Rory's room, Liora stepped over to the stove. *Lord, you'll have to be her protection today.* With a sigh, she lifted the pot roast into one side of her basket.

"That roast beef..." Tess inhaled appreciatively. "Smells deeevine. Makes a gal wish she hadn't et such a big breakfas'." She giggled.

Liora gave her forearm an appreciative squeeze. It didn't escape her that Tess was trying to lighten the mood.

"And that pie!" Tess's eyes sparkled as Liora tied a towel around the pie to help keep it warm. "Such a sight! I like how ya used extra crust to make them flowers for the edge." She grinned at Liora over her shoulder as she slipped on her coat and stepped over to wait near the door.

Liora smiled her thanks. It pleased her to see Tess relaxing enough to interact with her on such a level. This was probably the most Tess had said since her arrival.

It also pleased Liora to have her work appreciated. She had gone out of her way to make the top of the pie beautiful. She had cut varying sizes of flower shapes out of the crust and then layered them atop one another in a cascade around the edge. From the extra dough, she'd cut small leaves and pasted them on with egg whites to act as glue. The flowers, combined with the braid she'd done along the edge of the pie, had come together rather nicely, even if she did think it herself. Berry juice seeped through the holes, staining the edges a dark red that added to the floral effect. She just hoped it was going to taste as good as it looked.

She slipped the pie into the basket along with the rolls she'd baked the evening before and the fresh butter that she'd taught Tess how to churn while the rolls baked. A jar of apple butter that Dixie had helped her make last fall would add the perfect tart touch.

She gave Tess a nod. "I'll just grab my coat and be right out. Please let Joe know we are ready."

Liora made sure all the doors were locked tight and said one more prayer for Aurora's safety as they rode out of the yard.

When they arrived in town, Joe reined the horses toward the church. Liora started to hold out a hand to stop him, but it trembled something fierce, and she thought better of it and tucked it away before he could see. She had to proceed with caution here, for she knew Joe would not approve of, nor be pleased with, her plan for her contributions. But what he didn't know wouldn't hurt him. "I'm sure the ladies are preparing the food over at Dixie's. Why don't you drop Tess and me off there?" She held her breath, had he noticed the quaver in her voice?

He gave her a hard look, but did pull to the other side of the road and stop at Dixie's front door.

"Thank you. We'll meet you over at the church." Scooping up her basket, she motioned for Tess to follow her and scuttled inside before he could voice any of the questions she could see in his expression.

Dixie was busy in the kitchen putting the finishing touches on her chocolate cake. Her mother, Rose, leaned over a large pan of crispy golden chicken at the stove.

"Morning." Liora greeted. "You both remember Tess?"

Tess gave a little curtsey.

"Morning!" Dixie greeted them both with exuberant hugs.

Rose was more sedate, but no less welcoming.

"We were just about to head over." Dixie gave the frosting on her cake one last swirl with her knife and stepped back to eye her handiwork. "Flynn should be here at any moment to help us carry everything over."

Rose used tongs to layer the chicken into a cloth-lined basket.

Dixie suddenly spun toward them with a blink. "Aren't you supposed to have someone else with you?" Her voice quieted on the last few words as she peered behind them, obviously looking for Rory.

"The parson must have already spoken with you?" Liora figured caution was the better part of valor since she wasn't completely sure Dixie actually knew about Rory and she didn't want to break the parson's confidence.

Dixie grinned and nodded, her eyes sparkling with mirth. "He was in quite a state last night. Arrived here sometime well after midnight. Said he'd been trying to sleep, but simply couldn't, and he wanted to talk to Flynn and get his advice."

"And what did Flynn tell him?"

"Same thing as Joe did, from what we can tell. That he should simply come clean and that all of us know he would never touch the girl, or have her in his house if he'd known who she really was. So where is she?" Dixie dropped her frosting bowl and knife into the kitchen sink and spun to face them, removing her apron.

Liora gave a little shake of her head. "I think it was all rather much for her. Parson Clay was quite angry with her. And I think she'd been putting off mourning for her ma. She didn't want to come today, and I can't say as I blame her what with all the…" She caught herself just in time. She felt her face heat at the fact that she'd been about to mention the gossipy women in such a condescending tone. *Oh Lord, how I need to be more like you.* "Well, anyhow, I don't blame her."

"Neither would I." Rose gave a firm nod of her head.

Dixie looked sympathetic. "The poor dear. We'll have to remember to send her home a plate."

"Yes. I promised her as much."

Flynn entered the kitchen just then. "Mmmm. Smells like heaven in here! Morning, Liora. Tess." He nodded to them, and then gave his wife an unhurried, lingering kiss.

Dixie finally pulled back with a giggle and swatted him with the apron in her hand. "You scoundrel. Can you please carry food over to the church? You can start with the cake, but then come back for the chicken."

Liora set her basket on the sideboard. "And Flynn? If you don't mind, could you carry this basket over for me? I'm afraid Joe's gone down to the livery and the basket is some heavier than I first thought."

Tess gave her a frown of curiosity, but held her silence.

Flynn offered a little bow, apparently none-the-wiser to her little deception. "Happy to oblige." He left with the cake in one hand and Liora's basket gripped in the other.

When Liora turned back to look at Dixie, she found her friend's gaze on her. "You shouldn't let them get to you."

Liora swallowed. She couldn't talk about this right now or she would end up in a crumpled heap of tears on a day that should be nothing but celebration. She tugged her gloves from her fingers and tucked them into her reticule. "Is there anything I can carry over for you?"

Dixie's expression indicated the conversation was not over, but all she said was, "You could carry the stack of green tablecloths there. And Tess if you don't mind, bring the bucket of greenery?" She nodded toward it by the back door.

Dixie picked up a stack of lace linens and Rose lifted a crate full of crystal candle holders and candles. Together they headed across the street and past the empty lot to the church.

At some point this week the men of the town had emptied the church of almost all the pews and set up a long row of tables near one wall. There would be room to have food served down both sides of the tables, and still leave plenty of area for people to visit and mingle.

Mrs. King and Mrs. Hines were directing everyone to place their food on the few pews that lined the wall opposite from the tables. "There you are!" Mrs. Hines snipped at Dixie. "Goodness. Here we are with food arriving and no place to put it yet."

"I'm sorry, Pricilla. We're here now and it should only take us a moment."

Liora didn't meet Pricilla's gaze when she hurried past with the tablecloths. It didn't take her and the other ladies long to get the tablecloths smoothed, the lace squares laid out to form diamonds on the table tops, and the greenery woven down the middle of it all. Then they set to transferring the food dishes from the pews to the tables.

"I saw Flynn carrying the basket. Sorry about that. I should have thought to carry it for you."

Liora, who had leaned across the table to place a basket of rolls on the other side, started at the sound of Joe's voice beside her. She stood and found him so near that her shoulder bumped into his chest. His hand came to rest against the small of her back, and at the look of concern in his dark eyes, her conscience pricked her. She opened her mouth, but Tess, who was just setting a dish down across the table, beat her to it.

"Basket got some heavier the moment we reached Miz Dixie's kitchen. Ain't that something?"

Joe frowned. "What?"

Liora shook her head. "It's nothing."

"Wait a minute." His focus flashed to the two women in feather hats still gabbing by the church doors, before it flitted back to her. "Those two again, huh?" There was compassion in his voice.

Liora sighed. In as few words as possible, she explained what had happened the last time she'd brought a dish.

Joe's lips pinched into aggravation. "It's certainly a good thing the light of Jesus shines so strongly from those two, isn't it?" His wink urged her to good cheer.

She couldn't help but chuckle at his joke, even as she looked over at the two women. "You know... I think Ethel would actually be nice to me, but Pricilla influences her."

"You are some woman, Liora. Most women would meet them battle for battle. I admire your desire to seek peace. But you'll forgive me if I go to battle for you, hmmm?" She felt the gentle squeeze Joe gave to her shoulder before he walked away to join Flynn and the parson near the front.

Liora pondered as he walked away. Was it really her desire to bring peace? Or simply to avoid humiliation?

And what did Joe plan to do? She knew better than to fight him about that this time, but... *Lord, please don't let him humiliate me.*

Her cheeks burned. There was the answer to her question. Most definitely her motives had selfishly been to avoid embarrassment.

Lord, am I ever to be making decisions for the wrong reasons? Help me to be more like you.

She determined that at some point today she would go out of her way to try to make a true and real peace with both Mrs. Hines and Mrs. King.

And she was certainly going to need the Lord's help to make that happen!

oe could still feel the heat of his anger as he approached the parson and Doc. He needed to calm down. Giving Mrs. Hines too much space in his mind and thoughts could lead to no good. Indigestion. That was all he was likely to get. A burning case of indigestion.

Doc was speaking to Preston in low tones.

Joe hesitated. "Am I interrupting?"

The parson shook his head. "No. No. Please join us. Flynn here was just giving me a last-moment jolt of gumption."

Joe laid a hand on his shoulder. But he'd already said his piece about the parson's predicament, so he asked instead, "Where's Kin? I haven't seen him around today."

Preston scrubbed the back of his neck. "He hasn't come home for a couple nights. I'm afraid to think where he might be."

Flynn chuckled. "Teenagers. What is he now? Seventeen?"

Preston nodded. "Yeah. If only my sole concern for the lad was the normal insubordination common in that age. But I'm afraid... Well..." The parson's face paled a little. "Truth is, I'm afraid he's a lot like I was at his age. And he's going to be in for some rough lessons."

Joe exchanged a look with Flynn. This was the first he'd heard of the parson being a ruffian. Now was not the time to give him a hard time about it, however. "Wash generally gets through to him fairly well. Have you asked him to talk to him?" Joe nodded toward Washington Nolan, who was openly flirting with Zoe Kastain in the corner.

"No. Maybe I'll try that today. He's not in trouble with the law, is he? I half expected he might have been arrested again."

Joe shook his head. "Not as far as I know."

"Well that's a relief, anyway. By the way, Joe, you're handy with construction...any idea how the Kings' cat might have gotten into the sanctuary?"

"What?" Joe tried to catch up to the topic change.

Preston nodded. "Yes. You heard right. When I came over early this morning, their cat was in here, curled up under the stove. I shooed it out."

Joe chuckled. "Well, with your policy of leaving the doors unlocked so people can come in anytime to pray, it's likely that someone came in and the cat followed them, then got left inside. But we can check to see if there's any other way it could have gotten in also."

"Joe?" Liora approached. "Could you get a fire going? With all the in and out we've been doing, we've had the door propped open. We can't have the bride catching cold only a few weeks before her wedding. And they should be arriving soon."

Joe allowed a lazy smile. "Which bride are you talking about?" He was gratified to see a pretty blush sweep across her cheeks.

"Joseph Robert!" She whispered his name fiercely.

The parson and Doc both gave him congratulatory socks to his shoulders.

Joe realized he may have started something he shouldn't have. He chuckled. "Now don't go spreading rumors fellas. I'm still trying to convince her."

Doc leaned toward Liora. "How could a gal resist such a fine specimen of a man?"

Liora's face was even redder now. "Joe? The fire?"

He tipped her an imaginary hat, since his was hanging in the church entry. "Yes, ma'am."

She giggled and hurried off, and my how that sound did his heart good.

Tess sat on a chair by the stove. He gave her a nod as he approached. "You having a good time, Tess?"

She smiled. "Yessuh. Miss Liora said she didn't need no more help, and I'm just sittin' here ponderin' and enjoyin' the hubbub."

Joe opened the stove door as he scanned the room behind them. "Hubbub sure about sums it up, doesn't it?"

The church was full of townsfolk now. And the tables, laden with food, didn't look like they had a spare inch for another dish. David Hines dashed over to the desserts and snatched a cookie from one of the plates. In the blink of an eye, half of it disappeared into his mouth. Crumbs trailed down the boy's freckled chin. Mrs. Hines hoisted her skirts and scurried toward him. "David! I do declare! We haven't even had lunch yet. No more sweets! And I mean it."

David hung his red curly head, cookie dropping to his side, shoulders slumping. "Yes ma'am," he mumbled.

Joe was gratified to see Mrs. Hines give the boy an affectionate pat. "Very well then. Run along and play."

The moment her back was turned, David snagged another cookie off of the plate. Using his body as a shield, he kept the new cookie carefully hidden from his stepmother as he dashed past her to join his friends in the corner of the sanctuary.

Tess giggled.

And Joe couldn't help but grin, himself. "Guess that boy's bound to keep her on her toes."

Tess nodded. "Yessuh."

Joe's focus shifted to Liora. Would she ever change her mind about his proposal? Give him children that would keep them both scurrying to catch up?

She looked up then and met his eyes across the room, as though she'd been able to feel him watching her.

He let all the love he was feeling shine through his eyes.

Her face turned a pretty pink and she deliberately turned back to her conversation with Dixie and Rose.

He grinned as he turned back to the stove and found Tess's gaze fixed directly on him.

Her eyes sparkled. "You ever gonna ask her to marry you?"

He gave a roll of this shoulders. "Already did. She turned me down flat. Twice."

Tess hummed a thoughtful note. "She'll come to her senses one o' these days. My mama woulda said she looks at you like you done hung the moon."

"Does she?" Joe chuckled. "Could have fooled me. But if she asked me to hang it, I'd sure give it my best shot."

Tess gave a definitive nod. "She know that too."

Kin leaned over the neck of the horse he'd stolen from in front of the Timber Saloon. Pain punched him with each hoofbeat, but he was nearly to town now and wasn't about to give into the need for rest when he was this close to victory.

He searched the horizon, still half worried that at any moment he was going to see a huge black plume of smoke tower into the sky. But there was still nothing but the crystalline expanse of turquoise-blue.

"Hah!" He slapped the ends of the reins against the horse's rump, urging it to take the last hill into town at a gallop. The horse surged past the livery as a thin gray vapor wisped from the church stovepipe. "No!" He leaned so low he was practically flat against the horse's foam-flecked neck. "Hah!"

The horse flagged. Stumbled. He'd ridden it too hard. It stopped in front of McGinty's, sides heaving, staggering a bit.

Kin leaped from the saddle and surged toward the church, clutching at the pain in his side.

Another puff of smoke billowed from the church's chimney.

Terror stung Kin's eyes.

God, please. He didn't even have time to be surprised by his prayer. He just kept running.

Why had the parsonage been built so far from the other buildings in town?

Joe finally got the kindling in the woodstove to light. He'd almost had the fire going a couple times, but each time a gust of wind had blown down the chimney and extinguished the flames. This time, however, the blaze was going strong enough that it should catch. He shut the door of the stove almost all the way, leaving about an inch of gap so the stove could get a good draw of air. In a moment he would add the sticks of wood, he had waiting nearby.

Tess rubbed her hands up and down her arms. "That warmth sure feels nice."

Joe smiled at her. "We'll have this stove cranking out so much heat it will drive us all from the room in just a moment."

"All 'cept that one, I s'pect." With a grin, she nodded her head to where a small freckled hand reached slowly out from beneath the long green tablecloth at the dessert table and fumbled to find the cookie plate.

David Hines. Under the table. Attempting to sneak cookies.

Joe chuckled.

At the front of the room, Parson Clay cleared his throat loudly. "May I have everyone's attention? Before Reagan and Charlotte get here and we begin the festivities, I have something I need to...say to everyone."

A hush fell over the room as everyone turned expectant attention toward the parson.

He slipped one finger beneath the collar of his shirt, and it was almost more than Joe could do to keep a chuckle from escaping. He didn't envy the man the task before him, but at the same time, he knew that everyone in the town was going to understand. Well—Joe's gaze darted to Mrs. Hines—almost everyone.

Preston's volume was a bit thin when he continued. "Last week, many of you met a young man in my charge named Rory."

Murmurs of acknowledgment filled the room.

"Well... it turns out that—"

"Get out of the church!"

Joe frowned and glanced toward the double doors at the back.

"Everyone get out!"

Was that Kin? What was the kid up to now? Footsteps pounded up the stairs.

Everyone turned to see.

The double doors at the back burst inward and Kin stood between them. His hair stood up at all angles. He was covered in dirt from the smudges on his face to the mud that clung to his boots. And blood covered one side of him from hip to knee. He heaved for breath.

Joe felt his jaw drop open. What in—

"Out!" Kin's wild gaze found the parson's. "Get everyone out now!"

No one moved. Everyone was too stunned by the outburst and Kin's appearance to follow his instructions.

Kin stomped one foot, then hissed in pain and bent to clutch at his side. "John Hunt said he would blow up the church! Everyone out!"

A pregnant moment of frozen shock burst into chaos. Women screamed. Men cried out. Children wailed, and everyone surged toward the doors at once.

A veritable logjam of bodies crashed together in the exit, and Kin fought the current to wade deeper into the room. He was yelling something about the fire, but Joe's one concern was to get Liora and Tess from the building. Where were they?

He spun Kin around and nudged him back toward the doors, urging Parson Clay to move along with everyone else. He searched the room, almost everyone was out now, Liora and Tess must have already been swept outside.

Joe was the last to leave the room. A glance behind him showed the sanctuary empty. Relief coursed through him.

At the base of the steps, Joe grabbed Kin's arm. He needed to ask him some questions, but first... He searched the lawn. Only when he saw Liora huddled under the oak tree with Dixie and Rose, and Tess on the lawn just a few paces away, did he relax. Doc was making his way purposefully across the lawn toward Kin, his doctor bag in his hand.

Everyone faced the church and an expectant hush fell over the crowd. All eyes fixed on the sanctuary doors as if at any moment the building might ignite into a firebomb.

Parson Clay raised his hands and his voice. "All right, everyone, we're all safe now. Is everyone okay? Does everyone have all their loved ones? Back up. Let's all back up."

Doc stopped by their side. "Kin, let me take a look at that."

Joe returned his focus to Kin and stopped Doc from escorting

Kin away. "You can examine him right here." He propped his hands on his hips and gave the kid a hard look. "Out with it. I need details."

Kin swallowed, lifting one arm so Doc could get a look at his side. "I was in Hunt's saloon a couple nights back. He said I bought everyone drinks, though I don't remember it. Anyhow, he said I owed him thirty dollars but that I could pay it off by bringing nitroglycerin to this gathering." Kin trembled and winced when Doc probed his side. "I told him I would because I couldn't see any other way out of there, but then I hid the nitro by a tree. They saw me and captured me. Locked me in a shed... The ground was near frozen, but I managed..." He waved a bloody hand as if how he'd escaped wasn't important. "I knew I had to come and..." His gaze fixed on the church and his words trailed away in befuddlement as if even he was surprised the building was still standing.

Joe narrowed his eyes on the boy. "So you left your nitro by some tree, but you figure he had someone else plant some?" Joe's gaze also swung to the building. *The cat.* The cat could have gotten in if the door had been opened...

"He's John *Hunt.*" Kin let the words hang as though they should be sufficient explanation, but when Joe only gave him a hard look, the kid's shoulders slumped. "He told me to hide the nitro behind the stove so that when a fire was lit..." Kin's worried gaze turned to the smoke drifting up from the chimney. "I just figured... better safe than sorry. I didn't want anyone getting hurt."

"What a mess." Joe dropped a hand on Kin's shoulder. "You did the right thing. But that fire's been going for some time now. Likely an explosion would have happened already. Nitro is pretty volatile. I'll go back in and—"

Across the lawn, Mrs. Hines screeched. "Davey! Davey? Has

anyone seen David?" She lifted her skirts and twirled around, searching faces.

A low murmur lifted from the townsfolk as everyone glanced around trying to find the boy.

Jerry Hines leapt onto a stump and searched over everyone's heads for his son. "David, lad? Where are you?"

A queasy feeling suddenly dropped into the pit of Joe's stomach. He pictured the small freckled hand easing out from beneath the tablecloth and fumbling to find the plate of cookies.

"Dear Lord!" He offered the prayer even as he turned toward the church, but Tess was already disappearing through the double doors. "Tess! No!" Joe took the steps two at a time.

He landed on the top step, and reached for the brass handle on the righthand door.

BOOM!

A wall of hot air blasted him backward off the steps. He hit the lawn on his back, tumbled over a few times, then lay limp.

Joe fought for breath. Unnatural silence. Ringing ears. Smoke.

Everything...black.

The explosion knocked Liora off her feet. It took her a moment to be able to move. She rolled to her hands and knees and gave her head a shake. The grass was cool beneath her palms.

So much smoke.

She coughed, settled back against her ankles, and tried to see through the haze.

All around her, townsfolk who'd also been knock down, clambered to their feet. Beside her, Rose and Dixie helped each other stand. Dixie had a trickle of blood running down her face from a cut near her hairline. Rose cradled one arm.

A gust of wind cleared the haze momentarily and Liora blinked at the chaos all around. The Kings were just helping each other to their feet. Ewan McGinty, long hair all askew, had one hand to his forehead and was staring all around, mouth hanging open in shock. And in the background, the church burned.

Joe.

His name settled into her heart and mind like a little piece of home in a time of war.

Where was he?

Ewan reached down a hand to help her up.

He said something, but she couldn't make it out through the ringing in her ears.

Where was Joe? She couldn't think for the need of him.

And Tess?

They'd both been— Her gaze flew to the front steps of the church. Or more accurately, to where they used to be. Nothing remained now but a mangled mound of broken boards and jagged edges. She inhaled a gasp. The lungful of smoke bent her double with coughing.

A gap in the swirling smoke revealed Reagan and Charlotte running toward the church from town.

Sound crashed over Liora in a sudden wave. Screams. Cries. Wails. And the crackling of the ugly orange flames consuming the steeple that lay on the lawn a few feet away.

And through it all, only one thought, one need, pounded at her.

"Joe!" Liora lurched forward, staggering around clumps of people huddled together. "Tess?!"

The haze of smoke settled in again.

She waved a hand in front of her and squinted at each visage that came close enough for identity. "Joe?!"

She bumped into someone. The woman stood alone, sobbing, hands over her face.

Liora put an arm around her shoulders. "Everything's going to be all right." The rote words poured from her with no foundation of hope.

The woman looked at her, and with shock Liora realized it was Pricilla Hines.

Tear tracks streaked soot on the woman's face. "I can't find them," she sobbed. "Jerry...and David. I can't..."

Liora kept her grip around Pricilla's shoulders. "We'll find them. I'll help you. Have you seen Joe? Or Tess?"

Pricilla shook her head.

Liora searched the church lawn again. Some of the haze had dissipated now. And across the way, silhouetted by a backdrop of billowing smoke and orange flames, Liora spied Mr. Hines.

She nudged Pricilla. "There is Jerry. See?"

Just then a barrel of ten-year-old energy slammed into Pricilla's legs. "Ma!"

"Oh, Davey! Where have you been? We have to let your pa know you're all right." Pricilla rushed forward and Jerry cried out with joy and threw his arms around them both for a moment before he hoisted his son and cradled him against his shoulder. Pricilla wrapped them both in her arms and rested her head against Jerry's shoulder.

Jerry pushed David back from him. "Where were you?"

David pointed across the lawn to where a group of boys still huddled, staring at the burning church with jaws agape. "I was with the fellas."

Liora could only feel relief that he'd been found. She left the family to their joyous reunion and continued to search faces. And that was when she saw him.

"Joe!" Liora lifted her skirts and pushed past Bill Giddens.

Smoke swirled in to block her view again, but the image of Joe laying limp and unmoving on the church lawn, jaw slack, was seared indelibly into her memory. Liora pushed through the last of the crowd, then fell to her knees by his side.

One leg, bent at the knee, was pinned beneath him. And something had cut a long swath down one of his forearms. The arm rested across his chest, and blood pooled on his shirt beneath it.

"Joe, I'm right here. Doc!" she yelled, unable to take her eyes off the man she loved. She covered as much of the gash on his arm as she could with her palms and applied pressure. "Joe, don't you die on me, you hear? Doc!"

Someone knelt at her side. It was Jerry. "I think he thought David was in the church." Jerry set to rapidly undoing the buttons of his shirt.

Liora searched the lawn for Flynn.

Pricilla sat on the grass nearby with David cradled in her lap. Her focus was on Liora, and for the very first time ever, Liora felt no censure in the look. Only sorrow. Compassion.

Flynn bent over someone not far away, handing them his folded handkerchief.

"Doc!" Liora called again.

He looked up.

"It's Joe!"

He nodded. "Coming!"

Jerry stripped off his shirt. And Liora had only the briefest of instants to wonder what he was doing before he wadded the material into both his hands and then leaned over Joe's arm. He wanted to clamp his expensive store-bought shirt against Joe's wound.

"Thank you." Liora removed her hands and Jerry immediately applied pressure to the cut.

Liora looked next to Joe's leg. "His foot is pinned. Should we move his leg?"

"Yes." Flynn's deep baritone, coming from right behind her, filled her with reassurance. "Good thinking, Jerry." Flynn gave Jerry and his shirt a nod as he sank to his knees beside Liora. "Here. Help me roll him toward Jerry a bit and we'll get this leg straightened out."

Together they rolled him, until they could free his pinned foot. Flynn felt Joe's leg all up and down and bent it this way and that. He gave a relieved sigh. "I don't think anything is broken. He just landed on it awkwardly when he fell."

Tears of relief filled Liora's eyes. "Thank God."

Flynn moved to Joe's head next. He probed the skull from every angle and then sat back against his ankles.

Liora searched his face. "Will he wake up?"

Flynn gave a non-committal wag of his head. "I don't feel any obvious fractures but—"

Joe moaned. Rolled his head to one side. Fluttered his eyes open, and then frowned.

"Joe!" Liora leaned over him and cupped his stubbled cheek in one hand. "You're awake."

"What happen—"

"Joe, are you all right?" Reagan was suddenly there, leaning over them.

Kin stood behind him, a worried pinch to his pale lips.

Joe waved his good arm. "Everyone, please, back up."

He took hold of the hand Liora offered him and sat up slowly. He glanced around.

Jerry was still clumsily trying to hold compression against Joe's arm.

Joe's focus swept over Jerry's undershirt, and then dropped

down to the material pressed against his wound. "Thanks, Jerry. I've got it now."

Jerry backed off, and Liora was thankful to see that Joe kept the material in place with his free hand. "What happened?" He blinked at the chaos all around, confusion and pain darkening his eyes.

"There was an explosion. You were knocked unconscious," Flynn offered.

Jerry sank down beside Pricilla and put his arm around her. He bent forward and placed a kiss against his son's tousled head.

Joe's gaze landed on the boy, and then his eyes widened. "Tess and I thought David was in the church. She went back in to find him. Where is she?"

A hushed silence settled as everyone stood and looked around.

"Dear, God." Reagan exclaimed the prayer. "Flynn, help me."

Liora turned to look in the direction his attention lay fixed. Her heart stuttered to a stop. "No! Oh, Jesus, please no."

In the midst of the pile of jagged boards that had once been the church steps, a piece of material fluttered in the breeze. It was the cornflower blue color of Tess's new dress.

Chapter Twenty-four

Liora paced in Dixie's dining room, doing her best not to crumple into a heap of blubbering misery. Several of Wyldhaven's men were still digging Tess's body out from the lumber. Flynn and Reagan had uncovered her enough to confirm she had no pulse, but a heavy timber had prevented them from being able to extract her body right away.

Joe and Kin had wanted to stay and help with the task, but Flynn had insisted they come here and allow him to doctor them. They had both been upstairs getting cleaned and stitched. She had heard Kin come down and go out just a moment ago, but Joe still hadn't come down.

Liora felt hollow. Shallow. Used up. Numb.

All her efforts to help Tess. And for what? She'd actually gotten the girl killed. If Liora hadn't rescued her, hadn't angered John Hunt, none of this would have happened.

"Oh Jesus, what have I done?" Liora sank into a chair. It was the only prayer she had to offer. Nothing else would come to mind.

Dixie bustled back in with the tea she'd gone to fetch. She set a steaming cup before Liora, but the tea held no appeal.

Dixie sank into the seat beside her and reached over to cover Liora's hand. "I'm so sorry."

Liora nodded. Everyone was sorry. The table blurred beneath her gaze. "I killed her."

"No! You did not! You can't think like that. This was not your fault."

"I'm the one who angered John Hunt. The one who brought Tess to live with me. She wouldn't have been in that church if it wasn't for me. John Hunt wouldn't have blown the place up, if it wasn't for me."

Dixie shook her head. "Liora—"

Joe stepped into the dining room, his arm in a sling, his head bare, hair tousled. "You ready?" he asked.

"Yes." Liora stood. Gave Dixie a hug. "Thank you."

"Anytime." There was a sad look in Dixie's eyes. Liora knew that her friend was worried about her, but she had nothing to alleviate that worry at the moment. Not a particle of reassurance to offer.

She followed Joe out onto the porch in front of the boardinghouse.

In the street, several men stood talking. Reagan was there along with Zane Holloway. Kin and the parson, flanked Ewan McGinty and Washington Nolan.

In the distance, Liora could see Ben King and Jerry Hines lifting Tess's body into the back of a wagon. They laid her down gently. Covered her with a blanket Pricilla handed up to them. Liora entertained the fleeting bitter thought that they were giving her more respect in her death than they ever had while she lived.

Joe looked down at her and she realized she had taken hold of his arm and was squeezing it like she never planned to let go. "Where will they take her?"

He swept one hand down his face. "To the livery. Doc said Bill Giddens is already making the coffin."

Coffin. Such an unwelcome word. One that shouldn't have intruded on this day that was meant to be nothing but celebration.

"Give me just a minute?" Joe asked.

She withdrew her hand. Fiddled with her gloves. "Yes. Of course."

Joe walked over to the group of men in the street as the wagon started toward them from the church.

Liora watched the wagon start their way.

Dixie stepped out onto the porch, and stood next to her.

"Dixie, can I—"

"Yes. I've already prepared for it. We'll clean her up. And Jacinda is finishing the hem on the last dress you ordered for her. We can put her in that."

Liora's throat tightened up so that she could barely get out, "Thank you."

She stepped forward and met the wagon in the middle of the street, directing the men to carry Tess inside.

Tess may not have had much in this life, but Liora intended to see that she was buried proper, just like any other citizen of Wyldhaven would have been.

"What?!" John Hunt picked up a chair and hurled it across the saloon, an action he immediately regretted. For where this conversation had been a quiet, unnoticed affair before, now every eye in the room was on them.

He motioned for Samuel to follow him outside.

"You mean to tell me that only one person died?"

"Yes, sir. The girl, Tess."

Hunt grunted. "Well, at least she got what was coming to her for running out on me. Still... How is that possible?! All those lawmen are supposed to be dead!"

"It was the kid, sir." Samuel's face paled a little and he kicked his toe into a rut on the street. "Kin Davis. He escaped. Stole a horse and arrived in time to warn everyone to get out."

Hunt cursed Kin and then he turned the full ire of his anger on to Samuel. "You said he'd be dead by morning!"

Samuel trembled. "He must not have been as bad off as I figured. You want I should bring him around for a visit?"

Hunt cuffed Samuel upside the head. "No! You dolt. The kid can be dealt with any time. Right now we have bigger problems. All this trouble is because of that woman! And now the law is going to come snooping around."

"We could just lay low, sir. Nothing points back to you yet. Well..." His words trailed away as his eyes widened a little.

Hunt felt a pain in his chest as he cursed again. "Unless the kid talked." He slugged Samuel in the gut. "Do you think the kid talked?" He grabbed Samuel by the lapels of his collar. "Of *course* the kid talked!" Hunt thrust Samuel from him with all the emotion he was feeling. The man reeled backward and tumbled into the street, arms curled around his head. Hunt kicked a rock after him, and watched it careen down the street. "I trusted you! Took your word that the kid was already half way into boot hill. Now I have to think of a plan."

Samuel swallowed. Sat up slowly, not yet daring to rise. "We could just leave them be? Losing one or two women isn't going to hurt your business none. You head for the hills and lay low for a couple years and pretty soon they'll forget about you."

Hunt poured every ounce of hatred and anger he was feeling into a snarl. First he kicked his boot into the man's chest, knocking him onto his back, then he fell to his knees by his side and grabbed the man by his throat. "Are you a saphead?!"

Samuel's eyes bulged and he clasped at John's hand, gaping for air.

With a growl, John let him go. He would gladly have killed the man, but he still needed the dullard to do a few things for him.

Samuel coughed and gagged.

John rose and dusted himself off. He paced, kicked more rocks, ran through idea after idea in his mind, tossing them aside one by one. And then just as he was about to give up and start considering his man's idea that he make a run for it, the answer came to him.

Hands propped on his hips, he froze. Considered. Smiled.

He turned to face Samuel, stretching out a hand to help him off the ground.

Uncertainly, Samuel accepted his hand. Hunt could tell from his expression that he didn't know if he was being restored to his position or about to be killed. Good. Let him wonder.

Hunt dusted some dirt from the front of Samuel's shirt, and straightened his jacket by the shoulders. He smiled placatingly at the man. "If I let even one or two women go free, word will get out and soon they'll all be fleeing like rats from a sinking ship. Total control. It's the only way to run an empire such as the one I've built! And I've lost it. But I know just how to get it back. Now get me my horse. And get yourself one too. I need you to ride into Wyldhaven."

Liora sank down at one of Dixie's tables, and this time she did accept the tea Dixie placed in front of her.

They had done all they could. Washed Tess. Done up her hair. Dressed her in the fine, navy blue dress Jacinda had completed, and then laid her out carefully in the coffin Bill Giddens had constructed.

The service would be first thing in the morning. Surprisingly, not one person had protested when Liora requested that she be buried in the church's cemetery.

Dixie paced to the window and tugged the curtain aside. "Looks like they are still talking."

Joe and the Wyldhaven menfolk had been discussing strategy on how to capture John Hunt. Most had been ready to simply take the fight to Hunt. Give him a taste of his own medicine. But Reagan, Joe, and Zane had calmed the posse down and insisted they should do things by the letter of the law. They would ride out to Camp Sixty-Five and conduct a thorough search for evidence or witnesses who might testify to Hunt's involvement. Arrest him proper. Have a trial and pray to God he would hang like he deserved.

Dixie pressed her face closer to the window. "Looks like they are about to ride out."

Liora sighed. Best she go find Joe and say goodbye. Her heart pinched at the thought that it might be the last time she would need to do so. What if something happened to him? Her mind rebelled at the idea. Surely the Lord thought they'd all suffered enough today with Tess's coffin not five feet away and the church nothing but a heap of blackened debris across the street? Thankfully, the church had stood far enough apart from the other buildings of town that the fire hadn't spread.

She slid back her saucer and stood. "I need to go speak to Joe. Then I need to get back to the cabin. Aurora has been there on her own all day. She doesn't even know about Tess yet." The words choked her. Filled her throat with a lump that couldn't be vanquished. And to think, it had been Aurora that she'd been worried over this morning.

Dixie gave her a hug. "I'll see you again in the morning."

Liora nodded and pushed out onto the porch.

She didn't have to go far to find Joe. He and Reagan were having a heated discussion in front of the jailhouse.

"You can't keep me from riding along on this, Reagan!"

Relief immediately filled Liora. *Please God, make it true.*

Reagan's jaw was hard. "I can. And I just did. You and Kin both."

Liora noticed Kin standing off to one side, and he didn't look any more pleased than Joe did to have been denied permission to accompany the posse.

Reagan was still speaking to Joe. "You were knocked unconscious not more than an hour ago. And with that arm? Can you even shoot your gun?"

"You know I can." Joe ground out.

"Look, Joe, there's not a man here would doubt your grit..." Reagan's attention snagged on a lathered roan that wandered out from the alley by McGinty's. The horse's saddle was still strapped in place, and it held its head off to one side to avoid stepping on the trailing reins. "Whose horse is that?"

Kin glanced over and his eyes widened. He immediately headed for the horse. "That's just the roan I stole." He grabbed up the reins and led the mount toward the livery.

Reagan blinked at Joe. He opened his mouth, then gave his head a shake and started toward the other members of the posse who waited for him at the far end of town. "I'm not asking, Joe. I'm telling you. Sit this one out. Take Liora home. Make sure she's all right. There will be plenty more fights in the future."

Liora clenched her hands in her lap as she sat beside Joe on the wagon seat. He hadn't said a word since they'd left town. And in her present state of mind that was fine by her.

Only this morning they had ridden this very road with Tess jabbering excitedly about the beauty of the sun dancing through the evergreen treetops. Now they were headed home without her.

"I killed her." The words blurted out of her without her permission. She hadn't planned to have this discussion with Joe. He would only reassure her. Tell her it wasn't her fault.

Empty words with little truth behind them.

"S'pect the devil would like you to believe that. But don't let him lie to you. Evil is never happy when good tries to fight it. And that's what you were doing by helping Tess. Fighting evil."

Liora squirmed in her seat and fiddled with her gloves. Just as she had figured he would respond. Her heart wished she could believe him, but her rational side told her he was wrong. She let it drop. Changed the subject. "How's your arm?"

Joe gave her an assessing look, but then must have decided to allow her the topic change. He glanced down at the thick white bandage encasing his forearm. "It'll be fine. Doc said I was lucky nothing too critical got cut. Said it should heal up fine."

"Glad to hear it." And she truly was. When she thought of the terror that had clawed at her when she had first seen him lying on the church lawn... Her gaze drifted to the large blotch of dried blood on the front of his shirt. "Joe? When I thought I had lost you today..." Her throat closed off and she couldn't finish the thought.

"Whoa." Joe pulled the wagon to the side of the road and then turned to face her. His deep brown eyes searched her face. Searched seemingly to the very heart of her.

Tears welled and she forced herself to say the words that would make her oh so vulnerable. "I don't want to live without you, Joe." She swallowed, studying her hands in her lap. She held her breath. Now the truth would tell. Had he really asked her to marry him because he loved her? Or had he asked her, knowing she would turn him down and he wouldn't have to follow through? She waited, lower lip captured between her teeth. She could feel him studying her, but could not bring herself to check the expression on his face.

After a long moment, she felt him scoot a little closer. Felt his hand come to rest at the back of her neck. The gesture sent her heart racing. She looked up to search his face. And when she saw the genuine compassion and love shining in his expression, she loosed the fistful of skirt she'd been clenching.

"Do you mean it?" His thumb skimmed along the side of her neck.

She nodded. "Is your proposal still proffered?"

A softness tugged at one side of his lips. "Until the sky is no longer blue. Until the sun no longer shines. Until fillies and colts are no longer born in springtime."

She would have smiled, but the circumstances of this day and the life altering consequences of this moment prodded her to seriousness. "That's quite a long time, Joe."

He leaned forward until his forehead pressed against hers. "My invitation will stand until death parts us."

She pulled in a breath. Considered the guilt that chided her for feeling happy on a day like today, and the despair that wanted to drag her down into wallowing misery. She shook her head. "I should have waited. I shouldn't have… Not today."

Joe shook his head also, bringing both hands up to cup her face. "She would have wanted this. Been happy for us. She asked me just this morning when I was going to ask you to marry me. I told her I already had and you'd turned me down twice. She smiled and said you'd come to your senses one of these days." He chuckled. "I have to say I wasn't so sure she was right."

Liora relaxed a little, unable to deny that it eased her mind some to know Tess had been rooting for them. "All right, Joe. But I want you to consider one last time what it will mean for you to marry—"

Joe's thumbs slid across her lips. And he was already shaking his head. "Anyone who can't see what a wonderful woman you are doesn't deserve the time of day, as far as I'm concerned."

Liora looked deep into his eyes for the space of several heartbeats, then reached up and stroked her fingers down the side of his face. "Then yes, Joseph Robert Rodante, I will marry you."

He kissed her then, long, and slow, and sure. Their lips danced to a rhythm all their own. A dance Liora felt certain had been created solely for them from the beginning of time. And most miraculous of all, not one ounce of fear coursed through her.

Joe pulled back and rested his head against hers once more. "So when are we going to experience this most miraculous of days?"

Liora shook her head, feeling her energy drain right out of her merely at the thought. "I don't know. For now, let's just call the decision enough. I'm too weary to think beyond that."

He nodded. Gave her another gentle peck on the lips. "We'll get it figured out." He eased back and took up the reins, and Liora noted the wince of pain that creased his eyes as he did so.

"You are in pain? Did Doc give you anything for that?"

Joe waved a hand of dismissal. "Just a slight headache. And yeah, Doc gave me some powders. But..." Joe angled her a glance before quickly returning his gaze to the road. "I didn't take them because I want to have all my wits about me."

Liora felt something cold settle in the middle of her belly. "And why do you need all your wits about you?"

"Come on, get up." Joe clucked to the horses. "I'm going to drop you off at the cabin, and then I'm going to ride out to the camp, in case Reagan needs more backup than he took along with him. I don't want John Hunt escaping."

"Joe—"

"My mind's made up. It shouldn't take us long to arrest him. I'll be back before nightfall. We'll all rest better when the deed is done."

Liora gritted her teeth. So this was what she was in for? Always worrying about Joe when he rode off on a case? She rolled her eyes at herself. Who was she kidding? She had always worried about him when he rode off on a case.

"Very well. Why don't you just drop me at the top of the hill. Then you can simply keep on driving out to the camp without taking time to unhitch the wagon."

Joe nodded. "That sounds like a right smart idea, soon-to-be Mrs. Rodante." He took her fingers and drew her close to his side, tucking her hand beneath his arm.

The muscle beneath her palm rippled with each movement of the reins. She felt a slow curl in her belly. Her face heated, but she leaned close to him and pressed a quick kiss to his cheek, reveling in the freedom she had to do so. "Come back to me, Joe."

He gave her hand a quick squeeze between his ribs and his arm. "Always."

He pulled to a stop at the top of the hill that descended to her cabin—their cabin—and helped her dismount. He motioned for her to wait, then pulled his field glasses from his kit in the back of the wagon. He searched the hills all around before finally giving her a nod. "Looks safe. I'll watch you till you get in the cabin. Just be cautious if you need to come back outside for anything."

After another lingering kiss, she stepped back, gave him a wave, and started for home.

This short walk would do her some good. She still needed to plan how to break the news to Aurora about Tess's passing.

But first she would take time to send up some prayers for the safety of Joe and the other members of the posse.

Joe waited until Liora disappeared into the cabin, and then climbed back up to the wagon seat. He clucked to the horses and resisted a groan when the jostling sent a spike of pain through his skull.

Likely Reagan was right, he should be curled up on his bed right about now, but especially after seeing Tess's crumpled body this morning, there was a driving need in him to see to completion the job of arresting John Hunt.

The drive out to the camp took a good twenty minutes. But it didn't take him long to find Reagan and the rest of the posse. Their horses were all tied in front of Hunt's saloon. He pushed through the tent flap, expecting to see Hunt bound and being interrogated. Instead he found the posse with guns drawn, holding the patrons at bay, while Reagan demanded information from a man seated at the bar.

A man who from the looks of things, didn't seem to be talking.

"I tell you anything and he'll kill me," the man whined.

"He won't be able to kill you because he'll be behind bars!"

The man shook his head. "Hunt's got more than nine lives. I can't take the chance that he'll be set free. I seen what he does to... Well. I ain't talking no more."

Reagan looked up then and saw Joe across the room. His gaze narrowed and his lips thinned. "What are you doing here?"

"Figured you might need some help. Can't find him?"

Reagan shook his head. "We've been over every inch of the camp. I don't think he's here. And no one's talking."

Joe felt a cold wash of terror start at the top of his head and sweep all the way down to his boots.

"Liora's! And I left her home alone!"

He castigated himself for every kind of fool as he sprinted back to the horses. His wagon would be too slow, so he swung up onto the mount Kin often rented from Bill Giddens.

"Hey!" Kin yelled as the men barreled out of the saloon behind Joe.

Realization dawned. Kin was here? Joe tossed Reagan a look as he reined the mount to face the road. "Looks like I'm not the only one who didn't listen?"

Reagan tossed up his hands in a "what can I do" gesture.

"Bring my wagon," Joe called over his shoulder. He urged the horse into a frenzied gallop back toward the cabin.

He registered several other members of the posse mounting their horses and galloping along beside him, but in his mind all he could pray was, *Dear, God. Dear, God, please. Dear, God...*

Chapter Twenty-five

On the way down the hill, Liora decided that the straightforward approach would likely be best. She would sit Aurora down immediately and tell her what had happened in town.

She stepped up onto the porch, tugging off her gloves as she pushed into the house. "Aurora? I'm ho—" Liora gasped.

Aurora sat wide-eyed on the settee, bound hand and foot. And pressed to Liora's temple was the unmistakable cold round circle of a gun barrel.

"I'm disappointed." A voice drawled. A voice Liora would recognize even on a dark night during a windstorm. John Hunt.

Her eyes fell closed.

"I figured Rodante would enter first to make sure the house was all clear. He coming in after you?" Hunt kept his voice low and remained out of sight to one side of the door.

Liora's mouth went dry. What should she tell him? Should she tell him Joe had driven away only moments ago? Or should she say Joe would be right in?

She decided on neither. "What are you doing here? How did you get in?"

Hunt snorted. "Aurora there, let me in."

Aurora trembled, and the look in her eyes held apology. "I went out for just a moment and he grabbed me on my way back in."

Hunt cocked his pistol for emphasis. "Is Rodante coming in?"

Liora lifted her hands. "He's not here." She wouldn't tell Hunt that Joe had ridden out to the camp to arrest him.

Hunt chuckled. He gave a quick check of the yard to verify the truth of her words, and then slid the lock home and sauntered across the room to sink down on the settee next to Aurora.

Aurora scooted as close to the arm of the settee as she could get, revulsion in her expression.

Liora felt despair rise to the fore. Joe wouldn't be back for at least a couple hours. If they were going to get out of this it would be up to her.

Biding for time to think, Liora placed her gloves and reticule on the table just inside the door. Her gaze flitted to the mantle where her pistol should be.

Hunt laughed. "I took the liberty of...*securing* your pistol, if that's what you are looking for."

Liora spread her hands, willing herself to remain calm. "What do you want?"

His face lost all traces of humor. "First I want to know where Rodante is. Then we'll talk about the fact that I want you dead."

Liora swallowed. "Me and everyone else in the town of Wyldhaven, it seems."

Hunt sneered. "I heard my little surprise incinerated the entire church. Too bad Kin Davis got everyone out in time. Well, *almost everyone*." His laugh was calculated to taunt.

Aurora's eyes widened and she searched Liora's face.

Liora couldn't stop the tears that sprang up and spilled over any more than she could have stopped the sun from rising each morning. And it galled her to let Hunt see her emotions. She swiped angrily at her tears.

"Aw," he taunted. "Look at you. She can't have meant that much to you. You only stole her a few days ago."

Liora raised her chin. "I didn't *steal* her. I *rescued* her. And I loved her more than any man like you could ever understand if he had an eternity to study on it!"

Liora saw the moment realization dawned in Aurora's eyes. Her focus shifted to the door of the room that had been Tess's, and she returned questioning eyes to Liora's face.

Liora gave her a little nod.

Hunt *tsk*ed. "Such venom. Such biting wit. I think I'm going to enjoy this. I came here to get back at you for rescuing one of my girls, and what did I find when I arrived, but another little mouse hiding out in your hole." He slid the backs of his fingers over Aurora's arm and then over her hair. "Shame about all that beautiful hair, but it will grow back...in time. Until then, maybe I'll just let her service me, special like." He slid a lecherous leer from Aurora's hair to her knees and back, reaching out to brush his fingers over her cheek.

Aurora jerked away.

Liora's fists clenched. "Don't touch her!" She skimmed Aurora from head to toe, suddenly fearful of what he might have done to the girl before her arrival. "Did he hurt you?"

Aurora shook her head, blinking back tears.

Liora felt relieved at that. But being accosted, tied up, and forced to remain in the same room with this man was trauma enough. What she wouldn't give to be able to pull the girl into a comforting embrace, but she knew Hunt would never allow it.

She glared at him. "So what now?"

"You still haven't told me where Rodante is." There was a hardness in his demeanor now that told her he would be put off no longer.

Did he want Joe dead too? Of course he did. He would have

shot Joe dead the moment he stepped into the room, had he been with her. She threw back her shoulders. "Someone like you would never get the drop on Joe." If only that were true.

Hunt lurched off the settee and had her pinned to the wall by her throat before she could even blink.

Liora's pulse thundered in her ears, and she felt a wave of dizziness wash over her. But if she passed out, Aurora would have no one to protect her. She willed herself not to panic. Willed herself to meet him stare for stare, even though his fetid breath puffed over her face in nauseating waves.

His face only inches from hers, he trembled with anger and his skin was so red she could see blue veins tracing his bulbous nose. His hand tightened around her throat and though she fought and punched and kicked, nothing seemed to have an effect. Her vision was turning black around the edges and a pain stabbed through her temple. The need for oxygen made her knees weak.

"Let her go!" Aurora crashed into him from behind, but with her hands tied at her back and her ankles bound as they were, she lost her balance and crashed to the floor.

Liora closed her eyes. So this was to be her end?

But just as quickly as Hunt had attacked, he released her.

Liora gasped in precious gulps of air, coughing and heaving.

Hunt stepped back, giving his jacket and sleeves a tug. He heaved Aurora to her feet and plunked her onto the settee. Then he sank down beside her as though nothing out of the ordinary had just happened.

"Joe would kill you if he was here," Aurora spat at him.

Hunt ignored her. He angled his head and studied Liora for a long moment, then a slow smile broke over his lips. "He can't kill me because he went out to the camp looking for me, didn't he?" He slapped his thigh. "This is going to be even easier than I thought."

"What's going to be easier?" Liora rubbed at the raw skin of her throat, hoping he couldn't read her dread at the prospect of his answer.

Hunt seemed to ponder. "Well... as I've just proven, I could simply finish you off here and now. Leave you for the deputy to find the next time he swings by. And my, wouldn't he be disappointed? I hear you two have taken quite a shine to each other!"

Liora refused to acknowledge that comment with a reply.

"But the moment I laid eyes on you..." He made an appreciative sound, like a man tasting chocolate cake for the first time, and his gaze raked over her. "What an addition you'd be to my business. You remind me of...someone. A woman who used to work for me, maybe?"

Liora gritted her teeth. She would die before reminding him that her mother had worked for him up until a few years ago.

"Can't quite place who, though." He waved a hand. "Makes no never mind. Like I said... Right up until the moment I laid eyes on you today I planned to kill you. But now...I need to do some thinking." He gestured with his pistol to the chair across the room. "Sit."

His stomach rumbled loudly in the silence. "On second thought"—he motioned her toward the kitchen—"You can cook some vittles for me. I've been so worked up all day that I haven't taken time to eat properly."

Liora actually felt relieved. She would at least have something to do other than sit here and contemplate the end of her and Rory's lives. And maybe with her and Hunt in the kitchen, Rory would be able to find a way to escape her bonds.

But as if the very thought had just occurred to Hunt, he paused. "Up!" he said to Rory.

She stood slowly, her balance precarious with her ankles bound together and her hands tied behind her back.

He gestured her toward the table. "Jump."

Aurora rolled her eyes. But she did jump. All the way until she crashed against the table to keep her balance.

Hunt pushed one of the chairs away from the table with a shove from his boot. "Sit!" he barked at her. When she complied, he turned his attention on Liora once more. "Bacon and eggs. And biscuits. And be quick about it."

Liora felt the first rays of hope she'd felt since she walked inside. He was really going to let her have hot grease? She would cook for him with pleasure!

She built up the fire and set the cast-iron skillet on the hottest part of the stove. Then she lifted the lid on the icebox and retrieved the paper-wrapped packet of bacon. By the time she'd cut several thick slices, the pan was hot. She layered the meat into the pan, then looked at Hunt. "I've only got three eggs left. Will that do?" She tempered her voice to make him think she felt compliant.

He waved his pistol in a way that was at once a dismissal and an acceptance, then paced to the window to peer through the curtains.

While his back was turned, Liora quickly scooped up a large spoonful of bacon grease from the jar she kept by the stove and plopped it into the pan with the bacon. The more hot grease she had, the better, as far as she was concerned. She plunked the spoon back into the jar just as he spun to face her once more.

His gaze swept over her like a businessman assessing wares he planned to stock in his store.

A shiver ran down her spine and she turned her back on him. She had biscuits left over from last night's dinner. She put two into the warming drawer of the stove.

Hunt turned back to the window. His contemplative silence was even more unnerving than his assessing scrutiny.

Liora met Aurora's gaze across the sideboard.

Aurora looked pointedly at the block of sharp knives next to the stove.

Hunt pivoted to assess her again.

Liora poked at the bacon, hoping he hadn't noticed where their attention had wandered.

"Perhaps I could let you live. There might be a way."

Liora scoffed. "With what you pulled in town today? The law is going to pursue you till your last breath. And I've lived the life you are offering. I'd rather die than go back to it."

"We'll see if your tune changes when you are kneeling behind a tree with my pistol to your head. Besides..." He waved a hand in the general direction of Wyldhaven. "They have no proof."

"They have Kin's word." Too late she realized her careless proclamation might condemn Kin to his death, so she added, "And now mine."

"And mine," Aurora piped up.

Hunt cursed them all. "You're both making a very good case why I should let neither of you live." He prodded at the curtains, once more skimming the hills around the cabin. Was he merely searching for the arrival of the law? Or was there something else he was looking for?

Taking up a plate, she laid a cloth napkin, a mug, and a setting of silver on it. Lifting out the smallest knife in the block, she moved to the table and began to loudly set a place. Just as she'd hoped, Hunt gave her a cursory glance before returning his focus out the window.

She lifted the paring knife into her hand. She thought about simply thrusting it into Hunt's back, but it was too small and he would be on her before she could do enough damage to hurt him.

On her way back to the kitchen, Liora eased the knife into Aurora's bound hands.

The bacon was soon ready to flip and Liora set the eggs to cooking in a smaller pan—with more bacon grease.

She kept half an eye on Rory. Was she having any success sawing through the ropes? She sat so still, Liora couldn't tell if she was making any headway, or not. There wasn't anything they would be able to do about her ankles. If Aurora bent over to work on those ropes, Hunt was sure to notice. How were they to escape, then?

She watched the bacon bubble and splatter for a moment.

His eyes. The grease would have to go in his eyes. Then maybe he'd be blinded and in enough agony that they would have time to get the ropes untied or cut. She angled a look to where he still stood at the window. She felt guilty simply for thinking it. Not even a man like Hunt deserved such a fate, but what other option did she have? The parson had entrusted Rory into her protection. And it was Hunt or them.

She flipped the eggs over and checked on the biscuits.

Another check of Rory showed a slight smile on her face.

Liora lifted her brows.

Rory gave a subtle dip of her chin.

Sweet Jesus, be praised. The girl had done it.

Liora gave Rory a cautious nod that she hoped communicated she should be ready to move. Her heart beat so hard against her sternum, she feared Hunt would be able to hear it, but he remained focused out the window.

He was tall. She needed him to sit. There was no way she would be able to toss the hot grease from near his plate at the table all the way over to the window and be accurate enough to ensure some got in his eyes.

She took a steadying breath. "If you'll just come sit at the table, I'll serve up your plate." She pulled the warmed biscuits from the oven and balanced them on the edge of the skillet, then transferred the eggs over onto the slices of bacon.

Hunt didn't move. "Come get my plate, put all the food on it, then bring it back and set it down."

She stilled. Had he guessed what she was up to? Fear quaked through her. How was she going to get Rory out of this mess if the man was always one step ahead of her?

Rory remained calm. And again it was a small direction of her eyes that made Liora look to the pint jar of grease by the stove. Realization tingled over her scalp. The jar was small enough that she could hold it in one hand, and it had enough room for the hot grease in the pan. It was her only shot.

"Yes, sir." Liora scurried to the table and retrieved Hunt's plate. Back at the stove, she served up the bacon and eggs, and set the biscuits to one side of the plate. She wanted to pour the hot grease into the jar and immediately take it with her, but it was too soon. He was too much on his guard. She left the pan on the stove where it would keep the grease hot, and even set the mason jar up beside it.

Then she stepped over to the table. She used the walk to assess the ties around Rory's ankles. There was enough space between her ankles that she would be able to get a knife in between to slice the ropes. Thankfully, Joe had just stropped her large meat knife the other day.

Liora set the plate on the table, folded her hands before herself in plain sight, and stepped back. "Would you like some coffee?"

Please God, make him say yes.

Hunt turned, and slowly assessed her and then the plate of food. After a moment, he must have decided it was safe to sit, because he nodded and pulled out his chair. "Coffee. Yes."

Liora didn't dare look at Aurora. This was going to be their only chance. If they didn't escape from Hunt the first time, there would be no other escape.

Jesus, please forgive me for what I'm about to do...

Back in the kitchen, she hoped her back would block her actions from Hunt, but Aurora must have thought of that too, because she spoke suddenly into the silence of the room. "I'll keep silent, I swear. But please Mr. Hunt, you just have to let me live. I'm only seventeen. I have my whole life ahead of me. What can I do to make you keep me alive?"

Hunt's laughter grated. "Desperation does not become you, my dear."

Liora poured the hot grease from the skillet into the mason jar.

Rory added a few sobs to her repertoire. "I'm only desperate because you've made me so! Please, Mr. Hunt, you simply can't refuse me!"

Hunt slapped her. "I'll refuse anyone, anyplace and anytime I like."

The slap rocked Rory back in her chair. She blinked and spat blood from a split lip.

Liora flinched, but knew that Rory was sacrificing so they could make an escape. She forced herself not to react to what was happening at the table.

Rory remained silent for only as long as it took her to shake off the slap. "The law will never let you stay in business!" Anger bit off the end of each word.

Hunt snorted. "The law isn't going to be a problem for me."

Liora knew she needed to get back to the table. Rory had done an admirable job of creating a diversion, and everything was ready, but Hunt's comment had made Liora's heart stutter to a stop and then kick up like a team of stampeding horses.

Her gaze traveled to the window. Why *had* he been watching the surrounding hills so intently?

Chapter Twenty-six

At the cutoff road that led to the back of Liora's property, Joe pulled his mount to a skidding halt. "We should split up. Kin will need to keep the wagon on the road, and he'll need some help in case he runs into any trouble. Zane, Ewan, and Doc, you all go with Kin. Reagan, Wash and Preston, come with me." He kicked his mount into a gallop again, too late realizing that he maybe should have left the bossing up to Reagan. With his fear for Liora mounting with every minute that it took to get to the cabin, his only thought had been to instruct and keep moving.

Thankfully, none of the others seemed too taken aback by it, and everyone split off as he'd instructed. The group taking the road would arrive at the house about ten minutes later than the rest of them.

Joe could only hope and pray he and his half of the posse wouldn't be too late to save Liora and Rory.

All the while praying for Joe's safety, Liora took up a towel, wrapped the jar of hot grease, and tucked it behind her back.

"Kill me if you must, then!" Rory spat at Hunt, still doing her part to distract the man. "I would never work for you anyhow!"

Hunt lurched to his feet. "Kid, you'd better shut up or I'll—"

"Coffee's ready," Liora interjected. Lifting the pot, she started for the table, relieved to see Hunt sink back into his seat.

Hunt's attention transferred to her, immediately on the alert. He watched the coffeepot like a hawk, tense and ready to leap back if she tried anything.

Liora willed her hand not to tremble. She filled the cup to just below the rim. "Cream? Sugar?" she asked, drawing the coffeepot away from him.

His gaze sharpened on her other hand. "What's that behind your back?"

Liora's heart stuttered to a standstill. She blinked at him, feeling frozen. If she tried to throw it at him, would he simply leap out of the way? "Whatever do you mean—"

Aurora lurched to her feet and plunged the short knife Liora had given her into Hunt's thigh.

He bellowed curses, and the swing of his fist caught Aurora's collarbone and knocked her over. He started after her. "How did you get free you little—"

Liora dashed the pint jar of hot grease against the side of his face.

Hunt screamed and lurched back, clawing at his eye and swiping at his ear.

Grease dribbled down his cheek and onto his chest. The skin across his nose and around his eyes was already bubbling. The wounded eye closed, he staggered toward her and swung his arms wildly.

Liora dodged under his swing. She yanked the lid off the pot and followed the grease with the hot coffee. Straight into his face.

He staggered back blindly, screaming and clawing at his face.

"Rory, go! Jump for the porch!"

Rage purpling his features, Hunt fumbled to get his pistol out of his holster.

"Rory!" Liora only had time for that one word of warning before a bullet whined past her cheek.

She dove forward, and clapped one hand over Rory's mouth.

Where only a moment ago, Hunt had been screaming and writhing, now he stood perfectly still. He was listening. Listening for any sound to shoot at, head cocked, jaw rock hard, blood oozing down his leg from the knife wound. He swayed on his feet.

They huddled together. Rory's eyes were large and frightened.

Liora kept her fingers over the girl's mouth, her own heart a thudding tympani in her ears. Surely, he could hear them breathing?

But his own breaths were ragged with agony. Laced with torment.

He twisted toward them, and Liora had to look away from the grotesque visage of his blistered face and milky burned eyes. Guilt traipsed through her at what she'd done. Could they have escaped by another means? No. This had been her only chance to save Aurora.

Even now they were still too exposed! But what should she do? To move would reveal their location.

"Where are you?" Hunt's curses bellowed through the room.

Bullets sprayed.

One pinged off the stove.

Another cut a gouge into the log wall by the kitchen door.

Liora literally bit down on her tongue to keep from crying out. Any sound at this moment could be the end of them.

She needed to get Aurora's ankles unbound, but she'd never had a chance to get the knife from the kitchen. And trying to untie the hemp rope would make too much noise.

Her eyes fell to the lid of the coffeepot that lay on the ground a couple feet away.

Slowly, she released Rory, reminding her to remain silent with a finger laid across her lips. Then she eased forward, never taking her eyes off Hunt. She clenched her teeth and very carefully lifted the lid, making sure the metal didn't clink or scrape against the floor.

She tossed it into the kitchen. It clattered off the pump handle and clanged into the sink.

Just as she'd hoped, Hunt shot twice in the direction of the sound, and Liora urged Rory to crawl toward the front door.

But Hunt swung toward them!

They'd made too much noise!

"Go!" Liora urged Rory onward.

Bang!

Splinters chipped out of the floor and slashed against her cheek.

And then silence fell.

Eyes wide, Rory glanced over her shoulder.

Swiping at the sting on her cheek, Liora glanced back too. He was out of bullets! His fingers, burned and swollen from the grease he'd swiped at, fumbled to remove one from the bandolier around his waist.

Liora's focus landed on the heavy log table.

"Rory!" Liora motioned.

On their knees, together they shoved the table up and pushed it until it tumbled forward into Hunt's legs.

Cursing and roaring, he stumbled backward. Tripped by his chair and pushed by the weight of the table, he fell against the wall with the table lying halfway over his legs. Hunt's face was so red now, that it was a wonder he hadn't collapsed from his fit of rage. He thrashed once more, then went still.

Liora snatched up her long meat knife and yelled for Rory's attention. "Don't move!"

It only took her two strokes to saw through one strand of the ropes and that loosened them enough that they were easily removed.

"Run!" Liora shoved the girl toward the door.

Rory complied and Liora was fast on her heels.

They sprinted across the yard, and Liora wouldn't let Rory stop until they were all the way up the hill and onto the road. There they bent, propped their hands on their knees, and gasped for air.

And that was when they heard the cocking of several guns.

They looked up.

Burt Pike and four other men stepped out from behind trees.

"Well, look here," Pike drawled. "I didn't expect this. How did you escape the boss?"

Liora's shoulders slumped. "Aren't you supposed to be locked up in the Wyldhaven jailhouse? How did you get out?"

Pike offered a mocking grin. He swung a nod toward a small man off to one side. "Hunt sent Samuel there to blast us out, knowing all the law would be out to the camp looking for him. Guess it's a good thing he did." He gestured with his gun. "Now hands up and back to the cabin with you."

Joe was the first one to the top of the hill that looked down on the back of Liora's cabin.

His heart stilled. For there on the road leading down to the front of the house. he could see Liora and Aurora being prodded along at gunpoint by a group of men.

He tossed a glance at Reagan. "It can't be!"

Reagan swung down and stripped his rifle from his scabbard. They both fell to their bellies at the top of the hill, with Wash and Preston following suit. Reagan sighted down his scope, then gave Joe a grim look. "That's Burt Pike and the rest who were in the jail."

"What do we do now?" Wash asked.

Joe moved without reply. His only thought was that he couldn't let Pike get the women into the house. If he did it would be the end for them.

He was already sprinting down the hill before the thought hardly had time to register. He wasn't surprised to hear Preston join him. Joe knew Reagan would stay at the top of the hill as an overwatch, and that he would send Wash around to flank the outlaws.

Joe touched Preston's shoulder and indicated he should go left around the cabin, and he would go right. So far, the men on the road seemed to be so fascinated with the women that they hadn't noticed what was happening on the hillside behind the cabin. But their advantage wasn't likely to last much longer.

Even as Joe thought it, one of Hunt's men looked up and raised a shout of alarm.

Reagan put a shot into the dust of the roadbed before the group. "First man to move gets shot," he said into the stillness that followed. His words weren't overly loud, but Joe could tell they carried just fine. Each man in the group froze, hands half lifted. They looked at one another. They had obviously only seen Joe and Preston sprinting down the hill and were taken aback by the third voice. They likely couldn't see Reagan, covered as he was by the tall grass at the top of the hill. They were probably wondering how many other men there were.

Right on cue, Wash spoke from off to the right and back in

the trees. "Sure is a frustrating thing to be on the wrong side of the law, ain't it?"

Liora and Rory glanced around, eyes wide. Hopeful, yet fearful.

Please, God... Joe ignored the pain each footfall caused in his head as he and Preston kept sprinting.

Joe lost sight of the group for a moment as he descended far enough that the cabin blocked his view, but it only took him seconds to reach the side of the house and peer around past the porch rails. He drew his pistol, and using the foundation of the porch as cover, he pointed his Colt through the log posts. "Gentlemen, drop your weapons, if you please." He hoped they couldn't hear the pain and the need for air in his tone.

None of them moved.

From the other side of the house came the sound of another pistol cocking. "I'd do as he says, men."

If Joe was honest, he wasn't even certain that the parson knew how to shoot a pistol, but at least the man was putting on a good show of it. His voice had been rock-steady when he spoke just now.

And the addition of his gun seemed to have swayed some of the men. Three of them eased down to lay their weapons in the dust of the road.

"Hold your positions, men!" Pike snapped.

One of the three shook his head as they stepped back, knelt down, and interlaced their fingers behind their heads. "Don't got enough loyalty to Hunt to die for him, Pike."

Something eased inside of Joe. Maybe this wasn't going to be as bad as he'd feared. Only two left with weapons. They could take them!

"Well I do!" Pike lurched forward and wrapped a forearm around Liora's throat, pressing the point of his pistol to her temple.

And just like that, Joe's pulse was once again pounding in his ears. Without thought he stepped out into the open space in front of the cabin. He advanced toward the man, making sure to leave the parson a line of sight, as he did so.

"Whoa, Pike!" The other man tossed his gun to the ground and raised his hands. "You shoot a woman and you will condemn us all to the gallows."

"Shut up, Tom!"

Joe kept his advance steady and slow. He was a fair shot. Better than most. But the closer he got the more accurate he would be.

Pike backed up a step, dragging Liora with him. "Stop right there!"

Joe complied. "Easy, Pike. We can work this out without it ending in a death sentence for you."

Pike swallowed and glanced around like he was searching for help. But Wash was already there, kicking the weapons of the other men farther away, and Preston was rapidly approaching. He gestured for the four men to lay down on their bellies, and they complied. Wash and the parson bound them hand and foot. Pike's four compatriots were already out of commission.

Joe never took his eyes off Pike, even though everything in him wanted to search Liora's face. "It's going to be all right, Liora." He swallowed away the dryness in his mouth.

He heard footsteps behind him, and the whuff of a horse. Reagan had come down the hill.

"Pike...there's no way out of this." Reagan spoke in a casual tone. "Put down your gun and I won't even report this incident to the judge when he comes through tomorrow. You'll only be tried and sentenced for that first shooting. And since no one got hurt, you'll likely be out inside of five years. But shooting a woman? That's a hanging offense. And it will be swift and certain."

"Hanging nothing." Joe's voice was quartz hard. "You shoot her and I'm going to drop you where you stand with a shot through your heart, Pike."

He broke his own rule then, and shifted his gaze to Liora. Face pale and eyes wide, her gaze fastened on him like he was her lifeline in the midst of a storm-tossed sea.

Please, God don't let me fail her now...

Pike examined them from behind Liora's head. The gun in his hand trembled with impotent rage.

Joe took a step to his left to get a better angle on the man. Then another.

He heard Aurora speaking in low tones to Wash and the parson but couldn't quite make out what she was saying.

But suddenly Washington and the parson scrambled toward the cabin. "Sheriff, I think you better join us inside," Preston said.

And then it was only Joe, Pike and Liora left standing in the yard.

Joe assessed what he could see of Pike. Part of one foot. A bit of his hip. The hand that held his pistol. And every once in a while, part of one eye when the man peered out from behind Liora. Joe despaired. Would any of those shots maim the man enough to make him let Liora go? Or would Pike pull the trigger on reflex and take Liora from him forever?

Joe inched a little more to the left. Something moved behind Pike—some*one*. More precisely, Zane Holloway. The other members of the posse had arrived.

He didn't dare look, or he would direct Pike's attention to the man sneaking up behind him, but before that moment Joe would have disbelieved anyone who said Zane Holloway could move that quietly.

"What's your next play, Pike?" he asked, as a distraction to cover Zane's approach.

And then Zane was on him, pressing his pistol to Pike's head and greeting Joe with, "Looks like you could use a little help. Mind if I join the party?"

Pike rolled his eyes and lowered his gun.

"Liora, come." Joe held out his hand to her, and wrapped her in a relieved one-armed embrace as Zane ratcheted his handcuffs onto Pike's wrists.

Zane patted Pike on the shoulder and leaned close to his ear as if about to impart a very important secret. "Those handcuffs are brand new. Special new design makes them nigh impossible to get out of. Just thought you'd like to know. 'Course you're welcome to give it a try." He offered the man a grin that said he wouldn't mind shooting him if he did manage to escape.

Pike only glowered at him and slumped onto the stump that Zane shoved him toward.

Joe had never felt more relieved. "Thank you," he said to Zane, never releasing Liora.

Zane nodded.

Joe holstered his pistol and pressed a kiss into Liora's hair. "You're safe now. You're safe. I'm sorry I left you." He eased back from her and brushed the tangles of her hair away from her face. "Are you all right?" His gaze fell to a blotch of blood on her cheek, and his stomach dropped, but on closer inspection the wound didn't look very bad.

Liora rested one hand against his chest and looked up at him. "I'm glad you weren't here. He would have shot you the moment we walked in the door and I wouldn't have been able to live without you."

Joe frowned. He glanced over at the five men, all trussed and gloomy. "Who would have shot me?"

Liora tipped a nod toward the house. "John Hunt."

Heart almost stopping, Joe turned to see Reagan pushing a

cuffed Hunt out the door of the cabin. The man moaned and whimpered and limped. He could barely remain on his feet. And the thought that he'd threatened Liora and Rory only a bit ago made Joe want to finish him off.

Hunt's face was a swollen mass of blistered flesh on one side, and red burned flesh on the other. It appeared he could only see out of one eye, and not very well at that. And blood soaked one leg of his trousers.

Joe's eyes widened and he looked back at Liora with new respect for her tenacity. "You did that?"

Rory, followed by Kin, hurried to Liora's side as Reagan helped Hunt down the stairs.

Liora swept a hand over Rory's hair as through assessing whether she was all right, before she lowered her gaze. "I threw the grease in his face, but Rory is the one who stabbed him." She swallowed, apparently unable to go on.

Kin bumped Rory with his elbow. "Way to go, but..." His gaze slipped the length of her. "Want to tell me why my kid brother is suddenly wearing a dress and looking pretty as a picture?"

Liora smiled and Joe laughed.

Rory blushed. "Right." She looped her arm through Kin's. "Come on and I'll tell you. I know you'll take it some better than Parson Clay did." She accompanied the words with a glower in the older man's direction.

When they were once again alone, Liora looked up at Joe. He could read a world of sorrow in her expression. "I didn't know what else to do. He had Rory tied up and the way he looked at her... He..." Tears filled her eyes. "The man is a monster. I didn't want to hurt him, but I didn't..." She swallowed and looked down.

Joe touched her chin. "You gave him more mercy than he would have given you. You left him alive."

She turned sorrow-filled eyes on Hunt as Reagan led him by. "I couldn't think of any other way to fight him. He said he was going to kill us." Her gaze followed the man to the wagon that Kin had earlier pulled into the yard. "I think the only reason we're still alive is that he was waiting for his men to arrive from town."

Reagan loaded Hunt into the back, followed by the other five.

Liora's voice came out small when she said, "He confessed to me that he was responsible for the church. For Tess."

Joe pulled her close and tucked her head beneath his chin. He didn't have the energy to analyze all the emotions pumping through him in this moment. Anger. Fear. Relief. Pride. Horror. The list could go on and on. "You did what you needed to do to protect both yourself and Aurora. It's always the right thing to fight for life."

Liora settled against him, like she was meant to fit in his arms just so. He closed his eyes and relished the feel of her. Safe. Unharmed. Alive.

"Joe?" Her breath brushed warmth against his throat.

He swallowed. "Hmmm?"

"Do you think a posse would have been formed to go after Hunt, if Tess hadn't died?"

The words shot an arrow to his heart. He considered. They'd had Kin's word that Hunt was involved, but would that have been enough if no one had died? Especially considering Kin's history with the law? "We'd have gone to question him. Probably only Reagan and Zane, though. Not sure if I'd have ridden after them. Like you said earlier, I might have been killed by Hunt the moment we walked into the house. Reagan and Zane probably would have thought to come here looking, but maybe not as soon as I did." He shook his head. "Likely the outcome of this whole day would have been vastly different." A shudder worked through him at just the thought.

She was so quiet he didn't realize she was crying until he felt the dampness of her tears soaking through his shirt.

He curved his hand around her head, holding her close, wishing he could also absorb all her sorrow and take it on himself. "It's all right. Everything's going to be all right."

She swiped a hand across her cheek. "Thank you for coming back for me. For us."

He caressed one hand over her hair. "I will always come for you."

She leaned back and looked into his face. "Can we go inside?"

A wave of weariness and pain made his agreement fall quickly from his lips. "Yes. Let's go inside." And she needed some levity in this moment, so he added, "We can sit on the settee and discuss when you are going to follow through on your promise to become my wife." He winked down at her.

"What?! Congratulations!" Reagan, who had approached without Joe's notice, clapped him on one shoulder and grinned at him.

Liora blushed and quickly stepped away from Joe, kicking at a pebble on the ground.

Joe's arms felt bereft. He glowered playfully at Reagan. "Now look what you've done."

"Yeah, man. Sorry about that. Just wanted to let you know we're going to borrow your wagon to take the prisoners back to town."

Joe gave him a nod. "The Paint's about done in. Take it slow, would you? And make sure he gets a double portion of oats from Giddens? I'll pick him up sometime tomorrow."

Reagan nodded. "Will do." Then he grinned. "Getting married! Just wait till I tell Charlotte. She's going to be over the moon."

Joe reached over and took Liora's hand. "Well, nothing is decided yet. So maybe you should wait until—"

"Hey! I know!" Reagan's eyes brightened. "You two should get married on the same day as Charlotte and me."

Joe blinked at him.

From his peripheral vision, he saw Liora's jaw drop.

Reagan nodded, undaunted. "Why not? All the town will already be gathered together. And then"—he socked Joe in the arm—"You and I can help each other remember what day to bring home flowers every year."

Joe chuckled and rubbed his arm. "We'll let you know." He gave Reagan a pointed look and a jut of his chin toward the waiting wagon.

"All right, all right." Reagan started away, waving a hand over his head. "Get some rest, and good job today. Both of you!"

Chapter Twenty-seven

A week later, Liora awoke with a stretch and a large yawn. She squinted at the window with one eye half open.

Still just barely dawn.

She snuggled back into her pillows and pulled the blankets up around her ears. But returning to sleep would be nigh impossible with all of the swirling emotions pumping through her.

Sadness over the loss of Tess. So much sadness.

Her funeral had taken place on the church lawn the day after the attack. It had been appropriately gray and overcast. The entire town had turned out for it. Liora had fully expected to return home with just as heavy of a heart as when she'd left for the funeral, but surprisingly Parson Clay's words had uplifted and encouraged. He'd painted such a bright and joyous picture of heaven that Liora couldn't help but be happy for Tess to be free of all the burdens of this world. And when they'd all walked to the cemetery on the hill behind the church and Kin and Wash and two of his brothers had lowered Tess into the earth, Liora had surprisingly found peace in her heart. Tess was truly home now. Home where she belonged.

Another emotion still swirling through Liora was horror at what she and Rory had been through with John Hunt and his men. And marveling that God had brought them through unscathed.

She and Rory were still prone to starting at any loud sound or clatter. But Parson Clay had revealed Rory's story toward the end of Tess's funeral, and everyone had been more than understanding considering all they'd learned about John Hunt the day before. Both the parson and Aurora had been visibly relieved at the response.

Lastly, and most wonderful and consuming of all was the joy. So much joy over the fact that she would soon be Joe's wife. What a blessing was that? She still couldn't believe Joe had actually talked her into taking Reagan up on his offer of sharing his and Charlotte's wedding day. With so much to prepare between now and then, she really ought to rise early and get a jump on her work. But, for now, she just wanted to lie here and revel in the miracle God had given her over the last few weeks.

Her thoughts went back to the day of the attack...

She had been quite concerned about Joe. After the posse had ridden away, he had come into the house and talked with her for a little while but then he had gone out to the lean–to and slept clean through until noon the next day. She had been so worried, she had sent Aurora into town to fetch Flynn.

After examining Joe, and re-wrapping the gash on his arm, Flynn had insisted that Joe do absolutely no heavy lifting or strenuous work for at least two weeks. "Medicine still has a lot to learn about head injuries, Joe, but I've read several recent reports and I think it is better to be cautious. If in two weeks your headaches are gone, then we can reassess."

That had relieved some of Liora's concern, but Joe had been grumpier then a bear fresh out of hibernation about the whole affair.

Liora giggled and twirled a strand of hair around her finger, remembering how upset he had been the night before when she had insisted he stand by and watch her haul in the wood for the stove. It had given her great delight to tease him until he'd finally given up his frustration and allowed the smallest of smiles. And if some of the reason for his smile had been over the fact that she had linked her arms around his neck and batted her eyelashes at him... Well, she liked that too.

She stared at the bare finger on her left hand, hardly able to believe that in a little less than a week she would be waking up as Mrs. Joseph Rodante. *And* she was happy about it. That was actually almost more of a miracle than anything.

The Bible on her nightstand caught her eye, and she traced her finger over the cover.

God had indeed taken her ashes and supplied beauty in their place. Where she previously had felt terrible dread at the thought of a man's touch, now she looked forward to each gentle brush of Joe's fingers. Each quick wink he sent her way. Each soft kiss that he trailed across her knuckles.

Last night when he had come in for dinner, there had been so much appreciation in the gaze he swept over her that she'd felt like the last dark room of her past had just had the shutters thrown wide open. She had blushed and spun away from him, but he caught her hand and gently tugged her back against his chest, wrapping her in the safe cocoon of his arms. His lips found the soft spot just behind her ear.

She giggled when his lips descended to the curve of her shoulder and his whiskers tickled the sensitive skin of her neck. She smacked his arms and spun away from him, shaking one finger. "Behave yourself, Joseph Rodante."

He spread his hands with an unrepentant grin. "What?"

"You know exactly what. I called you in for dinner and not a thing more."

He folded his arms and leaned into his heels. "Disappointing.

Mighty disappointing. I'm sure there's got to be something I could do to change your mind."

He crooked one finger at her, gesturing her closer.

Liora giggled. Tempted. Oh so tempted. But instead of giving in, she gave him a look. "Rory's right in the next room."

His brows lifted. "Oh, so am I to understand that if Rory wasn't in the other room things might be different?"

Liora had felt herself blush to the roots of her hair, because she knew that the answer to that question was in fact an emphatic yes.

Aurora came around the corner. "Did I hear my name?"

Liora started to deny it, but Joe interrupted her with a distinct gleam in his eyes.

"You did in fact hear your name, Aurora. I was wondering if you would mind taking that bucket of oats there out to my Paint. After all his running the other day, I've been pampering him a little."

Aurora glanced back and forth between them, confusion wrinkling her brow. Joe had never asked her to do his chores before. It was only a moment before realization dawned on her face. Her brows shot up and her face turned pinker than spring cherry blossoms. "Oh! Yes. Of course. I can do that." She scurried outside so quickly both Joe and Liora were left chuckling in her wake.

Even now as Liora remembered the incident, she felt her face heat. Because Joe had taken distinct advantage of Aurora's absence. And a very pleasant time had been had by all. Well, except for maybe Aurora who'd only been afforded the pleasure of feeding the Paint oats.

Liora giggled and pushed back the covers. Much as she would like to lie about and dream of Joe all day, she had things that needed tending.

She had just slipped on her day dress and done up her hair when a knock sounded on the front door. She frowned and glanced out her window again. The sun was barely up. Joe never came to the house this early. Who could be at the door? She hurried through the chill of the living room and cracked the door a little to see who would be on the porch.

To her surprise it *was* Joe. But he wasn't alone. Behind him stood three women.

Liora opened the door farther.

Joe gestured to the women with a sweep of his hat. And there was a light of something gleaming in his eyes. Was it pride? "Came out of the lean-to, right as they walked into the yard. Seems they were employed by John Hunt up till a couple days ago. They want out of that life. They heard about your place, and wondered if you had room for them?"

Liora covered her mouth with one hand, blinking back tears. All she could think about was something Tess had said to her just a few days ago.

Them other whores back there workin' for Mr. Hunt? If I could sacrifice somethin' to give them a chance to have a better life, I would want to do that too. Like you done for me.

These women would not be free from John Hunt had Tess's death not happened. Had Tess not had that very attitude—one willing to sacrifice herself for others—she would be here today, but these women likely would not.

Beauty from Ashes...

Father God, I lack so much faith.

She stepped back and swung the door wide, smiling at the women through blurred vision. "Of course I have room. We'll make room. Please, come in. I was just about to start breakfast. I'm sure you are all hungry."

harlotte couldn't help but grin at Reagan and Jacinda who were both pacing the train platform like caged tigers. Due to Father's previous banking commitments, he and Mother had not been able to get away from Boston until this week. So now, here they stood, the night before the wedding, waiting for the train to arrive.

Charlotte wasn't sure who was more nervous, Reagan or his mother. And that didn't even take into account the jitters squirreling through her own middle. She hadn't seen her parents since she had left Boston over two years ago. Well she remembered her first impression of Wyldhaven, and she so wanted her parents to love her new home and the man that she would spend the rest of her life with. Would her parents be able to let go of their citified expectations with only a few hours before the wedding? Her mother was nothing if not set in her ways, and Charlotte feared that the culture of Wyldhaven might just be too much of a shock for her system.

Charlotte flipped open her fan and tried to cool herself, even though the day had not been overly warm. She knew that her stresses were likely partly responsible for Reagan and Jacinda's edginess.

Reagan was doing his best not to look nervous. But the tapping of his boot toe gave him away.

In the distance, the train whistle pierced the air. Reagan glanced over at her and smiled. But it was a bit strained around the edges. Stepping to his side, she looped her arm through his and looked up at him. "They're going to love you."

He grinned. "Of course they are. I'm the hero who saved you from that fiend Patrick Waddell! It's you I'm worried about. You've changed a lot since coming to town, you know."

She slapped his arm in accompaniment with Jacinda's chuckle. "Oh do get on with you. Now you've made me even more tense than I already was!"

Reagan covered her hand and gave it a gentle squeeze. "You can't be even half as nervous as I am. Is my tie straight?"

Charlotte paused in front of him and patted his perfectly tied bow. "You look just as handsome as ever."

"As do you." He took her hand and pressed a kiss against the back of her fingers.

"Here they come." Jacinda tapped Reagan on the shoulder in indication they should pay attention.

They all turned then to watch the train glide into the depot. With a release of steam, it came to a halt. And only a moment later, Mother and Father descended the train steps.

Mother held a handkerchief to her nose and glanced the length of the platform and back, eyes wide. Charlotte grinned even as she hurried towards them. If she thought this was a backwater, wait till she arrived in Wyldhaven. She wouldn't know what to do with herself.

Mother saw her, and her eyes widened and burgeoned with tears. "Charlotte! Oh, Charlotte!" Her hanky waved like a white flag of surrender. Mother hustled toward her and threw her arms around her neck. "Oh, my baby, Charlotte."

Charlotte chuckled a little and patted Mother's back. "Hello, Mother. I trust that your journey has not been too tiring?"

Father approached more sedately. But Charlotte could tell by the gleam in his eyes that he was just as happy to see her as her Mother was. She released Mother and held her arms out to her father, relishing in the strength of his embrace as he tugged her close and wrapped his strong arms around her. The familiar combination of his cologne and the soft whiff of cigar smoke washed her with a melancholy longing.

"Ah, child. 'Tis so good to see you again."

Charlotte stepped back, laughing at herself as she dashed tears from her cheeks.

Both her parents were looking at Reagan now and she realized that she hadn't made introductions yet. "Mother, Father"—she slid her arm through Reagan's—"I'd like you to meet Reagan Callahan. And this is his mother, Mrs. Jacinda Callahan. Reagan, Jacinda, my parents, Bertrand and Etta Brindle."

Father reached out a hand to Reagan, while Mother and Jacinda shared an embrace.

"I trust that I don't have to tell you what I will do to you if you ever hurt my daughter?"

Charlotte gasped. "Father!"

Reagan didn't even chuckle. He shook his head. "No sir. You sure don't."

Charlotte reached over and slapped her father's arm. "You stop that." She laughed. "There's no fear of Reagan mistreating me."

Father gave her a rapid-fire wink. "I figure with only a few hours till the wedding, I better make myself plain and clear right up front. I would hate to have to deny my permission when the minister asks for it."

Reagan's feet barely had time to shuffle in consternation before Father broke out into his signature belly laugh and socked Reagan in the arm. "I'm only funning with you, son. Lord knows my Charlotte has had plenty of beaus in her day. And if you're the one that makes her happy, then I'm happy."

Charlotte felt her face flame. "Father really!" The way he said "plenty of beaus" made her sound like a downright floozy. And now there was a slight furl between Reagan's brows. She gave him a shake of her head and a subtle eye roll.

And when Father turned his attention to Jacinda, Reagan leaned close to whisper in her ear, "We're going to have to talk about all these beaus of yours someday." His quick kiss of her cheek let her know where he really stood. "I'll fetch the carriage."

He was off before she could even get a word in edgewise, and she grinned as she watched him go. Life with that man would certainly never be boring.

Reagan was only a little way down the platform when Charlotte heard someone call her name, and her heart went cold in her chest. It couldn't be! But when she looked up, her fears were confirmed.

Kent Covington scurried toward her from the rear of the train. He wore a white linen suit with a crisp square of red silk peeking from the pocket. He brushed past Reagan, who stopped where he stood and spun to watch Kent rush toward her.

Charlotte squeaked as Kent fell to one knee before her and clasped her hand. His coat was cut so long that the hem brushed the depot platform, and with one hand he kept his light gray bowler pressed to his chest.

Jacinda took a step back and flapped her fan.

Mother and Father gasped.

"Covington, what under all of heaven are you doing here?" Father demanded.

Charlotte tried to step back and withdraw her hand, but

Covington held on and scooted after her awkwardly on his knees. He tossed a glance at Father. "I followed you." With his gaze fastened to Charlotte, he beseeched, "Charlie, please, when I heard you were getting married, I just had to come. You can't do this. You know we were meant to be together. You'll never be happy if you marry this western fool, whoever he may be."

Beside them, Reagan cleared his throat. Loudly.

Charlotte glanced up. He'd returned from down the platform and now stood just behind Kent. Nudging his Stetson back and raising his brows at her, he folded his arms and leaned into his heels.

Charlotte was still so in shock that all she could seem to do was stand there and gape back and forth between the two men. Everything seemed to slow. Each breath took forever to fill her lungs. Each beat of her heart took minutes.

She looked first at Kent, with his pale city skin and his bowler pressed to his chest, so much entreaty in his eyes. His waxed mustache quivered in anticipation of her answer.

Her gaze next fastened on Reagan, who towered over her, broad, brown and muscled, his expression demanding to know what was going on here.

The moment of suspended time snapped, and Charlotte forcefully withdrew her hand and backed away from Kent.

"Kent—Mr. Covington. No! Stop!" She held out a finger when he crawled forward to recapture her hand. "*Mr.* Covington"— she deliberately emphasized the formality which put distance between them as she looked down at him—"I fear you have made this journey in vain. I left Boston to escape you, and I've never for even one moment regretted it." She looked over to find Reagan smiling at her, a good deal more relaxed in his stance. She couldn't pull her gaze from his. "God knew just the man for me and I found him when I came to Wyldhaven."

Without caring that they were standing on a public platform for all to see, she stepped around Kent, wrapped her arms around Reagan's neck, and kissed him full on the lips.

He grinned down at her. "I'm mighty glad to hear you say that. But"—his gaze hardened just a touch and he held up one finger—"there's one thing I need to do."

Before Charlotte could react, Reagan drew his pistol and leveled it at Kent's chest.

Everyone gasped including Kent, who scrunched his eyes shut, bowler still clutched to his chest.

For all the world, down on his knees like that, he looked like a man about to be dispatched to meet his maker.

"I'm not going to kill you!" Reagan's tone conveyed disgust. He leaned down and hauled Kent to his feet. "But the train's about to leave and we don't want you to miss it." The words left no room for negotiation. Reagan escorted him to the nearest passenger car and handed him on board. Then he gave the conductor a few bills from his wallet. "For his ticket back to Boston," he said. With that, he spun to face Charlotte, with a huge grin on his face. "Right, I guess I'd better fetch the carriage now. Unless you have some other beau that's about to hop off the train? Am I going to have to challenge someone to a gun battle before the day is through?"

Mother gasped and Jacinda, who had started to laugh at Reagan's joke, quickly smothered her humor. "It was— He was joking."

"Oh," Mother forced a smile, but put her hanky to good use blotting at moisture on her face and throat. "Oh dear, Bertrand, I think I'm might need my smelling salts."

Charlotte felt her face heat. She gave Reagan a pointed look. "Just fetch the carriage, would you?"

The morning of the weddings dawned with gorgeous sunshine that puddled rectangles of warmth through Liora's window. With her quilt wrapped around her shoulders, and a warm cup of coffee in her hands, she hunched her shoulders into the wonderful feel of it and eyed her dress hanging from the hook Joe had put in for her the day before.

Jacinda had outdone herself. The gown was all creamy silk, and lace, and pearl buttons, and gleaming beads. It filled Liora with awe that she should be privileged to wear such a concoction. And she couldn't imagine the late hours Jacinda must have put in to complete the dress on time for her.

Joe had very reluctantly agreed to stay in town last night. He hadn't wanted to leave her, but all the men who had been a threat had been sentenced just a few days previous—most of them, including Burt Pike, to several years in McNeil Island Prison. John Hunt and the man who had planted the nitroglycerin in the church had both been sentenced to hang for their part in Tess's death. It had been small consolation, but Liora was at least thankful that she didn't have the dread of Hunt getting out of jail in a few years hanging over her head.

Ewan had rented out his room above the alehouse already, so Joe had stayed with the parson and Kin.

Zane Holloway was supposed to arrive in a couple hours to pick her up and take her to the church.

Her stomach swirled and dove like a veritable butterfly garden.

A knock sounded at her door.

"Come," she called.

Rory poked her head in. "Ready to start getting dressed? Ruby is cooking breakfast. She says for you to just relax and she'll take care of everything. And I'm here to do your hair." Rory blushed and ran a hand over her short mop. "You wouldn't know it to look at me, but Mama taught me quite a lot about hairstyles and I know just the one that will be perfect for your wedding day."

Wedding day...

Liora smiled. "I'd like that very much." She tugged the girl into a one-armed embrace. "I'm so glad both you and Dixie will be standing up with me today." She would have asked Charlotte too, but of course Charlotte would be a little busy.

Charlotte had also asked Dixie to stand with her, along with Jacinda. She had claimed that she never would have stayed in Wyldhaven were it not for them, and she wanted them to have the best view of what their friendship and encouragement had brought about.

The morning passed in a flurry of hot hair irons and button hooks, and before she knew it, Zane had pulled the wagon right up to the porch.

He clapped his Stetson to his chest and smiled at her, one hand extended to help her climb aboard. "Joe is sure one lucky man, Miss Liora. One lucky man. Mind now that we don't muss your dress or Jacinda will have my hide. I've laid out a clean blanket. Just sit down right there and I'll get you to the church, before you know it. Joe, he's already pacing like a caged tiger. Don't suspect he'll be able to stop till he sets eyes on you and sees you survived the night without his protection."

Liora smiled and thanked him, settling her skirts around her as Aurora and the other newly arrived women climbed onto the back seat.

Zane would drop them off on the way into town before they stopped to pick up Charlotte and her family.

Liora inhaled deeply and tipped her face into the sun. She was on the way to her wedding!

"Charlie, baby, are you *certain* this is the man you want to marry? The place where you want to spend the rest of your life?" Mother's words were almost a whimper. She stood at the window of Charlotte's room on the upper floor of Jacinda's house. With the curtain slightly parted, she stared down at the gaping hole that was all that remained of the near side of the jailhouse. The explosion that had freed Pike and the other men, had demolished nearly the entire back wall of the jail and had even broken out one of Jacinda's front windows. It was a miracle that none of the men in the cells had been killed.

Charlotte, who sat before her vanity while Jacinda worked on her hair, could hardly blame Mother for her concern. She well remembered how shocked and outraged she'd been when she first arrived in Wyldhaven.

"Don't worry, Mother. I've been collecting money for boardwalks and that will give us a good start on rebuilding the church. And Reagan has decided that this time when he rebuilds the jailhouse, he's going to do it out of river rock."

"This time?" Mother's shocked exclamation barely rose above a whisper.

Charlotte nodded, angling her head so Jacinda could remove the last paper curler that she'd slept in the night before. "Yes, so if anything like this happens in the future it will be much harder for someone to break out of the jail."

"Oh dear." Mother sank onto the settee by the window.

Charlotte met Jacinda's gaze in the mirror. "Was I that bad?" she mouthed.

Jacinda's eyes widened and she nodded emphatically.

Charlotte rolled her eyes at the petite woman who would be her mother-in-law, but was already a friend. She needed to distract Mother from her worries or they were going to have to run for the smelling salts. "Mother? Why don't you go down and see if you can find Father? He might need help with his...tie."

"Yes. Of course. That's a good idea. I'll do that." She scurried from the room, but not before she parted the curtains once more and tossed one last glance toward the jailhouse. On her way from the room she murmured, "Lord, preserve us."

Charlotte inhaled a lungful of quiet and eased it out on a long slow exhale. Today she would become Mrs. Reagan Callahan. How lucky could one woman get?

Jacinda squeezed her shoulders. "Very lucky."

Charlotte met her gaze again. "Did I say that out loud?"

Jacinda smiled. "You did. Now up with you. We have to get you into your dress. It's almost time. Zane will be here to pick you up at any moment."

Charlotte couldn't stop herself from jumping in a few circles. "I'm so excited."

Jacinda chuckled. "So I see. Now into the dress."

"Yes, Mama." Charlotte batted her eyes at the woman, who promptly pulled her into an embrace.

"You can call me that anytime. Just don't let your own mother hear it until she's had some time to adjust to your new status."

From outside, they heard the creak of wagon wheels.

Both their eyes widened and Charlotte hurried to the dress that waited for her in the corner. "We'd better hustle. Reagan doesn't like to be kept waiting."

"That is certain." Jacinda's fingers worked swiftly, first to tie the waist of the hoop-slip and then with the silk ribbon that laced up the entire back of Charlotte's dress.

Jacinda squeezed Charlotte's shoulders as she settled the silk shawl trimmed in beads around her and pinned it at the front with the diamond brooch Father had presented to her as a wedding present. "My, you look like a dream!"

Zane waited for them on the front porch. His gaze skimmed over Charlotte and he smiled. "Good thing this town has more than one lawman. I have a feeling our head honcho is about to have trouble breathing, the moment he lays eyes on you." His gaze swept past her to Jacinda who was just pulling her own dusty-blue organza shawl around her shoulders. "Kinda like I am right now." He swallowed.

Charlotte stood on her tiptoes and pressed a kiss to Zane's cheek, drawing his attention back to her.

"What was that for?"

She grinned up at him and whispered. "We'll be happy to welcome you to the family, *Papa*, when you finally get up the courage to ask her."

Zane's focus darted back to Jacinda for the briefest of seconds. He swallowed, stretched his neck, and slipped one finger beneath his collar. "Best we get you loaded up. Reagan doesn't like to be kept waiting."

Charlotte chuckled.

Zane helped Charlotte onto the back seat of the wagon, then he helped Jacinda up beside Liora, and Etta and Bertrand into the back next to their daughter. "Right," he said as he climbed up to the front bench and took up the reins. "We're off."

Both Charlotte and Liora gasped as Zane drove the wagon past the mercantile and turned the corner to take the block toward the church. Both of them had resigned themselves to outdoor weddings with a burnt church as the backdrop, but it appeared that the town of Wyldhaven had other ideas.

A large white tent had been pitched on the lawn, and swags of greenery draped elegantly on either side of the tied-back doorway.

Zane helped them both from the front seat and extended an elbow to each of them. "Ladies, shall we?"

Liora did her best not to tremble as she walked toward the tent.

When they stepped into the back of the tent, both of them drew in breaths of awe. Several benches that still had a new-wood shine lined both sides of a center aisle. All along the aisle, buckets of sunflowers and evergreen branches lined the way. At the front of the tent, two tables on either side of a newly constructed pulpit held tiers of candles that filled the area with a golden glow. The men of the town had even transferred Ewan's Alehouse piano to the front and Rose Pottinger sat before it on a bench.

Both Joe and Reagan waited off to one side, hands clasped behind their backs, impatiently rising on their toes every once in a while.

Charlotte met Reagan's gaze with a grin of excitement. He tossed her a wink.

Liora felt all her nerves suddenly come to life. Everything inside her trembled as she looked at Joe. Her rescuer. Her friend. Her confidant. Her first and only love. A soft smile played over his lips and his brows pumped. If propriety would have allowed it, Liora would have run down the aisle to him right then and there.

Zane gave Rose a nod and she started to play a soft melody. Jacinda led the way to the front, followed by Etta. Each of them took a seat on the front bench of each side. Dixie and Rory went next, and Liora grinned to see Parson Clay fiddling with his collar and seemingly unable to tear his eyes off of Rory. She did look lovely and petite and fairy-like in the gauzy moss-green gown that heightened the color of her eyes to perfection. Jacinda joined Dixie and Aurora once they reached the front, and then every eye in the room turned to fix on the two brides.

Rose broke into a more exuberant song, and Bertrand stepped up beside Charlotte to offer her his arm.

It was only then that Liora realized her lack. She felt it as surely as she would have felt a knife to the ribs. She had no father to walk her down the aisle. Joe immediately noticed too and started toward her, but Zane waved him back.

As Charlotte and her father started down the aisle, Zane offered Liora his arm and bent to speak in her ear. "I'd be honored to escort you to your husband, if you'll allow me, Miss Liora?"

Liora slipped her hand into the crook of his arm, feeling a wash of thankfulness toward him. "That's very kind of you. Thank you."

"My pleasure."

Liora couldn't take her eyes off of Joe after that. The ceremony was a bit of a blur. Reagan and Charlotte stood on one side of the pulpit, and Liora and Joe took the other. But from the moment Joe wrapped her hands in his, everything else seemed to fade away. His palms were warm against hers. His soft brown eyes, taking her in from head to toe, were home. A home she never wanted to part from again.

None of the pomp and circumstance mattered. All that mattered was this man, this miracle that God had given her.

This beauty that God had rendered from her ashes.

Please Review!

If you enjoyed this story, would you take a few minutes to leave your thoughts in a review on your favorite retailer's website? It would mean so much to me, and helps spread the word about the series.

You can quickly link through from my website here: http://www.lynnettebonner.com/books/historical-fiction/the-wyldhaven-series/

Now Available...

CONSIDER THE LILIES

Book Four
WYLDHAVEN

You may read an excerpt on the next page...

acinda Callahan stood next to Marshal Zane Holloway on the train depot platform with a smile fixed on her face as she waved goodbye to her son, Reagan, and his wife Charlotte. Their train had been late. But it hadn't dampened their enthusiasm. They had boarded only a few minutes ago and were even now grinning at her from behind the grimy window of their boxcar.

"Goodbye! Have a lovely time! Don't worry about a thing!" Jacinda blew a few kisses their way, truly hoping Reagan would be able to leave the pressures and concerns of his job as sheriff behind.

Charlotte flapped her hanky in response and literally bounced up and down from what Jacinda could see through the dingy glass.

Jacinda saw Reagan say something to Charlotte and they both laughed, then leaned close to relish in a lingering kiss.

Jacinda kept her smile in place, but as the train belched a column of steam and chuffed a slow exit, she couldn't keep up pretenses any longer.

Her shoulders slumped as she watched the train shrink into a small speck on the horizon.

Lord, keep them safe. Bring them back to me all in one piece.

Something tightened in her chest. What would she do if something happened to them? And there were certainly any number of things that could happen!

There were outlaws and gangsters and train robbers. Murderers and thieves.

And that was just the beginning of the list!

Not to mention that Reagan and Charlotte were headed right into the heart of godless San Francisco. Oh, why had she ever agreed with them that this trip was a good idea?

When they'd gotten married late last year, they'd planned to take a wedding trip within a couple weeks of the ceremony— after Charlotte's parents returned to Boston. However, one delay had led to another and now here it was early March and they were just setting off.

Jacinda would have preferred if they'd never gotten around to the trip.

Beside her, Zane cleared his throat. "Ready to head back? Or shall we stand here staring at the tracks until they return next month?"

Jacinda gave him a deprecating look. She'd almost forgotten that he was beside her. Almost. But not quite. Because it was nearly impossible to forget about the handsome Zane Holloway, even if he was only a friend.

She looked down and fiddled with the lace at her cuffs, willing herself not to give in to the tears that suddenly begged for release. "Yes. I suppose we should get going. It will already be near dark by the time we arrive back in Wyldhaven. I wouldn't want us to be caught out on the road after dark, especially since that new gang of outlaws has been raising such a ruckus in the area." Her heart rate increased merely at the thought. "I'm just not certain it's a good time for Reagan to be away. On the other hand, maybe it's the best time for him to be away—for his own protection. With the new bank being built in town..."

Zane settled a hand at her back and gave her a nudge down

the platform. At the same time, he gave her a sympathetic look that was almost her undoing.

The look told her to buck up, but it also said she could confide in him.

Was there any other man who could say so much without speaking a word? She felt thankful that he'd come with her, because he was such a good listener and she really needed someone to spill her concerns to.

Jacinda stepped out at a smart pace. "Of course, I'm not doubting that you and Joe can protect Wyldhaven, you understand? But do you think the outlaws might try something?"

Zane's only answer was a bit of a squint around his eyes and the uptick of one corner of his mouth.

Jacinda released a huff. "I know what you're going to say. You're going to say that I shouldn't worry. That I should trust that the good Lord has good plans for everyone. Even better plans than I could ever hope for."

She glanced over her shoulder.

Zane said not a word, but there was a glint of humor in his blue-gray eyes as he followed in her wake.

"The problem is—"

"Mind the steps," Zane said.

Jacinda faced forward, lifted her skirts and took the stairs down to the flat area. Then she turned to look at him again. There was something comforting about the man's soulful eyes. "The problem is that one can never know if God is done with a person on this earth. I understand that—"

"Look out for the wagon."

Jacinda spun just in time to avoid crashing into the tailgate of a farm wagon.

With that hurdle cleared, she twisted to face Zane again, but before she could resume her speech, he lifted a hand.

"I think things will be safer if you come here." He reached out and wrapped the warmth of his fingers around her own, then tucked her hand into the crook of his arm. He glanced down at her with a smile. "Now...you were saying?"

But the impact of that smile, combined with the knee-weakening assault of his long-lashed blue eyes, knocked Jacinda's thoughts six ways from Sunday.

She pressed her lips together. Tore her attention to the path before them. "It doesn't matter, I suppose."

Zane rubbed the back of her hand where it rested on his arm. "Matters to me."

She swallowed. And how well she knew it. His affection for her was part of her current barrage of worry. Always in the past, she'd been able to put off his attentions with excuses of being busy helping Charlotte or Reagan with this or that. But now that they were going to be out of town for a month, what excuse was she going to offer?

She gave a flap of her free hand and then settled it over the crimp in her middle. "I know it does. And I appreciate that. You've been a good friend, Zane." She layered a little extra emphasis onto the word "friend," hoping he would hear it.

Needing him to hear it. Because, heaven help her, the man was a temptation. She'd known from the moment he walked into her dining room just over two years ago now, asking for information about a couple of murderers he was tracking, that if ever there was a man who could make her forget her promise never to love again, it would be Zane Holloway.

After she'd lost Wade to that outlaw's bullet, she never wanted to go through the pain of something like that again! It was better not to love at all, and certainly loving another lawman was out of the question! So far out of the question that it shouldn't even be a consideration.

The last time Parson Clay had preached about worry, he'd said it was a sin because it was a lack of trust in God.

Jacinda would be the first to agree with that. But how did one get back to a place of trusting a Being who'd had the power to save the man she loved, but had chosen not to do so?

She only realized they had reached their wagon when Zane stopped next to it. "Oh, and here we are." She forced a smile and made to climb aboard, but Zane's hand on her arm stopped her.

"You know you don't have to pretend to be strong with me, right?"

Jacinda blinked at him. Something inside her curled up a little.

"Pretend?" Did he think she was weak?

Zane grimaced. "I didn't mean it like that. Trust me, Jac, you are one of the strongest women I know. I just meant…you don't have to hide your real feelings and struggles from me."

Jac. Everything in her stilled. Zane had never called her that before. But "Jac" had been Wade's affectionate name for her. And Zane had said it with a hard C just as Wade always had. If she didn't know better, she would swear the two men were conspiring against her. But Zane had never had the opportunity to meet Wade. Nor had Jacinda been afforded the opportunity to meet Zane's first wife, who had died in childbirth when he was just a young man.

Jacinda hoisted herself up onto the wagon seat without even waiting for Zane's help. "I don't have anything I need to confide. We'd best get going if we're to beat the dark."

Zane pressed his lips together, traversed the back of the wagon, and swung up onto the driver's seat. With a click of his tongue and a snap of the reins, he set the team to trotting down the road.

He'd been patient with Jacinda Callahan for several years. Especially since he'd been attracted to her from the moment he'd first laid eyes on her in her dining room all those months ago. At first, he'd flirted with her a little, but it had been clear from the start that she wasn't interested in jumping into a courtship with an old codger like him. He'd thought maybe she had another beau in the wings, because surely a single woman as attractive as her would have men buzzing around like bees to clover. And a few had tried. But Jacinda had always put them firmly in their place—which was anywhere other than in her life.

Zane had proceeded with caution after that, never wanting to make her take enough offense that she might put him out on his ear also. But in the past few months since Reagan had married, Zane had found his patience with the whole tiptoeing around their feelings growing thin. He wasn't getting any younger, and neither was she.

And there were times when he could sense that she was attracted to him.

There would be a softening of the cornflower blue of her eyes. Or a little release of breath which reminded him of the way that Daniella used to respond when he took her hand. But then Jacinda would give herself a little shake and in a blink, it was as though she had dropped a mask back into place and reconstructed a wall between them.

Zane canted her a look. He shouldn't have let that endearment slip out. But Reagan had mentioned it to him not long ago—how his father had always called her "my Jac"—and ever since then he'd not been able to think of her as anything else. It was diminutive, just like her, but also implied the strength that embodied her.

Even now he could tell from the pinched pucker of her lips that she was fretting about something, but he knew she wouldn't say anything. She would battle through her fears alone and with a smile and a word of dismissal for anyone who questioned if she was all right.

So he simply wouldn't ask. "The trains are quite well protected these days. I'm sure Reagan and Charlotte will be fine."

She straightened and dusted at her skirt. "Yes. I know. I'm certain you are right."

"And that gang of outlaws has been quiet for several weeks. Joe and I think they must have moved on to a more lucrative area. The bank will be fine."

He swallowed. Had she heard the hesitation in his voice? Because the truth was more like *hoped*. Hoped they had moved on. Hoped the bank would be fine. They shouldn't have any trouble there for a while anyhow, because it was still being built and had no money or even a vault yet.

She fidgeted and glanced toward the rapidly setting sun. "That's good."

He felt her worry as palpably as if she had screamed it aloud. And if he was honest, the concern echoed in his own heart. It was why he'd urged her back to the wagon so quickly after the delayed departure of the train.

It would be dark inside five minutes, and they still had a good thirty minutes till they arrived back in town.

Maybe he could take both their minds off it with conversation. "So, what do you plan to do with your time while Reagan and Charlotte are away?"

Jacinda smiled at him and he knew she had immediately perceived what he was up to. "Charlotte's material that she ordered for their drapes arrived just the other day. I suppose some of my time will be spent in getting those sewn up for them."

"And how are they settling in at old man Jonas's place?"

She tipped her head. "Well, I think. His son was relieved to sell it to someone who would care for it after Mr. Jonas's funeral."

"I'm sure your house seems empty now that they've moved out?"

Jacinda cleared her throat. "Yes. But I don't mind being alone so much."

Ah, yes. He'd wandered too close to the taboo. "I suppose it is easier to keep everyone at arm's length when you can keep your distance from them."

He jutted his jaw to one side. He hadn't meant to say that.

Her mouth dropped open. "Zane Holloway! Whatever you might—"

A puff of gray dust kicked up in the roadbed before them. The horse neighed and reared. The echoing sound of a rifle shot bounced along the steep hills on both sides of the road.

Someone was shooting at them!

"Jac! Get down!" Zane grabbed her arm and urged her to the floorboards at his feet all while trying to maintain his grip on the reins and get the horse back in line. They were going to have to make a run for it!

But just as the horse's hooves hit the road once more, another bullet slammed into the ground.

"Whoa!" Zane tried to keep his voice steady to calm the panicked horse.

Jacinda cowered next to his leg, but when he glanced down, he did a double take. She had a pistol held at the ready in her hand and was searching the surrounding hills with a practiced eye.

"Don't move!" A voice called out of the darkness on the hillside to their right.

Jacinda pointed her gun in that direction and Zane reached down to slowly cover her hand.

She looked up.

He shook his head.

They couldn't just go shooting at voices in the dark until they learned more.

She gave him a nod of understanding.

"We don't want any trouble!" Zane called.

"Well ain't that just dandy? 'Cause we don't want no trouble neither...just your money!"

Several voices laughed, each coming from a different direction.

Zane swallowed. They were surrounded.

"Zane?" Jacinda whispered. "What are we going to do?"

Find out more about this series here:
http://www.lynnettebonner.com/books/historical-fiction/the-wyldhaven-series/

Want a FREE Story?

If you enjoyed this book...

...sign up for Lynnette's Gazette below! Subscribers get exclusive deals, sneak peeks, and lots of other fun content.

(The gazette is only sent out about once a month or when there's a new release to announce, so you won't be getting a lot of spam messages, and your email is never shared with anyone else.)

Sign up link: https://www.lynnettebonner.com/newsletter/

ABOUT THE AUTHOR

Born and raised in Malawi, Africa. Lynnette Bonner spent the first years of her life reveling in warm equatorial sunshine and the late evening duets of cicadas and hyenas. The year she turned eight she was off to Rift Valley Academy, a boarding school in Kenya where she spent many joy-filled years, and graduated in 1990.

That fall, she traded to a new duet—one of traffic and rain—when she moved to Kirkland, Washington to attend Northwest University. It was there that she met her husband and a few years later they moved to the small town of Pierce, Idaho.

During the time they lived in Idaho, while studying the history of their little town, Lynnette was inspired to begin the Shepherd's Heart Series with Rocky Mountain Oasis.

Marty and Lynnette have four children, and currently live in Washington where Marty pastors a church.